IMAGO

IMAGO

A MODERN COMEDY OF MANNERS

JAMES McCLURE

PENZLER BOOKS · NEW YORK

Penzler Books, 129 West 56th Street, New York, N.Y. 10019

Printed in the United States of America

First Printing: January 1988

10 9 8 7 6 5 4 3 2 1

Library of Congress Cataloging-in-Publication Data

McClure, James, 1939–
  Imago.

  I. Title.
PR9369.3.M394I43   1988   823   87-22020
ISBN 0-89296-273-9

For John Hamill

IMAGO

1

When she became woman, and Tom Lockhart saw her standing there, serene on the doorstep of her father's house, he partly understood. It alarmed him so much he wanted to turn and run.

"Ginny, dear," said his wife, Sylvia, crossing the threshold, "how lovely to see you again. Why, it must be *years* . . ."

She smiled. "Years and years," she agreed. "I probably had pigtails, and my teeth in a brace! Mum and Dad are weeding the patio."

"No, you'd—" he began.

"Tom?" said Sylvia, turning.

"Lead on!"

Ginny went first through the house. She'd not had pigtails; her hair had been in a ponytail, caught back by a velvet ribbon. Her teeth, nibbling corn from a buttery cob, had been very even.

My God, thought Tom Lockhart, I can remember it all, that long-ago summer's day which seemed utterly forgotten. I can see the moment of our first meeting.

She, gangling in gingham, glancing up at him as he came down the garden path, his arms outstretched in welcome to her parents.

"Hugh, you old bugger! So you managed to find us."

"Beautiful place you have, Tom! Isn't it, Moira?"

"Lovely," said Moira. "I'm jealous."

"Oh, and this is Ginny, by the way," Hugh said uneasily. "You weren't expecting all three of us, I know, but she's been allowed

1

out this Sunday by the school, and we hoped you wouldn't mind if—"

"Hello, Ginny," Tom said, kissing Moira's cheek. "Like horses?"

Moira laughed. "Show me the twelve-year-old who doesn't!"

"Then come on up to the house—Sylvia's got about a ton of windfalls in the scullery, and around the back, in the top paddock, are two of the fattest, *gutsiest* ponies you've ever clapped eyes on. They'll do anything for an apple."

"Names?" asked Hugh.

"Adam and Eve."

"Tom," said Moira, delighted, "you've not changed a bit!"

But he had, irrevocably, in just those few seconds.

"What an attractive child Ginny is," murmured Sylvia in the kitchen, topping the prawn cocktails with sprigs of parsley. "Have you noticed her eyes?"

"Oh, that extra one in the middle, you mean?" he said, taking the wine from the refrigerator.

Sylvia frowned. "Even for you, that's unusually facetious."

"Sorry! No, I'd not noticed her eyes."

"They're huge, and a soft gunmetal gray I've never seen before. So shy."

"Shy?" He paused, corkscrew in hand.

"Well, has she given you a direct look yet?"

"No," he said.

Lying hurriedly, and not knowing why.

"And her skin," said Sylvia, tossing the salad, "is extraordinary. Smooth and goldenish, like the bikini models' in *Vogue*."

"She doesn't take after Hugh, then. He's still leaving patches of his chin unshaved."

"The eternal boy," said Sylvia, smiling. "One shoelace not properly tied either. It's a wonder he can earn enough to send Ginny to boarding school."

"Ah, but they say, you know, the lad's a marketing genius."

"Tom, hasn't that cork been corkscrewed enough?"

"Oh, Christ, now I've got bits floating in it."

Perplexed by his preoccupied behavior, he decanted the wine into a mixing bowl basin, and then back into its bottle through a tea strainer.

"Delightful body to it," remarked Hugh, and then held his glass against the light. "What year would you say?"

"Sixty-three," replied Tom from the head of the table. "More cold beef anyone? Corn on the cob's all gone, I'm afraid."

"I'm sure Ginny could manage another mouthful or two," said Sylvia, taking their young guest's plate and passing it over.

"There we go!" Two slices of beef dropped from his carving fork. "And now you, Moira? Hugh?"

Strawberries for dessert, and the clotted cream the Ashfords had brought with them.

"More of both?" he asked Ginny.

She gave a polite shake of her head.

"Moira? I'm not going to have to twist your arm, am I?"

"No fear!"

In the kitchen, while he stacked the dirty dishes and Sylvia made the coffee, she said to him, "Tom, why don't you ever call that child her name? One couldn't help being aware of it."

Ginny . . . It was true, he hadn't uttered her name more than once. He couldn't account for this, although he did have a feeling it'd be a little like giving a secret away.

"Don't know, Sylv," he said, breaking a dish.

Then, after lunch, Ginny tried to ride Adam and had a fall, skinning her knees. She wept and had to be comforted, given a Coke and fussed over. She was only a child and this showed.

An odd shame assailed him.

Yet, at the back of his mind was the look she had given him when, gangling in gingham, she'd glanced up for a moment.

Now his alarm turned to a curious, predatory excitement as he approached the patio, a pace behind Ginny. Hugh and Moira were down on all fours, grubbing up the weeds between the cracks in the crazy-paving, looking like a pair of earnest, single-minded sheep.

They bleated greetings and lurched to their feet.

"I've just said to Ginny," remarked Sylvia, "it must've been years."

"Six," said Moira, nodding and giving her knees a brush. "I worked that out by which car we had."

"Yes, our old yellow Renault known in the family as the Banana

Split," added Hugh, chuckling. "Things are a bit different now, of course."

Of course. Tom had seen the brand-new Volvo estate, left ostentatiously outside the double garage. It was already very obvious, as Sylvia had said, why they'd received this surprise invitation to lunch: the Ashfords had finally bettered the Lockharts when it come to worldly goods, and wouldn't rest until the point had been driven home.

"Shall we take our drinks down to the pool?" suggested Hugh, handing Sylvia her gin and tonic. "Must catch the sun while we can . . ."

Tom, dizzied by the realizations crowding in on him, was watching Ginny and taking very little notice of the others.

So Ginny must have *known*. She must have understood intuitively what had happened to him as soon as he set eyes on her, and had accepted the enormity of it all quite calmly. That's what her glance had meant.

"Tom, are you coming?" asked Sylvia.

He began to move, irritated by his wife's hearty, graceless walk. I'm in love, he was thinking. And I've been in love all the time, which explains everything. It'd been love at first sight.

"I'm going inside for a while," said Ginny.

Yet the excitement stayed with Tom, and he thought of double agents seated at café tables with their dupes, feeling as he felt.

"Care for a nut, old chap?" asked Hugh, proffering the bowl of cashews.

"I've still half a handful. You were saying?"

Hugh, visibly anxious a moment ago that he might have begun to bore, lit up with pleasure and continued his tedious history of the new swimming pool.

It allowed Tom time to reflect. This wasn't easy, not while he was still too stunned to snatch whole ideas from the swirling confusion in his head, but even fragments seemed to make sense. Take the past six years, for instance. Thinking back, he realized with a jolt that this was pretty well as long as he had been drifting off course, never getting where he'd planned to go, or finding himself becalmed for long, bleaching months in the doldrums. And no matter how carefully he'd taken new bearings he had still gone wrong, passing instead with Sylvia through storm and tempest, down to the icy wastes and back, finding it all so inexplicable. But consider for a moment, the effect of a gleam of soft gunmetal gray lodged in a compass, teasing the needle around.

"Surely, you've *not* got rid of the cottage," Moira was saying.

"It'd become a bit of a bore, to be honest," pretended Sylvia, for in truth they had needed the money. "And some of the people we lent it to last summer let us down rather badly. We even had a police raid in August! They came looking for drugs."

"Goodness, and did they find any?"

"None. Only, Mr. Grantham, the farmer next door, was very upset."

"But those adorable fat ponies, you can't have sold them as well?"

"They were his, Mr. Grantham's."

"Oh," said Moira. "I'd not realized. It'd all seemed so idyllic."

Hugh harrumphed and broke off his swimming pool saga to remark, "Idyllic? A bloody awful lot of work! We've a couple of 'em now ourselves, you know, and the back of the Volvo is always knee-deep in straw and things."

"An odd place to keep ponies," murmured Tom. "Still, if one hasn't the room, then I suppose . . ."

"The *room*?" echoed Moira, stung. "We've over four and a half—" But Sylvia's delighted laugh stopped her, and she tried to laugh too, rising as she did so.

"Good old Tom!" applauded Hugh. "I had been waiting for one of your cracks, wondered when it'd come! You'd not seemed your usual self, if I may say so, not until then."

Wife-person Sylvia, the double agent noted, had been put more at her ease as well.

"I'm hot," declared Moira, bouncing on tiptoe in quaintly athletic fashion. "I vote we all take a dip before lunch."

"Hear, hear!" said Hugh, getting up. "Changing rooms, just off to the left. Ladies this side, and gents—"

"Hold on," said Sylvia. "You two have a swim by all means, but we haven't brought our—"

"Guests are provided for," cut in Moira. "You'll find a selection of the latest in swimwear, all laid out and waiting."

Tom smiled, as always beguiled when Moira let slip a phrase from her secret years as a shop assistant; it was the one thing he liked about her. "You're on," he said, ducking out from under the big white sunshade over the round cast-iron table. "I've been working up quite a sweat out here."

And he used a sweeping gesture, which allowed his eyes to travel swiftly over the house, hoping for a glimpse of Ginny. She was there, brushing her hair at a high window.

"Tom," said Hugh, when they were all alone in the changing room, "Tom, it's damn good seeing you again! No, really, we ought to do this more often."

As often as possible, thought Tom, gripped by even greater excitement. But what he said was, "It isn't as if we live quite so far apart any longer."

"No distance at all," agreed Hugh. "Well, you know how Moira always had a hankering to live in your neck of the woods. And I'm sure she'd love to see more of Sylvia too. You've no idea how often she mentions her."

"Oh? In what—"

"Admires her taste terrifically. Go shopping for curtains with Moira, and it's, 'I'm not too sure Sylvia would approve of that pattern . . .' All that sort of thing."

"Ah," said Tom.

Hugh unzipped and sat down to drag off his jeans. "It's one of the things one learns when one's getting on a bit," he remarked. "The importance of old friends. They connect one, I suppose, with memories of happier, more carefree times."

"Getting on a bit?" mimicked Tom, and laughed. "Bloody hell, Hugh, don't be so pompous! The pair of us have only just topped forty!"

"You make it sound as though that's young."

"Young enough, for God's sake!"

Pulling his shirt off over his head, Hugh exposed a boyish, hairless chest, little changed from his punting days on the Cherwell, when they were both up at Oxford. "That's another thing about old friends," he said, winking at Tom, "they like one enough to give it to you straight: 'Christ, your breath's awful!'—or 'You're talking balls, old chap!' I deserved that."

But I don't like you, thought Tom as he began to undress. I don't think I've ever liked you. Loathed being your best man at that fiasco of a wedding at St. Michael and All Angels in Marston, where the priest, in a stained cassock, had spent the entire sermon waving a yellow 1958 Litter Act sign about, warning of the evils of confetti.

"Those trunks may seem somewhat on the small side," remarked Hugh. "But the black ones are able to stretch a good bit. Why not give them a try?"

Tom ignored the black trunks and picked up the red pair. New College aside, he thought, you're a common little man, Hugh Ashford. Passing through the living room in Ginny's wake upon arrival, Tom had seen Hugh's row of fake leather-bound volumes of the kind used to store videocassettes in, God forgive him.

He had also noticed hips on Ginny, whereas once she had been one schoolgirl width from the shoulders down. Hips that, from behind, tilted with each step she took, lithe and easy, proclaiming her womanhood even more emphatically than the unexpected press of breasts upon the threshold.

Tom went cold. The red swimming costume was cutting deep into him, squeezing his scrotum. He looked down, aghast, to see his midriff protruding like a pregnancy. And suddenly, for the first time since puppy fat had made a torment of his early teens, inciting girls at the seaside to snigger at him, he felt deeply ashamed of his body. A body which, until a moment ago, he hadn't given a serious thought to in years, but had treated like a kid brother who just tagged along, kept acquiescent by overindulgence. He heard the sniggers again and the same panicky feelings set in, the same churning fears of instant, ruthless rejection.

"Jesus Christ!" he gasped, making himself stumble. "Not that bloody thing again." Then he dropped to the duckboards and grasped his left ankle.

Startled, Hugh rushed over to him, stark naked. "For God's sake, Tom! What the hell's happened?"

A good question. The same panic had bred the same sort of childish, potentially disastrous solution it used to do, replacing one problem with another far worse.

But, committed in that instant, he could only blunder on.

"I can't bloody believe it," Tom grunted through gritted teeth. "Keeps doing this to me. Sprained it badly two years ago, jumping onto a jetty on the Broads, and ever since—just like that!—over it goes. Pain shoots right up into the groin, like a poke with a rusty saber."

Hugh winced, cupping himself. "Er, anything I can do for you?" he asked.

"No, not really, thanks. I'll just massage it a bit, and then find somewhere to rest it for a while, the only answer. You'd better join the others, old son, and make my excuses."

"Well, you'd know best. You're sure there's nothing . . ."

"Quite certain. Don't worry, I'll hobble out shortly and shout encouragement from the sidelines."

Left alone in the changing room, Tom felt old, older than he'd ever felt, and his heart sank so literally there was a dragging ache in his chest.

Then he gave a short, bitter laugh and said, "Right, you poor pathetic bastard, what next?" Gone was the excitement, his absurd joy over Ginny; all that mattered now was somehow saving face, having landed himself in this adolescent mess.

He stood up and practiced a hobble, making the duckboards creak beneath his weight. Pretending lameness, he realized, would not be enough. Again he glanced down, compounding his self-disgust by noting the veins like sprigs of blue fern on the insides of his ankles. He dipped a corner of his towel in a puddle near the door and began flicking at his left ankle. It stung. He was pleased to be hurting himself, even just a little.

His mind wanted to strip the flesh from his back, lash by furied lash.

Sylvia, dripping, heaved herself from the pool and came over to the sun bed to touch his ankle. "My," she said, surprised, "it *is* red—and already a bit swollen."

So she'd suspected something despite the limp, as anticipated, but he felt no pride in the success of his deception. Only dull relief.

"By the way, what was this about you having a fall on a jetty?" Sylvia asked. "Hugh had me stumped there, not that I was going to admit it."

"God knows. What's the water like?"

"Gorgeous! You're really missing something."

He watched Sylvia turn and take a running dive back into the deep end. He wondered why she had picked such an inappropriate swimming costume, cut high in the thigh, making far too much of her long white shanks. The frills and flounces weren't her either, and looked as absurd as a lacy lampshade on a lamppost.

"Tom, chuck that ball in, will you?" Hugh called out, hanging by an arm from the diving board. "I'm going to take the girls on at water polo."

"Must we?" complained Moira.

Petite, and at thirty-eight only a slightly melted version of the wax doll Hugh had chanced upon behind a counter at Marks and Spencer, Moira looked very good in her shiny black bikini—as well she knew. Tom picked up the ball from beside the sun bed and punched it, catching her in the face with the splash.

She laughed, as though favored.

A ladybug alighted on Tom's knee. It began making small clockwork rushes that ended in bewildered turns, bringing it back to where it had started.

You bastard, he thought, that's really rubbing it in.

And wondered at the range of emotions he'd passed through so swiftly in so short a time, until reality had finally, not an instant too soon, reasserted itself, sparing him further embarrassment. Emotions which, for the most part, he'd almost forgotten existed, thank God.

Love? That was a good one!

Dirty old man, more to the point.

No, that wasn't right either, he decided, sending the ladybug on its way with a touch. Dirty old men had vigor, a goaty, rutting glee, an abandon, not this taste of ashes in the mouth.

Then, strangely calm, detached, he reviewed his behavior, and accepted what he had become: a magazine cliché, a typical male in the midst of a midlife crisis, hopelessly vulnerable to any fantasy of youthful potency regained. There was nothing remarkable in this, and no doubt it would pass. The important thing, he told himself, was acknowledging as much.

Food: he was beginning to feel peckish, and hoped there'd be plenty for lunch. Drink: he could do with another gin and tonic. Large.

"What's the score?" he called out.

"Eight-nil to me, old son," said Hugh, holding the ball out of reach of Sylvia, high above his head, "but they won't give up."

"Like hell we will!" said Sylvia, pushing at his chest.

"Grope him!" urged Moira from the goal at the other end, and giggled. "That always makes him bring his hands down!"

"But what if it doesn't?" Hugh asked Sylvia, smiling.

She went very red.
And Tom found himself feeling tenderly toward her.

He dozed. He half heard Hugh declare himself water-polo champion, and Moira asking him to take a look at a suspected patch of algae on the pool bottom. He half heard Sylvia saying the patch was slippery to the touch, and the three of them discussing problems of pool maintenance. He sensed someone very close by and opened his eyes.

The ladybug—it had to be the same one—was back, motionless on a slim brown forefinger that moved into view from behind him.

"What is it," murmured Ginny, "you're meant to say to ladybugs? 'Fly away home, your house's . . .'?" The brown hand withdrew.

He glanced around at her. That one fleeting glimpse engulfed him. Oh, Jesus Holy Mary, she was beautiful! He noted no detail, just the numinous silhouette of her poised, unclothed it seemed, in a white cotton wrap against the sun. He turned to face the others. They were all treading water, and it glinted like a silver tray on which three severed heads were laid.

Moira, black curls and lilac stare; Hugh, deep-set eyes and dimpled chin; Sylvia, long auburn hair spread flat, pale lips slightly open.

All yours, so come dance the seven veils, my love!
My Ginny . . .

2

On Monday morning, a storm began just before dawn and rain was still falling heavily as Tom Lockhart arrived at the hospital. Hodgkins, the security man in the staff car park, hobbled from his booth in streaming waterproofs and snatched up the pair of plastic traffic cones in a reserved space, acting like a Cornish fisherman recovering lobster pots in a Force Eight. Tom parked, buttoned his raincoat, and covered his head with his briefcase as he climbed out.

"Good mornin', Doctor, sir!"

"Thanks, Hodgkins," he said, hurriedly locking the car door. "You'd better get yourself back under cover."

"Very good, Doctor, sir!"

And off the old reprobate shot, after taking a wild look around him as though dodging heavy mortar fire. Tom smiled. He remembered having once said to Geoff Harcourt, "Hodgkin's disease, in this instance, manifests itself as chronic inflammation of the mundane, infecting each and every situation with almost toxic levels of high melodrama. One way, I suppose, of converting what could seem a very dull, senseless existence into a life exciting and meaningful enough to be worth living—a divine gift, of a sort."

Running for the steps to the side entrance of the hospital, Tom Lockhart also remembered how often, during the past six years or so, he'd envied Hodgkins his gift. That was all changed now.

* * *

11

Between thunderclaps Sylvia, staring up at a heavy oak beam in their bedroom ceiling, had said, "Surely you weren't serious when you said that about us and the Ashfords getting together again soon?"

"Whyever not? You said how gorgeous their pool was, and I naturally—"

"I've never been so humiliated!"

He rolled over then and was surprised to see Sylvia biting her lip and the tears welling.

"It's raining, bucketing down, the sky is a heavy, leaden gray, the traffic's appalling even at this ungodly hour . . ." said Geoff Harcourt over the top of the *Daily Telegraph*.

"I'd noticed," said Tom, pausing on the way through to his office.

"Then you do surprise me, coming bouncing in here, at the start of another frightful day, all bright-eyed and unrepentantly bushy-tailed."

Tom grinned. "Could it be I just wasn't born an Eeyore?"

"I fear," said Geoff, disappearing behind his newspaper to add with a shudder, "it could have rather more to do with the state of your gonads, old chap . . ."

"Prognosis?"

"Well, I certainly won't last long, not if you keep this mad gaiety up, dear me, no. I've left an interesting little something on your desk, a Mr. Fred Buckland. Tell me what you think of it."

Tom wavered. He had a lot he wanted to tell Geoff, who came as near to being his closest friend as anyone—and some of it, had he the voice, he'd want to sing, there was such joy in him. But when Geoff lowered the *Telegraph* momentarily, to turn the page, his bland and bloodless face—which would have become the young abbot of a particularly ascetic order—imposed its own rule of silence.

"Humiliated?" Tom had repeated, looking up at the same oak beam in their bedroom ceiling. "By what? By whom? I can't remember anything that . . ." He had to search hard, having been obsessed for the best part of a day and a night with thoughts of nobody but himself and Ginny Ashford. "Oh, you mean that stupid remark of Hugh's, when you were trying to get the ball away from him and—"

"No!"

"Then what, then?"

Rain began striking the leaded windows and tears slid down the pane of Sylvia's cheek, disappearing beneath her earlobe.

The wire tray for general reporting contained several cases left over on Friday night plus a batch of new ones that had arrived over the weekend. Tom pushed the tray to one side, annoyed that someone had left it so pointedly in the middle of the blotter, and reached for his diary.

"Oh, sod it . . ."

He was down to give a lecture on heart size in high kilovoltage at three. Which meant his half-formed plan, of being in the area when Ginny went for her interview as a part-time waitress at Falstaff's, would have to be abandoned.

And for an instant he regretted having idled his time away the night before, lost in imaginary walks with her along an empty shore, when he should really have been doing his preparation. Now he would have to fudge up something from the Bart's piece in the RCR journal, and the sooner he made a start on that the better. His head of department had an unpleasant habit of suddenly materializing at lectures, tapping his teeth with the wax pencil he used for tart little memos.

Tom took down the Yellow Pages and found a florist's shop near to Tuppmere, the Ashfords' village. A dozen red roses and a card saying *Best of luck, sweet Ginny, from Tom and Sylvia* ought to help boost her self-confidence. He dialed the florist's number, but before being connected, put the receiver down. *Best of luck from Sylvia and Tom*—did that sound better? No, he just couldn't do this, much as he wanted to. It'd be seen as a gross overreaction, and Moira was certain to ring up and create complications. What was worse, Ginny herself would probably be embarrassed— making any attempt to draw closer to her difficult and this was already fraught with enough problems, as yet to be surmounted.

"That *bitch*," Sylvia had said, teeth gritted. "That common little . . ."

"Not your secret admirer, surely?"

"Moira? You must be joking!"

"No, honest, Hugh says his missus uses you as her yardstick in matters of taste, as her arbiter of—"

"Does she just!" said Sylvia, turning to him for a moment before facing the lightning beyond the windows. "Oh, she knows my taste all right, you could see that! Not one, not bloody *one*, even remotely suited me. All carefully chosen to make me look as ridiculous as possible in front of—"

"We're talking about . . . ?" interrupted Tom, irritated.

"Bathing costumes—what else? You can be bloody obtuse at times!"

That brought him up with a jolt, and he regarded Sylvia admiringly. By God, she had guts. Nobody would ever have guessed, from her carefree performance in and around the pool, that she'd been anything but thoroughly enjoying herself.

Then, hearing her sobbing, poor old lamppost, he almost confessed to his own agony of humiliation on the floor of the changing room. Instead, he patted her shoulder.

"I'm not asking for your pity," she snapped.

Tom paused and thought. You won't have it again, he decided.

He couldn't concentrate on compiling his lecture notes. When in doubt, as long had been his motto, take a nibble at general reporting—the staple diet of every diagnostic radiologist.

The first X-ray pictures, slipped under the clips on his viewer, gave four routine angles of the same human skull. *No lesion seen*, he wrote, after careful perusal, and left it at that.

No lesion seen covered the next set as well, and the same applied to the third: three views of a knee joint, more simple routine radiography. As with the vast bulk of his work, this was his first and last sight of the patient.

The fourth had him bending forward, looking closely at the stomach of a sixty-one-year-old plumber he'd dealt with himself. He picked up his ballpoint, ignoring the word processor that waited stubbornly at his right elbow, and scribbled:

Report: Barium Meal
Esophagus, no lesion. There is a neoplastic lesion invading the stomach from just beneath the cardia to about an inch short of the pylorus. Appearances suggest a lesion of the "linitis plastica" type. The duodenal cap and 2nd part of the duodenum appear natural, but the 3rd part is narrow, relatively rigid and indented from above, suggesting a mass of glands in this situation.

In short, the patient was doomed. And so on to the next one, a quick mammogram.

"Hmmm . . . anyone I know?" asked Ric Stephens, tipping his head to appreciate better the faint curve of breasts seen in profile on the viewer.

"I doubt it, no indication of rough handling," muttered Tom, who had taken an increasing dislike to this new cardiology registrar since his appointment a month ago. "And if you've come to remind me I've an angio this morning, I've already noted that. Just let me know when you're ready."

"*Sir*," said Stephens, and went off jingling change in his pocket.

"Definitely destined for private practice, by the sound of it," remarked Geoff Harcourt, as he replaced him in Tom's office. "Horrible smarmy little object. I just wondered whether you'd had time to—"

"Mr. Whatsit Buckland?" said Tom, hunting guiltily for the envelope under the untidy pile of reports he'd made. "Ah, the good Fred . . ." He clipped the X-ray pictures to his viewer.

Instantly, against the light, the dark, glossy sheet of acetate yielded the familiar silhouettes; images in subtle shadings of gray from almost white to nearly black. They had a particular beauty all their own, as delicate as the inside of a seashell.

"Well?" said Geoff.

Ginny had spoken only once during lunch on the weeded patio, while Hugh was cross-examining him on what a consultant cardiac radiologist *did*, as distinct from the senior registrar he'd known six years earlier.

"Radiologists are either diagnostics or therapists, and I'm still the former," he said, "just somewhat more elevated in rank, that's all."

"So there's this decided split between you chaps?"

Tom nodded. "Mind you, change is on its way. Diagnostics are beginning to establish their own areas of therapy where our—er, expertise—with catheters comes in handy. Embolizing, for instance. Or, say, giving blood vessels in the leg a rebore."

"Oh, don't!" Moira protested, putting down a drumstick.

"I warned you not to encourage Tom," said Sylvia, lancing a tomato with her fork. "But if you want to hear something really revolting, then ask him—"

"From what you were saying earlier," Ginny cut in quietly, "mostly you look for things in people you never meet, never see—at least not from the outside like the rest of us, with their skin on."

"Sorry?"

Hugh laughed apologetically. "That's our Ginny, Tom! Gets a bit deep for us too at times . . ."

She smiled at Tom. "Only skin-deep," Ginny said, with his gaze upon her.

He adjusted the position of one of the X-ray pictures. "Well?" Tom echoed, mimicking the cardiologist's tone. "You know I don't like pretending I read tea leaves. Tell me a little about Mr. Buckland and I'll trade you an informed opinion."

"He's a chap of sixty-five," said Geoff Harcourt, "who had apparently been well until six weeks ago, when he began to complain of breathlessness. Then a week ago he was seen by his GP, obviously in cardiac failure. That's been treated fairly successfully, but he continues to have substernal pain."

"Uh-*huh* . . ." said Tom, toying with a wax model of a human heart, known to radiologists as a "phantom."

"Can I have that in just a few more syllables?"

"I think he's got a cardiac aneurysm," said Tom, then pointed with his ruler. "If you look on that lateral view, do you see that rounded protuberance posterially, which is hidden in the A/P? And . . . looking closely, I fancy I can see some calcification on it. This unexpectedly white area of fine stippling."

"Which would explain a lot."

"He needs 'coronaries' and an LV angiogram."

"Fine, we might fix that for tomorrow. And speaking of tomorrow, how would you and the delightful Sylvia care to join me for a small flat-warming at eight?"

"You've moved in?"

"On Saturday. Nothing ostentatious planned: just Harry Coombes, his latest young lady, plus yourselves. Five take-outs from the Bengal Tiger—lobster mughlai—and a portion each of best French champers. Confess now, you're more than tempted . . ."

Tom hesitated. Sylvia, he felt like saying—what the hell has Sylvia to do with me? What about *my* young lady?

"You're not going to make some excuse, are you?" said Geoff, bland no longer but looking unhappy. "I know it's short notice, only the place is still so soulless and—"

"We'll be there, of course we'll be there," Tom interrupted him. "It was simply I thought we'd promised the Ashfords we'd all—"
"But you hadn't?"
"No, that's not till next Tuesday," said Tom, wishing it were true.

Once he was alone again, Tom wished that Hugh and Moira were in fact the sort of people whose company he sought, for that would make what was to come so much easier. Or would it? Presumably, no decent parents of a teenage girl would welcome the attentions of a much older man, and when he made off with her, even though to a future he *knew* would be good and beautiful and fulfilling, it'd break their hearts. And the nicer they were, the harder this would be to live with.

So there was at least this to be thankful for, even if it complicated the initial stages, to which he had so far given no serious thought. Such a love as possessed him could be very careless of time, practicalities, and circumstance.

"But enough of that, Lockhart," he told himself, turning to a fresh page of his notepad. "This is going to take some planning."

He sat for a long while with his ballpoint pen poised. He did not care for the succession of thoughts that followed. He ducked quite a few of them, not wanting to entertain fleeting mental pictures of Ginny in the midst of a giggle of girlfriends; Moira raising an arched brow over the increasing frequency of his visits; Hugh beginning to suspect something, and taking him aside for a quiet talking-to. Neither did he like how he began to feel about himself; at best, low, cunning, and scheming; at worst, as some sort of deviant—sweaty-palmed and glib, wholly indifferent to shame or risk, determined only to slake a raging thirst. And if his imaginings sometimes became grotesquely sentimental (for an instant, he also saw himself as a slavering beast, stalking a trembling fawn in the forest glade) then this only underscored the perverse nature of what he was proposing.

Perverse, he wrote, *WRONG!!!*

His shoulders slumped.

But loving someone couldn't be wrong. Moreover, he knew nothing could ever take that love from him.

So be it, he scrawled. *I will love, love with all my heart, now and forever, but nobody need ever know it.*

Although Ginny, of course, was already aware that . . .

"Sweet Christ!" he sighed, seeking some way out of his confusion; having been so trained, he resorted to cold logic.

The plain fact of the matter was, the risks—to his professional status, social position, and above all, to his self-esteem, should Ginny Ashford reject his advances with an incredulous laugh—were simply too great. Yes, that was it, and whatever she had realized instinctively, those six long years ago, was beside the point. He had *himself* to look after, Numero Uno, and when he died he would inevitably die alone—he had to remember that.

This settled, he slipped another set of X rays under the clips on his viewer, and jumped when the telephone rang almost immediately.

"Isobel, Dr. Lockhart, angio room—we're ready for you now."

"On my way," he said, grateful for the distraction.

The angiogram room had no windows. The patient lay supine on the couch, above a hidden X-ray tube and below an image intensifier on an overhead gantry. A nurse wearing, like the cardiac registrar, an off-white lead-lined poncho to protect her from radiation stood by the patient's head. She was prettier than most; a strawberry blonde with a whipped-cream complexion that suggested she was as nervous as the man she was meant to be reassuring.

"Who's this then?" the patient slurred as Tom walked in, dark-suited under his unbuttoned white clinical coat, adjusting a face mask. "Not that I care, s'long as it's not the bleedin' undertaker!" And high on premedication he laughed delightedly, jerking his legs.

"Hold still, man!" snapped Ric Stephens, who had inserted a thin plastic catheter in the femoral artery at the groin, and was trying to push it upward through the body.

Tom glanced at the notes and said, "Good morning, I'm Dr. Lockhart, Mr. Finch—that is, I believe, this patient's name, Dr. Stephens."

Stephens flushed slightly but said nothing. He glared at the black-and-white screen of the small monitor. His handling of the wire guide inside the catheter was as clumsy as always. The last registrar, a Nigerian, had seldom taken more than two minutes to reach the heart, whereas this morning it looked as though half an hour would be needed.

"I understood you girls were ready and waiting for me," Tom couldn't help remarking to the radiographers.

"Bloody hell, what's this?" cut in the patient. "You lot going to indulge in a bit of naughty, take me mind off—"

"Shhhh, Mr. Finch!" remonstrated the nurse. "You're the one being naughty! Try and be good, like the other patients we've had in this mor—"

"Been good all me life, luv! Time for a change, I reckon . . ."

The patient's face fell then, despite the effects of the Omnipon, and Tom took another glance at the notes. The man was forty-one, married, a fingerprint clerk at police headquarters.

"Cheer up, Mr. Finch," he said. "This shouldn't really take all day."

"It hasn't taken all day," announced Stephens, withdrawing the wire guide and smiling smugly. "Catheter *in situ*, one mil of contrast coming up."

"*In situ* where?" asked Tom coldly.

"There," said Stephens, jerking his chin at the monitor screen. "In the coronary. This *is* an angiogram, isn't it, Dr. Lockhart?"

"It is indeed, Dr. Stephens, but you may recall we had agreed in conference to begin in this case with a routine left ventriculo-gram, enabling us to see the size, contour, and activity of the left ventriculum. Our exploration of the coronaries come later."

What stung the registrar most, in all probability, was the two radiographers biting down on their smiles behind the lead-glass screen shielding the control panel in the corner. And yet, from the look he gave Tom, it was clear they weren't the ones who had just made an enemy.

Not much of an enemy, admittedly, for consultants were Goliaths who dropped boulders on the careers of impertinent stone-throwers; but Stephens had a very sly, devious side to him, as evidenced by how well he'd come across at his interview. Geoff had taken his usual approach, a quick run-through of the man's clinical experience to date, followed by an extended exploration of his other interests; which had turned out to be deep-sea sailing, early Polish cinema, and an avid interest in military history, with the emphasis on Balkan campaigns. All topics of which Geoff was completely ignorant, leaving him to be impressed by whatever Stephens chose to say with such enthusiasm, and to see in him the sort of well-rounded personality specialist medicine needed most, rather than an overdedicated professional. Not until a little later, Geoff had admitted to Tom, when the new registrar's true character emerged, displaying a mixture of superficiality, ignorance, and general insensitivity, did it strike him that such a catalogue of interests could've been craftily calculated to confound and impress practically *any* interviewer, giving Stephens the whip hand even though he'd fabricated every word of it.

Which, when seen from a slightly different angle, more than suggested that a degree of psychopathology was involved. And this, in turn, was probably why the look Stephens had just shot Tom carried a curious charge, a frisson that gave a boost to his adrenaline level, making his heart thump. In itself, this was of no consequence, being a purely reflex response to implied threat, but how good it was to feel again how he had felt the day before, as he'd followed Ginny out onto the patio.

God, it was going to be hard, giving up that sense of being so alive, so much part of a glorious creation, when even the traffic lights that morning, on his way to work through the rain, had glowed with colors so rich they'd made him marvel. Excruciatingly hard, but for his own sake, not impossible.

"What you starin' at?" the patient demanded, his wavery, Omnipon smirk back again. "Don't you fancy me moustache or something?"

Tom, who barely noticed patients' faces from one day to the next, removed his stare immediately, switching his attention to the monitor. Stephens, his sharp features honed even sharper by intense concentration, and his clumsy, nail-bitten fingers twisting the guide all too impatiently, was again having trouble.

Let him sweat, Tom thought, and joined the radiographers behind their lead-glass screen. He wanted to make sure there would be no further delay, though, once the catheter was positioned.

"Film loaded?" he asked, motioning to the Arriflex cine camera attached to the image intensifier. "I don't relish a repeat of last Tuesday."

"Yes, Doctor, it's loaded," said the more senior radiographer. "Ten to fifteen seconds?"

He nodded, then asked for the X-ray voltage they had chosen. This, too, was satisfactory. He watched the catheter nose its blindworm way past the aortic valve and into the left ventricle of the slow-pumping heart. He caught himself staring at the patient again.

"We're ready, Dr. Lockhart," said Sister McTaggart, joining him in the safe area behind the lead-glass screen. "My, you've got quite a tan this morning, I must say! Been swimming?"

"Proceed!" he snapped.

The pressure injector, working far faster than any thumb could depress a syringe plunger, slammed forty milliliters of contrast medium into the catheter so that it almost instantly spurted out the other end, transformed by X rays from a clear, colorless fluid into a blossoming, opaque cloud. The cine camera chittered its forty-eight frames a second, collecting up the data available.

"Stop!" ordered Tom.

A sudden silence, broken an instant later. "Phew," said the patient. "Was that all there is to it? It's over?"

"Not quite," said Stephens, preparing to switch from the pressure injector to the ordinary syringe needed for the first stage of a coronary angiogram.

"Yes, it's over, Mr. Finch," said Tom, emerging from behind the lead-glass screen. "You can go back up to the ward." He beckoned to Stephens.

"Smashin', Doc! Ever so grateful—and can I have me a cuppa tea now?"

Outside the angiogram room, Tom said to Stephens, "That left ventricle just bloody well doesn't contract, bar the proximal part of the superior border."

"Oh," said Stephens. "I thought—"

"He's a goner, *kaput*, so let's just admit how relieved we both are at having been spared another of your hamfisted sodding angios!"

Tom could not recall having allowed himself to give vent to such anger in years, but was even more uncomfortably conscious of the irony that Stephens and his incompetence, however provoking, had not sparked it off. Damn and blast Sister McTaggart!

Damn and blast Ginny, to be even fairer. God knows what she was going to do to the rest of his day. He'd have to find a cure for this.

3

His head of department, Professor Andrew Hughes-Sinclair, waylaid him before he could return to his office. "Ah, the good Thomas," he growled, an avuncular arm coming up, "a quiet wee word in your ear, if I may . . ."

Tom, with that arm across his shoulders, was drawn firmly to one side in the corridor. This seemed all very ominous.

"You know that I've attracted certain notoriety with my views on examining the temporomandibular joint by direct sagittal computed tomography?" said Hughes-Sinclair.

Oh, Christ, thought Tom: there's a paper touching on that in the current RCR journal and I've not even glanced at it. "Why, yes, of course, Professor."

"I'm wanted in Toronto."

"Wanted, sir?"

"Special conference, one of the main speakers, should be away a good ten days or more, depending."

Then he made a suggestion that left Tom Lockhart wanting to grin from ear to ear. God—or something equally providential, long-neglected and neglectful—was on his side again.

A snippet of that conversation had obviously been overheard.

"I'm waa'nid in Toronno," Geoff Harcourt drawled out of a corner of his mouth, with an accent straight from *The Godfather* "I'm waa'nid in Dee-troit, Kalamazoo, an' Clevelan', Ohio—you name it, bud! Dis is one *bad*-ass mother, y'know?"

22

Tom laughed. "Oh, I know," he said, "you irreverent bastard. But did you get the rest of it? The boss's going to deliver a paper, and wants me to deputize in his absence, starting next Monday."

"Good God," exclaimed Geoff, with a startled flicker of an eyelid. "Keep the old voice down, lest your fellow radiologists do mischiefs to themselves as an expression of protest. Or are Hunt and Williams already aware of this ghastly snub?"

"Hell, no. I'm sworn to secrecy, pending my decision. The Prof has told me to sleep on it, and I'm to see him in the morning."

"When you'll no doubt feel compelled to graciously decline his offer?"

"No, I think I'll accept it."

"What?"

"You heard."

Geoff stared at him. "Completely out of character," he said. "You are definitely beginning to trouble me, Lockhart. There's something about you today I can't put my finger on."

"Fear not," said Tom cheerfully, making for his office again. "Method in it . . ."

Running the department would be a horrendous, totally preoccupying ordeal, guaranteed to force his mind off all other matters, including Miss Ginny Ashford.

And in the meantime, he had that lecture to prepare for the afternoon.

But the cobalt-blue cover of *Clinical Radiology*, the RCR journal, which should have been easy to spot among the heap of the other journals, unread sales matter, and conference papers on the windowsill in his office, was nowhere to be seen.

"Buggeration," muttered Tom, and fell into a dither, trying one unlikely drawer in his desk after another.

He turned up a half bottle of Gordon's gin he'd quite forgotten was there, and then an early birthday present he had bought Sylvia at Orly Airport, hidden away safely until October. It was a flask of expensive French perfume with the name *Jini* on its label, which shook him.

Then he had an inspiration: he would go up to the hospital reference library and study its own copy of the current journal in a quiet corner there, sparing himself the inevitable interruptions he'd have to endure if he remained in his office. With only four hours or so before the lecture began, and with his other work to squeeze in somehow that day, this was clearly the ideal solution.

"Oh, by the way, Betty," he said to his shared secretary, popping his head into her cubbyhole of an office, "hold the fort, will you? I'll be up in the library for a while, but keep that to yourself unless it's something utterly vital."

"Fine, Doctor," said Betty Earnshaw, pressing the "pause" button on her audiotyping machine and directing her motherly smile at him. "Only, does that mean personal calls, too, like the young lady if she rings again?"

Tom froze, denying the wild, joyous leap in his stomach.

"What young lady?" he managed to say, possibly all too casually.

"Blessed if I know! Didn't wait to leave her name, not when I said you'd be busy in the angio room an hour or more, now that nice dark Dr. Onsulu has left us and—"

"Just how young a 'young lady' was this?"

Betty shrugged. "Not sure. Eighteen, nineteen, maybe? At least—"

"Did she say she'd ring again?"

"It was on the tip of my tongue to say try again later, but she said, 'Thank you!' and—boomp!—put the phone down."

Steady, Tom cautioned himself, steady. During an average day, I must answer the telephone to half a dozen young ladies or more. Radiograpers, ward sisters, admission clerks; Christ, the hospital was awash with them.

"Ah," he said, "this call must have come through on the internal system."

"Can't tell no longer," said Betty, "not since they put this newfangled switchboard in. Mind you, it wasn't a voice I sort of recognized, if you know what I mean. Something a bit unusual about it, really."

"Low and a trifle husky, like honey caught in her throat?"

Betty laughed. "Couldn't have been for us, then—it'd be ENT she wanted!"

"Very droll," said Tom, forcing a chuckle, "but I understood this wasn't a patient; you described it as 'personal'."

"Well, it sounded like one, but I never got a chance to—"

"Tell you what," said Tom, "I think we could be talking about a young cousin of mine, who's threatened to pass this way on a biking holiday and could be wanting a bed for the night."

"So if she rings again, shall I give her your home number, and your wife can—"

"No, no, Sylvia's away today, so just bung it through to the library," he said in airy haste, immediately wishing he'd invented a lie less fraught with complications. "Won't be much of a distraction."

It was a total distraction.

Tom almost shot from his seat each time the library telephone rang, and it rang far more often than he could believe possible. He tried to make a joke of this. He told himself that the stereotypical librarian, a self-righteous-looking spinster with a sniff, was actually doing a little sly bookmaking on the side, taking bets from the porters for the two o'clock at Epsom. But he remained shaky, churning, and quite unable to assimilate the data before him.

Yet another sinking feeling set in.

"Tom," Sylvia had said, as he was crossing to the breakfast table with their toast that morning, "you're not limping."

He stopped and looked down. "You're right! Can't have wrenched it as badly as I thought. Marvelous what a good night's rest can do for something like that."

"Sweet dreams?"

"Hell, no. I went out like a light, and slept like a log until the storm began." He tested his weight on his left ankle, wincing slightly. "And you? Are you feeling any better now that all that nonsense about the bloody Ashfords has been sorted out?"

"You've not limped since after lunch on the patio yesterday," said Sylvia.

The telephone rang again.

Tom glanced up, catching the librarian's eye. She looked back at him with a coolness that dropped ten degrees now each time this happened, obviously resentful of him monitoring her every conversation.

"Library here," she said.

It's Ginny, thought Tom. It bloody has to be.

Betty Earnshaw no fool, she'd sensed something about that earlier call, which was why she'd made such a thing about it. In fact, on reflection, she'd been far too intrigued by it for his liking, and it was a relief that she'd not be able to eavesdrop on the library line as she sometimes attempted to do on the one down in the department.

"I'm sorry," said the librarian into her receiver, "you're Mrs. who, did you say?"

Please Lord, not Sylvia! begged Tom silently, having no idea how he was going to explain away the twin mysteries of why his secretary thought his wife would not be at home that day, and the precise identity of the young lady wanting a bed from him.

"Mrs. Bentley? Oh, the field nurse, of course. Yes, the photocopier has been repaired now."

High kilovoltage. An air gap was simply the distance between the . . .

Tom found he was fighting to keep a grasp on the most elementary concepts. But even then, the journal's pages hardly made sense at all, remaining outside of him in curious way, as though radiology had never been any part of his existence.

Meanwhile, paradoxically, thoughts and feelings normally quite foreign to his experience seemed to have set up camp inside him. Three or four times that day already, for instance, he'd behaved as though there were a God after all, shamelessly beseeching and imploring the granting of favors. On top of which, he was now being dragged down by an alien sense of guilt, and it kept being compounded. Never, so far as he could remember, had he practiced as many deceits in so short a time. All this, when taken with the distractions he'd suffered in the angiogram room, confirmed in him a loss of control that was frightening.

The librarian unwrapped two rye biscuits, separated by slivers of pale cheese and a wan lettuce leaf, then poured herself a mug of clear soup from a Thermos flask with worn patches in its thin tartan pattern.

It was one. One o'clock on the yellowing dial above her head; one o'clock on Tom's wristwatch.

I'll cancel, he thought, closing the RCR journal without having made a single note from it. I'll do what I've never done in my twenty-two years in medicine, including those endless, exhausting stretches as a houseman in casualty: I'll fake D and V and go home.

Or I could first trot along to Falstaff's, of course, and see if I can't catch a glimpse of Ginny, when she turns up for her interview . . .

No, *straight home*, he instructed himself firmly. Take a bloody pull at yourself, Lockhart!

"Tom?"

He looked up and saw a pair of frank green eyes and a wide, lopsided smile he'd always liked.

Oh, Christ, he thought, now how do I pretend I've had diarrhea and vomiting, when the librarian, who can overhear us, knows bloody well I've not left this seat all morning.

And sure enough, Felicity Croxhall's next question was, "How are you? I don't seem to have seen you for ages."

"Oh, bearing up," he said. "Battling to cobble together a talk for this afternoon. And yourself?"

She shrugged. "Surviving, I suppose." Then she hesitated before saying, "It was today, wasn't it? Your secretary hadn't a note of it, and so I waited around for a bit, not certain, until she finally—"

"What was today?"

"I thought we'd made a date to discuss the Richardson case."

"Good God, I'd completely forgotten!" he said, jumping to his feet. "And it should've been at twelve-thirty, unless my memory's failed totally."

She nodded, smiling.

"Dreadful, unforgivable of me. Look, what are you doing for lunch?"

"I'd not really thought. I usually dash into the canteen and grab whatever's nearest."

"I'm having none of that! Come, we'll go to lunch together, and it'll be my treat. Is there anywhere you particularly like?"

"Are you sure?" she said. "Because I—"

"I'm adamant. Now, choose . . ."

"Well, what about that new place which has just started up?" she suggested.

"Falstaff's, I think it is."

This is crazy, decided Tom, opening the menu at the Purple Cockatoo. I should still be in the library, jotting things down furiously, not assuaging a guilty conscience in this reckless, time-wasting manner. It was further evidence of a loss of control, of course, when one's priorities all went to pot. And yet, just as a roller-coaster ride was frightening because one couldn't control what happened, there was something equally exhilarating about the state of mind he was in. He actually liked having thrown caution to the wind for once, and didn't really give a damn what dizzy, gut-lurching drop lay around the next corner.

"So much for poor Mr. Richardson," said Felicity with a sigh, apparently unconscious of how she was excising the fat from her steak with the evident technique of a surgeon. "We'll just have to find a way of breaking it to him gently."

"Correction: *you* will," said Tom. "I dread those confrontations."

"Which is why you went into radiology?"

He smiled. "I've always thought it was because I wandered into the department one afternoon and saw a particularly scrumptious junior registrar there."

"And?"

"Alas, there wasn't an 'and'," he said, starting on his own steak. "By the time the Prof let me join the firm, too late!—she was four months pregnant, never saw her again."

"You could always have done the decent thing."

"Ah," said Tom, "but I hadn't done the indecent thing, and naturally suspected her morals. Talking of which, how are you and Jolly Joe the Cutter getting on lately?"

Felicity made a face. "He's as awful as he ever was, but I've put a stop to his pawing me. By the way, he'll be at your talk this afternoon. Said he'd a couple of questions to bring up; his usual snide bit of axe-grinding."

"Oh, Christ," said Tom, putting down his knife and fork. "Why? What's it on?"

"Heart size in high kilovoltage chest radiography, unquote."

"Thought so. I've just been reading about that. Fascinating."

"Why on—"

"Oh, while I was waiting in your office, I picked up the RCR journal on your desk for something to flick through. The page was marked."

"On my desk?" he said.

Felicity raised one eyebrow. "What's so odd about that?" she said. "Can I tell you what struck me in particular?"

"Do," said Tom from the roller coaster.

It was extraordinary how well informed Felicity Croxhall had made herself in so short a time, notwithstanding her reputation as no beauty but decidedly a brain to be reckoned with. She talked on and on with her customary enthusiasm, citing one finding after another, and left Tom to simply nod in an interested way at intervals while he finished his steak.

By which time, he found he was in fact interested in the points she made, and that he had absorbed far more of the paper in the journal than he'd realized while running his eyes, again and again, over apparently impenetrable sentences like some layman. Moreover, Felicity's repeated deference to his years of experience encouraged him to show off a little. He began dredging up all sorts of apt snippets, and almost without thinking invented some very pithy ways of getting across trickier aspects of the cardiothoracic ratio values.

"That's marvelous!" she applauded, laughing at a phrase he suggested for his concluding remarks. "Mind you, isn't someone likely to find that a touch risqué?"

"Risqué? God, let them try one of Harry Bell's gynae lectures after he's been to a reps' luncheon!"

"But what about Hughes-Sinclair?"

"Aye, there's a thought," he said gratefully.

And looked at Miss Croxhall afresh, wondering why else he was so enjoying being there in the steak house with her. Or indeed why, on reflection, his instincts had probably played a larger part in inviting her to lunch than his guilt had. He had somehow known she'd be good for him.

There was that lopsided smile, of course, which expressed so well her outlook on life, a mixture of ready warmth and reluctant cynicism. A smile hidden for most of the day behind a surgeon's mask, leaving just her green eyes to convey a blunt pragmatism, and occasionally, with a sudden sparkle, a sense of humor that poseurs like Jolly Joe learned to dread. For the rest, it was close to being a child's face, very round, with a definite Gretelish cast to the almost pug nose, and far younger than her thirty-odd years. Her hair, a nondescript brown, had never been cut, making it seem a remarkable feat that she could coil it all so neatly away beneath a green cap in the operating room. Ordinarily, like now, she let it simply hang all the way down her back, soft and shining, inviting a fleeting fantasy of how it would look divided and drawn forward over her shoulders, hiding her full, pendulous breasts beneath its thick flow.

Tom looked back at her face and saw there a serenity, a sureness of purpose that calmed him; a friendliness, too, that felt like a gentle hug, making him want to tell her things, spill out his heart to her.

"What is it, Tom?" asked Felicity, laying a hand briefly on his own. "You're not yourself today."

"Aren't I? Whatever makes you think that?"

She waited, saying nothing.

So he resisted his greatest temptation, for surely a woman would be able to explain why Ginny had stood brushing her hair at a high window, and whether that lady bug had meant anything, and said instead, "Hughes-Sinclair wants me to deputize for ten days, starting on Monday. Dead secret, by the way, in case Hunt and Williams get wind of it before it's *fait accompli*."

She still said nothing.

"I've got to give him my decision tomorrow," he said. "That's all."

"That's all?" she said. "I'd . . ."

"Yes?"

Felicity reached briskly for the menu. "A sweet?" she said. "And this will be my treat, to even things up a little. Thank you, the steak was delicious!"

"I'll have whatever you're having, or I'll only be jealous."

"Two gateaux," she said to the waiter, and then to Tom, "Remember Miss Avery?"

For the rest of the meal they talked about Alice Alison Avery, the last case they had shared, and it wasn't until they were walking through the hospital grounds that Tom said, "Well, what do you think? About the deputizing business?" Felicity had seemed eager to drop the subject, arousing his curiosity.

She glanced at him. "I suppose it bothers me. Nobody can easily fault you as a diagnostic. There are times when you're not far short of inspired in your imaging, everyone says so, noticing subtleties the rest of us practically need our noses pushed in. But—well, administration isn't you, somehow. I can't imagine why you're even considering it."

"In short, I'd be making a big mistake?"

"I could be completely wrong, of course."

"Ah, no, feminine intuition," he said. "I set a lot of store by it."

Felicity Croxhall paused at the entrance to the operating room area. "You do?" she said.

"Definitely."

"Then if you ever want to talk about what was really on your mind today, Tom," she said, "you know where to find me."

Ker-thump! went the roller coaster, then started up another slope again.

Geoff Harcourt caught him trying to sneak back into his office, walking on tiptoe to avoid attracting the attention of Betty Earnshaw, who was bound to have thought up new questions concerning the young lady and her phone call.

"Hoping to join the Bolshoi's corps de ballet next season?" Geoff inquired. "Betty's been looking for you."

"She has?"

"Some phone call or other. She's gone to a late lunch now, so she's left a message on your desk for you, she says."

"Oh, good."

"Didn't spot you down in the canteen."

"No, I went out."

"Foolish boy," said Harcourt with a shake of his head, "you really ought to be more careful."

"Meaning what?"

"You'll find out soon enough, and I trust it'll be a lesson to you."

"I'm still none the wiser!"

But Geoff simply walked away, leaving Tom bewildered.

"Sod you, Harcourt!" he muttered a moment later, remembering he had that message waiting for him, and hurrying on.

Betty had weighed down the sheet from her memo pad with a phantom heart he'd been preparing to test some new equipment. The message read:

NO MESSAGES BUT YOUNG LADY RANG AGAIN AFTER ONE, NO NAME, NOT STAFF, NOT COUSIN, YOURS B. EARNSHAW.

4

Pocketing the message, Tom Lockhart left his office to walk blindly around the quad in the old part of the hospital until shortly before three, not knowing what to think.

On the one hand, he had no evidence to suggest this really was Ginny trying to get in touch with him, and so he could be allowing his day to be totally disrupted quite unnecessarily.

On the other, he had no evidence to prove it wasn't, and this made it impossible for him not to consider the probable implications.

Why would Ginny Ashford be trying to get in touch with Tom Lockhart? For only one reason he could think of: to convey to him, however obliquely, that she felt as he did; and to arrange, somehow or other, for them to meet again.

He pictured Ginny dialing the hospital from way up there in Tuppmere, across miles and miles of gray skies and green countryside, ignoring the years that also lay between them. He saw her smiling at the very thought that blue veins in ankles mattered, and wanting to reach out to embrace him.

Only that's one hell of an assumption to make at this range, he reminded himself, smiling ruefully at the all-too-obvious analogy which then occurred to him.

On impulse, he used it to conclude his talk in the lecture room, some ninety minutes later. "The crux of the matter being," said Tom, "that an air gap in high kilovoltage of the chest results in

32

magnification." Then, setting aside a phantom made from tissue-equivalent material, and the lead marker he'd been holding against the back of the heart at roughly the anatomical midline, he moved to the edge of the platform.

"I'll not spell out the melancholy moral this points to," he added, and there was surprised laughter. "I'll simply repeat the same warning, in a slightly different way, with a quote from the current RCR journal: Remember, gaps cause 'an additional *subjective impression* of a large heart'—something the more romantically inclined among us should all be on our guard against!"

Oddly enough, once he'd stated this publicly as it were, Tom found he had no difficulty whatsoever in dismissing all further conjecture regarding the two telephone calls.

It made him think of his wedding day. He and Sylvia had been married, in their view, since the autumn afternoon they'd first slept together, rendering the church ceremony a mere formality, a concession to parental notions of propriety. But the ritual had nonetheless wrought a change in him. By having uttered in public what had hitherto been avoided in private—to wit, a solemn promise of remaining forever faithful to her—all his furtive doubts about being able to honor this pledge had mysteriously fallen away. Perhaps it had helped to have something as clear-cut as the difference between black and white to deal with: either one was a man of one's word or one wasn't, and sexual mores as such didn't come into it.

Perhaps now, for much the same reasons, having committed himself to heeding his own caution, he was experiencing this identical sense of relief at having been released from choice, from the *ifs* and *whethers* and *maybes* of endless speculation, from those subtle shadings of gray that so bedeviled him.

Brisk, sensible, capable, feeling once again in full control, Tom returned to his office and sat down at his desk to plan the remainder of the afternoon. First, he decided, he would clear the general reporting tray, which had been steadily accumulating further cases during his absence; then he'd check to see whether his diary for the rest of the week was properly made up, lest he overlook another important appointment.

Lying beside Sylvia, as the lightning had stabbed closer and closer that morning (making him worry about the thatch overhead and whether it was really fireproof), he had placed his hand gently on her left shoulder, hoping to comfort her as she wept. She had shaken it off.

"Is it really just the bathing suit that's upsetting you?" he'd asked.

Sylvia laughed, not making a pleasant sound.

"What's wrong now?" he said.

"Isn't it a bit redundant, this sudden profound insight of yours?"

"You'll have to explain that."

"Once, Tom, I'd have been overjoyed had you seen beneath the excuses I made. But now I can't help feeling, what does it matter? We've drifted too far apart."

"That doesn't mean I no longer care about you."

She reached around for his hand and replaced it on her shoulder. "There," she said, "we're touching."

"And so?"

"Exactly," she said.

Tom switched on his X-ray viewer but reached for the flask of perfume in his desk drawer. He had to look at that label again, and make sure he hadn't been seeing things. No, there it was, in curling, elegant letters, the word *Jini*. God knows what had possessed him not to make a more obvious choice, such as the Chanel No. 5 Sylvia had worn on their wedding night. Naked properly for the first time, and heady with its fragrance, she had made a shy joke about Marilyn Monroe, and he had said that, being of lusty rustic stock and far from a gentleman, he much preferred redheads. This wasn't a term she usually liked—and it was true, Sylvia's coloring was really auburn—but she'd giggled in a surprisingly sexy way, before sliding her hand across under the sheet to squeeze him. The Chanel had been stolen the next day, presumably by the Spanish chambermaid. They'd not replaced it, having little enough money to last the rest of their honeymoon, and comforted themselves with the thought there was always the duty-free shop on the way home again. He had sneaked off and bought her a bottle of white wine with his remaining change, and she'd sneaked off and bought him a bottle of white wine with her remaining change. Both bottles had been of the identical cheap vintage, making a real exchange of gifts impossible.

"Jini? That's a new one on me!" said Ric Stephens.

* * *

Tom twisted around, startled.

"What the hell do you want?" he demanded.

Stephens affected a hurt expression. "Only came to tell you I thought that was a cracker of a talk you gave—and I'm not the only one who thinks so. For the lady wife, is it?"

"You've never heard of knocking?" said Tom, fumbling the flask back into the drawer.

"Door was wide open, boss, so I thought—"

"Knock in future," snapped Tom. "And stop addressing me as 'boss'—this isn't a bloody steel yard!"

"Sorry! You didn't happen to notice the tasty blond bit sitting over on your left? You know, in the lecture room?"

"No," said Tom, more icily than truthfully.

"Pity, I'd like to know what department she hides herself in. Quite fancy trying for two falls and a submission!"

"If you don't mind, Dr. Stephens, I've work to do."

"I know," he said, propping that morning's angiogram film against the telephone.

Then he went away without another word, looking most contented.

Before this intrusion, Tom had been just about to put the perfume aside, with the thought that here was another present he couldn't give Sylvia, and make a start on his general reporting. So he tried to carry on from about where he'd left off, and slipped three X-ray pictures under his viewer clips. But the images failed to signify anything. He sat, vexed and perplexed, getting angrier and angrier. God rot Stephens! Did he had to behave like a bloody adolescent? Did he seriously think a grown man had the time to waste on "tasty blond bits" and other teenage crap? Did he have to come sneaking into the room at that exact moment, filling the air with the stink of his pestilence? Didn't he have a home to go to? For it was after five, and the department should have emptied by now, leaving Tom to some proper peace and quiet.

He looked again at the three X-ray images, but nothing registered. His mind wouldn't work, neither could he seem to sit still. He decided he needed some coffee, black coffee, and he was damned if he was going to go through to the coffee room and make it himself.

He got up and walked out, fuming.

"You got troubles, chile?" asked the kindly-faced, elderly West Indian woman at the serving hatch of the hospital's main kitchen, pouring him a huge mugful of boiling water and adding a tablespoon of instant coffee. "Oh, the sweet Lordy Jesus, how he do try us poor mortaal crea-chus . . ."

Taken aback, and wondering how the woman could possibly have failed to realize she was addressing a senior member of staff—so clearly identifiable by his dark suit and clinical coat—in this extraordinarily familiar fashion, Tom said nothing. Then, with a pang of shame, it occurred to him that he was having his common humanity recognized.

"If I were a Christian," he said, "yes, I suppose I'd agree with you."

"All are God's chillun."

"You may be right, but why put us on trial when—"

"You wantin' sugar?"

"In a mug that size, four should do it!"

She laughed, showing how few teeth she had, and heaped each spoonful, stirring so vigorously that some of the coffee splashed out. "All dem angels," she said with a heavy sigh. "All a-pullin' and a-tuggin' to keep you from da big bad Debil!—gettin' dem *hooky toes* proper digged in. You go careful now, you hear?"

Tom was still smiling slightly when he turned into the west-wing corridor leading eventually to the radiology department. If nothing else, he thought, that exchange had added weight to a dubious theory which had been growing in the back of his mind all day. A theory that postulated there were times in people's lives when they appeared to become subject to a cosmic conspiracy, to a bombardment of chance remarks, unexpected encounters, simple coincidences, and trivial twists of fate all calculated to push them in a certain direction, according to some divine plan or other. Then again, it was possible to argue that certain states of mind merely made people alert to trifles which would normally have passed unnoticed, denying them any spurious significance.

Which view did he subscribe to? To be sure, it was wonderful to think one could be the target of so much magical good will, and that one's whole life was about to change, becoming infinitely happier. But should the reverse happen and everything go quietly to hell, then the folly of such a belief showed plain, for it could only needlessly intensify the pain of an already painful situation.

Tom took the theory by the scruff of its neck and threw it aside, wishing now he'd not been reminded of it by an entirely inconsequential conversation that had nonetheless seemed part of a process which was altering his emotional patterns in strange and—

Stop this! he told himself.

The scalding-hot coffee did him good. It made a back tooth ache a little, and that was a feeling a man could trust.

He balanced his cup on the word processor and looked once again at the three X rays on the viewer. This time, he recognized them immediately: they were a set upon which he'd already written a *no lesion* report. "Buffoon!" he muttered. "You're in a right bloody muddle . . ."

In fact, he'd no business tackling general reporting until he had examined the film taken in the angiogram room that morning, and delivered to him at the end of the day by Ric Stephens.

"I'll get you yet," growled Tom, "you sinister little bastard . . ."

Then he had to admit to himself that he was stalling, finding any excuse to delay placing the film of George Finch's left ventriculogram in his cineviewer. Already, he'd half an idea of why.

For much of the day, Finch's face had been haunting him, peering at him through the cracks between sentences. The face was waxy, white, and too smooth, making the head of wavy brown hair look artificial and the man's eyes seem altogether too glassy. The latter were of two slightly different blues, suggesting one had been taken from the wrong box.

Yet, it was a friendly face, with good bone formation, a dependable sort of nose, and a square chin that complemented the quirky line of the mouth. A face which, if the truth were admitted, wasn't entirely unlike Tom's own face, give or take a laughter line or two and the strawberry birthmark.

And if the expression seemed somewhat inane, then this was almost certainly attributable to the effect of Omnipon, while the same applied to the facetious remarks Finch had persisted in making.

Bar that one remark, of course, when his face had fallen.

"Been good all me life, luv! Time for a change, I reckon . . "

Too late, Mr. Finch.

Thank God it was no part of a radiologist's job to tell him so. Geoff Harcourt might have done so already, although the most likely person would be his family GP, who'd know him and his circumstances far better.

A 6:15 appointment, Tom imagined, so the GP could go straight home to chili con carne and recover. The last people still in the waiting room. "Do come in, Mr. and Mrs. Finch! Yes, I'd prefer to see the pair of you, and yes, it would be best if you both took a seat. Comfortable? Now, I have something to tell you . . ."

The GP looking down at the case notes, and then up again, ill at ease and wishing he'd had time to prepare properly for this moment. Opening his mouth and then shutting it again. And George Finch, noting his hesitation and obvious discomfort, saying with a smile, "What've you decided to talk about, Doc? Not the birds and the bees, is it?"

"No, the flies and the worms, Mr. Finch."

There had been a fly in the bedroom that morning, aroused in some primordial way by the storm, and sizzling in a fold of the curtains.

Tom knew damn well why Finch's face and that one remark had remained with him throughout the day. They had tempted him to identify with them, to cry out in turn, "Been good all my life, too, my love—and look where it's got me. Time for a change, I reckon!"

Because there was no guaranteeing that Thomas Matthew Lockhart had a second longer to live than George Arthur Finch. Any moment, anything could happen, from that airliner over-head dropping its undercarriage on him through the hospital ceiling, to a freak aneurysm going pop in his circle of Willis.

"Oh, balls," said Tom, purposefully out loud, and threaded the film into his cine viewer.

It was grotesque, utterly bizarre, to even suppose for an instant that he might see himself in this patient, however remotely. Admittedly, they were both male, both married, both in their early forties, and shared certain hardly unique facial characteristics. But there any resemblance ended, without their having a single specific thing in common. Not one.

The cine viewer's screen flickered, then filled with a slow-motion X-ray picture of Finch's left ventricle. It proved such a good image that Tom grunted with pleasure, adjusting the contrast control just a fraction. And when the proximal part of the superior border, the only section still pumping on that side, contracted, he froze the picture and sat back, simply to admire it. The shift in his viewing position revealed several fingerprints smeared on the glass covering the screen, superimposing them on the ghostly heart behind it.

Sweet Jesus, thought Tom, shocked. Finch worked as a fingerprint clerk. This meant that he, too, scrutinized photographic negatives images for a living, wrote up brief reports, and often sealed an unseen stranger's fate for him.

The fly, trapped in the bedroom curtains, had led to one of the most ludicrous and cruelest exchanges Tom had ever entered into with Sylvia.

"Tom, kill it," she'd said, pushing at him with the calloused sole of her right foot.

He ignored her.

"Kill it, Tom! Kill it this instant!"

"No."

"For pity's—why not?"

"You killed my spider."

"*Your* spider?"

"My spider," said Tom. "He had his web up there, where the beam almost touches the light fitting, and early these summer mornings, I'd watch him. We'd greet each other, say what a fine day it was going to be. You'd be snoring."

"Christ!"

"Well, you do bloody snore. Just try sleeping with someone else, and see what they've got to say in the—"

"Perhaps I could think of a better reason for sleeping with—"

"I don't doubt it! But the point is, if you'd had the decency and good sense to leave my spider alone, he'd have gobbled down that bloody insect days ago. Why did you have to—"

"Cobwebs! You know I've always hated cobwebs! Filthy things, full of—"

"Dead flies," said Tom mildly, and was momentarily distracted by how soft a smooth young foot would surely feel, caressing his calf muscle. "Sylvia, there is something I ought to tell you."

A high buzzing came from the curtain as she turned to him, raised herself on one elbow, and looked, even in that light, very pale, "What must you tell me, Tom?" she asked, dread in a voice muted by resignation.

"The spider you sucked into your vacuum cleaner had just become a daddy."

The short length of film in the cine viewer rewound swiftly. Tom set it running again. Pump, pump, pump, went the heart, very slowly. He touched the "freeze" button. The heart stopped, the picture jittering frantically.

"Dead, Mr. Finch," he said.

He pressed the "play" button and half closed his eyes, obscuring the defects in the heart and robbing it of its individuality. He gradually increased projection speed until the heartbeat matched his own. He increased it further, simulating the high pulse rate of youthful lovemaking, watching the heart beat faster and faster, more furiously, more joyously, then brought the speed down again. Down and down to the dull, plodding pumping going on inside him. He touched the "freeze" button.

"And that," he said, "is Tom Lockhart when the music stops." It was a terrible thing to look at.

Yet it did a man good, he felt, when beset by too many abstractions, to come face-to-face with something a little more concrete.

He switched off the viewer and sat back, sensing another irrevocable change in himself. He had suddenly understood and accepted the wisdom of a trite truism he'd overheard: *This life is for real, it isn't a rehearsal.* And so, if there was something he craved here and now, would give his right arm for, then to hell with convention and every other inhibition, *go for it!*

Moreover, through having given in to his impulse to treat a patient's film so unprofessionally, he'd learned something else. The secret of survival, when apparently under siege by strange forces, probably lay in simply letting go, in following one's instincts, and not in continually trying to second-guess everything. Detecting the patterns in grand designs and other such fancies were all very well, but they took up valuable time and one couldn't go to bed with them.

The moment had plainly come to make up his mind once and for all about Miss Ginny Ashford. Did he want her or didn't he? It was as simple as that. But somehow he could no longer picture her as clearly, and his thoughts had too little to focus on, other than a hazy, vague image which failed to move him in any special way. Here again, something more concrete was needed, something he could actually look at, but although surrounded by thousands of pictures of people, he had none of G. Ashford. Then he thought of mammograms.

Sylvia herself had killed the fly in the end, crushing it, still trapped in the curtain fold, with the bottom of an old wine bottle kept as an ornament. "There," she said. "And who knows, maybe in its next reincarnation it'll progress a step up the ladder! I've a feeling it was one of my miscarriages."

Tom held up one mammogram after another in front of his X-ray viewer, hoping for near enough the identical profile. He hardly knew himself; what he was doing wasn't merely shameless, but unforgivably unethical. Yet this didn't stop him.

All day he seemed to have been breaking with convention left and right, doing things he would normally never contemplate. He had finally reached a point where this no longer bothered him in the least, for his soul, if it existed, had long since been damned anyway. Then he began to have second thoughts about that, for something inside of him was still protesting in a faint, shrill voice, calling on him to acknowledge his wanton, foolish behavior, and to—

"Ginny!"

Oh, Jesus Holy Mary, there she stood . . . The pale gray curve of the X-rayed breast appeared perhaps a trifle less pronounced than her own. But the erect nipple he'd glimpsed, pert beneath a white cotton wrap against the sun, was duplicated exactly, engulfing him.

And seconds later, convinced that he loved Ginny Ashford beyond any doubt, loved every ounce, every cell of her, deeper than skin-deep, deeper than the very core of her, Tom Lockhart turned to his work, eager to rid himself of it as quickly as possible. That done, he'd drive up to Tuppmere, fabricate some excuse for a visit, and begin his secret wooing of her. It would never do, of course, for his intentions to be known by anyone at this stage— but otherwise, how simple everything had suddenly become, how wonderfully uncomplicated.

Drawing his writing pad over to him, he leaned forward to scribble the first of his reports. The light caught a series of indentations on the pad, left there by the pressure of his ballpoint when he'd last used it. He could read what the first line had been: *Perverse—WRONG!!!* He could remember having gone on to confess his adulterous intentions. He could not see that incriminating top page anywhere. Neither could he remember having removed it, before hurrying off to the angiogram room that morning.

"I can't sodding believe this . . ." he murmured, trying to remain calm as he started to go through those unlikely drawers in his desk again. "Surely, nobody would have bloody whipped it. Betty?" No, she'd have immediately given herself away, just by the look on her face afterward. "But who else could've bloody been in here and—can't have been Croxhall!" He happened on the perfume flask once more and noticed how tainted the name on its label seemed. He went icy cold and gasped, "Oh, shit, no!"

Yet Ric Stephens must have called at the office at least once while he'd been up in the library, to drop off the Finch case notes.

Instinctively, Tom panicked. He flung the perfume flask into his wastebasket, snatched the mammogram from the viewer, delayed only long enough to return it and the rest of them to the records office where they belonged, and then fled the building.

5

Sylvia laughed and laughed when she heard about it. She was still laughing when Tom arrived home late the following evening, in a hurry to change for Geoff's flat-warming at eight. "I hear your office's reeked like a brothel all day!" she said. "Betty's had me in fits! Dear God, how one's sins will out . . ."

He glared but said nothing, going over to the kitchen sink, where he could turn his back on her while he washed his hands. Bloody secretaries, Tom thought; having somehow survived one of the worst days of his life, he was in no mood for this kind of surprise homecoming.

"Who was it for?" Sylvia asked in an abrupt change of tone.

"What?"

"This ghastly cheap scent you had some sort of extraordinary accident with."

"The bottle had somehow become cracked without my noticing," Tom said stiffly, his toes curling as he recalled, yet again, having been stupid enough to hurl it so hard into his metal wastebasket. "This morning, it became apparent it'd been leaking out all night. Nothing too extraordinary about that, surely?" And then, because Sylvia remained silent, seemingly chastened, he was tempted to add, "Besides, it was an expensive French perfume, not 'ghastly cheap scent,' and I bought it for your birthday, as it happens."

"What rubbish! My birthday isn't for months!"

"I'm perfectly aware of that, only I—"

"Just how expensive? I've a right to know! That's *our* money you've been squandering on some little bitch! Do I know her?"

"For Christ's sake!" he said, soaping his hands.

"How expensive, you bastard? Very?"

"Didn't Betty tell you?"

"She said you'd got rid of the bottle before she got a chance to see it. Why? What was so secret, so *personal* about it?"

"Oh, you know . . ."

"No, I don't!"

"Yes, you do."

"I bloody don't! Come on, what kind was it?"

He hesitated, then said, "Chanel Number Five."

There was a sharp intake of breath behind him.

He rinsed his hands, switched off the taps, and turned to reach for a tea towel. Sylvia was standing stock-still, staring at him, stricken.

"Oh, Tom," she said. "Tom, I'm so desperately sorry. I've ruined everything again, haven't I?"

Once, he would have crumpled with guilt then, unable to forgive himself. He'd not foreseen how changing the brand name, simply to avoid saying Jini, could mislead Sylvia into drawing an understandable if wildly wrong conclusion. Once, all of two days ago, he might have been almost pleased to learn that she was still open to the idea of a reconciliation between them, and was eager to credit him with feeling that way, too. But this was Tuesday night and he was no longer the same Tom Lockhart, which meant that he reacted quite differently.

He simply walked out of the kitchen.

And it was only later in the car, as they drove over in silence to Geoff Harcourt's new flat, that Tom wondered for a treacherous instant whether he'd not been unconsciously cruel to be kind, as much to deaden something in himself as in Sylvia, before the time of parting came.

"I loathe Harry Coombes!" she said with sudden vehemence, as Tom parked outside the flat beside their fellow guest's macho Renegade Jeep. "His effing and blinding is tedious and I've never liked any of his common little 'dolly birds,' either. I do wish Geoff wasn't so keen on inviting him to his parties."

"Oh, Harry's all right, a little flash and repetitive, that's all," said Tom, much relieved the silence wasn't going to cross the threshold with them. "I think Geoff enjoys the contrast. You know, a bit like a monk fancying the idea of having a sailor's parrot for a pet—titillation without responsibility."

Sylvia gave an astonished laugh. "You do say some unexpected things," she said. "But you're right, Geoff *is* rather monkish in his way. Only I'd always imagined he was simply a latent queer, and Harry Coombes was his idea of rough trade or whatever the term is."

"Good God!" said Tom, his own astonishment making him turn to look at her. "Wherever did you get that idea? Geoff's no more a queer than I am!"

"I got it," said Sylvia, getting out of the car, "from the way I've noticed him stealing glances at you sometimes. Coming?"

Hastening up the flight of stairs to Flat 2A, Tom tried to collect himself. He'd never heard Sylvia offer an opinion anything like that before, and he was staggered by this startling change in her. It'd been like having her suddenly strip off her kitchen gloves and hit him below the belt with a hidden pair of knuckle-dusters.

"Why the face?" she demanded, waiting for him to catch up with her on the landing. "Something else I've ruined?"

So that was it. "Look, Sylvia," he began.

"No, *you* look," she said. "And you might see for yourself what I mean. I still like Geoff, for heaven's sake; I adore his sense of humor. And, I suppose, I can't help being flattered that my choice of man should attract such a discerning and eligible—"

"You unbelievable bitch!"

"You've got it in one," she said. "Now, which doorbell do I ring?"

"You can't seriously think I'd still want to—"

"Oh, grow up," said Sylvia, with her prettiest smile in years.

And the nearest door opened. "Gate-crashers," said Geoff Harcourt, looking out and shaking his head. "Thought I heard a noise. Well, I suppose you'd better be invited in, or you'll only—"

"Geoff, darling," said Sylvia, touching her cheek to his. "Lots and lots of happiness in your new home!"

"My thanks, the delightful Sylv!"

"Um, yes, same here," said Tom, holding out a tissue-wrapped bottle. "Nothing special. A modest malt akin to Glenfiddich."

"But cheaper?"

"Of course."

"See, Tom," whispered Sylvia, as they followed their host into his flat, "back at your usual boyish banter in under a minute! Didn't hurt a bit, did it?"

She was right, but only because he had withdrawn deep inside himself.

I can't *believe* this day, he was thinking, which had begun with the entire department being permeated by the smell of that bloody perfume, making everyone want to know its name—yet Ric Stephens, who could surely have revealed it to them, had said nothing, only winked at him.

Worse still, for it'd only increased the tension to an unbearable degree, Stephens had not dropped a single hint about the missing page from the report pad. For a short while, Tom had been able to convince himself that this was because he'd neither seen it nor removed it. But twice, by looking up quickly from the controls in the angiogram room, he had caught Stephens smiling at him. It had made the hair at the nape of his neck rise, and he'd been deeply shocked, never having felt so vulnerable at work before.

Not surprisingly, he had then started to make mistakes. These in turn had affected his temper, robbing him of his usual equanimity. In no time, all hell had broken loose, as though the fates had darkened his world using a pressure injector.

First, the row with the pompous idiot responsible for seeing that the cleaners did their jobs properly and emptied all the wastebaskets overnight; followed by the row with another pompous idiot, whose job it was to know that the ventilation system in radiology had been acting up for weeks; followed by yet another row, when both idiots turned out to be union officials, and Hughes-Sinclair had been compelled to appease them at enormous cost to the taxpayer by retracting some management proposal or other; followed by the most regrettable row of all, when the suggestion that Tom Lockhart should deputize as head of department had been acrimoniously withdrawn on the one hand, while on the other, rejected with utter disdain.

At least that had settled something. But wedged in between all this had been five visits to the angiogram room; three case conferences; endless general reporting, including what he'd abandoned, still untouched, the previous night; Betty showing a lively and unwelcome interest in all incoming calls from young women, even when she knew them well by name; and having to show around a party of visiting Japanese radiologists, with whom he'd also been obliged to have lunch. Not once had he had the time to finally make up his mind how to deal with Ric Stephens, or even to console himself with thoughts of Ginny, until, very briefly, in the car on his hurried way home.

And now this, Sylvia running amok, threatening to increase the level of strain in him to breaking point.

"So this silly ol' git," Harry Coombes was telling his new girlfriend, "the kind what won the war for us an' all, gets out and comes over to me motor, and he's dead stroppy, call us 'a young layabout' and all that, right? Then he wants me name, me address, and bleedin' insurance details—I mean, it's not as if I done more than shunt his effin' bumper, right? So I says to him, 'Look, granddad, that's a load of paperwork to get involved in, right? So I'm going to have to make it effin' worth me while, right? Guess what? I'm gonna give yer motor another doin'—only this time it'll be deliberate! I'll smack an effin' big soddin' dent in it!'"

"You never!" gasped the new girlfriend.

Harry smoothed down his quiff, transferring the grease from his nail-bitten hand to his embroidered shirt under an armpit, and let the tension build. "No, I never," he said, grinning, "but you shoulda seen 'is face! Tears in 'is effin' eyes there was, and he was pleadin' with us, right? Please, kind gen'lman, sir, spare me crappy Morris Minor! Stupid old sod."

"Fascinating, Harry," said Sylvia, approaching. "Lovely to hear your voice again. But *who* is this gorgeous creature?"

She was certainly a gorgeous creature, straight out of the radiology porters' collection of the *Sun*'s Page Three girls on the wall of their office, all bare bosoms and discreet crocheted tablecloths. Her gold spandex dress made little difference to this impression, for her breasts were so pronounced they'd have defied chain mail to conceal them. Not only that, but she was showing enough curvaceous leg to put a convoy of army lorries in the ditch, and her face had the classical features of any adorable young creature (puppies and kittens included): big round eyes, big rounded brow, and a cute little mouth with a hint of pink tongue showing. Oh, and she was a true blonde too, Tom noted.

"Carole, say hello to the lady," ordered Harry. "She's Sylvia, whose hubby—Tom, how are you, my son?—also saved me bacon the time I effin' near croaked it, only Geoff here—"

"Hi!" said Carole, with immediate friendliness, offering her hand to Tom. "I'll be honest, I imagined you lots older, being so clever and all! But you're nearly the same age's our Harry, right?"

"Wrong," said Sylvia, "although I'm quite sure the wanton flattery's deeply appreciated."

"Ooo, nasty!" said Carole, and laughed delightedly. "I got an Auntie Edith just like you! Always *terrified* me dad, but had us in stitches!"

And Tom, still with her silky paw in his grasp, couldn't help laughing too, as did everyone. Including Sylvia, who laughed possibly loudest of all.

There were no other guests.

This meant Harry Coombes's operation story could be happily avoided for once. He had inflicted it upon total strangers at various functions so remorselessly that Tom had once said it suggested he'd had an albatross removed, rather than bypass surgery. Instead, while Geoff handed out the drinks, Harry recounted two more of his motoring tales (neither of which had much point to them), and began a fourth.

Tom didn't mind. It gave him the opportunity to sink back into his chair, start getting some alcohol inside him, and take another, more critical look at Carole, who had lifted his spirits enormously. Small imperfections showed up: the tapering of her fingers was largely illusory, helped by the length of nail protruding over what were in fact rather stubby fingertips; a dim, azure tracing of broad blood vessels spread beneath the pale skin of her breasts at a point just above where the gold spandex cupped and began to cover them; she had a brown mole at the left corner of her lower lip, and from it grew a tiny hair, close-snipped. Even so, gorgeous was still the only word for her, and he marveled at how his loins had shown no response of their own to such a winsome wench. Why, only a week ago, he mused, I'd probably have been struggling with gross engorgement by now, and flat-warming etiquette notwithstanding, an immediate desire to mount.

"Oh, very good, Harry!" said Geoff, taking a seat beside Sylvia on the sofa. "No, I'd not heard it before. Had you, Tom?"

He shook his head, and turned to Harry. "By the way, how's the work going on that bungalow you'd just begun last time we met?"

"Got to first lift, didn't we? Only the QS'd ballsed up, and the footings round the back isn't even started yet."

"Typical," said Sylvia.

"Now, don't you start on about the buildin' trade," warned Harry. "I get enough of that down me effin' local!"

"No, what I meant was, how totally incomprehensible men can be when they discuss their work. You'd think they did it deliberately to exclude us! Wouldn't you agree, Carole?"

"I'm sorry?" she said.

"I can't entirely agree, Sylv," said Geoff. "The more romantically inclined among us—unquote!—have been known to use talking shop as an excuse to impress a girl and get to know her better."

Very aware of how intently Ginny had listened to him describing diagnostic radiology on Sunday, it was all Tom could do not to give Harcourt a sharp look. But he was unable to check the involuntary start he gave.

Then it really began, whatever it was. Tom knew only that he'd become the target for an onslaught of sly, casually dropped bombshells, each devastating in its effect.

"Right, everyone," said Geoff, beckoning them to the table in the alcove. "Dinner is served—nothing so grand as you'd get at Falstaff's, I fear, but reasonably exotic."

"Falstaff's?" said Sylvia. "Yes, that's the place to go these days, I hear. I know someone hoping to be a waitress there."

"Ideal," said Geoff, "for a cozy tête-à-tête, wouldn't you say, Tom?"

And Tom, unable to avoid looking back at him, saw a glint in his eye that could have come off a gun barrel. "I don't go in for them a great deal," he said, shrugging, "so you've got me there."

"Yes, I think I rather have," said Geoff, picking up a champagne bottle. "Bubbly, everyone?"

There was a lull. But Tom, unnerved even further by it, remained constantly on his guard, drank rather a lot, and barely heard Carole's comic anecdotes from the world of ladies' hairdressing. Then she switched to asking him about X rays, to which her Auntie Edith had been a martyr for many years.

"You are in a mumbly mood, Tom!" said Sylvia from the other end of the table. "I don't think I managed to catch any of that last sentence."

"Tom said," relayed Carole, "that he doesn't think X rays is why Auntie Ede's gone sterile. Mind, me mum's always said it's my Uncle Norman what wants lookin' at in that department."

"Your Uncle Norm wants effin' lookin' at, full bloody stop!" said Harry with a leering wink for Sylvia. "Should meet 'im, luv!"

"Why's that, Harry?"

"Maggots," said Harry. "Pockets full of 'em soon as season starts! It's disgustin'."

"What, does he throw them during football matches?" asked Sylvia.

Carole burst out laughing, and so did Harry, giving Tom a moment in which to check Harcourt's expression. But although slightly flushed after a large helping of vindaloo curry, his face was as bland as ever.

"It's *fishin'* season, Harry means," explained Carole.

"Ah," said Sylvia, sweetening an uncertain smile. "I'll remember that!" And there was something vengeful in her tone that Harry, still laughing, possibly missed, although Tom didn't.

"Time we adjourned to seat ourselves somewhere more comfortable," said Geoff, rising. "More champers is on its way, but I hope everyone got enough to eat?"

"Ta, it were smashin'!" said Carole.

"Aye, and a good laff!" said Harry.

"But Tom's only picked at his," said Geoff, tut-tutting. "Wonder what's been ruining the poor chap's appetite? Can't be young love at his age!"

"Oh, dear, couldn't it?" said Sylvia.

That did it. Tom got Geoff Harcourt alone in the kitchen while he was taking the champagne from the refrigerator, and demanded to know what bloody silly game he was playing at. Being fairly intoxicated by now, it was either that or batter the bastard.

"Not really a game," said Harcourt. "More of a warning shot across your bows, foolish boy, and so much more effective with your good wife present."

"Look—!"

"Careful, keep the old voice down. She *is* in the next room, as I said."

"Then tell me," said Tom, between clenched teeth, "what all these weird cracks you've been making have been in aid of!"

"Tom, you know damn well you've been having the frighteners put on you, in the hope it'll nip this ridiculous business in the bud."

"What ridiculous business?"

"These adulterous designs of yours upon a young female."

Tom, feeling as though an icicle had just pierced his innards, put out a hand to steady himself against the refrigerator.

"Yes, your secret is out," Harcourt went on, stripping the foil from the champagne cork. "Although how you expected to keep it much longer, considering how criminally careless you've been, I can't even begin to imagine."

6

"Look," said Tom Lockhart, fighting to steady his voice and keep it from being heard beyond the kitchen, "just what gives you the preposterous idea—"

"Don't start blustering, Tom. It doesn't become you, and besides, you know as well as I do that I'm right. A half-wit could have spotted the changes in you yesterday morning. You were your usual self at squash on Saturday, so I'd say you must have spent time with this person on Sunday, and ended up allowing a schoolgirl crush to get the better of you."

"What bloody changes?"

"Oh, you know, bouncing in on that manic high I remarked upon at the time; all sorts of little things. Not that I made anything of them at first, not until I began to sense there was more to it than sheer boyish high spirits. Call it intuition, if you like, but the usual trite symptoms—silly grin, a tendency to daydream, allow one's work to go to pot—weren't difficult to put together. My God, I realized, the fool thinks he's in love! And I saw immediately what this might do to your marriage if allowed to continue unchecked. It's simply that I love you both too dearly to sit back and—"

An incredulous laugh escaped Tom as he glimpsed the picture Harcourt must have of Sylvia and himself, against all the evidence.

"That's true," said Harcourt. "You do both matter a great deal to me, however amusing you may find it."

52

"No, I didn't mean—" began Tom.

But Harcourt cut him short with a wave of the hand, and continued: "The point being, I didn't want to go off half cocked until I knew who else was involved, or until at least giving you a chance to tell me about it. So I saw Betty, and went up to the library to suggest lunching together, only to be told by the librarian that you two had already departed to Falstaff's. That did give things away a bit, didn't it? And I must say, discovering who she was—a sound character, I'd always thought, hardly given to seducing married men—came as something of a profound shock to me."

"Who she was?" said Tom. When he caught Harcourt's drift, it came as a profound shock to him too. "Felicity Croxhall? You can't be serious!"

"Oh, but you looked serious enough, Tom, as you two strolled soulfully back through the hospital grounds afterward. Yes, I admit spying on you, and I'll give you this, her parting smile can be remarkably poignant."

"Nonsense! We—"

"And you saw me at your talk, where I heard that tailpiece so obviously inspired by—"

"That was just a joke, for God's sake! I was trying for an easy laugh!"

"But you were certainly very serious and rather troubled when you penned this, weren't you?" asked Harcourt, reaching into his breast pocket. "And, so far as I was concerned, it clinched matters, while at the same time offered a glimmer of hope—for it showed your conscience was far from happy with what you were involving yourself in."

He handed Tom the missing sheet from his report pad.

"So it was you who took it! You bastard, what right—"

"I'd a perfect right to return to your desk to retrieve my case notes on Mr. Fred Buckland, and you'd left it out for all the world to see, including Ric Stephens—or, God forbid, poor Sylv, had she popped in for a moment to say hello. Now do you understand what I mean by criminal carelessness? And isn't that what Miss Croxhall would call it, too?"

"But this hasn't anything to do with—"

And there Tom stopped, suddenly properly aware that Ginny had never been in fact any part of this conversation, and mortified by how close he'd come to disclosing the actual truth of the matter. He shuddered, thought again, saw only one way out—and dropped Felicity Croxhall's head on a silver platter.

"All right, I admit everything: her, me, the lot," he said, sighing.

"Excellent," said Geoff, giving an approving nod, and twisted the wire off the champagne cork. "Always been honest with each other, and I'm delighted it's to remain that way. Well, not much more to be said, is there?"

No, there isn't, Tom agreed silently, but felt he ought to put on a front of some sort, all the same: "Yes, there is, Geoff. What do you expect me to do now?"

"I leave that to you, my son. Although I'm fairly sure, what with all the worry you must have had overnight wondering where that paper'd got to, you might already have started to have very grave doubts about the wisdom of the whole business yourself."

"Too right! In all fairness, you ought to know she hasn't any idea I—"

"Don't let's prolong this unnecessarily. I really don't need to know the details; in fact, I'd much rather not know them. The crux of the matter is simply, having had cause to face up to the sordid reality of the situation, and bearing in mind, too, how Sylvia—or indeed, Felicity—would feel if she could overhear us, surely a lot of the magic's gone out of it? Don't you wish you'd never become involved in the first place?"

Tom nodded.

"Then there's your answer, the good Thomas," said Geoff, making a loud pop with the champagne cork. "Now toss that silly piece of paper in the waste disposal. We'll forget all this, rejoin the others, and see if we can't cheer you up a bit!"

Unbelievable luck, however, was something that Tom Lockhart had never trusted, and so his return to the party was accompanied by a sense of deep misgiving. He felt he'd been let off the hook too easily, too quickly, and this suggested that somewhere along the line he must have missed some ominous implication or other he had yet to identify. Having blundered as he had, there was surely a much higher price still to pay. The fact that he'd been absent from the living room for only five minutes, and that the terrible mystery of the missing page had lasted such a short time didn't really prove anything, except that life didn't always imitate soap operas and spin everything out endlessly. Indeed, perhaps the time factor itself had nothing to do with his unease, but lay instead with the character of Geoff Harcourt, a true friend with a consummate bloody cheek. What an old-fashioned thing to do, real *Boys' Own Paper* stuff, to try bringing a wayward chum to heel like that! But that was Geoff Harcourt, always had been, and as Tom had once said jokingly in the coffee room: with Geoff, appearances could be deceptive; he was invariably behind the times, not the *Telegraph*.

"Where did you leave your glass, Tom?" asked Geoff. "Ah, got it, good man!"

"Thanks, and I won't say 'when.'"

"Hark at this!" said Harry. "Bit of an alky on the sly, are we?"

"You've seen nothing yet," said Tom, having realized he had now to get very drunk indeed if he were to disguise the sudden confusion of feelings welling up in him.

There was anger, for Geoff had manipulated him outrageously; there was filial affection, because the silly sod had meant well; there was shame, over what had been done to Felicity's reputation; there was elation, at knowing his love for Ginny hadn't been discovered after all; and there was still the gnawing suspicion that he'd overlooked, possibly quite deliberately, some dreadful threat to his future happiness.

Harry then launched into another of his stories, allowing Tom to concentrate on the goal he'd set himself, a goal for which champagne seemed ideal. He had one glass after another. He began to think of weddings.

He thought of brides in virginal white, and of the old men at receptions, guzzling cheap bubbly, dropping almond icing into their shriveled laps, showering their stiff knees with crumbs of cake, all goatily agog at the prospect—for they stuck to a traditional outlook when it pleased them, no matter how much the realities of life had changed—of the deflowering.

"Be gentle, be gentle . . ." young brides used to plead in the dark, old men said, chuckling at the memory of their drunken fumblings. "Be gentle, be gentle with me . . ."—dear God, the last words their mothers ever taught them.

Tom couldn't recall being drunk at his own wedding, which, when he glanced across at Sylvia, didn't make any sense now.

* * *

Then someone burped, rather amusingly like a puppy.

"Ooops, pardon!" said Carole with a giggle. "But I do like a good curry, y'know, anythin' hot and spicy."

"Aye, aye!" said Harry, raising his coffee cup. "Hear that, Tom?"

Tom, who had been watching Ginny, all in white, brushing her hair at a high window, opened his eyes and looked around at him, raising an eyebrow.

"Sounds," said Harry, "like I'm all set for a right knackerin' tonight! Oi, Carole, your place or mine, luv?"

"Now, now, none of that," she said. "Remember where you are, Harry Coombes!" Then, turning to Sylvia, she said, "Aren't you lucky, not havin' the likes of 'im to put up with, Tom bein' such a gentleman and all?"

"It'd make a change," said Sylvia.

"What's this, Tom?" asked Harry. "Not a touch of the Uncle Norm's, I 'ope?"

"Thank you, Harry!" said Geoff, rising uncertainly. "And now, anyone for more coffee? A brandy? The hour is getting fractionally late . . ."

"No, not for me, thank you," said Sylvia, picking up her handbag. "And as for Tom, he's made a big enough pig of himself for one night, and so I really think we ought to go, while you've still—"

"Tom's never a pig," said Carole with a slight slur but very firmly. "He's lovely, all curled up like that, dead cuddly."

"Watch yerself," said Harry, warned her, lurching to his feet, "you're forgettin' he's the fella with the X-ray effin' vision! Oh aye, looks like butter wouldn't effin' melt, but I bet yer, last hour he's been starin' smack through yer knickers and—"

"Thank you again, Harry!" said Geoff curtly. "Sylvia, my dear, if you give me a moment, I'll just fetch your shawl."

"But one can't see into their minds, though," Tom said sadly to Harry. "That's the problem, you see. It'd make all the difference."

"Too right, squire! Er, Carole, ready for the off?"

Carole rose unsteadily, and with great care, removed a peanut from her cleavage. "There," she said, handing the peanut to Geoff as he returned with the shawl, "for yer sparrers. I've ever such nice sparrers at me own flat, and they like them, they do." Then she swung around and said to Sylvia, "If you ever wants yer hair styled and all—y'know, loads cheaper than that right poser's place yer usually go—just give us a bell, okay?"

"How kind," said Sylvia. "Nice to have met you, Carole."

"Oh aye," said Harry, leering at her, "and if ever yer fancies that change you were on about, Sylv—nudge, nudge, and say no more—you've only got to give us the nod, like. Play yer cards right, and yer could even get to see me soddin' great effin' scar and all!"

"Goodness, Harry," said Sylvia sweetly, yet with a vengeful look in her eye, "how the fuck did you scar yourself effin'?"

Twenty minutes later, on the journey home, Tom was still snortling at the deeply shocked expression on Harry Coombes's face, and savoring Carole's peal of wicked laughter. He'd not felt as warmly disposed toward Sylvia in ages.

"What an odd evening that was," she remarked, changing down to leave the divided highway. "Geoff, I had the feeling, was up to something, and your behavior at the table was a little strained, to say the least. Why?"

Tom said nothing. The champagne bubble around him, shielding him from the world, had popped suddenly.

"And then, when you two disappeared into the kitchen for what seemed like hours, I began to have some very nasty suspicions."

"Ah! You thought he had me bent over the waste disposal?"

Sylvia laughed. "No, that wouldn't have taken half as long, surely!" she said. "But you're right, my mind was running along those lines."

"Oh?"

"Those rather weird remarks of his. Poor Geoff, I think you were making him dreadfully jealous. He must've hated the way you lit up the moment you saw that lovely creature, started trying to impress with your 'X rays can be fascinating' bit, and then ignored him almost completely . . . bar the odd guilty look now and then."

"Really, your imagination knows no—"

"Now, Tom, be honest," she said, overtaking a bus rather dangerously. "Given half a chance, a few minutes ago, you'd happily have gone off with little Carole to her flat and her sparrers, wouldn't you? And you'd have been in bed, the pair of you, feverishly having it away, even before I'd driven this back into the garage."

"No, I would not," he said.

The car dropped speed as Sylvia turned to glance at him. "I do believe," she said quietly, "you actually meant that, didn't you?"

Sylvia's manner changed then, and she relaxed behind the wheel, smiling slightly. "All right, Tom," she said, "you tell me what was going on there tonight."

"For a start," said Tom with care, "yes, I liked Carole, her lively vulgarity especially. But if you remember, I didn't volunteer any of that stuff I told her about the job—she asked me a question."

"About her aunt," said Sylvia, nodding. "But what about the odd remarks and you two going into cahoots in the kitchen?"

"One and the same thing," said Tom. "I asked him what the hell he was playing at."

"And?"

Hang on, I'm still trying to invent a reason, thought Tom, then laid his second head that night on its silver platter. "Well, I suppose you could be right about Geoff. He was absurdly miffed about something. I had a working lunch with one of the surgeons yesterday—"

"—at Falstaff's?"

"No, the Purple Cockatoo, as it happens, but he got hold of the wrong end of the stick. And the rest, seeing your intuition's so good, you can make up yourself!"

"Ah, a female surgeon?"

Rather shaken, Tom nodded.

"Not that dowdy little Croxhall woman?"

He nodded again.

"And Geoff got in a huff because you'd not invited him to join you? Or—I know!—it was because *he* wanted to take you to lunch yesterday?"

"You've got it. I mollified him by fixing a lunch for tomorrow."

"Hoo!" said Sylvia, grinning. "Not bad in four guesses!" Then she took her eyes off the road to look at him directly. "Tom, do you realize what's just happened? You've actually given me credit for not being a total idiot for once—and just listen to how we've been happily chatting . . ."

Then she turned away and fell silent, having to concentrate now on unlit country roads. But also because, he supposed, she wanted to savor the moment; not knowing he'd presented her with a cheap lie that she'd decanted and handed back in an exchange of identical bottles.

* * *

The leather fob dangling from the ignition key bobbed and swayed, reminding Tom of something he'd seen recently. He settled back in the passenger seat, his head swimming, and propped his feet against the dashboard.

He stared at the fob.

Sylvia changed gear.

The fob bobbed and swayed.

His eyes began closing. How different he now felt. It was as though the past twenty-four hours had never happened, and that he'd been released—like a balloon escaping the grasp of a nasty, spoiled child—to go soaring up, with the sky his limit and Ginny his rainbow.

Tomorrow, he promised himself, I'll see her again. One way or the other, I'll see her. He made that a solemn vow, and knew he'd not break it. He also knew, with sudden insight, why Harry Coombes's new girlfriend hadn't made him want to go to bed with her. That would be a little like expecting a man with a Botticelli on his wall to swap it for a saucy seaside pinup on a postcard.

Sylvia swore softly and swerved.

Tom opened his eyes and saw the crinkly-leather fob bobbing and swaying, just like Hugh Ashford's genitals had done, when he'd hastened, stark naked, across the duckboards to a fallen friend's assistance in the changing room on Sunday. It seemed impossible that anything so gloriously beautiful, so God-given as Ginny, could ever have come into this world, not rising on a great scallop shell from a sparkling blue sea, but through that stubby, meaty tube and its thick-veined foreskin.

Impossible, yet true, as every doctor knew. And this, Tom Lockhart also conceded, was a fact he'd just have to reconcile himself to. But that could wait until morning.

7

Sylvia was still asleep when the note was propped against her bedside radio at 7:30 A.M. the next day. The note said that Tom had made an early start as he'd a lot of catching up to do. It was not signed *Love, Tom,* but ended with an X.

He set off for the hospital in no great hurry. The morning air was as fresh and crisp as a lettuce leaf, and the sky already a deepening blue. At the crossroads, he turned left instead of right and drove toward Tuppmere, where the Ashfords lived.

He did not think about it. He just went.

The approach to Tuppmere was down a steep, wooded hillside with a sharp bend every seventy yards or so. The road was a slow descent that yielded a series of vignettes, each having the vivid intensity of a pre-Raphaelite: a glimpse of sun-slanted glade, another of toadstooled log and tumbling stream, then a slack-slung web sparkling with dewdrops. They made Tom want to give thanks, for the beauty to be found in natural things always had this effect on him. But as usual, not knowing where to direct his thanks, he grew edgy. He accelerated.

Which was idiotic, he conceded, when he had to brake hard through the next bend; he dropped speed again. A bright yellow flash in the wings of a bird startled from an overhanging branch awed him. This was when it seemed obvious he could thank Ginny for all this, as she personified everything he was feeling at that moment, including his yearning to somehow merge with such beauty, to become part of it himself. When very young, he had often wished he'd been born a baby otter in the snug riverbank below his father's farm.

A milk tanker suddenly appeared, horn blaring, grinding up the slope and crowding him off the narrow road. He had to slew sharply, stopping with his nearside wheels almost in the ditch.

As he started moving again he began to question what he actually intended doing once he reached Tuppmere, now a scant half mile off. But even as he did so his thoughts were drawn back to the extraordinary fancy he'd had, to this notion of giving thanks to Ginny. On reflection, its whimsy proved even more pronounced and worthy of dismissal, yet he couldn't deny a strong appeal to the pagan in him.

So he said aloud, "Thanks, Ginny . . ."—and smiled, both at himself and because of how right that had sounded.

A barn, mossy-tiled and of rough gray stone, marked the beginning of Tuppmere; and was followed immediately by a farmhouse built almost on the road. The farmer was cranking an old tractor in the yard and did not look up. Next came a row of small cottages with uneven tiles, facing a small playing field, and beyond them stood some larger cottages, several houses, a village hall, a doctor's office, a shop-cum-newsstand, a pub, and a pottery with a white cat in its bow window.

Tom did not stop. His intrusion had already attracted a glare from Tuppmere's sole pedestrian at that hour, a jodhpured woman being tugged along by an Irish wolfhound big enough to catch (and possibly bury in its garden) passing motorcyclists. Cloud Hill, the Ashford property, was not in the village itself but situated a few hundred yards farther on, screened by a small plantation of Scots firs near a rest stop—an area situated, he soon confirmed, to the south of Cloud Hill's gates, and this meant, as Hugh turned north to drive to work, he'd not spot a possibly familiar vehicle parked there.

"Perfect," said Tom, braking beside a picnic table.

It excited him, simply being no distance at all now from Ginny. His pulse rate rose, making him feel intensely alive once more, and he liked that. What else he had to gain, however, was still none too clear. The firs on his left, rising from a billow of fern and bracken, were far too close together to allow so much as a corner of the house to show through, let alone anyone standing at a high window.

Again without thinking he climbed out, stretched, and started to follow the line of the three-strand wire fence bordering the road.

Soon the cuffs of his trousers were sodden with dew, and mud was caking the soles of his polished black shoes. But he took little heed of this, being too intent on finding a gap in the trees somewhere.

He began to curse so much bloody greenery. He reached a corner post, where the fence went off at a right angle from the road, and started down the slope, soaking his trousers to the knees in the undergrowth.

"You're bloody mad, Lockhart," he muttered, yet had to admit he was thoroughly enjoying himself as he stole stealthily along like an Apache, watching out for dead branches that might snap beneath his feet.

A good way down the slope the impenetrable screen of firs ended and a rough meadow lay stretched before him. Only the house was now hidden by a distant windbreak of yew trees, every bit as impenetrable themselves.

He glanced at his watch. Good God, 8:20—he was going to be late for work!

His mood changed abruptly. He started back up the slope, feeling increasingly appalled by his foolish and irrational behavior. The juvenile impulse that had tempted him to play truant for the first time in his life now promised to make his entire day a hideous muddle and a hell of self-reproach.

"Idiot!" he hissed at himself, sickened. "You incredible bloody fool! And all for what? You *knew* this—oh, bollocks!"

He'd slipped, landing on his knees, and realized he would just have to stop and remove the mud from his shoes if he were to climb the slope. He used the lowest strand of the fence as a boot scraper, setting up a loud rattling in the iron fence posts on either side of him. A moment or two later there was a heavy thudding sound, and he looked up in alarm—only to see two ponies, attracted by the noise from behind a clump of willows, approaching at a trot. They came right up to him, whinnying and snorting, and stretched their necks over the fence to nuzzle hopefully at his pockets.

"Cheeky little sods!" he said. "You've no shame at all, have you?" Then he laughed despite himself as they persisted in trying to extract a tidbit from him. "Sorry, you two!—not a thing on me . . ." He stroked and patted them, delighting in their warmth and firm, satiny feel. "Ginny. You're Ginny's, aren't you? Too right you are, you jammy buggers, and it's Ginny you give rides to. I don't suppose you've ever heard her say she—oi, you behave!" Tom grabbed the tubbier pony's halter and dragged its velvety muzzle from inside his jacket. "We'll have less of that, you greedy bastard! Oh, got a name, have you?" He reached for a brass medallion he'd just this moment noticed attached to the halter.

The name on this medallion was *Gutsiest*, and on that attached to the other pony, *Windfall*.

Geoff Harcourt put his head around the office door. "Ah, Señor Gonzales, so you made it after all," he said. "Betty gave me a bad moment on arrival, saying you'd rung to report you'd had a puncture and mightn't be here until God knows when."

Tom, who was scrubbing at caked mud on his trouser cuffs with a nail brush, looked up for a moment and grinned. Too true, he must have established some sort of land-speed record on the way in from Tuppmere, handling his car superbly; he'd never felt such a sense of wild exhilaration, of such cocky confidence in himself.

"I see," said Harcourt, "came a cropper in the ditch, did we, changing tires?"

"Something like that!"

"And there was I, convinced you were romancing."

"Romancing?" repeated Tom sharply.

"Last night's Bacchic excesses, dear boy. I've a bloody awful head myself this morning, and thought you might be still languishing abed, fabricating yarns to disguise your exact whereabouts."

"Not a bit of it! Been up for hours."

There was a pause, as though Geoff wanted to say something about the party, then he apparently changed his mind and remarked, "I'll be in the angio room in fifteen minutes."

"Fine!" said Tom, and went back to brushing at his cuffs.

But Harcourt lingered. "Everything all right?" he said.

Oh, Christ, thought Tom, he's noticed I'm on a so-called manic high again, and this could get complicated. "Better than all right, Geoff!" he said. "Thanks mainly to your good self, I suppose, although naturally it hurts to say so."

Harcourt looked at him inquiringly.

"You know, that talk we had last night?" said Tom, still brushing, as it gave him an excuse to keep his eyes averted. "Feel I've got my head screwed on the right way round now, and yes, I had a quick word from a call box with a certain someone on the way in this morning, and that's all taken care of. A bit upset, but really as relieved as I am, she's not really that kind of—"

"Does she know I—?"

"Hell, no, I've more sense than that!"

Harcourt smiled, quite obviously for once. "A relief to me, too, I suppose. I wouldn't want to get a reputation for—well, not minding my own business. But as I said, you and Sylvia—"

"Talking of which," Tom cut in, seeing a chance to spike the interfering bugger's guns once and for all, nipping *this* nonsense in the bud, "you must've realized things can't have been too idyllic between Sylv and me for this to have happened in the first place. But that seems to have changed too. Noticed it after the party. Happiest evening we'd spent together in ages, all in all, and you've no idea how one thing tended to lead to another after we left. Got you to thank for that, I think. In fact, Geoff, I've another confession to make: it's true, part of the reason I was late had to do with a spot of languishing we—"

"Mind you," Harcourt said hastily, coloring as he swallowed whole this load of old cod's wallop, "the gods probably had the major hand in things, so I can hardly take all the—"

"The gods?" said Tom, smiling.

"Or whatever," mumbled Geoff, moving toward the door.

"No, seriously, I was sort of thinking about them only this morning. Do you think they really do intervene occasionally?"

"What, sit about on Mount Olympus, saying to themselves, 'Here's an idea, let's have some fun and games with that mere mortal down there, young what's-his-name . . .'—that sort of thing?"

Tom nodded.

"Hmmm," said Geoff, shrugging. "I suppose one could be tempted to see them as having put one into an intolerable situation, hoping one'll squirm and wriggle entertainingly, while they all watch it reflected in some magic pool or other, tossing in a pebble from time to time to ginger things up."

"Oh? I had in mind a more benign collection of divine beings who, provided there'd been sufficient placatory sacrifice beforehand, now and then dreamed up a special treat for one. Something wonderful, breathtakingly—"

"There are no gods," said Geoff Harcourt brusquely, the pain fleeting on his face like a raven's shadow.

Left alone again in his office, all Tom could think about was the choice of names for those two ponies.

Pure chance, insisted the most cynical side of him. The names had been picked at random, and had no significance whatsoever.

Fat chance, retorted the most logical side of him. Nobody would dream of giving names like that to ponies in the ordinary way, and for Ginny to have picked on Gutsiest and Windfall entirely at random was—well, the odds against this happening would be astronomical, unimaginable.

Not chance, but equally not anything to make too much of, argued the most sensible side of him. That long-ago encounter with the ponies Adam and Eve had simply made a strong impression on a young girl who, wanting to recapture something of the moment while exercising some originality, had merely chosen two other words which had stuck in her memory of her introduction to them. The fact that these two words had been uttered by Tom Lockhart was in itself immaterial; she'd have done the same if Sylvia had used them.

GINNY LOVES YOU—*that's what those names mean!* shouted the rabble rest of him, and this voice was by far the loudest.

Threatening to drown out his day.

So Tom decided, with great firmness, to turn his attention to breadwinning for a while, setting such imponderables aside for the time being.

He expected this to be difficult.

But having made a start on his pile of general reporting, he found himself whisking through diagnosis after diagnosis, phrasing each report with elegant precision and tremendous self-confidence. His zest and energy astonished him; he felt ready to take on anything from a hundred more angiograms to a fire-breathing dragon. By ten to one, he had cleared not only the backlog but that morning's radiography as well, leaving him free to study the case notes for the tricky examination of a cyanotic infant at two-fifteen.

Instead, he felt again a satiny firmness, warm against the palm of his right hand, and daydreamed until a quarter to one, not of ponies.

* * *

Felicity Croxhall brought her lunch tray over to his table in the canteen, and with a thoughtful frown on her face, sat down opposite him.

"Oh, hello," he said, flinching as guilt plunged its knife in him. Then he hurriedly tapped the cyanotic's case notes, which lay beside his plate. "Just briefing myself on what sounds like it'll be the bluest blue baby ever seen in the department."

But Felicity was not to be so easily sidetracked. "I've just had the strangest two minutes with your friend Geoff Harcourt," she said.

"He's not—?" said Tom, quickly looking around.

"I've no idea where he is," she said. "He came up to me, outside the main entrance, and said what a glorious day it was. I said, yes, it was. I waited, thinking he must have something else he wanted to say, but he just stood there, stroking the side of his cheek, looking at me. I mean, I find he makes me uncomfortable enough without this sort of behavior."

"Uncomfortable?" said Tom. "I don't understand."

"You would if you were female," said Felicity, lifting her long hair away from her face. "He has this . . . this aura."

Tom took a sip of his coffee, rather noisily.

"It's some form of yearning, I suppose," Felicity went on, with a more brisk, professional tone to her voice. "You can almost feel it nuzzling against you at times, but when you turn to look at him, his eyes shoot away. It's awful. You feel they've somehow left some sort of mucky mark on you, and yet at the same time you're feeling dreadful for frightening someone like that. I just wish he could find himself someone he could spend a very long and dirty weekend with and finally get whatever this is out of his system."

Tom's coffee cup clattered back into its saucer.

"Why so surprised?" said Felicity. "I'd have thought your wife must have mentioned it to you ages ago! But I'm digressing."

"Look," said Tom, "I'm not sure this is either the time or place to—"

"Then," said Felicity, dipping a stick of celery in her mayonnaise, "he suddenly asked if I was 'all right.' I didn't know what to make of that at all, because from the way he said it, you'd think I'd been on his conscience half the night! I said, yes, I was fine, thank you, and that was it—off he went, quite happily. Now tell me, whatever does one make of that?"

Tom reached for his coffee cup, but he'd already drained it.

What worried him most at that moment was that here was someone who'd already proved her intuitive powers weren't to be trifled with, making a swift fib imprudent.

"Obviously, what you sensed must be correct," he said. "A bad conscience. Only could it've been from a dream he had?"

Felicity laughed. "That's even worse! Makes me feel I've become a part of his fantasy life, poor man! And don't keep blinking at me like that. Honestly, Tom, as horrible as it is of me to say it, there are times when I think that if Geoff weren't quite so inhibited and frightfully civilized, he'd probably be out every night in a grubby mac, doing his heavy breathing bit." Then she smiled her lopsided smile, and added, "Not that, given the same lack of restraints, we'd mind giving him something really worth peeping at, I suppose! What chaos life'd be without our taboos and our hang-ups."

Then it was Betty Earnshaw's turn to contribute to his confusion.

"Doctor!" she called out, intercepting his hasty return from the canteen. "Doctor, a message for you! That young lady's phoned again, and this time she's left a number."

Tom took the proffered slip of paper and, noticing his hand start to shake, quickly buried them both in his jacket pocket. "Er, thanks," he said. "I'll see to it later."

"A right little Miss Mystery, isn't she?" said Betty, falling into step beside him. "Still didn't leave a name or anything."

"She didn't?"

"No, didn't you see? I'd have writ it down as well, wouldn't I? I mean, that's three times she's rung you, and you'd think—"

"Actually, I believe I know who this is now," Tom heard himself glibly ad-lib, wanting to put an end to the bike-hiking niece story before it reached Sylvia in the same way as the perfume incident had done. "Number rings a bell. Must be that hypochondriacal pest of a girl we did an angio on last month, and who won't accept there's nothing the matter with her. She knows you might recognize her as a patient if she gives her name, and that's why, the last time she rang, she also just gave her number to the night switchboard."

"*Sounds* just the same one to me," said Betty.

"Be that as it may," said Tom, "I don't have the time right now for all this, as I've a blue baby's notes I've still not properly looked at, and the angio's only about twenty minutes from now."

"Like me to ring her back, Doctor? I could say—"

"I'll attend to it, I said, Betty!"

"Only trying to help," she grumbled.

Tom closed his office door behind him, took the slip of paper from his pocket, and propped it against the telephone. His hand was still shaking. Then, with a pencil poised to begin dialing, he reached for his receiver.

In seconds, he'd be speaking to Ginny. He just knew it.

8

Tom Lockhart did not touch his telephone until twenty past two, when Isobel Craig, the senior radiographer, rang through to remind him he had a cyanotic infant waiting in the angiogram room.

It wasn't simply that he'd taken fright again, as he had on Sunday when Ginny Ashford opened her parents' front door. Tom had begun wondering what right he had, as a mere mortal, to pursue happiness at the cost of others.

Just say he was correct, and Ginny had been trying to contact him. Just say he deliberately did all he could to consolidate what appeared to be the uncanny bond between them, and this led to their going off blissfully together, into the sunset. What then? Like a great rock dropped into the pool on Mount Olympus, the lives of a great many people would be devastated, destroyed even, and among the first casualties would be Sylvia, his parents, in-laws, Hugh and Moira, their parents, if any . . . On top of which, dare he think it, what about the effect it could ultimately have on Ginny's own life? At best, she'd certainly end up a young widow, because of the disparity in their ages, and would be left to grieve for a score of years or more, tragically alone. But all this was really peripheral to the crucial question before him. Had any mortal the right to act simply as he wanted to, casting aside all other considerations in the interests of his own gratification? Surely, only the gods were entitled to willfully inflict so much misery in the pursuit of joy.

"And I'm not a ruddy god," muttered Tom, as he hurriedly changed into a green gown, mask, and cap, glad of the distraction but wishing he'd given himself longer to study the far-from-abstract problem about to confront him. "So forget it."

"Bloody part-timer," said Dr. Darby Freeman, by way of greeting.

Tom followed his gaze to the angiogram room's wall clock. "Only eight minutes adrift, but that's enough to give you the impression I've been idling my time away while you've been slaving away all day over a hot oxygen cylinder?"

Freeman, down from the intensive care unit to provide specialist help with the anesthetics, waved two rubber-gloved fingers at him, each the size and color of uncooked pork sausages, and resumed his check on the respiration rate.

"Australia's loss," Tom said to Geoff Harcourt, inclining his head at Freeman, "has hardly been England's gain, would you think?"

"Hmmm," responded Geoff, intent on the monitor screen as he directed a wire guide, sheathed in a catheter, through the small blood vessels.

"Although," added Tom, "I suppose one has to admit that the hospital rugby team has benefited marginally from certain uncouth colonial tactics no true gentleman would dream of using."

"Benefited *how much*?" Freeman boomed indignantly, making the young nurse beside him jump. "I'll have you know, my little Limey poofters, that when Darby's killer knee comes up in the bloody scrum, the—"

"He will mix business with pleasure, you see," Tom interrupted. "Three more of the opposition being carried off utterly insensible last season, I believe. So for God's sake don't provoke the brute, or this luckless infant may find itself being booted into touch!"

Freeman's happy growl was cut short by Sister McTaggart, issuing a rebuke in a tone only she'd risk adopting: "The patient's name is Annabel, Dr. Lockhart, knowing what importance you usually place on such details."

Chastened, Tom moved to the side of the examination table. This blue baby, he confirmed, was blue all over, and not just blue to the halfway mark, as sometimes occurred to heighten interest. So far so good, and despite his perusal of the case notes having been all too hasty by his usual standards, he had taken a look at the straightforward chest X rays made by the radiographers and saw no reason to feel inadequate to the task ahead of him.

Only take care, he cautioned himself. You once became overconfident in a situation like this, skipped the contrast test, and killed the poor little bugger. "I rather fear," Geoff Harcourt had murmured, glancing up compassionately from the tiny fists clenched in cadaveric spasm, "young Wayne here will not be playing the piano again, contrary to parental exhortations . . ."

And Tom, looking down on Geoff as he expertly withdrew the wire guide from the sticklike left leg of yet another small cyanotic, felt the same rush of pure gratitude—almost love for the man— that he'd experienced when, with those few words, he had been granted total absolution.

So total, as it turned out, he'd not had to confess to Sylvia what he had done, even though this had been back in the days when each had seemed the other's only true friend and comforter.

Could it've been that same compassion, the same urge to forgive a wrong, which had made Geoff seek out Felicity that day? He must've had *some* good reason . . .

"Doctor?" said Sister McTaggart.

They were ready for him to now take charge of this delicate, dangerous exploration, made all the more uncertain by the evident distress of the drowsy little creature beneath the image intensifier.

"All set!" he said.

Exhilarated, because that's what teamwork of this caliber did for him, Tom moved to the foot of the table. Yet he was also suddenly fearful, what with Windfall and Gutsiest and the mystery telephone number still claiming every other second of his thinking, that he might again need absolving.

The infant, lightly premedicated, moved its blue-tinged, under-developed limbs in a sluggish imitation of what healthy babies did when held on their backs too long, but uttered not a sound.

"Right, young Annabel, and what is your RV pressure?" asked Tom.

"About arterial," said Geoff.

"Isobel, her weight again?"

"Three kilos."

Tom, acutely aware he was about to introduce toxins to a faulty system incapable of diffusing them too readily in the blood-stream, made a careful mental calculation. "Half a mil," he decided.

The test injection of contrast medium brought an immediate reaction. The infant's blood pressure dropped, its pulse rate fell, and Tom's shot up. But these effects proved momentary.

Good girl, Annabel, he thought, confirming that the catheter was in exactly the required position in the right ventricle, and making sure the contrast medium was drifting from its tip, unimpeded by contact with any tissue. This was crucial, because medium under pressure could puncture almost any part of the heart the end of the catheter rested against, blowing a hole in it just like a shotgun pellet.

"Lovely piece of work, Geoff," he said warmly, and noticed for the first time that Isobel's hair was the same color as Ginny's, if half a shade darker. "Four and a half mils. Ready to go, Darby?"

"And a half," echoed Isobel, preparing the pressure injector.

Freeman belched. "Ready to go?" he said. "My guts is in such a state of flamin' uproar, any minute they'll—"

"I think I'll move out of earshot," said Tom, and retreated behind the lead-glass screen of the control booth. "Five seconds."

"Five," echoed one of the radiographers.

"Camera loaded?" he asked. "Video all set?"

"Yes, everything's ready, Doctor."

He found himself standing and looking at Isobel's hair again, now that she had her face turned away. Get thee behind me, Ginny!—he wanted to say out loud. Not now, lass, *not now*.

"Proceed!" ordered Tom, then suddenly wasn't sure how many milliliters of contrast medium he'd stipulated.

But the pressure injector's piston had already slammed home, and the camera chittered as Annabel's blood pressure plunged and stayed down. Her heartbeat, made audible by the monitoring system, faltered.

You're expecting Fallot's tetralogy, Tom Lockhart, he reminded himself in a desperate attempt to remain calm. Think about it, go through it step by step, review how essentially simple it all is.

Fine, the heart was divided by a muscular wall called the septum. The left-hand half contained red arterial blood, bound for the brain, torso, and extremities. The right-hand half carried blue venous blood destined for the lungs, where oxygen would turn it red again. As for pressure, that on the arterial side was normally higher because of the resistance it met in reaching those extremities, while on the venous side it was lower to prevent it seeping through the thin membranes of the lungs. And naturally enough, red and blue blood weren't meant to mix.

But observe the action of the contrast medium in this instance. Like the blue blood it's dispersed in, the medium is finding the exit from the heart into the lungs restricted by an abnormal narrowing of blood vessels known as a stenosis. The stenosis is creating a buildup of pressure in the right-hand side of the heart, just as a whistle makes a referee's cheeks bulge, and venous blood is being forced into the heart's arterial side through a congenital defect in the septum wall, hence the blue skin tone. There was also—the camera had stopped.

"Fallot's," said Geoff. "Subvalvar stenosis."

"Valvar, too, I think!" said Tom.

"Boom, boom, and she's off again," grunted Darby Freeman, jerking his thumb at the heart and respiratory traces on his oscilloscope. "BP recovering nicely. She's a tough little sheila, this Annabel! Could do with a few of her in the bloody team, instead of—"

"We know, ducky," said Geoff Harcourt, quietly camping it up. "Instead of us little Limey poofters, right?"

Dear God, thought Tom, looking at Geoff. Two women, two totally opposed views of the same man; so much for feminine intuition.

He knew which view he preferred, even if it would give half the world's population every right to exclaim indignantly, "You men!" But what women shouldn't overlook was that lusting after them, no matter how overtly, was something the average normal heterosexual male could at least regard as natural; whereas the thought of sodomy, especially with another male, simply made the flesh crawl.

Granted, Sylvia had in fact branded Geoff as only a latent gay— but as Felicity had claimed the opposite was true, accusing him of what amounted to latent lechery, there were still some very curious contradictions at work here.

"Tom," said Geoff, turning to the control booth, "video all right?"

"Spot on."

"And what about developing the film? Any chance of having it in, say, an hour from now? The ambulance brought the parents in, too, from some godforsaken place in the country, and I imagine I'll have to deal with the pair of them fairly soon."

Tom raised his eyebrows inquiringly at Isobel, who nodded.

"Excellent," said Geoff.

"But," said Tom, "I think we'd better do an LV angio as well." He wanted to give all the information he could to the surgeons, and still wasn't completely sure of the exact location of the leak in the septum wall. "Can Annabel cope, do you suppose, Darby?" he asked.

"You're after the VSD? Well, *if* Butter Flamin' Fingers can get a shift on this time, I reckon me and Annie can hang in a little longer."

Geoff began immediately to prepare for an arterial puncture. But as he did so, he glanced up at Tom to let him know that he didn't share Freeman's confidence in the patient's capacity to withstand the violent shock of another pressure injection.

Geoff and I do a lot of glancing into each other's eyes, Tom realized, and especially when we're masked up and forced to resort to these discreet exchanges. All part and parcel of the job, Sylv!—and presumably, a habit that's hard to kick after hours, you know. Ponder that a moment, while I take another look at what we've managed to pick up on video.

It wasn't a bad image at all, once the contrast was adjusted, and so he emerged from behind the control booth and said, "Hold on, everyone. I'm not certain its worth going for the LV after all."

"I know I'd be happier, leaving it at this stage," said Geoff, glancing up gratefully.

"Darby?" said Tom.

Freeman shrugged. "I'm only the hired help, boss! Jesus, wasn't that stew at lunch a diabolical bloody mixture?"

"Good, then let's unplug her," said Tom, "and I'll see if I can't use the film to pinpoint the site for the cutter."

"That was the one going to do it, with the salad?" asked Darby.

"Hmmm?" said Tom, distracted by a sudden insight.

Glances! Certainly, his work must have made him unusually adept at this form of communication. And was this why a single glance from Ginny, six long years ago, had persisted so vividly in his memory? Had he been able to read into it far more than most people might? More, perhaps, than even she had been aware of at the time? And had Ginny herself caught up with those innermost thoughts yet, or did they still lie as though asleep, deep in the unconscious, made manifest only in her choice of names for two fat ponies? Was he then her errant knight in armor, fated to finally awaken her with a gentle kiss beneath a golden bower? And would they, could they, *please* live happily ever after?

"Oh, isn't she sweet?" one of the radiographers was saying, as she left the control booth to take a closer look at Annabel. "Just like my sister's youngest!"

The tension in the room had vanished, and smiles were appearing all around. Professionalism, Tom had long been aware, although an effective shield against most forms of harrowing experience, could never quite block the emotional strain of dealing with a young life that could be ending before it'd scarcely begun.

"Phew," he said, letting his shoulders drop.

"As good an answer as I'll get, I suppose!" said Darby enigmatically, and began packing up.

Geoff still had his thumb pressed down on the punctured vein through which the catheter had been passed. After another thirty seconds, when the blood vessel had performed the minor miracle of resealing itself, he lifted his thumb away and began closing the wound. As the stitch went in, Annabel gave her first whimper and started crying, very feebly.

"Hush, my lovely," soothed Sister McTaggert, her scrubbed face pinked by rare emotion as she supervised the nurse replacing the tiny nightdress. "Don't you fret, you poor little thing . . ."

"I'll try my best not to, Sister!" said Geoff, winking at Tom. "You off?"

"Might as well, I've probably a whole heap of reporting piling up. I'll give you a shout the minute the film arrives and I've had a proper look."

"Good man."

Tom had just reached the door to the passage and was reminding himself that no, having decided against returning that telephone call, he couldn't go back on his word and risk behaving like a god, when Annabel abruptly stopped crying. With hollowed belly he twisted around, aghast lest something terrible had happened.

It hadn't. The minute patient was being gently rocked, eyes closed peacefully, in Sister McTaggert's freckled arms. Caught completely out of character for once, she noticed his amused smile of relief, and said gruffly, "Well, mine were all lads, Doctor; never had myself a Sleeping Beauty!"

"Christ, not et tu," muttered Tom under his breath.

Then, back in his office, it suddenly became really all too bloody much. He had only to think of Ginny, it seemed, to come under sniper fire from piffling coincidence. He felt worn out by the endless, fevered hypothesizing going on inside him, by his wild hopes and crushing doubts. So he seized on the fresh X-ray pictures in his general reporting tray and vowed to drive from his mind everything but good, cold, hard, clinical fact.

This patient, Tom saw instantly, pen in hand, was doomed.

There is a mass lateral to the right hilum with patchy consolidation in the lateral segment of both right upper and right lower lobes. Appearances suggest a neoplasm with associated infection.

And this patient was not.

The heart is normal in size and shape. There is a small area of consolidation in the dorsal segment of the left lower lobe. Presumably, simple inflammatory.

And this patient . . .

It was like plucking petals from a daisy. Ring her; don't ring her; must ring her; mustn't.

Tom couldn't stop himself.

But just as he drew the last set of X rays out of their big brown envelope, with fingers crossed that they weren't going to reveal a carcinoma, the developed film of Annabel's ventriculogram arrived.

"Well done, Isobel," said Tom, "straight to the head of the queue it goes! Like to take a look yourself?"

"Love to, Doctor, only I've another to deliver to the Prof."

The film proved superb. In no time, Tom had a very precise idea of where the ventricular septum defect was sited and whether surgery would be successful. He reached out to telephone Geoff, brought his hand back, thought a moment, then set off down the corridor to barge into Harcourt's office, intent on inviting him down to see such fine images for himself.

"And this is Dr. Lockhart," Geoff said, quite unperturbed by having his door thrown open without Tom having first knocked on it, "the consultant who saw to young Annabel's X rays this afternoon."

Oh, no, thought Tom, finding himself face-to-face with a pathetically distraught-looking couple. "Ah," he said. "Good morning—I mean, afternoon."

"Mr. and Mrs. Woodley here," said Geoff, waving him into the chair beside him, "are not unnaturally rather keen to hear what news you may have. Have we the results of the ventriculogram yet?"

Tom nodded as he sat down. "Yes, and it's goodish news, I'm pleased to say."

"Good news!" said Geoff, his greater experience in these matters evident as he did away with the hint of reservation. "Did you hear that?"

The Woodleys stared even harder at Tom. They did not look like the parents of an Annabel. Mr. Woodley was plainly some form of farm worker, sunburned and gaunt, with hair as stiff and bleached as the straw poking out from under a scarecrow's hat. Mrs. Woodley, whose sole piece of jewelry was a thin wedding band, had a strangely translucent, very white skin, peeling in places, and her figure was not unlike an onion in shape. She had a sharp odor as well, and there were large damp patches in her wrinkled pink dress beneath the unshaven armpits.

"Our bebby," said Mr. Woodley, "can tell us about bebby?" And his voice shook, unmanning him, for he then bit into his lower lip, fiercely.

"Yes, of course," said Tom. "Well, from what I've seen from the X rays, I would think a hole-in-the-heart operation should set matters right, provided it's carried out in . . ." At the mention of the operation, the Woodleys had linked hands on the edge of Geoff's desk, as tidy as an altar top, and Tom found he'd dried up.

"Ah, but why do we recommend surgery?" said Geoff, taking the baton from him to forge on, quite effortlessly. "Some children with this abnormality do survive into their teens, I grant you that, but in Annabel's case, we're really facing something more severe.

Without surgery, one probably couldn't count on more than a few months."

Mr. Woodley squeezed his wife's hand tightly. "The missus . . ." he said, then swallowed, changing tack. "A few m-months, you say, Doctor?"

"To be blunt, she could die at any minute."

Mrs. Woodley inhaled sharply, and Tom saw two more stains appearing in her dress. Her fat round breasts were expressing the milk a well baby would have suckled hours ago.

"Oh, Tom . . ." Sylvia had sobbed into her pillow one long-ago night, when it'd been their custom to unite against a dark world in light embraces after lovemaking. "Oh, Tom, I do so want your child. I don't care what it is, boy or girl, any sort of baby!" And he had said, his day returning to him, "No, not *any* sort, Sylv . . ." Making her sob all the more, most mysteriously.

"Only, this operation . . ." said Mr. Woodley.

"Mr. Matthews," said Geoff, betraying nothing of his personal antipathy for Jolly Joe, "is a very careful and experienced surgeon, of that I can assure you, and we've had some excellent results."

"But, but afterward, like?" asked Mrs. Woodley timidly, the weariness in her voice suggesting the strain she must have been under, trying to cope night and day in poor circumstances with a very sick child. "I mean, I'm not sayin' it might be for the best if Annabel . . ."

But she was, so she stopped, and her husband looked ready to weep for her.

"Afterward?" said Geoff, smiling. "Afterward—and I apologize if we've not already made this clear—you will of course have yourselves a normal child."

The bedazzled expression on the Woodleys' faces was extraordinary. Then they tried to express the way they were feeling, and out came a muddle of awe, gratitude, rejoicing, belief and disbelief, laughter, tears, and stammered thanks that bordered on sheer adoration, forcing Tom to withdraw hurriedly from the room. They're treating us like gods, he thought angrily, and I've always hated that side of medicine, it's bloody ridiculous.

Then again, he said to himself as he returned to his office, who am I to talk? There I was at Tuppmere this morning, offering up thanks to the Goddess Ginny! Which could of course mean, from one point of view at least, we're both perfectly entitled to behave just as we please, up here on Mount Olympus.

Smiling wryly, Tom tossed high the phantom heart that Betty had used as a paperweight, caught it, made to drop it, and then with the other hand, lifted his receiver.

9

The ringing tone went on and on, an interminable eleven times, before the receiver at the other end was snatched up, banging hard against something. "Whoops!" said a young, very feminine voice. "Sorry about that! Print workshop, Fay Trotter here."

"Print what?"

"Workshop. Are you a wrong number?"

Tom read out the digits on the slip Betty had handed him.

"That's right, that's us. Can I help you?"

"Er, I've had a message that someone wanted me to ring her at this number."

"Yes?"

"Is . . ." But he couldn't bring himself to ask outright for Ginny; that might be saying too much at once. "Um, is there another young woman on the premises?"

There was a pause. "Who is this speaking, please?"

"I'm ringing from the hospital. The message was taken by my secretary and left on my desk—only just found it."

"Who's this speaking?" she repeated, suspiciously.

A fine sweat prickled over Tom's brow. "Dr. Lockhart," he said, his throat tightening. "Ring back, if you like, and the switchboard will know where to find me. The person didn't leave a name."

"I can't. They put a lock on this phone when the technicians aren't here," she said, but her voice had lost some of its edge. "Anyway, I'm all on my own, so obviously whoever this was must have gone. Sorry!"

Well, that was that, thought Tom. The dignified, sensible, face-saving thing to do now was to put the receiver down before he compromised himself any further "No, don't!" he begged.

"Don't what?"

"Don't hang up. It's vital I—" Then he switched to his iciest professional tones and said, "I don't think you properly appreciate the possible urgency of the call we received. We've an idea it could be essential to the welfare of this patient that we contact her."

"Oh, a *patient*. I see. Lunchtime being at about one?"

"Or slightly after."

"Well, I didn't arrive until three-thirty, and there was nobody here then either, but I'll look in the diary, see who's been in today. You've got to put down the paper and stuff you use, so they can charge you."

"I'd be very grateful," said Tom, and listened to some large pages being turned noisily. The sound stopped.

"It's Wednesday, isn't it? Here's today's ones: Sarah Blinkhorn, Nell Overton, Dylan Jones, Herda Schwartz, Barbara Gonzales."

"Oh."

"None of them ring a bell?"

"Afraid not."

"I've had an idea!" she said. "Why don't you get in touch with John Wilson, the technician who was on this morning? He'd have to have given permission to anyone using this phone—you know, unlock it. He'd know."

"Excellent! And his number is?"

"Oh, John hasn't a phone; you'd have to go round to his studio. It's the old stables in Waite Square."

"I'll do that right away. Thanks very much, you've been very helpful."

"Good luck," she said.

But Tom stayed where he was, staring at his unlit X-ray viewer, trying to decide what he really ought to do next.

Part of him was smarting over the start of that conversation, when his reluctance to name names had made him sound like one of Felicity's heavy breathers, placing him on the defensive. He hated being thought of in that way, even temporarily. Another part of him was applauding how cunningly he'd extracted all that information without having given anything away—aside from his own name of course, which doubtless had been forgotten by now. That had been masterly, real cloak-and-dagger stuff.

And yet, where had it got him? He now knew his mystery caller had to have some connection with a print workshop, whatever that meant, and that he'd been far too late in ringing back. A great deal of good that did!

Hang on, he told himself. As Ginny's name hadn't been among those read out from the diary, and as he knew of nothing linking her with such a place, he had at least proved that the call couldn't have been from her.

"Ah, but!" said Tom, rising to pace his office. "There's a *reason* I can't just accept that . . ." And it wasn't just the crushing disappointment involved, which he doubted he could bear.

Then he had it: he knew nothing *whatsoever* about Ginny, not the real, live Ginny Ashford, not a thing.

She could have spent her last six years in that workshop, for all he knew, and could be intending to spend the next six—or even sixty!—there.

"Oh, Christ, Tom . . ." he said, sitting down again.

It was a shock to realize, with a very belated and sickening thump, quite how grossly self-centered he'd been, feasting on skin-deep images of her like some fantasy-ridden schoolboy pawing over pictures of a favorite pinup. Even more shattering was the further realization that he'd been entirely content to ask no questions, to find out nothing about the person he'd allegedly fallen in love with. Instead, he had opted to deny Ginny her individuality, her humanity, her very soul—come to that!—in order, presumably, to create her in his own image of exquisite femininity and keep her there.

"No," he said. "*No!* Sodding hell, Ginny, it wasn't like that!" And he got up, resumed his pacing, reached into one pocket after another, and found himself in such a state of agitation that the room could no longer contain him.

He looked at the wall clock, saw it was well after his usual going-home time, and without even pausing to pick up his briefcase, walked out. He had in mind going straight to a large park, where he'd run and run and run.

Geoff Harcourt was the last person he wanted to see at that moment. Tom wished he'd thought to take the shortcut through the coffee room, and tried switching direction before being spotted in the corridor. But Geoff's hand came up, palm first, indicating he wanted a word with him.

So he stopped and turned back, tapping the face of his wristwatch. "Sorry, Geoff, have to fly!" he called out, while there were still ten yards of corridor separating them. "You won't mind if we leave this until—"

"It won't take a moment, Tom. I just thought you'd want to know."

"Oh?" he said, halted in his tracks by something now evident in Geoff's face; a certain stiffness around the mouth, and an extra degree, perhaps, of pallor. "Know what?"

"She didn't make it. End of story."

"She?"

"Sleeping Beauty."

"God, not Annabel?"

Geoff nodded. "Ten minutes ago on the ward."

"Shit! But she—"

"At least we'd warned the Woodleys, told them it could be any minute."

"We'd also raised their hopes!"

"And our own," said Geoff, with a shrug.

"Were the parents there?"

"They'd just slipped down to the canteen for a cuppa and a sticky bun."

With a lurch, the lift began its descent. Tom leaned back and closed his eyes. He'd had enough, more than enough. He was throwing in the towel. He hoped the lift would carry on going down, down and down and down, down to darkness and silence and oblivion.

The lift stopped.

Pfffft-sssssss

He opened his eyes, saw the lift doors sliding away, and with an effort, walked out into the ground-floor lobby. He was passed by a pair of young nurses chattering brightly, the idiots. Hadn't life taught them its one important lesson yet? The one he'd learned over and over: the Lord only giveth so He could taketh away again, the mean, shitty bastard, amen.

Talking of such, what about Tom Lockhart? There was a fine figure of a shitty bastard, for you: poor Ginny, a two-dimensional cutout against the sun, all Botticelli and no bloody bowels! No dreams, hopes, aspirations, no needs, no fears of her own to make a real, living person.

Perhaps it's not too late to make amends, Tom thought for an instant. No great harm had been done, surely. So, go on, start discovering things about her! Begin with Sylvia when you get home; she's always encyclopedic when it comes to facts about other people, the good and the bad. Or, for a bit of excitement, even if it does prove a wild-goose chase, why not follow up Fay Trotter's suggestion and visit the workshop technician in Waite Square? It was perfectly possible he might know something about Ginny, because *you* certainly aren't able to say why he shouldn't!

And for that selfsame instant, Tom was tempted, very tempted, to do just that.

But, as he started down the steps of the hospital side entrance, he had to admit he really had had enough, both of the world and of his absurd attempts to find joy in it. A man could take only so much loss, so much self-delusion, before finally giving up.

There was someone hovering near his car, holding a large flat parcel, and so, being determined to avoid further conversation that day, he kept his eyes averted by studying the leather fob on his key ring.

"Hello, Tom! I hope you won't mind . . ."

He glanced up.

It was Ginny.

Ginny, in full color, flushed, tanned, gaily dressed, and the only gray now, lit from behind, in her eyes.

Ginny, actually standing there, feet braced wide, hips tilted, hugging the parcel to her, one breast flattened behind it, the other raised to him, caught on the parcel's edge.

"Hello!" said Tom with a laugh. "You hope I won't mind what?"

"Me lying in wait for you."

He very nearly laughed again, but realized he might not be able to stop. "No, not one bit," he said as casually as he could.

"It's this," she said, indicating the parcel. "I was worried about getting it home on the bus."

"Oh?"

"This print. Cross your fingers they're going to like it!"

"Who's they?"

"Mum and Dad. It's their twentieth anniversary the day after tomorrow."

"Ah, so you've got them a present."

Ginny nodded. "I know it's a terrible cheek," she said, "but I'd hate to bump it on the bus accidentally and break the glass. Would you mind terribly giving me a lift home?"

"Don't be silly," said Tom with a nonchalance that greatly impressed him, "no trouble at all. Hop in."

The flusters hit him moments later.

Tom slipped behind the wheel and then wondered why Ginny simply stood at the passenger door, making no attempt to slide in beside him. She had to point politely to the door lock before the penny dropped. In reaching across to open the door for her, he gave it such a shove he almost bowled her over.

"Sorry!" he said, curling up his toes. "Sorry! Not thinking!" He fumbled with his seat belt, struggling to engage its catch between the front seats. "Damn!"

"I think you're trying to get your thing into mine," said Ginny.

"Oops!" he said. "Ah, now I've got it!" His safety belt clunk-clicked, the engine started, and he took his foot very carefully off the clutch—the engine stalled, he'd left the handbrake on. "Sorry!" he said. "I can't imagine why I'm making such a mess of things!"

"Had a bad day?" said Ginny.

The tale of Annabel steadied Tom. It was like making one of the confessions he'd made long, long ago. Ginny listened in silence, and without attempting to say what couldn't be said, just nodded. He looked at her directly then, and she at him, and he was astounded by the color of her eyes: from as close as this, he could see not one gray but slivers of silver, flakes of slate, peat smoke, distant raincloud.

"Why do you suppose," she said, "that sort of people gave their baby . . ."

He knew immediately what she was thinking. "Such a grand, upmarket name as Annabel?" he said, facing the traffic again. "Do you know, I've wondered that myself. Perhaps they wanted something special for her out of life. Or maybe it was a touch of Tess of the D'Urbervilles!"

"Unkind," said Ginny, laughing.

And already he'd established one remarkable fact about her:

she had a mind that ran along quirky, inquisitive lines identical to his own.

Tom breathed in deeply. As if the sight and sweet sound of Ginny Ashford were not enough, he was now becoming dizzied by the smell of her, not something he'd noticed before out in the open at Tuppmere. His MG Metro, left parked in the sun all day, still had its windows up and a fragrance grew and grew in that hothouse swelter like a blossoming of orchids, ousting the scent of his deodorant.

"You enjoyed Tess?" he asked, joining the tail of the rush-hour traffic jam. "It became the bane of my life at school. We were expected to have read it right through three times before the exams."

"I've only seen the film," she said.

"Oh, yes, made by that Polish chap who got into hot water for—" Tom searched frantically for an immediate distraction. "God, look at that maniac!"

"Where?"

"Fifty yards ahead, cut straight across two lanes!"

"You were saying?" said Ginny.

"Was I? Sorry, I've forgotten."

Like hell he had, and was still cringing at the thought of having so very nearly trotted out Polanski's reported indiscretion with a twelve-year-old. Why, in the the name of Christ, had he even *begun* to come out with that?

"Your day," said Ginny, with an apologetic smile, "can't have been helped by people leaving you telephone numbers to ring in the middle of everything."

He glanced at her. "So that *was* you?"

"You'd guessed?" she said, sounding surprised, even pleased.

"Er, not exactly. Well, I don't know many young—um, a hunch, that's all. You must've said something about a print workshop on Sunday."

"Don't think I did, did I?"

He shrugged.

"Actually, I first rang you a couple of times on Monday," said Ginny, "when I was still trying to make up my mind about what present to get, thinking you might have an idea, having known

Mum and Dad for so long. But your secretary was a bit off-putting and I—"

"Off-putting?" Tom said, ready to fire the bitch. "In what way?"

"Oh, I'm sure she didn't mean to be! It was just hearing you called *Doctor* Lockhart like that, made you sound too important a person to—"

"Rubbish!" he said with a laugh.

"Anyway, you were obviously very busy," said Ginny. "Then I thought of getting them a Nell Overton, which seemed brilliant—until lunchtime today, when I wondered how I was going to get it home safely. That's when I rang again."

"But forgot to leave a name!"

"That was on purpose. What if you hadn't got the message until very late, missed me at the workshop, and then thought you ought to ring home? Mum'd be bound to want to know all the ins and outs, and bang would have gone my surprise for them!"

And my surprise for *me*, thought Tom, very relieved things hadn't happened that way. But he said, "Surely, a little white lie would have done the trick, Ginny?"

"I never lie to my parents," she said unaffectedly.

"Never?"

"Never ever."

His heart definitely sank then.

"And so," Ginny said, "when you hadn't rung back by the time everyone was leaving the workshop, I realized you must be tied up again and decided to try to catch you in the car park after work."

"Talking of work," said Tom, easing off the handbrake as the cars in front of him began to move at last, "any luck with that waitress job you were after?"

"Falstaff's? The manager tried pinching my behind—if you call that luck!"

"The bastard! Who is he?"

Ginny shrugged. "I didn't wait to find out," she said. "I hate lechy old men like that. Do you mind if I wind my window down?"

"The *bastard*," said Tom.

Then the cars in front of him began traveling even faster, and he realized to his dismay that something must have happened to unblock the usual bottleneck at this hour on the route north. He had counted on at least fifteen minutes in the queue with Ginny, finding out things about her, admiring her profile, not having to think about the road but concentrating on her entirely.

"Oh, good, they must've opened the new section of the beltway at last," she said. "Dad's usually never home till six, and Mum's always late back from her golf lessons, so we could be in time for me to smuggle their present in without them seeing. I'm dying for it to be a total surprise on Friday."

"Hmmm," said Tom. "But it's nearly six now. Couldn't they both be at home already?"

"Yes, I suppose so. Damn, I should've thought of all this before! What I could do, is find somewhere else to hide it beforehand."

"Good idea," said Tom, taking the next exit from the beltway and joining the main road, where the signpost to Tuppmere would appear any minute now. "Only it's got to be somewhere really safe, of course."

"If only I knew someone I could trust in the village," murmured Ginny. "But we haven't been there long enough. Don't know anybody living anywhere nearby either, come to think of it."

"What about old family friends . . . ?" said Tom, and smiled.

Ginny looked around at him. "You don't mean—I couldn't! You've been kind enough already."

"Rubbish! It's their wedding anniversary after all, and I was best man, remember!"

"No, I . . ."

"It'd be the perfect hiding place," Tom urged her. "Then, on the morning in question, I'll whip it over to Tuppmere and you can collect it from me at the gate or something."

"But wouldn't that be an awful lot of trouble for you?"

"Not at all."

"Honest?"

"Honest."

"And Sylvia won't mind?"

I'd kill her! "Of course not, why ever should she?"

"But oughtn't I to ask her myself?"

"You'd feel happier if you did?" asked Tom, accelerating as the turnoff to Tuppmere came in sight, hoping to shoot past it.

Ginny nodded. "Will Sylvia be at home now?"

"Of course," he lied.

10

Tom had just remembered that this was a Wednesday. Every Wednesday, come hell or high water, toothache, the decorators, or raging blizzard, Sylvia set off at nine to visit her parents at a genteel home for the elderly and incontinent. Trade Winds, as it was called, with what he considered a sublime hint of unconscious irony, stood behind a high hedge on the far side of the next county, making the journey a day-long expedition. Seldom, if ever, was Sylvia back before half past seven in the evening. The time, he noted, stood at only five fifty-seven.

"All right," said Ginny. "If you promise Sylvia won't mind."

She was too late anyway with that reply: the turnoff to Tuppmere had already come and gone.

"Tell me," said Tom, dropping back out of the hectic pack of commuters rushing home at seventy, "what exactly is a 'Nell Overton'? The name rings a bell. A type of reproduction, like a Medici print?"

Ginny smiled. "No, Nell's an artist I know, and it's not that sort of print. I mean an etching, one of her latest. I think her work's marvelous, really lovely! You've never seen any of it?"

Tom shook his head. "Don't actually know a thing about art. I subscribed to a Time-Life series on old masters once, really enjoyed poring over each new book when it came, but that's the closest I've ever been to—"

"You don't go to exhibitions?"

"Never even crossed my mind."

"Oh, but you should, Tom! Even locally, lots of it is really worth seeing. Nell Overton's going to be at the library next week, and Len Tullet."

"Who?"

"He's a sculptor, mainly in welding rods."

"And you, Ginny?"

"Me?"

"Well, you're speaking as though you know a lot about all this," said Tom, "so I naturally thought you must be an etcher or something, too."

"Wish I was, but I'm hopeless even at drawing! It's just I love looking at images, and watching people make things. I hang about the workshop quite a bit."

"Then if you're not into art in that sense," he said, feeling pleased with his unstodgy phrasing, "what are you hoping to do?"

"I'm still thinking," said Ginny. "I'd like to travel, though."

"Oh? Anywhere special?"

"Not Greece," she said firmly. "Greece's gorgeous, but Dad's been taking us there year after year, till it's grown really boring."

Dear God, thought Tom, of course. Hugh Ashford must have seen *Zorba the Greek* at least thirty times as an undergraduate, and had then insisted on performing an excruciatingly bad imitation of Zorba's dance at every party he went to, bringing several of them to a premature end. Only an impressionable young sales girl from Marks and Spencer, such as Moira had been, could possibly have ever felt he had to be enormously "cultured" even to attempt such an outlandish thing.

"Not Greece," said Tom. "Then where? Africa? India? The States?"

"Somewhere Third World, probably."

"Ah."

"Are these your tapes? May I look?"

"Do!" he said. "Help yourself. There are a few more scattered about on the back seat, too."

Ginny took a batch of tape cassettes from the dashboard shelf and shuffled through it. "Brilliant!" she said. "You've got Verdi! I love nearly all his things."

"Old Giuseppe?" said Tom. "So do I." Then he grinned and

remarked, "Mind you, can a properly classical composer really have a name like Joe Green?"

"I'd never thought of it like that before!"

"Neither had I."

And they laughed together.

Which gave the world a sound, Tom decided, more incredibly beautiful than any sodding music. He wanted to hear it again and again.

But before he could think of an even wittier follow-up, Ginny slipped the Verdi cassette into the tape deck, and sat back to listen, closing her eyes.

His own eyes pounced then, first at the caramel cleft separating her breasts, just visible above the neckline of her loose-weave white cotton shirt, and then at her nearest nipple, which showed through the cloth like a pink sun rising behind ground mist. He looked back at the road for a moment, slowed down a fraction, made sure her eyes were still closed, and lingered his gaze along the line of her mouth, delighting in its minutely upward-turned corners.

The road still ran empty and straight.

Her upper lip, he explored swiftly; it was smooth and elegantly shaped, like one edge of a young willow leaf. He looked at the succulent fullness of her lower lip, emphasized by how its redness grew deeper the further it curved out, turning like a subtly shaded petal. His next glance at the road and back seemed to catch a tiny light between her smoky lashes, as though she'd opened her eyes very slightly, so he looked away quickly.

He counted his heartbeats to ten, and gave her a casual glance. Her eyes were closed; he must have been imagining things. Then, as he was looking up to check the road again, he noticed that the nipple nearest him had engorged and was pressing against her shirt as distinctly as a wild cherry.

Tom didn't know where to look after that, and almost missed his turn.

Ginny circled the drawing room like a kitten straight from the pet shop. She touched this and that, sniffed cautiously at the potpourri on the piano, shied away from a gong that boomed very loudly at a touch, and finally curled up on one end of the sofa, her feet tucked neatly away beneath her.

"Wherever Sylvia's got to, I'm sure she won't be long," said

Tom, opening the rolltop desk he'd converted into a liquor cabinet. "Probably dashed out for a sprig of parsley or something to add a final touch to tonight's whatnot. May I offer you something?"

"I'd love a coffee, if that'd be all right."

"Of course!" He took two paces toward the kitchen. "With milk?"

"I—" began Ginny, then glanced back at the desk. "You haven't Bacardi and Coke, have you?"

"No Bacardi, but most other things. How about a gin and tonic?"

"Lovely," she said, smiling across the room at him.

How totally she *belonged* on that sofa, he thought, justifying at last the ridiculous amount he'd been obliged to pay for it, and how perfectly she graced the room itself, adding a warmth that made its four walls seem to draw cozily closer together, squeezing out the empty chill. Tom smiled back at her, then turned to pour the drinks.

"You've aroused my curiosity," he said over his shoulder.

"I have?"

"Yes, you must teach me a bit about how etching's actually done. All I know is, it involves using acids to eat lines into copper plates or something."

"Zinc plates mostly, these days. They're cheaper."

"Ah."

"Or you could use any metal really, I suppose. It used to be steel in the beginning, because etching was started by armorers— you know, putting those gorgeous intricate patterns on knight's breastplates and things. Only they used vinegar instead of nitric acid, believe it or not, and it took them ages to get a proper bite."

"Must've," he said, adding a splash more gin.

"Why the smile?" asked Ginny, finding a flat spot on the sofa's arm where she could stand her drink.

"Oh, nothing special," said Tom, sitting down. "Just a remark an Australian anesthetist made in the angio room this afternoon."

In fact, he was smiling at convention, somewhat crookedly. Back in his MG Metro, he had sat rump to rump with Ginny, a bare eight inches apart, and hadn't had to give the matter a second thought. But a moment ago, as he'd turned from the rolltop desk with his own drink in his hand, he had felt compelled to choose the seat farthest from her.

"This remark the anesthetist made," prompted Ginny. "What was it?"

"Hmm? Just something about 'little Limey poofters.' Darby tends—"

"Yuk!" said Ginny with a quick frown. "You should hear Nell getting stuck into bigoted pigs like that—she's brilliant."

"Nell's your special friend at the print workshop?"

"No, Pat—who'd probably just sock him one!"

"Pat?" he said, resisting the thought of a virile young rival for her favors entering the lists.

"You know, more the same age as me."

Tom took a mail-fisted blow to the head. This was the inevitable moment he'd been dreading and trying not to think about; the terrible moment he had managed to avoid so far only by never asking questions. His fragile illusions shattered by that blow, he toppled, crashed down heavily, and just lay there, made helpless by his weight of armor. "Mind you," he said, taking one feeble lunge at his phantom vanquisher before the coup de grace, "perhaps you'd better warn this Sir Galahad of yours that Dr. Freeman's a bloody sight bigger than I am, with the muscle to back up his prejudices!"

"My what?" said Ginny, then laughed in sudden amusement. "More like Joan of Arc, you mean! I think Pat's probably a bit too feminine to want to be compared to a—"

"Whoops!" he said joyfully. "I beg her pardon."

And now let that, he growled inwardly, be a lesson to you, Tom Lockhart. You're far too prone to paranoid extravaganzas that excel, when it comes to grotesquely melodramatic romanticism (not to mention a sheer sickening sentimentality), the very worst examples of Victorian art. You'll be imagining yourself being pursued in the nude by the Furies next, with nothing save a mere wisp of muslin to shield your unmentionables. But what he actually pictured, as Ginny turned to take up the glass he'd handed her, offering the classical innocence of her profile, was himself as a debauching, beaming Bacchus with Kew Garden vine leaves in his hair.

Ginny blinked and set her drink down again on the arm of the sofa after just one sip. "Wow," she said. "What were we talking about?"

"Etching—oh, and your friends," said Tom lightly. "I suppose, having only recently come to live down this way, you must still be . . ."

She nodded. "I hardly know anyone," she said. "Even Pat isn't a close friend—you know, if I'm honest about it."

Wonderful! cheered Tom behind an expression of solemn sympathy. "Still," he said, "there's the other side of that coin. Making new friends at least gives one a chance to—well, you know."

"Right," said Ginny, looking at him very directly.

Dear God, it was there, still there in her eyes, he was sure of it: that same elusive whatever-it-was that had haunted him down the years. And Tom wanted to leap up and caper, dance and stamp his feet. He stood up and strolled over to the rolltop desk, put the screw cap back on the gin bottle, and this time came about and sat down in the easy chair nearest to the sofa.

"Etching," he reminded her, nudging the parcel propped against his left armrest. "We'd got to using zinc plate because it was cheaper—and nitrochloric acid's the active agent, I gather."

"The mordant," she confirmed, taking an evident and endearing pride in her grasp of the right technical terminology, "which is usually diluted eight to one. Do you want to hear how a plate's made?"

Tom wished he could think of something else to keep the conversation going, something a great deal more personal, but for the moment this would have to do. At least it'd so far kept Ginny from looking at her watch and asking awkward questions about where Sylvia might have got to.

She's in the cellar, buried deep beneath a patch of new cement flooring, my love—so, OFF with another veil, if you please!

"Yes, just how is a plate made?" said Tom, settling back and downing half his gin and tonic in one swallow. "No, really, do tell me—I'm fascinated."

"Well," said Ginny, "first you . . ."

The occasional word and phrase caught his ear: hard ground, soft ground, bite, scrim, press, bed.

But he wasn't really listening at all, not to each individual note, as it were. Instead, he was allowing her voice, with its husky clarinet tones, to play soft and low in the smoky back rooms of his mind, improvising its rhythms from his heartbeat. And all the while, he looked, looked, looked, finding new subtleties of skin tone, new perfections of form to marvel at, fixing each silver-grained image in his soul.

"Aquatint is how you get all the grays," went on Ginny.

"Grays?" Tom repeated, leaning forward and putting down his empty glass.

"Tonal areas. You use rosin, but the process is a bit complicated to explain if you're not in the workshop."

"Any chance of my seeing it done sometime?"

"Oh, yes, I can ask Pat."

"Would you?"

"Tomorrow, if I can."

Even though he'd heard these four wonderful, magical, unbelievable words perfectly clearly, it took him several seconds to absorb their full impact. They meant that he, Tom Lockhart, in his very first proper encounter with Ginny Ashford, had found a way of ensuring not only that he'd definitely be seeing her again, but that this second meeting would take place almost immediately!—give or take an agonizing day or two.

"That'd be marvelous, Ginny," he said. "Ring me at the hospital, would you?"

"Fine," she said, looking just as pleased.

Looking, in that instant, very like she had at the poolside when reaching out to show him the ladybug, the blunt notch of her crotch backlit by the sun.

"And I could of course," added Ginny, "let you see some now, so at least you'll know exactly what's meant by aquatint." She pointed to the parcel.

Tom, momentarily preoccupied by visualizing the gentle curve of her belly beneath the lap of her bunched-up red skirt, and having just reached where its golden down thickened into dark springy hairs, looked up abashed into that sweet, innocent gaze of hers. "But," he said, swallowing, "but are you sure you don't mind unwrapping it? You've done up this parcel so neatly."

"Oh, that won't be any bother! Here . . ."

Ginny uncurled and came lightly across to fetch up the parcel and take it back to the sofa. There, she carefully removed the sticky tape from the back, opened out the brown paper, drew it aside, then turned the large frame around, balancing it against the sofa's backrest.

"Isn't that amazing?" she said, stepping away to allow Tom to see past her.

The etching was of a female nude, her limbs long, strong, and slender, her hair a honey-gold nimbus, confronting what appeared to be her own image in a tall, rectangular mirror; the right hands were raised and just touching, fingertip to sensuous fingertip, while the left hands each cupped a firm breast.

"Tom?"

"Yes, amazing," he agreed faintly, needing to clear his throat.

Ginny was at his side in an instant, crouching to judge his viewpoint and tickling his cheek with a stray strand of hair. "This isn't any good!" she said. "The glass is catching all those reflections from the picture window—no wonder you can't see properly. Come!" And she caught his fist in her cool slender grip and tugged him out of his chair and across to the sofa, where she knelt at his feet.

"Look," she said, touching a fingertip to the nude's pubic hair, "that's a mid-tone, with the highlights brought up by burnishing. Then up here, where the bark of the trees is, Nell's used the same mid-tone, only with the ink being blue . . ."

Once again, Tom Lockhart wasn't really listening. He was staring at the wild cherry shape of the left nipple.

"What fun," said Sylvia, with one of her sweetest smiles, strolling into the room at that moment and dropping a bag of shopping on the piano. "I'd been dreading the thought of coming home to an empty house."

"Hello!" said Ginny. "I hope you don't mind, but Tom—"

"Not in the least," said Sylvia, coming over. "And what's this he's got you so absorbed in? Oh, hasn't she a *divine* figure . . ."

"It's, um," said Tom, "an etching."

"Really?"

"Hugh's and Moira's. You see, it's their wedding anniversary on Friday and Ginny here wondered if—"

"Tom," Sylvia interrupted him. "I haven't seen you blushing in years, and no wonder! There you two are, happily pigging away at the gin, and yet, after my perfectly ghastly day, I haven't been offered one tiny drink yet."

* * *

Ginny smiled all the way through Sylvia's wry account of a day spent trying to reorganize commode-emptying procedures at Trade Winds, and twice laughed out loud in exactly the right places. But Tom, with so much else to distract him, took no particular comfort in this, much as he wanted Ginny to show she was intelligent adult company.

"So you go to see to your parents every Wednesday?" asked Ginny.

"Yes, every Wednesday, unless Tom's at home with the sniffles, demanding endless bowls of chicken broth, poor little soul. Mark you, I don't usually leave there until well after—"

"Another gin?" Tom cut in amiably, concealing a frantic need to shut her up before he lost all credibility.

"No, not for me, thanks," said Ginny. "I've still got some."

"Yes, just a drop, Tom, and even less tonic," said Sylvia, handing him her glass without looking around. "And as I was saying, both the darlings were so exhausted by all the fuss, I simply gave them an early supper and whisked them into bed."

"Yes, I'm sure that was the right thing to do," agreed Ginny.

"But here am I," said Sylvia, crossing her other leg, "going on and on about nothing at tedious length, when I'm actually dying to know more about this marvelous etching. Has it a title, Ginny?"

Bloody hell, thought Tom, as he poured Sylvia's drink, that had been close, and he sighed with relief, now that the topic of her Wednesday comings and goings had thankfully been dropped.

"And so," Ginny said, as he handed Sylvia her recharged glass, "I took a chance and waited in the car park outside the hospital."

"You were lucky not to have to wait all night," said Sylvia. "Tom had left me one of those notes this morning that generally mean I won't see him again for days, hence my expecting to be on my own when I got home earlier than—"

"I went through the backlog like a whirlwind!" hastened Tom. "Had it cleared before this afternoon's angio! Don't know what it was, couldn't go wrong today."

Sylvia shrugged. "I do wish I could say the same. I'm seriously beginning to wonder whether Trade Winds is a good idea."

"You don't mean—" began Tom.

"Damn!" said Sylvia. "The phone. No, let me get it in case it's for you, and I'll say you've gone to a meeting tonight—agreed?"

"Please," said Tom with a grateful nod, then waited to be left alone with Ginny before coming out with what was most pressing in his mind.

"Ginny, this etching . . ."

"I'm so glad that Sylvia likes it, too!"

"Ah, that's just it."

"What?"

"It's just struck me that your parents' tastes differ quite a bit from ours." He didn't like to see her face fall like that, but felt compelled to say the rest, no matter what it cost his conscience. "I'm not at all sure you'd not be wiser finding them a landscape or a still life or something."

"But I've already paid Nell for it, and I can't very well—"

"I've thought of that."

"Oh?"

It was all Tom could do, not to reach immediately for his checkbook and hand over anything he was asked, *for he had to have that picture,* come what may. "Ginny," he said, "how about this for an idea? You could sell us the—"

"Tom," said Sylvia, coming back into the room.

"Yes?" he said, glaring around at her. "What?"

"That was Professor Hughes-Sinclair in quite a state. It seems something could have gone wrong today, after all—you're wanted urgently at the hospital."

11

"**O**h, I hope it's not anything—" began Ginny, looking around at Tom. Then she caught her bottom lip between her teeth, and held it there.

"Not what?" asked Sylvia, looking sharply from one to the other.

"I've no idea," mumbled Tom.

"Not anything too serious," said Ginny. "I've only got to think of hospitals, that awful smell they have, and my tummy turns over!"

"Tom's tummy's probably doing exactly the same thing," said Sylvia, smiling.

Out on the road again, traffic had lightened. The evening sky was still a clear blue above the first crossroads, with only a slight buildup of clouds in the northwest. A solitary cyclist, an old weathered man with a bag of potatoes tied to his carrier, pedaled by slowly from the right.

"Come on, come on!" urged Tom, tapping his steering wheel impatiently, his right foot ready to jump from brake to accelerator. "Right—now, go!"

And he went, racing off down a lane he used as a shortcut, laughing out loud. "Oh, Ginny, Ginny!" he said to the seat where she'd so recently sat. "You are amazing! You're perfect . . ."

Perfect to have instantly sensed in which direction Tom's own thoughts would turn, having heard the news from the hospital.

Perfect to have bitten back on any mention of the confession he'd made to her about Annabel. Sylvia, seldom privy now to any of his secret fears, would have been hurt, desperately.

Annabel. Yes, this urgent summons had to concern Annabel. But in what way—or why, Tom could not imagine. He and Geoff and Darby had conducted that angiogram procedure with all due care, thought, and attention, a few witticisms not excepted, for these had increased efficiency by lowering the level of tension. The fact that the luckless infant had then expired on the ward was altogether unrelated, as Geoff had already pointed out, and entirely consistent with their general prognosis.

Of one thing, Tom felt certain: no mistakes had been made. The amount of contrast medium introduced by the pressure injector had been a modest . . .

"Oh, sod it," he said. He still couldn't remember how much he'd stipulated, not exactly, or even calculating the amount, come to that, but was almost positive it had been well within safe limits. "Three mils, four? Something like that."

No good. He could no more make a decision on this than on what he now made of Ginny.

It was odd, he mused, how both these areas of confusion produced the same sensations in the pit of his stomach. But whereas thinking of Annabel made them feel like dread and the ghostly scrambling of spiders, trapped down there in the dark, he had only to switch to thinking of Ginny for the feeling to become an ecstatic tickle, filling him with excitement.

And as he drove, with what he knew was a silly grin on his face, he struggled to reconcile Ginny, as how he'd once imagined her, with the tantalizing paradoxes now evident in the *real* Ginny. Paradoxes that on the one hand confirmed his original impression of chaste artlessness—while on the other they offered more than a suggestion of unashamed earthiness, sensuality, and pride in her naked young body, as made explicit in that astonishing etching.

Above all, Tom wondered why she had shown the picture to him. Didn't she realize he would instantly recognize her? Or was she really such an innocent that the fact she'd modeled for it—as he had no doubt she must have done—was of no consequence in her eyes?

He arrived at the hospital without really having given Annabel Woodley another thought, which shocked him. Not only because of how indifferent to her tragic death this made him seem, but also because he ought to have properly prepared himself for any possible attack on his professional competence.

So Tom remained behind the wheel of his car for a few minutes, trying very hard to review his recollections of the entire procedure, but finding them constantly cross-cut with lingering shots of Ginny in the seat beside him, Ginny on the sofa, Ginny behind glass in a narrow aluminum frame.

"Ginny Ashford . . ." Tom said with a sigh, getting out to lock his door.

And, for a fleeting, unforgivable moment, he felt decidedly irritated by her and by what she was doing to him.

"Good evening, Doctor," said a tired-looking ward sister, arms folded tightly under a short cape as she came down the steps of the side entrance.

"Evening, Claire!" he said. "What, another half-day?"

She poked her tongue out at him.

Smiling, he pushed open the double doors in sudden good humor and felt himself back in his familiar, self-assured role as a senior consultant well liked by most people he worked with, and surely, give or take the odd lapse, above any serious criticism.

"Hello, and how are you?" he asked the next person he met.

"The Lord he do try us, but . . ." And the elderly West Indian kitchen worker, pushing a food trolley, laughed her gap-toothed laugh.

"Watch out for those hooky toes!"

"Oh, right!"

"Evening, Nurse!" Tom said, half recognizing a face.

But the young nurse, stepping from the lift, looked away and pretended not to hear him as she hurried off.

Premenstrual tension, Tom decided generously; a deliberate snub from junior staff was, of course, unthinkable.

Then, as the lift doors closed, it struck him that she had been the nurse in the angiogram room that afternoon, the one who'd jumped when Darby Freeman made a joke right near the start of the procedure. And come to think of it now, she had remained pretty poker-faced after that, as though thoroughly disapproving of the behavior of her betters. Poor kid, Annabel's death must have hit such an obvious beginner very hard.

Tom Lockhart went cold.

He could see it, there before him: the weeping parents, the distraught young nurse blurting out her anger, her irrational, self-righteous fury. He could even hear her as she stormed: "I was there, and the doctors didn't care! They were laughing and joking, not watching what they were doing!"

And he saw the Woodleys looking around in disbelief, asking if she'd swear to this. Demanding to see whoever was in charge, threatening to talk to the newspapers, to the television, to every likely powder keg of outraged indignation if they were not immediately reassured that this was not so, God help them.

No wonder the nurse had refused to look at him. No wonder Professor Hughes-Sinclair had been called in, and had then telephoned Tom's home like that, too furious to waste words.

The same self-righteous Hughes-Sinclair, Tom recalled, wincing, with whom he had crossed swords over half-witted bloody cleaners not two days earlier.

"Ah, the good Thomas!" said Professor Hughes-Sinclair warmly, as the lift doors opened on the third floor. "I've been at the window, watching out for your arrival." And he beamed in his most avuncular manner, while dropping an arm across Tom's shoulders. "A man I can so totally depend on . . ."

"Sir?"

"Aye, a great comfort," rumbled Hughes-Sinclair, lowering his voice to a whisper to say, "A terrible, terrrrible sight, it is; most pitiful and most tragic."

"Sir?" Tom said again, even more disconcerted. "You don't mean Annabel?"

Hughes-Sinclair drew back from him, raising an eyebrow. "Annabel? No, no, it's not one of the female staff, dearie me, no. But I knew you would surely be the person best qualified to render the right assistance." Then, as always thrice the Scot when visibly stirred by emotion, he said, "Would you no go in and see Dr. Harcourt in his room, have a wee chat?"

"Geoff?"

"Aye, Geoff," replied Hughes-Sinclair, before remarking with a faint, pained smile, "and I fear it was one of the cleaners who found him."

"But—"

"I was working late on my Toronto paper—I'd said to Mrs. Hughes-Sinclair not to wait supper—when there was a knock at my door, and in burst that awful wee man Pearson, waving his confounded mop at me. I went immediately to Geoff, but, alas, there was little I could do. It was your name he kept repeating, an' I ken fine you two were guid friends an' all, so I—"

Tom shrugged off Hughes-Sinclair's arm and hastened along the corridor.

Geoff Harcourt was nowhere visible in his room at first. Then his feet, protruding from beneath his desk, led Tom to crouch down and peer into the gap between the two sets of drawers. Geoff was sitting there, hunched up, a gin bottle in his lap, repeatedly bumping the crown of his head against the underside of the desktop.

"Stop that," said Tom. "You'll hurt yourself, you silly bugger."

"Excellent! Fool that I am!"

"Bloody stop it, Geoff! Here, let me give you a hand out of there."

Geoff looked at Tom with no immediate sign of recognition. "Give a man a hand, and he'll take an arm," he slurred.

"Then crawl out on your own."

"Crawled enough, Christ knows, so sod off!"

"Geoff, what the hell's this all about?"

"Tom? That you, Tom, you bastard?"

"Yes."

"Ah! And your question was?"

"I want to know what's making you—well, do anything as bloody ridiculous as this."

"Your happiness."

"You've got to be joking!"

"*Happiness!*" Geoff bellowed at him. "Work it out for yourself, you sly, fornicating bastard!" Then he collapsed.

Deeply shocked, without knowing entirely why, Tom carried out a quick examination, decided it would not be necessary to use the stomach pump, and then wondered how on earth he was going to get Geoff back to his flat to sleep this off. Calling an ambulance was all very well when one wanted to transport an unconscious person from home to hospital, but a request to reverse the process was surely out of the question. And yet, unless something fairly discreet like an ambulance and its stretcher were used for the removal, far too many eyes would witness the undignified departure of a consultant in his cups, making it impossible for Geoff to remain on the staff—and indeed, at Tom's side in the angio room.

"Turned rather peaceful," said Hughes-Sinclair, peering round the door.

Tom rose from the floor, where he'd been kneeling to loosen Geoff's collar, and gave a wan smile. "Out for the count," he said. "It's a pity there's nowhere here we can find him a bed for the night."

"God forbid! Could we not perhaps commandeer a wheelchair and get him into the service lift? Then, away with him down to the basement, where you can have your motor vehicle waiting."

"They lock the basement car park after six, so that'll mean having to get permission from security to open up and God knows what else."

"Then we'll use the other service lift, take him down to the mortuary and you can use the special entrance for hearses and the like. That's never closed."

"Perfect, Professor!"

"Aye, and how salutary it might be," murmured Hughes-Sinclair, looking down at Geoff Harcourt, "should our colleague here chance to open an eye during the proceedings!"

Yet the professor's face was as troubled as Tom knew his own must be.

One thing went overlooked in this otherwise straightforward enough plan to get Geoff Harcourt home: he no longer lived on the ground floor, but had moved the previous weekend to his new second-story flat.

"Oh, bollocks!" said Tom, as he turned the last corner. "How the hell could I have forgotten that?"

Geoff, slumped at his side, made no response. He was still out cold, and patently beyond caring.

He was also, when Tom tried to pick him up in a fireman's lift, a dead weight far heavier than he'd seemed with Hughes-Sinclair helping to carry him. And so, the sensible thing to do now was obviously to contact Harry Coombes, whose own build matched that of his Renegade Jeep, and who probably would give any assistance only too gladly. But when Tom looked around him, he couldn't see a public telephone anywhere—and all that would take time anyway, increasing the likelihood of Geoff being sick in the car.

"And you'd better not do that, you silly bastard," Tom warned. "I've still to get Ginny to Tuppmere."

* * *

This sudden thought made him look at his watch. It was unbelievable!—he'd already lost the best part of an hour away from her.

"Right," he said grimly, heaving Geoff's limp body back out of the car and onto his left shoulder, "no more of this pissing about: you're on your way up those sodding stairs, my son!"

Over the first ten yards, he was surprised by how much lighter his burden seemed, and started on the first flight of stairs without pausing. He staggered a little on the landing, but kept going. Midway to the second floor, he missed a step, barked his shin painfully, and stopped, gasping for breath. It was extraordinary how much his leg muscles hurt, especially the rectus femoris in his right thigh, and he even felt slightly dizzy, a trace nauseated. God, now Geoff really did weigh a ton, and he wanted desperately to put him down. If he were to do that, however, Tom wasn't at all sure he'd have the strength to pick him up again, and so he just stood there, feeling Geoff warm on his shoulder and a tapping pulse in the wrist he was gripping so tightly. It was a curious, comradely type of intimacy he'd not experienced before, and for a stock-still instant, he was reminded of a World War I bronze he'd seen in a square somewhere: a statue of a defiant British Tommy, steel helmet tipped cockily back, carrying his fallen chum to safety under shellfire. Tom smiled, braced himself, and started up the steps again, very uncertainly, holding tightly to the banister with his free hand.

They made it.

Nine and a half minutes later Geoff was in bed, with a plastic bucket from the kitchen on the floor near his head, and a roll of lavatory paper, for wiping any stray sick from his lips afterward, at the ready on his bedside table. He was still unconscious, and snoring gustily.

"Best leave you a note," murmured Tom, arranging Geoff's clothes a little more neatly over the back of a chair. "Can't have you thinking the fairies did all this."

So he went through into the living room, and brought down the flap of the elegant antique writing desk. Every pigeonhole had torn scraps of paper sticking from it. Tom plucked one out and found printed on it, in Geoff's own hand, *IWTFS*. He looked at another, and another. He found only two with anything different on them: *IWTFCY*

"Christ . . ." he said.

Then, checking the time on his watch, he quickly replaced the scraps and tore off the corner of a magazine cover for his note. But he couldn't think of what he might write that would reassure Geoff and keep him from doing any further harm to himself before . . . Before what? Help came?

Tom went back into the bedroom, found Harry Coombes's number in Geoff's personal index beside the telephone on his chest of drawers, and dialed it.

"Harry's gone down the offy for some lagers and crisps," said Carole. "But he won't be long."

"You're sure?" said Tom.

Carole sighed. "Got another of them blue viddies off one of his mates," she said. "Can't wait to see it, can he? Honestly, some fellas are worse'n kids!"

"Well, in that case . . ."

"No, Tom, if there's owt you want, you've only got to say, luv."

God, he hated doing this, being so selfish, but there were the minutes ticking away, on the traveling clock at his elbow. "Carole, Geoff's gone and got himself very upset about something, and he's sort of overdosed."

"Never!"

"I'm afraid so, but on neat gin, thank God, nothing more dramatic. I've just brought him back to his flat, and I naturally ought to stay, because of the condition he's in, only I've got this very urgent—"

"You want Harry 'n' me to stop by?"

"Er, keep an eye on him for a while, yes. But if you're—"

"Do anythink for Geoff, he would!"

"What about yourself, though?"

"Do anythink for *you*, Tom me love—thought you woulda noticed that!"

Tom looked at his reflection in Geoff's mirror and saw how delightfully surprised he was. He also felt a decided twitch in his loins, and this surprised him even more. "Um, well," he said, "would it be all right, then, for you and Harry to zoom over and start the vigil?"

"Pardon? Soon as Harry's back, I tell him. You can explain a bit more then, okay?"

"Fine," he said, but his eyes had darted to the dial of the traveling clock. "No, what I meant is, I'll leave the front door off the latch. Oh, and I promise to catch up with you later."

"See you do, pet," said Carole.

* * *

Tom got into his Metro and reached out to start the engine. But his hand dropped with the ignition key back into his lap. He had just visualized what might happen if Geoff started throwing up, and because of the position in which he'd been left, choked himself to death.

"Can't leave him," Tom told himself. "Not like this. Only take a couple of minutes more."

So he rushed back up the two flights of stairs, went crashing into Geoff's flat, and searched for something he could use to prop up the foot of the bed. It would ensure that any vomit ran on downhill, as it were, and not back into the lungs. He used a couple of leather suitcases from on top of the wardrobe. And on returning to his car, he noted that he'd accomplished all this in not two but five and a quarter minutes.

Oh, sod it, that won't matter, he decided, really putting his foot down.

The first turnoff to Tuppmere on the divided highway flashed by.

"Funny!" said Tom, who had become perfectly used to thinking aloud by now and found it, in the circumstances, immeasurably comforting. "You can see that signpost coming up from a good way off . . ."

His next thought was altogether too startling to put into words immediately. And yet, the more he stalked it, and the more he tried to believe he must simply be imagining things, the more convinced he became that he was entirely correct: he hadn't manipulated Ginny into going home alone with him, but *she* had.

That signpost was the dead giveaway. Ginny must have been able to see for herself when it would be too late to leave the highway, and so she must also have procrastinated quite deliberately before making a reply, encouraging Tom to take the initiative.

And once this delicious deviousness in her was recognized, everything else seemed to fall neatly into place, producing an entirely different picture.

For instance, it had struck Tom right at the outset that Ginny seemed to be making rather heavy weather out of getting her parcel home in one piece, the suspension on rural buses notwithstanding, but he'd been much too eager for her company to dwell on this point. Now, however, he could afford to acknowledge what a lame excuse it had been, and to smile at the gall of the girl. Had Ginny known all along that he'd not have dreamed of challenging her reasoning? She must have! God, how excited this realization made him.

Next, there had been Ginny's remark about not knowing anyone who lived near her village, even though she had to be aware of how closely Tom was situated. He'd glossed over this in his mind before, content to suppose that she'd been using polite pressure on him simply to provide a hiding place for the present. But with hindsight, he could see now that Ginny had been feeding him lines that would result in their having longer together! Took the breath away.

"Damn . . ."

Tom had found a glaring defect in his entrancing new theory: how had Ginny known that Sylvia would not be at home on a Wednesday evening, supposing she wanted to be alone with him? How had she known he was only lying when he'd pretended otherwise?

Why, of course! She must have overheard Sylvia talking about her visits to Trade Winds at lunchtime on Sunday, very possibly after he and Hugh had left the table to inspect the swimming pool's filtration plant. Sylvia invariably brought up the topic at every social gathering she attended, partly because she had a tried-and-true piece of patter to go with it, which most women found gruesomely amusing, and largely because she enjoyed a martyr's role and had really nothing much else to talk about, being bone idle the rest of the week.

From that, it followed Ginny had been fully aware of Tom's plan to get her to himself under false pretenses, and that she'd actively aided and abetted it. Moreover, as it was she who'd insisted on going to speak to Sylvia, knowing she'd not be there, it'd all been her idea in the first place!

Then, to top it all off, she'd shown him the etching to unveil . . .

Tom stopped short there, afraid all this sounded far too good to be true. With so much ambiguity involved, his original view could equally be the correct one—that he'd been the sole manipulator of events. In fact, his only hope of knowing quite where he stood would be to get Ginny back into the car beside him as soon as possible, and then, perhaps, to just ask her.

So he pressed down on the accelerator even harder.

12

When he reached home, Tom Lockhart walked into an empty-seeming house, dreading what he might not find there. To be sure, not only had Nell Overton's etching disappeared from the living room, but so had Ginny and Sylvia.

Then he saw a note propped against the potpourri bowl on the lid of the grand piano:

7:45

Tom darling,
Popped out to take G. home. Will pick up a Chinese so don't
start boiling eggs or anything. Hope you're home from hosp.
before it gets cold!!!

Love, Sylvia

He went icy, and his fists clenched. "You *bastard*, Harcourt!" he exploded. "You selfish, drunken, stupid, sodding bastard!"
Tom had missed Ginny by slightly over five minutes.

In a fury, quite the like of which he'd not been possessed by before, he began storming from room to room, trying to find where the anniversary present had been stored. It was all he had left to draw comfort from, and he was going to get that etching out and take a bloody good look at it. He was going to examine every highlight and shadow, explore every line. Now that there was nobody else around to see him do so, he intended a very much closer look at that left nipple—the right one as well—and a lengthy scrutiny of the pair of delectable dimples revealed in the small of the back.

He searched and searched. He opened cupboard doors, went down on his hands and knees to peer under things, pulled back curtains, lowered the attic ladder and climbed it, even ripped aside the counterpane covering the bed in the guest room. He searched on and on, long after he had proved to himself the etching had gone, and was often quite destructive.

At 8:05 the telephone rang. "Hello, Dr. Tom, me old son?" someone said in a hoarse whisper so uncharacteristic it was impossible to place immediately.

"Oh, Harry! Yes, Tom here. D'you get to Geoff's all right? Or are you—"

"No, we're here, no danger, but we're buggered if we knows why. Old Geoff—can you hear them snorings?—looks like he's just had a skinful, be right as effin' rain in the mornin'!"

"Um, there's rather more to it than that, Harry."

"Oh aye?"

"Look, I'd rather not discuss this over the phone. If you could keep an eye on Geoff until, say, nine, I'll be along to relieve you, and we can have a chat about it then. All right?"

"Suits me!"

"What about Carole?"

"Oh, she knows her place, me old son, never you worry. I've got her sat through in the lounge, watchin' the telly, good as effin' gold she is."

That wasn't quite what Tom had been concerned about, but to save bother, he said, "Fine. See you in a short while, then."

"No need to break a leg," said Harry.

Tom did almost that the moment he put the receiver down, by stepping on an old wine bottle he'd knocked over in the bedroom. But he caught his balance just in time, and having restored the wine bottle to its place, made this the start of some tidying up he had to do.

His mood had changed, tipped to another extreme by Harry's telephone call. Now he felt overwhelmed by everything, crushed and beaten back, weighed down by the responsibility he had toward Geoff, and incredibly sorry for himself. He also felt he'd rather Sylvia knew nothing of this.

So he was outwardly jaunty, positively ebullient, when she came in through the front door carrying a large paper bag.

"You managed to pick up a Chinese all right?" he asked. "Not one, I trust, of an uncommonly demanding nature?"

"Tom," said Sylvia, "even for you, that's—"

"—unusually facetious?"

She smiled, going through to the kitchen.

He'd noticed before how these small ritual exchanges, established over fifteen years of married life, could so quickly reassert the status quo, making everything seem quite relaxed and normal. This pleased him, for there were several questions he had to have the answers to. A row would only make this more difficult, while further delaying his return to Geoff Harcourt's.

"What an odd evening," said Sylvia, as he joined her in the kitchen, "but a very pleasant one. Ginny's such a dear child, isn't she?"

Tom shrugged, wishing she wouldn't *use* that word.

"But before I get sidetracked," said Sylvia, opening the first carton and releasing the aroma of sweet-and-sour, "whatever was that panic call from the Prof in aid of? He did sound alarmed, and I imagined at the very least you must have done away with another of your patients."

"Done away?"

She gave him a sidelong glance. "It's happened before," she said quietly. "A very long time ago."

"No, no, nothing like that. It concerned, er, a cleaner."

"Oh, of course, you went and upset their union the other day—how very tedious," said Sylvia, then laughed. "I'm sorry, but what happened to you and that perfume still tickles me! I've been telling Ginny about it."

"You've what?" protested Tom, as though he'd suddenly had his ankles exposed.

"She adored it! Giggled like anything."

"Ginny doesn't—"

"Doesn't what?"

Giggle, he'd been about to say, loathing the schoolgirlish connotations of the word. "She doesn't strike me as someone so easily amused," he said, "by what amounted to a rather poignant . . ." Then he decided to really hit back: "You've already forgotten why I'd bought the Chanel for you?"

"Naturally I haven't," said Sylvia. "I told her that as well, and her very words were: 'Oh, you do make me jealous! Isn't Tom so wonderfully romantic?' "

That sent him diving through into the breakfast room with the table mats and cutlery, too divided in his feelings to know whether to scream with frustration or jump for joy. Frustration, at having been misrepresented as a remarkably happily married man; and joy, at having heard something about himself that rang so sweetly in his ears it almost deafened him. He put down both knives on Sylvia's side of the table, both forks on his own, and nearly walked off before noticing this and quickly changing them.

"You'll be glad to know," said Sylvia, as he entered the kitchen and was handed the bowls of fried rice to carry, "you won't have to struggle out of bed at the crack of dawn on Friday to go dashing off with that etching."

"But Ginny was particularly keen to—"

"Yes, she explained all that to me, and I've arranged things so you needn't be bothered, while her surprise for Hugh and Moira isn't spoiled one bit. I've had Mrs. Vincent put it somewhere safe until Ginny calls for it. You must remember her? The vicar's wife who got me to give a talk to the Tuppmere Women's Institute last autumn on the subject of private homes for the aged?"

Tom gave an acutely bitter laugh.

"Now, now," said Sylvia, "don't let's have your uncharitable views on the Church of England this once, if you please! And anyway, Molly Vincent's a very nice woman, and terribly broad-minded."

"Jesus, you don't mean she might sneak a peep at the—"

"I'm sure she will," said Sylvia. "Sauce?"

"But," said Tom, "but . . ."

"Here, I'll put some on for you," said Sylvia, tipping the polystyrene cup over his prawns in batter. "Mmmm, doesn't that smell absolutely yummy?"

Which was Tom's cue to complete another ritual, dating back to the earliest of their days, when bread and gravy had been a highlight of each Sunday's so-called dinner. His expected response was: "Triple yummy!"

He said, "Christ, Sylvia, but what happens when this Mrs. Whatsit recognizes it?"

"Recognizes what?"

"The—um, figure in the etching."

"Figures," Sylvia corrected him. "Which one?"

"Which one?" he repeated, losing patience. "The one in front of the mirror, for God's sake!"

"What mirror?" she said.

Tom sat back. I must be going mad, he thought. Quite mad. Or else this is somehow her idea of a joke, utterly unfunny in the extreme.

"Let's begin again," said Sylvia, popping a prawn ball into her mouth with her fingers. "Just who is Mrs. Vincent expected to recognize?"

"Ginny, you idiot!"

Sylvia nearly choked. "Oh, Tom," she said, coughing and laughing all at once, as she jumped up and dashed for the kitchen, "whatever—God, I've got to have some water—gave you that idea?"

"I absolutely insist on knowing," she went on, breaking the heavy silence filling the breakfast room, as she returned to her seat with a half-filled tumbler.

"You've only got to—" began Tom, then paused. "Look, it's what I understood," he said, "probably from something she said to me. You know, in the car. When we were on our way here. Just a chance remark she made."

"Out of the question," said Sylvia, sitting down again. "In fact, thinking she had a rather lovely figure herself, I actually asked her if she'd ever thought of doing any nude modeling for her arty friends. I think she was shocked."

"Shocked?"

"Perhaps even appalled. There's a very prim and proper, not to say wonderfully unsophisticated side to Ginny, and I had it made quite clear to me that taking one's clothes off in front of other people was *not* something she'd even contemplate. Hers is, and one can tell this with hindsight by the way she sits, a very *private* body, compared to those flaunted today by most teenagers."

"But—" Her blouse had been sheer enough!

"Tom, do start eating. Chinese food tends to cool down so—"

"Ginny needn't have been telling you the truth."

"Why ever not?"

"Perhaps, well, Hugh and Moira are pretty stuffy and straitlaced in some areas, despite their frenzied attempts to appear otherwise, and if they knew their one and only—"

"Oh, bosh, Tom! By the same token, if that were Ginny in the etching, would she invite their whatever by actually giving them a copy of it?"

"Er, sounds to me like that could be typical teenage-rebellion stuff."

"Maybe that's why she's chosen that type of picture for them, agreed; the same idea occurred to me. But—this stir-fried beef is too, too delicious—it simply can't be Ginny in the picture, I'm sure of it."

Tom had just forced himself to take a mouthful of rice and it'd stuck to his dry palate. "Mmmm-mmm," he replied with a shake of his head, trying to convey he'd now concurred with her— which wasn't true, but he could hardly pursue the topic much further without sounding unduly interested in it.

"You still think that's Ginny in the picture?" said Sylvia, misreading him. "Left or right? Neither looks virginal enough to me, and that's another quaint thing about her, in this day and age: Ginny's strong views on keeping herself intact until the man of her dreams comes along. Oh, we girls did have a lovely chat together, especially in the car."

Then, after looking up at Tom, rather quizzically, for a few seconds, Sylvia laughed louder than she had done all evening. It was a delighted, peal-of-bells laugh, almost affectionate and loving.

"Oh, Tom," she said, "oh, Tom . . . I've just worked out why you thought there was a mirror in that picture! Do you know, for all your supposed earthiness and doctorly cynicism, you really must be as much a puritan at heart as little Miss Ashford."

Tom drove empty-bellied back into town, having explained to Sylvia he'd returned simply to have supper with her during a break in cleaners' union negotiations. He had not told her about Geoff Harcourt because he'd feared what her response might be, and he needed to keep seeing Geoff in the very best of lights for a while. Neither had he made any reference to her final remark on the subject of the etching, when she'd said something so extraordinary about himself and Ginny that his brain had abruptly switched off, unable to cope any longer. He had toyed with his food, watched her speaking about Trade Winds, looked at the electric wall clock, pleaded no appetite, made his excuses, and left.

He borrowed her car, though, for its vestiges of fragrance.

"Lovely evening," said one of Geoff Harcourt's neighbors, a man with a dog.

Tom nodded, and waited for the dog to be dragged away from its attempt to piddle on the first step of the stairs.

Then he started up them, and his thigh muscles ached in protest at having to make the climb again so soon. He tried to realign his thoughts to deal with what lay ahead of him, none of which he expected would be very pleasant. Midway on the second flight, he was reminded of the bronze memorial and recalled it in greater detail than before. The soldier with a fallen comrade on his back had had a cloth flap over his eyes, as though he'd been blinded.

"Mustard gas," muttered Tom, but was still left with a ridiculous sense of unease.

That vanished the instant Carole threw open the flat door and her arms, too, all in one. "Tom!" she said, and seemed about to hug him. "About flippin' time too, if I may say so!"

"Sorry, sorry about that," he said, smiling weakly back at her, feeling probably the way a dead moon did about the sunlight it reflected. "Geoff's not being too much of a nuisance, I—"

"Not being nothin', so far as I know," she said, closing the door behind him. "Harry's in there, keepin' an eye, that's all, and so it's been dead borin'."

"Sorry about that too," he said. "But I can take over now, so you two can go off and—well, lagers and crisps, wasn't it?"

"That Lockhart?" said Harry, lumbering out into the living room.

Carole turned away and went and sat in front of the television.

"Poor Harry!" said Tom. "I've just apologized to—"

"You been bitchin' again?" Harry said to Carole, not as lightheartedly as he might have done. "Now, I told yer, Geoff's—"

"I never," retorted Carole, and started using the remote control to jump continuously from one television channel to the other.

"You just cut that out, Carole, you hear?"

She ignored him.

"Look," said Tom, "I think the sooner I relieve—"

"He wants us to stay," interrupted Harry, wrenching the

control from Carole's fingers and switching to a police series on a commercial channel. "There, you stick with that crap and behave, you hear?"

"Er, Geoff wants you and Carole to stay?" asked Tom.

"No, just me—he never said nothin' about sulky-face there. Y'know, he's awake, like."

"Then I'd better have a word with him myself, and see if I can't—"

"Wouldn't do that, old son," said Harry.

"But I—" Tom suddenly realized his way was being barred by the big bricklayer. "What in hell's name is . . . ?"

Harry Coombes then had enough decency to look undeniably embarrassed, while at the same time, rather perplexed himself. "When Geoff come awake," he said, "he first thought he was back at the hozzie, till he saw me stood there, with his bucket at present arms, like. Then I tells him you must've brung him back from there, only you had this emergency to go to, and next thing, he's tellin' me he don't want you back in his 'ouse. I rung your place to say, but your missus told us you were already—"

"Oh, Christ," said Tom, his shoulders slumping at the thought of what sort of reception he could now expect upon his arrival home. "You really know how to do a friend a favor, don't you, you silly bastard?"

Harry's jaw tightened and he wiped back his quiff with a very large, ring-knuckled hand. "Goeff's me only real mate around 'ere," he said with a definite warning note in his voice. "'Specially since I heard he don't want to see you no more, not never."

"Oh, rubbish! The bugger's drunk—can't you see that?"

"What's stickin' out a mile, squire, like a blind cobbler's effin' thumb, is that *you*"—and here Harry prodded Tom in the chest with a forefinger as thick as a broomstick—"has upset me best mate, and I want yer effin' out of 'ere, chop-chop!"

Tom heard himself swallow loudly. "Jesus, this is so bizarre I—"

"Listen," cut in Harry Coombes, "piss off or I'll belt yer."

Tom left immediately, ashen-faced, and Carole caught him up on the stairs. "Give us a lift home, would yer, luv?" she asked.

"Home?"

"To me flat—s'not all that far to walk, but I'm not dressed really."

And for the first time, Tom became aware that Carole was in a light raincoat with some frills of a sheer negligee visible at the neck and below the hem. He also noticed, for the first time, the musky impact of her perfume.

"I'm afraid that it mightn't be such a good idea, sorry. Harry's not too well disposed toward me at this—"

"Harry? Sod 'im, for a start! Anyway, it was his idea—said to ask yer, or he'd get a taxi for us, only I didn't want some dirty old—well, would yer, Tom? *Please?*"

Tom dithered, struggling to untangle one confused thought from the next, then gave in on such an unimportant issue and said, "Come on, then—why not?"

Carole slipped an arm inside his own, giving it a squeeze.

Now there, thought Tom, in a distant, unbombarded corner of his mind, something like a remote suburban air-raid shelter, was a prime example of one of life's cruelest ironies. If Ginny had done that to him, he'd have capered joyfully down both flights of stairs, probably breaking his neck in the process and being perfectly content to die with a supremely grateful smile on his lips. And indeed, if Ginny had merely looked about to hug him, or had called him "love," he'd have turned cartwheels across the carpark. But she hadn't, Carole had; right things, wrong person; and he was slipping the key into Sylvia's car door with a calm, steady, joyless hand.

"I know I've gone a bit quiet for me," said Carole, as they drew near to where she lived, "and I don't want yer to think I'm bein' rude, like. It's just, well, y'know . . ." She tried to laugh, make a joke of it, but her laugh sagged in the middle. "Fact is, I've said nowt since we come down them stairs, have I?"

"Nor have I," Tom reminded her quietly. "All a bit too much for the pair of us, I think, what was going on in that flat."

"Couldn't understand it, could you, Tom? I mean, Harry'd been a bit stroppy with me earlier, like, when I had the telly on a bit loud, but to come out the bedroom and start on at you and me as if we . . ."

"Beyond me," said Tom. "Big block of flats, is it? The one we're looking for?"

"No," said Carole, pointing. "See those shops? Mine's the place over the launderette. Don't look much, I know, but . . ."

"It has friendly sparrows."

Carole gave a surprised laugh. "My," she said, "fancy you rememberin' that!" And this time she gave his left knee a quick squeeze. "Oh, they're such pigs with them bread crumbs, you'd never believe it."

"There you are," said Tom, pulling over and berthing amid a small sea of discarded fish-and-chip wrappings, "our door-to-door delivery service."

"Lovely, I'm ever so grateful. Comin' up for a coffee?"

"Um, not tonight, perhaps, Carole—but thanks anyway."

"See you around, then," she said, keeping her gaze on him as she slipped out of her seat and then gently closed the door.

Tom waited at the curb for a minute longer, watching to make sure she let herself safely into the building, and saw her beautiful blond hair catch the unshaded light as she disappeared inside with a flash of rounded calf. Then he stopped squeezing his thighs together for decorum's sake, and drove home in high spirits, having just realized that at least one thing precious to him had survived the day.

Tomorrow, of course, Ginny had promised to try and contact her friend Pat, so that she could take Tom to see aquatinting.

13

Hodgkins took a desperate backward leap and flattened himself against the side of a minibus in the car park, as wide-eyed as any hunter trying to evade the terrifying charge of a rogue rhinoceros. Fully thirty feet away, a black MG Metro tapped aside the traffic cones in its reserved space and stopped. Dr. Lockhart was late again.

"Why," Sylvia had said casually over breakfast, "did you lie to me last night?"

Tom, acutely aware of quite how many small evasions of the truth she could be referring to—ranging from the reason he was certain Ginny had modeled for the etching, to the excuse he'd given for leaving his stir-fried beef uneaten—pretended to have a mouthful.

"Or am I to believe, Tom, that Geoff somehow ran afoul of the cleaners himself yesterday, to end up in a state that Harry Coombes described to me on the phone as 'bleedin' pitiful'?"

"Well, he *was* found by a cleaner, funnily enough! Dead drunk under his desk. Hughes-Sinclair didn't want any scandal, so he insisted we make up a yarn to disguise what we were doing back at the hospital."

"Wasn't I to be trusted?"

"No—I mean, yes, of course you're to be trusted! But I don't think the Prof was thinking of you when . . ."

"Dead drunk?" said Sylvia. "*Under* his desk? Why?"

"Couldn't get any sense out of him."

Sylvia shuddered, and pushed her plate to one side. "I think I'd understand all this a little better," she said, "had you stayed in town until you were finished dealing with him, but you shot off back here to have supper with me in the middle of things. That wasn't like you."

"Well, there was a temporary hiatus and—"

"Harry was under the impression you'd an emergency call which had called you away."

"Supper was the emergency!" said Tom.

"Or was it," said Sylvia, "you wanted to take another kick at the linen closet door? I went to get a towel after my shower a few minutes ago and found quite a nasty scuff on it."

Tom left the lift at a half run, making straight for the angiogram room, and almost collided with Sister McTaggart.

"There's no need to hurry so, Doctor!" she said. "The first angiogram this morning, the special one, has been canceled from on high."

"Wonderful!" said Tom, who wanted to remain as close as possible to the telephone that day, in case Ginny rang about the aquatinting. "But, er, for what reason?"

"I've not been given one as yet."

"No? I'd better see the boss, then."

Tom went to drop his raincoat in his office first, and found Hughes-Sinclair seated there at his desk, swirling the dregs in a cup of black coffee.

"Morning, sir! I gather you've canceled—"

"What option had I?"

"Sorry, I don't . . ."

"You don't what?" said Hughes-Sinclair, producing a photocopied letter. "You weren't aware we'd be receiving this?"

Tom took the letter, and found himself almost unable to bear the disintegration evident in Harcourt's handwriting, which skipped and zipped and wobbled. But its message was plain enough. "Geoff's resigned, just because of last night?" he said. "I can't believe that!"

"Aye, and note the addendum, Thomas. He informs us he's taking sick leave for the period of his notice."

"But he can't not come back at all. What the hell does he think this'll do to his career?"

Hughes-Sinclair shook his head. "It's a sad, perplexing business," he said. "Dr. Emmanuel certainly can't accept he's lost Dr. Harcourt in such a precipitant manner, and naturally, as his head of department, he feels a certain responsibility for the man's welfare. He dropped in to see me a few minutes ago, hoping you'd provide him with some idea of what the actual position is."

"I'm sorry, but I can't really help you, sir. I had to leave Geoff not long after I got him home, although I did arrange for someone—"

"A belligerent young man of uncouth manner?"

"How did you—"

"Oh, he delivered the letter by hand to Dr. Emmanuel's office, first thing this morning," said Hughes-Sinclair. "Talking of whom, I made a promise we'd do what we could to throw light on the matter, and as your angio's off, I—"

"I do have quite a bit of—"

"I've studied the amount of work outstanding on your desk," Hughes-Sinclair broke in firmly, "and can see nothing that can't wait a wee while. I'd like you to go around to his home and assess the situation. Tell Dr. Harcourt of Dr. Emmanuel's concern, will you? And of course, we'll be relying on you to do your damnedest to bring this unhappy man to his senses."

"Blast you, Geoff!" cursed Tom, getting back into his car and starting it up. "The one bloody day I've *got* to be near a phone, and you do this to me, you bastard!"

For Harcourt really did seem determined, in an uncanny, diabolically circuitous way, to frustrate every plan he made involving Ginny. There he'd been, all set to spend the morning at his desk, an arm's length from snatching up his receiver the instant the telephone rang—and now he was stuck in his car, compelled to leave Betty Earnshaw, God help him, taking messages.

And so, when Hodgkins suddenly threw himself against the minibus for the second time that morning, Tom had to admit he'd fairly good reason to.

"I must find myself something *very* distracting to do today," Sylvia had said, buttering her third piece of toast. "I may even tackle tidying the garage. You've still not answered my last question, Tom, and I've so many others buzzing around in my head now. Like, for instance, why on earth did you give Ginny such a whopping gin last night? I picked it up by accident, took a tiny sip, and almost choked. Were you hoping to elicit something from her?"

"Pardon?"

"Oh, you never know, the details of Hugh and Moira's relationship could be utterly fascinating. I've a suspicion she's having an affair with that golf coach of hers. She will keep mentioning him, quite unnecessarily."

Tom laughed, much relieved. "Go on! Moira?"

"Thought you'd be heartened by that," said Sylvia. "And now you'll have to wait while I iron you another shirt—you've just got some egg on that one."

Eleven minutes after leaving the hospital, Tom was standing outside the door to Geoff Harcourt's flat, thumbing the bell hard and often, with fast-growing impatience.

"Won't do yer no good, mate," called across a milkman, putting down two pints outside a flat on the opposite landing. "Not even if yer played Beethoven. Gone on 'is 'olidays, 'asn't 'e?"

"How do you know that?" asked Tom.

"Got a note, didn't I?"

"Oh?"

"Down there," said the milkman, pointing.

Taking a step backward, Tom saw a scrap of paper he'd been standing on. He picked it up and read: *No milk til 8th. Ta.*

"Not his writing," he said.

"Nar, and 'e didn't wash 'is bottle this mornin', neither."

Good, thought Tom, as he drove back to the hospital. Excellent! That simplified things enormously. With Geoff out of the way, he felt he could breathe again. This seemed a shameful way to be thinking about a friend and colleague, however, and he wondered what had come over him.

His professional self began whispering first. It quoted fragments from a medical journal in which a paper had been published that discussed the well-known phenomenon of what appalling patients all health workers made, with doctors being among the very worst of them. This was almost certainly because, the paper had decided, basing its conclusion on an extensive survey, health workers had a very pronounced "them and us" outlook. An attitude which led them, albeit covertly and often unconsciously, to view the sick with contempt for being "weak" and, unarguably, victims. Therefore, when one of the "strong, nonvictim" group became ill, the enforced change of status was seen as intolerable and immediately denied by such statements as, "But I'm not sick—and I should know!" Moreover, when one of the "strong" became a "victim," the rest tended, subconsciously in the main, to turn their backs, expelling the runt of the litter from their midst. And never was this more obvious than when mental illness struck those not engaged in psychiatric work, the blood-and-guts brigade to whom a severe depression meant a dent in a fractured cranium, something tangible one could place one's thumb in.

Seen in this context, thought Tom, Dr. G. J. Harcourt, B. Chem., M.D., FRCP, more than qualified to be ignored, forgotten, treated with . . .

No, that's isn't it, came a different, very personal whisper. It's utter nonsense to suggest Geoff has become a victim in your view; you've been too close to him for too long. Perhaps this very closeness is the thing—perhaps you're afraid of him! Yes, it could be as simple as that. Afraid of how quick he was to detect and classify the changes in you after Ginny on Sunday. Afraid, too, of what else Geoff might learn. Remember how you felt you'd overlooked something after the kitchen conversation during the party? Well, you had. You turned a blind eye to the fact that if Geoff Harcourt could react so ruthlessly, self-righteously, and destructively over that imaginary indiscretion with Felicity Croxhall, then God knows what sort of threat he presented to Ginny Ashford.

"No, I don't think matters should be left there," said Hughes-Sinclair. "If anything, they've become more worrying. You must know this, er, Coombes fellow to have contacted him last night, so I suggest you do so again. See what he can tell us."

"Ah, but there's a snag to that, sir," said Tom. "He's a self-employed bricklayer and will be out on some building site or other at this time of day."

"No notion of where?"

"None, I'm afraid. I don't know him that well."

"Hmmm, but try ringing him anyway."

"Very good, Professor."

Tom strolled back to his office, borrowed a telephone directory off Betty Earnshaw on the way, and was soon dialing Coombes's number. No answer.

"Superb," he murmured, and hung up.

He started going through his desk drawers, prompted by an idea he'd not yet formulated properly. Interestingly enough, something seemed to be missing. He searched through them again and realized that his half bottle of gin had vanished. With a dull click, one piece of the previous evening's mystery fell into place, and from it, he deduced that Geoff Harcourt must have acted very much on the spur of the moment in taking to drink. Or, to look at the same thing another way, it now seemed obvious that some sort of incident had occurred, right there in the hospital, to spark off such an act of aberrant behavior. Not too long before, when Tom had met him briefly in the passage to discuss Annabel's death, Geoff had been perfectly friendly and normal.

But what sort of incident, and involving whom?

I left late, Tom remembered, and was not necessarily expecting to meet anyone on the way out, which is why I didn't go through the coffee room. Geoff, having no ties, often hung on a while, so encountering him made sense. But who else, bar Hughes-Sinclair, drafting his Toronto paper, would still have been about on the third floor? Drs. Hunt and Williams shot from the building on the stroke of five, while Ric Stephens was usually gone at least a minute before them. That left nobody really, other than the juniors—none of whom would normally come in contact with Geoff, far less dare to upset his equilibrium.

The telephone rang and Tom snatched it up.

"Part-timer?"

"Oh, Christ, you," said Tom, seeing the picture of Ginny fade. "How's the stomach and its wailing walls?"

"We need to talk," said Darby Freeman.

"About?"

"Yesterday's cyanotic. Truman's done the p.m., and the word is, he's going to call for reports from us."

"God, it's not going to become an inquest job, is it?"

"Need to talk," repeated Freeman. "Geoff's lot say he's not in today. Is that right?"

"Er, yes."

"Just you and me then. Twelve-thirty, across at the 'Dead' Lion?"

"Er, I'd rather canteen it."

"Bit of privacy's indicated."

"But I'm waiting for a phone call. Crucial one, really."

"Then tell switchboard to bleep you," said Freeman, ringing off.

He'd not uttered a single profanity during that exchange, which in itself should have been very worrying, had Tom not so much else to think about.

The strategically sound thing to do would be to borrow a standard text on etching from the public library, he'd just realized. It was bound to explain the various techniques, including aquatinting, and once he'd boned up on them, he would be in a position to ask what appeared to be unusually intelligent questions. Much the same approach had worked superbly well when he'd decided to switch from straight medicine to radiology, leaving Hughes-Sinclair enormously impressed.

"Betty," said Tom, putting his head into her cubbyhole. "Still such a thriller fan as you used to be?"

"My goodness, yes, Doctor! Can't beat a good murder, I always say!"

"No chance then that you might have a spare library ticket?"

"Will have, this lunch hour, 'cos I'm taking a whole lot back, see?"

"In that case," said Tom, seeing such luck as confirmation of an inspired idea, "I wonder if you could do a great favor for me . . ."

Then at twelve-thirty, with something of a spring in his step, and having made arrangements with the main switchboard to be bleeped if and when Ginny rang, he crossed the street behind the hospital and went into the Red Lion.

"Hello, Tom," said Fred Grose, the owner, "long time, no see."

Tom nodded and smiled, looking around for Darby Freeman, who hadn't apparently arrived as yet. "They keep us at it, Fred. You know how it is."

"You mean all those lovely young nurses?" said Harvey Meldrum, the chief copy editor from the newspaper next door, putting down a pint mug. "Shocking, the liberties doctors take— abuse of power, I call it!"

"Yes, my usual lunchtime tipple, please, Fred," said Tom, seeing him reach for the Worcestershire sauce, "and a pint for our imaginative friend here, when he's ready."

"Well, it pays to have a vivid in my game," said Meldrum, with his inbred tendency to trim unessential words from sentences.

"Dross we get! Should've seen main lead we've ended up with, noon edition—God, *another* famine in wherever! Who cares, I ask you, who really blood-dy cares?"

"A famine in London would be interesting."

"My point exactly, Tom! Cheers . . ."

Tom paid for his tomato juice and the beer, then wandered over to study the instructions on the slot machine. Usually, he much preferred the Red Lion to the Fox and Grapes, which stood outside the hospital's main gates and attracted most of its custom. Fred Grose was one reason. A former petty officer fitter in the Royal Navy—which had given him a mastery of piping that transferred well to the intricacies of modern cellarage—Fred had the beam and bearing of a battle cruiser, and conducted himself with equal dignity. He was also a man of considerable intelligence, masked by a mischievous twinkle, and when nobody else was about, his dry comments upon a great range of topics—Fred was an omnivorous reader—were always worth savoring. The other reason was of course that the Red Lion gave one a chance to avoid talking shop, even if this did mean putting up with someone like Harvey Meldrum, whose executive position on a responsible newspaper was one of life's enduring mysteries. But on this particular day, Tom wondered whether yet another pub wouldn't have been a wiser choice of rendezvous: Meldrum had the ears of a jackrabbit and just as few morals.

"With you in a tick, soon's I've got a drink," Darby Freeman said quietly over Tom's shoulder, as the slot machine reels spun. "Bloody cardiac arrest kept me back."

"Look remarkably fit on it!" called out Meldrum.

So Tom and Darby went out into the small walled beer garden at the back to hold their own inquest into the death of Annabel Woodley. After thirty-five minutes, the jury's verdict was unanimous: death by natural causes. Not a single piece of evidence suggested it could have been otherwise.

"Except," said Darby, "we've not got Geoff as a witness here."

"Geoff?" said Tom. "You're not suggesting he could've made a cock-up with the catheter? I personally double-checked the position of—"

"Yes, in the heart. But what about on its way there?"

"Geoff would have said, that's why! And he'd have been bloody upset, that I can tell you, especially when she snuffed it, but he wasn't. Well, no more than one usually is with a fatality."

"Then obviously you didn't see him afterward," said Darby, dipping a finger in some spilled lager and drawing a cross on the tabletop.

"Oh, yes, I bloody did! Caught me leaving about five-forty and gave me the bad news, was very philosophical about it. Christ, he was calming *me* down."

"Five-forty, you say, cobber?"

Tom looked hard at Darby Freeman. "Why the accent on the time, for God's sake?"

"Because," said Darby, "about five minutes later, he's up at intensive care, in a helluva state, wanting a word with me. I told him I already knew about the poor little sheila, but that wasn't it. At least, that was the impression I got. Geoff hung about, chatted, did all the small talk, asked if my guts was better, about eating in the canteen and all sorts, then it's like he's got kangaroos in the top paddock. Fair dinkum, Tom, he had the bloody shakes, but I couldn't get it out of him, what it was, y'know. Started being bloody airy-fairy, said it was nothing, and then he buggered off. Personally, I didn't believe a word of it. I thought he'd suddenly realized he had made a balls of something—suddenly, as in right after he'd seen you, it seems."

"Christ," said Tom.

A large library book entitled simply *Printmaking* was lying on his desk when he returned to his office. He didn't get a chance to open it, for the telephone rang at the very same moment.

"Isobel, Doctor, we're ready for you in the angio room."

"On my way," said Tom, then added, once he'd replaced the receiver, "Damn and blast it! What's happened to you, Ginny?"

Neither was his mood improved by the first of the patients. She had blood vessels with more twists and turns to them than the illustrator of Gray's *Anatomy* had ever had nightmares about. They looked, on the monitor, like a fistful of wiring ripped from an old radio set and then squashed flat, making directing a catheter through them a long and tedious business.

"Third time lucky," Sister McTaggart murmured, giving Tom a smile clearly intended to smooth the deep frown from his forehead. "You'll see . . ."

"Bloody incompetence," he grunted, glaring at Ric Stephens through the lead glass of the control booth.

"Now, be fair," said Sister McTaggart, "even Dr. Harcourt would've had his work cut out with this one."

Tom's frown deepened. He had a strong feeling that Darby Freeman had been hinting that somehow or another he'd played a part in Geoff's sudden realization and abrupt change of manner the evening before. But try as he might, he could think of nothing he'd said or done which would have triggered off such a reaction.

"Doctor?"

"Yes, Sister?"

"Your secretary's at the door, trying to attract your attention."

Tom turned to the porthole in the door, and saw Betty Earnshaw miming a telephone call. "Hold everything!" he said. "Back in a minute or two."

"It's a young lady, only—" began Betty.

"Where, which phone?" demanded Tom.

"The one on the wall there, I've had it put through. But as I was—"

"Later!" said Tom, lifting the receiver. And then, because Betty wasn't quite out of earshot yet, he said gruffly, "Dr. Lockhart, here. Can I help you?"

"Ooo, you do sound a right misery, pet! Like Carole to come round and kiss it better?"

Tom laughed, which rather astonished him.

"Carole?" he said. "To what do I owe . . ."

"You dunno?" she said.

"What?"

"Harry 'n' Geoff have 'opped it!"

"Well, I'd gathered something was—"

"It's amazin'," she said. "I went round to Geoff's flat in me dinner hour, to see how he was an' all, and this neighbor, see, fella with a dog, says the pair of them'd put suitcases and everythin' in Harry's jeep at seven-thirty and gone! So I phones Harry's mum, and she says, that's right, he'd told her him and a mate had decided sudden, like, to go on this trip, see? Never said where, 'cos Harry never does, and they'll be back Saturday. I mean, I'm beginnin' to wonder about them two!"

"Be back on Saturday? This one, or the next?"

"Oh, next, 'cos it were for ten days, his mum said. Not a word to me, not one word! Could've given us a bell or summat."

"Yes, they both could have," agreed Tom. "Very mysterious."

"Only I wondered if you knew more, luv."

"No, I'm afraid I don't, Carole. If I do hear something from Geoff, would you like me to get in touch? Tell you how Harry is?"

"Him? He can sod off, far as I'm concerned—every girl has her pride, y'know! Mind, I'd be interested, like, there's no pre- tendin'."

"All right, then, I'll get in touch."

"Promise?"

"I promise. What's the number of the place where you work?"

"Oh, there's no need for that, Tom, my luv," said Carole. "You know where me flat is now, so anytime yer fancies, jus' come round—all right? Always be a welcome for yer, an' I mean that. Be good!" And she put the phone down.

It was the only call from a young lady that Tom had that day. And on the following day, Friday, he had none at all.

14

Friday repeated and repeated itself in Tom Lockhart's dreams, well into Saturday. He wrote the same reports on the same X-ray pictures; answered the phone many, many times; heard nothing more from Darby Freeman, nothing from Geoff Harcourt; found *Printmaking*, in his present state of mind, incomprehensible; and took himself to the Red Lion for a couple of hours after work, in search of much-needed consolation. And now the telephone was ringing again, but he let it ring, the hell with it.

He awoke, and it was still ringing. Sylvia reached over him and lifted the receiver.

"I'll come at once," she said.

Then the rummaging in the wardrobe began, as Sylvia made a careful selection of clothes to fling on. "Sister Pinkerton," she said.

"Mmmm," said Tom, recognizing the name of the matron at Trade Winds.

"She says Mummy was taken very poorly during the night. The doctor suspects a stroke, and if she's not shown signs of an improvement by ten, he's having her admitted to the hospital."

"Mmmm," said Tom.

"Poor Mummy!" exclaimed Sylvia, deciding between a dark blue blouse or a light blue one. "Poor Daddy, too—you know how dreadfully upset he becomes whenever she's ill. He can't *bear* to be parted from her."

With any luck then, thought Tom, the miserable old sod would have the decency to follow her into the grave, but he doubted this was anything like the dire emergency it sounded.

"Tom? Are you awake? Did you—"

"Yes, I heard," he said, taking care to mumble sleepily. "I don't suppose you need me to come with you?"

Sylvia hesitated, standing on one leg with an unbuckled sandal ready in one hand. "It'd be nice to have someone share the driving," she said. "But what would you do with yourself all day, while I'm busy?"

"That's a point," he agreed, then felt he ought to add: "I could always take your father for a walk in his wheelchair, buy him half a cider down at the local."

"And repeat what happened the last time? No, I think not, thank you! If you want to be useful, you can always finish tidying the garage for me."

"You still believe his story, that I left him sitting under the dart board?"

She slipped her sandal on, hopping to keep her balance. "We'll not start that all over again, if you don't mind," she said. "Daddy's not quite as ga-ga as you try to—"

"Fine, we'll not start all that again! Any further instructions?"

"No, I don't think so. Oh, food . . . I know, there's a rabbit pie that just needs popping into the microwave. The one us girls made yesterday."

"What was that?" asked Tom, only just stopping himself from sitting bolt upright. "You and who made?"

"Ginny. She rode over to tell us how the etching had gone down, but you were out pub crawling."

"You didn't say a word about this last night!"

"If you remember, Tom, you came home in the most awful mood, glowering at me and not wanting any supper, so I wasn't going to allow that to spoil a good story on such a complete Eeyore. It would wait."

"What good story?"

"Moira's reaction to the etching," said Sylvia, sitting down at her dressing table to apply her makeup. "By the way, they've hung it on their landing, where none of their cocktail-party set are likely to see it and start asking wherever did they get it. Poor Ginny, she didn't say as much, but I'm sure she's worked that out for herself."

"And?"

"It was priceless. Moira apparently took one look and said, 'Oh, it's beautiful, my sweet, and such a surprise—but should, um, the ladies in really artistic pictures be *unshaven*?'"

"Hmmm."

"Oh, come on, Tom! Isn't that too, too marvelous? We girls giggled about it for ages!"

If Sylvia said "we girls" or "us girls" just once more, deliberately excluding Tom with all the subtlety of a door slammed in his face, then he was going to take an axe to her.

She did exactly that, not two minutes later.

But by then, feeling too confused, too weary, too old, feeling he had spent the last six days somehow making a terrible fool of himself, Tom was beyond caring. He lay curled tight in a fetal ball, the bedclothes over his head, and feigned sleep until at last Sylvia's car left the drive and the house closed its silence around him.

Us girls have made you a pie, Piglet, out of Rabbit and ALL Rabbit's friends and relations! Isn't that just too divinely triple-yummy?

"Bollocks!" exploded Tom, hurling aside the bedclothes and jumping out of bed, galvanized by fury. "What in Christ's name are you bloody playing at, Ginny?"

He dragged on his dressing gown, put on his slippers, and stumped through to the kitchen. He slapped the switch on the electric kettle, then dropped two slices of bread into the toaster, banging its lever down.

"Sodding women," he muttered.

Clatter! The toaster, as temperamental as ever, had ejected the two slices even before its elements had heated up.

"Look, you bastard," hissed Tom, replacing the bread and depressing the lever less violently. "Try that again, and I'll kick your backside the length of this bloody kitchen! Got that?"

Next, he put an egg in a saucepan to boil, and opened the refrigerator to take out the orange juice. There wasn't any. The refrigerator was almost bare; a reminder that on Saturdays he was usually expected to help Sylvia with her "weekly shop" at a supermarket out in the country. Well, he thought, at least I'm being spared that today. He detested having to trail around after her with the shopping cart while she fretted over the prices of things, determined to spend no more than her housekeeping money. This, being an arbitrary sum fixed by Sylvia herself, after having subtracted her personal extravagances and the vast amount it cost them to keep her parents at Trade Winds—that repulsive nursery for infantile nonentities, who sat around all day soiling incontinence pads and clapping hands in time to the matron's honky-tonk piano playing—while Tom, who'd not had a new car for several years now, sweated his guts out. God, he felt bitter that those two half-witted, peevish old snobs were the children the Almighty had finally blessed them with.

Then Tom noticed the pie, which had been covered with clear plastic wrap and left on the top shelf in the refrigerator. "Good God . . ." he said.

This was a pie unlike any he'd seen made by Sylvia before. To be sure, her pies usually had a fairly appetizing crust on them, but that was the limit of their visual appeal. She certainly never troubled to decorate them; much preferring, he'd always thought, to impose their wholesome plainness on the world almost as some form of reproach, like the well-scrubbed faces of certain orders of nun. But here was a pie with its crust crimped all the way around the brim of the dish; a huge X, made of two wide strips of pastry, centered over the hidden egg cup in the middle; and surmounting that, a large heart, also of pastry. Plus, there were four more hearts, smaller ones, each placed in one of the quadrants formed by the big X, and any number of tiny pastry crosses.

"Sylv?" said Tom. "What on earth made you . . ."

Then he stepped back suddenly, as though from a physical blow, so great was the force of the idea that had struck him. This piecrust wasn't Sylvia's work, it was Ginny's! And she hadn't forgotten him after all, for there it was, spelled out in pastry hearts and pastry crosses, made with such tender care: *LOVE & KISSES.*

Tom was still grinning at the pie when the toast burst into flames behind him.

"Olé!" he cried, shaking out the little red fire blanket, kept for just such an emergency in the cutlery drawer. "Olé, olé, olé!" he shouted, and stamped his slippered feet and pirouted. "Sí, and now El Lockharti will keeeeel you, you cunning li'l bastardo!— *OLÉ!!!"* He sidestepped the toaster's next rush, flung his cape over its smoking nostrils, and plunged in the bread knife.

There was a blue flash, a bang, and Tom was thrown back, colliding with the edge of the drain board.

"Sweet Zeus," he said, sobered, his right arm tingling. What a moment to almost kill himself!—now that he'd so much to live for.

And he turned back to the pie, expecting just the sight of it to restore the great joy of only a few seconds before, but found that, instead, he experienced a decided sinking feeling. Had those pastry decorations really the significance he'd like to attribute to them? Or was this just another example of his gift for rather pathetic self-delusion?

You're right, said that small, stubborn part of him which would not let go its puritanical rationalism. Look in the baking drawer over there. More than probably, the only pastry cutter you'll find is heart-shaped, leaving Miss Ashford little choice of decorative symbol. And as for crosses made of pastry, it would be difficult to think of an easier, more rudimentary form of trimming, surely?

Tom did not look in the baking drawer. He went through to the fuse box in the cloakroom and began to repair the damage he'd done.

But the larger, less stubborn part of him wouldn't let go either. It still liked the say-it-with-piecrust idea, and was wondering how this could be reconciled with the facts, as Tom knew them. Fact One: that Ginny had called on Friday evening; and Fact Two: that she'd done so to report on how the anniversary gift had gone down.

Or had she?

Tom froze, fuse wire in hand. Why, of course Ginny hadn't! And he silently cursed himself for having ever allowed something so obvious to escape him before. The anniversary present must have been no more than the *pretext* for her visit, while her actual intention had been to see him again and give him that message about the aquatinting.

Then the rest fell abruptly into place, making sudden sense of everything he'd found so bewildering and upsetting, and how simple it all was. Ginny obviously hadn't managed to contact her printmaking friend until it was too late on Friday afternoon to telephone him at the hospital. Realizing this, and being naturally hesitant to ring him at home, lest Sylvia reached the telephone first, she had decided to call on Tom instead. It would then have been easy enough, while Sylvia was out of the room, making tea or something, to have a quick word with Tom, and arrange their meeting at the workshop. Plainly, Ginny was no keener than he was for Sylvia to know of their date together, or else she would have asked her to pass on the details.

Tripe, said a small, puritanical voice. You're making this all up, just to suit yourself.

Sod you, thought Tom, I know I'm right, and I'll bloody prove it!

Because Ginny wasn't stupid. She would have anticipated his perhaps not being there, or his being difficult to get on his own, and so she must have made a contingency plan. That's right: she would have come armed with a note or something she could slip to him, or possibly leave somewhere, should that too prove problematic. The whole business of the pie had been providential at best, and never any part of her overall strategy.

Only what sort of note would Ginny have left behind? Certainly, it wouldn't have been too personal, lest Sylvia chanced upon it and started asking awkward questions.

"I'll just to have to look . . ." said Tom, tossing the fuse wire aside.

He explored the pockets of his three coats, hanging in the cloakroom, and then checked the pile of opened mail, awaiting replies, that lay on a brass plate on the hall table. He went into the living room and felt down the sides of the sofa, concentrating at the end where Ginny had sat once before. He lifted the lid covering the piano keys. Still nothing. His confidence began to waver slightly. He glimpsed something, lying half hidden by the brim of the potpourri bowl.

It was a card printed in three shades of green with its lettering in purple. The lettering announced the opening of an exhibition of recent work by two local artists—Nell Overton, printmaker, and Len Tullet, sculptor—at the main public library in town, and it invited the bearer to attend the private viewing that very Saturday between 12 noon and 2:30 P.M.

But that's wasn't all.

On the back, a firm, young hand had hurriedly scrawled: *SEE YOU!!*

15

Tom Lockhart drove into town much too early, arriving there before 11:30 despite the heavy Saturday morning traffic. He took one look at the length of the queue waiting outside the multistory car park nearest the public library, and decided to carry on to the hospital, where he parked in his usual place. Hodgkins didn't work weekends, so it was like entering the eeriness of an empty amphitheater, with his booth as the boarded-up box office.

And it was still only 11:32.

The borrowed copy of *Printmaking* lay opened on Tom's desk, behind the window three floors above him, but he was not in any mood for that now. Instead, he turned up the Verdi on his cassette player and propped up the private-viewing invitation on his dashboard. Then he sat back, fingers interlaced behind his head, to admire the card's abstract patterns and to read once again every word printed on it.

Nell Overton . . . Nell? Now there was a fine old English name one didn't come across very often. In fact, he couldn't recall having seen it on any patient's form, and the only Nell he'd ever known had switched to using her second name, Evelyn, having tired of too many Nell Gwynne jokes. That she had been uncommonly buxom *and* a mistress—albeit at a school—hadn't helped, of course. And what about this Nell, the printmaker? Was she a comely wench herself, perhaps, with breasts as round as oranges and skin like angels' milk? If so, what a surprise awaited her this lunchtime, when she'd be confronted by a man who simply didn't care, couldn't be less interested were she a toothless hag with hairs growing from her chin. For this was the most remarkable thing about being in love with Ginny: all other women virtually ceased to exist. It was probably how a monk hoped to feel, thought Tom, if he said his Hail Marys often and loudly enough.

"Hello, boss!"

Tom turned, stomach knotting. "What are you doing here?" he demanded.

"On call," said Ric Stephens, crouching beside his car door. "And you? Off to that?" He nodded at the invitation card.

God, it was chilling how quick his eyes were. "I'll have to, I suppose. My wife insists—I'm meeting her there in a few minutes."

"Should be good."

"Oh? Another of your more arcane interests?"

"Like to keep in touch," said Stephens, smiling. "Well, better get to work, I suppose. Traffic accident; hit-and-run victim."

Tom nodded curtly. He felt rather like one himself.

And he had to walk to the library very quickly, very energetically indeed, to dissipate the rage threatening to boil over in him. This had been going to be a perfect day, and already it'd suffered its first blemish. Correction: its first and *only* blemish, he told himself, and sneaked another look at the back of the invitation card, before thrusting it once again deep into his pocket. Instantly, *SEE YOU!!* had restored much of his joie de vivre.

He arrived at the library at the stroke of noon, precisely when the private viewing began, thought better of it, and circled the block a number of times. He did not want Ginny to be embarrassed by his seeming too eager in front of her printmaking friends. At 12:23, however, he decided the auspicious moment had come, and entered the library's main foyer, where the exhibition was signposted beside a large green and purple poster. Even before he started up the stairs, taking them two at a time, his heart had begun beating faster.

The last cardboard arrow pointed through glass doors at a long, low, very brilliantly lit room already filled with a surprising number of people. None appeared at first sight to be the sort he normally associated with, being either too flamboyantly dressed and hirsute, or too decidedly young and trendy. This should have been a relief in its way, for it offered him a form of privacy when it came to his meeting Ginny, but Tom was much more aware of feeling acutely alienated. For an instant, he debated rushing home and changing out of his suit and tie—a private viewing, he'd imagined that morning, being a very grand affair—and into his odd-job jeans and moth-eaten black turtleneck. Then he saw three or four obviously professional people, modestly attired in expensive agricultural clothing. He took heart from this, knowing they'd understand a man having had to dress in a manner befitting his calling, especially when his Saturdays weren't sacrosanct. "You're a senior consultant? Why, of course . . . !" they'd say, and raise their wineglasses to him slightly. Everyone in the room seemed to be holding a wineglass, which was possibly why the gathering had formed so quickly, especially as the wine—or fruit juice, for the more virtuous—was apparently free.

Tom took a deep breath and entered the gallery. "Red or white?" asked a stunning black woman with the most attractive American accent he'd ever heard. "And if you say white, honey, I promise I'm not going to take offense."

"Er, red, please," said Tom, and for some ridiculous reason (possibly dating back to his prep school, where good-conduct cards had to be produced at every visit to the candy store) he showed her his rather creased invitation.

"My," she said, "you been sleepin' with that under your pillow nights? You're a *real* art lover, right?" And she laughed, making her head of beaded braids jiggle.

"I thank you," said Tom coldly, taking his glass from her and turning abruptly away.

He couldn't see Ginny anywhere in the crush, nor anyone with breasts like oranges and a complexion like angels' milk. His high spirits, already fragile enough, teetered.

"Tom?"

He half turned and there was Ginny, right in front of him, her gray eyes lit with excitement and her lips slightly parted. She was dressed quite unlike he'd ever seen her before, very formally in a deep claret dress with a necklace of cultured pearls, and high-heeled shoes. Her elegance was astonishing, and he'd have burst with pride to take her simply anywhere.

"Ginny . . ."

"I'm so glad you could come!" she said, touching his shoulder.

Then she added, doubtless remembering where she was, with so many people around them who might be eavesdropping: "But where's Sylvia? Isn't she here, too?"

"Shot off early this morning to look after her mother."

"Really? Not anything—"

"—too serious?" said Tom, completing her sentence for her, and smiling at the memory of when last she'd used those words. "Oh, no, I very much doubt it. Look, thank you very much for your—"

"Ginny, my love," said a middle-aged, dark-haired man with a goatee, pushing his way between them, "do you think you could discover where the spare catalogues have got to? We're almost out already, and I hate to actually *announce* the prices of my pieces—one feels such a tradesman, if you know what I mean."

"Poor soul," said Tom.

"This is Len," Ginny said quickly, plainly hiding her laughter, "Len Tullet, the sculptor. And this is Tom Lockhart, Len—a radiologist at the hospital, an old family friend."

"Really," said Tullet.

But he didn't go away after Ginny had left with a promise to return in a twinkling, and Tom, tickled by how she'd so cleverly made her presence appear wholly innocent of any clandestine undertones, decided it was incumbent upon him to play his own role in this to the hilt.

"Lovely child," he said. "Known her, well, since she was twelve."

"Not in any biblical sense, I hope," said Tullet loftily.

"Another crack like that," warned Tom, using a low and confidential tone, "and I'll knee you in the goolies."

Tullet laughed. "I like it!" he said. "But what a man of your sensitivity could be doing at a shindig like this beats me."

"And me, to a degree," admitted Tom, smiling back. He was very surprised by the aggression he'd shown Tullet, but had really rather enjoyed it. "Conned anyone into buying anything yet?"

"No, but the customers are still only on their first glass of El Cheapo. I've high hopes, though, of getting rid of this one fairly smartish."

"What is it?" asked Tom, looking at the object under the spotlight.

"Title? *Third World Requiem*."

"Hmmm. Give you this, the welding rods are skinny enough, but you seem to know as much about the human rib cage as a—"

"Please, I couldn't *bear* to be figurative," protested Tullet, "and especially *not* with figures! Fancy another dollop of the same?"

Good God, thought Tom, my glass is empty already. "Thanks very much," he said, holding it out. "But, er, white this time."

It must be the adrenaline making me so thirsty, he reflected, as he went on waiting edgily for Ginny to return. The stuff had begun coursing through him the moment he'd started up those stairs, and when Tullet had started ordering her about, he'd received a triple booster shot. Fight or flight, that was the classic tag which went with adrenaline, and without a moment's thought, he'd opted for the former. Why? Perhaps because, as he'd noticed before, Ginny's femininity was so strong it intensified the sense of his own masculinity to Neanderthal levels, leaving him fearful, a wielder of clubs in an age of chrome. And yet, awed by the magical metamorphosis of erectile tissue, a brute beast too, aching to mount her there and then. Tom was glad he'd at least had the sense to put on the right kind of tight underpants that morning.

"You've hit it off with Len!" said Ginny, looking very pleased as she reemerged from the crowd, and this time she touched his arm, very briefly. "How did you do it? He usually *despises* people so."

Tom gave a laugh, overjoyed by her delight in him. "Not sure," he said.

"But who you really must meet is—"

"Ginny, just a second. First, could we—"

"Cheers," said Len Tullet, stepping between them again, and handing Tom his recharged glass. "Now it's Nell that wants you, Ginny honey, and don't say I didn't warn you!"

Tom watched Ginny disappearing, recorded one vivid impression of her delicately classical profile—not for his cave wall but for the Sistine of his longing—and then turned to the sculptor. "You've warned Ginny about what?" he asked.

Tullet shrugged. "Dangers of becoming a groupie."

"Groupie?" echoed Tom, finding even the taste of the word on his tongue abhorrent. "In what, er, respect?"

"You know, hanging around the workshop, always such a willing kid if there's a sod-awful job to be done, framing for shows, typing up résumés, scrubbing silk screens, guard duty at exhibitions, all sorts. There are always those ready to take even bigger advantage, know what I mean?"

Tom stared at him. "No, I'm not quite sure I do," he said unevenly. "In what way, exactly?"

"Len, darling!" cried out a circus tent of a woman, whirling her long necklace like a trick lariat and pouncing with a fanfare of gin fumes. "Will you believe me if I say I've quite, quite forgiven you?"

"Sorry, mate, a cash customer," Tullet said to Tom out of a corner of his mouth, and met the circus tent head-on, delighting her by scolding: "Not pissed again, are we, Gwenners?"

There was a high level of noise in the room. Tom was able to see that simply by the way people kept leaning toward one another and turning an ear, clasping at a lapel or drawing someone closer by the arm. It was also apparent in the pious, closed-off expressions of those with nobody to talk to, and so were pretending wrapt self-communion in the Presence, capital P, of Art. Tom could himself hear nothing but the thud of his own very loud heartbeat.

He was on the move, edging his way through the crush, making for where he'd last seen Ginny disappearing. He had to talk to her, talk to her properly, find out what Tullet could have been hinting at. The worst of it was, somewhere deep inside him, he had a terrible feeling he'd known all along.

Ginny was nowhere to be seen.

Perhaps the American at the door would know where she'd got to, as she faced what seemed to be the only door. Tom made for her, and had to pause for a moment, his path blocked by a chattering trio who hadn't noticed him yet. In that same instant something caught his attention so completely he forgot everything else, and remained rooted to the spot even after a gap had been politely provided for him to pass through.

Ginny, his Ginny, *was* in the room, and that wasn't all either.

She was for sale, naked, up there on the wall.

I don't believe it, decided Tom Lockhart.

Which made the rational part of his mind lose patience entirely. Listen, you idiot, it snapped, whose fault is it that you've kept thinking of that anniversary present as a picture, one picture, first on your sofa and later on the landing at Tuppmere? You must have known, from what you learned about printmaking from

Ginny, or even before, that one of the chief virtues of the technique is the fact one can make a whole series of etchings from the same plate, if one chooses to. Why has this taken so long to penetrate? Why all the fuss, when you found it missing that night, and went around kicking things? Why try to buy that copy off her, hurting her feelings in the process? For heaven's sake, you only needed to have contacted Nell Overton and you, too, could have been a proud possessor!

Days ago.

Tom shuddered. He couldn't tolerate the idea of anyone with enough money *possessing* Ginny as though she were some kind of . . . And yet, he knew, the fact remained: all the dirty old men in that room could have her right then and there, without having to do anything except reach for their check books.

He looked around for a catalogue to see what obscene price had been placed on her, but was struck, almost in the same moment, by the sheer absurdity of his response.

And he smiled wryly as he approached the etching, having remembered how Sylvia had denied, quite categorically, that Ginny had been portrayed in it, still less that she'd ever modeled for her artist friends. On top of which, Hugh and Moira had patently not recognized in it their very own daughter; Ginny, with her proven sweet nature, would never have dreamed of giving them such a shattering gift anyway.

So, the girl hanging here wasn't Ginny, couldn't ever have been. All this agonizing on his part, based on a furtive glance or two back in his living room, had been for naught. If only, Tom told himself, he'd not been too embarrassed that night to examine the picture for longer in front of her, then he too would have surely concurred with the consensus of opinion and seen what a fool he'd been to suppose otherwise.

Yes, just look at those heads. Neither was Ginny's; the jaws were too square and the ears too small. The feet weren't like hers, either; although similar in their narrow elegance, the toes were too long and the anklebones too pronounced. The hair was also much shorter, of course, even allowing for artistic license.

It amazed him to note how wrong he'd been.

And the figures were indeed two separate women, just as Sylvia had said: the nearer one standing in the light; the other, far darker and slighter, in shadow. What had thrown him, Tom concluded, were the trees in the background. They made strong vertical lines that suggested the sides of a looking-glass frame topped off by an overhanging branch, and the fact the figures were *mirroring* each other's posture simply compounded the illusion at a glance.

"What a buffoon . . ." he murmured happily.

But he still couldn't get why Sylvia had made that joke about him and Ginny being puritan, so he looked to see if a clue to this lay in the name of the thing, which he'd never got around to. It was written on the print in pencil: *Imago.* He looked over someone's shoulder at a catalogue, saw it listed at one hundred pounds, framed, and then back at the picture again, raising an eyebrow.

"Oh-oh," said the American woman, wandering up with her own wineglass and stopping beside him. "The title got you, too?"

Tom shook his head. "Imago," he said, remembering his biology, "the final and most perfect stage of an insect after all metamorphoses . . ."

She threw her head back and laughed. "God, you British," she said, "your humor's so *dry*. I'm Nell, by the way—Ginny said for me to come right on over, introduce myself."

Tom had to look at her all over again.

Nell Overton was about his height but less than half his weight, being willowy and light-boned. Her hips weren't obvious, and the only suggestion of oranges about her breasts were the pip-sized nipples holding her turquoise silk blouse out, an inch or so from her sternum. Her eyes were lustrous yet keen, like a leopard's, and her lips had a strong, woodcarver's curve to them, making one want to touch a finger to them for their texture. The many subtle tones of her complexion were astonishing, ranging from topaz, where the collarbones stretched her skin tightly, to a deep, almost sooty black on her upper eyelids. She made the very idea of milk, any form of milk, seem monotonous.

"Do I pass?" she said, raising a mocking eyebrow.

"I'm sorry!" said Tom. "How rude of me! It's just Ginny—"

"Now, there is a truly special person," said Nell. "The goodness starts right deep in her soul, and works its way clean through to the outside."

"You think so?" said Tom, elated.

"Which is *English*-English for damn right!—right?"

They laughed loudly, and were frowned at.

* * *

"Your work," said Tom, turning to the etching with the intention of flattering Nell into telling him much more about Ginny, "is absolutely marvelous." Then he searched his memory for some means of prompting her. "The way you've handled this plate is amazing, just as—"

"Why, thank you, kind sir! All I know is, you're a guy who takes X rays. So is art a kind of hobby for you? You go around to a lot of shows? Maybe draw, even paint a little?"

"Good grief, no! If our cartoons didn't come ready-drawn, I doubt I could even manage my job."

"You have to make up funnies about your patients?"

Tom laughed and shook his head. "No, what I meant is—well, a cartoon is jargon for the printed outlines of hearts and other bits and pieces we're required to scribble findings on, the position of lesions and so on. It's the hack side of imaging."

"Imaging?" repeated Nell, tipping her head to one side as she savored the word. "Hey, that's beautiful . . ."

He suspected a joke, then saw she was serious.

"Beautiful," she repeated. "And, I guess, it's another name for what I also do all day. Who knows, maybe we've got a whole lot in common."

"Oh, no," said Tom, turning to look at the etching. "Different worlds!"

Nell regarded him thoughtfully. "I wonder," she said.

Tom glanced around the room. Still no sign of Ginny. A pity that, as he'd have liked to have her with him to hear how well he was getting on with this, another of her friends. The only features he recognized were those of Len Tullet, sharply focused in the midst of a general blur.

"Sorry, what was that?" said Tom, having only half heard the last remark, but knowing it had intrigued him.

"Let's see how many touch points we can dream up," said Nell. "We both earn our living from images—right?"

"Very contrasting ones, surely!"

"But you must," she said, "see X rays that give you a kick sometimes. You know, aesthetically?"

Tom shrugged. "One's bound to, I suppose, if the tonal range is there, with good exposure and good darkroom work, but whether that's—"

"How about the patterns, the shapes?"

"Yes, they're important, but the real skills lie in perceiving what most people wouldn't see without you pointing it out to them, and to do this you often have to use your instincts, even your intuition, before you can—"

"Uh-huh, just like an artist does."

"Steady on," said Tom, enjoying this. "If you're not careful, you'll have me wearing a beret in the angio room, and I'm not at all sure the patients are going to be too reassured by that!"

Nell laughed. "I've thought of another thing," she said.

"Hang on," said Tom, "so have I! We both work primarily in a metal."

"We do? Okay, mine's zinc, but . . ."

"Mine's film."

"That's what I thought, so how come—"

"The tiny dark grains in it, making up the image, they're silver."

"Hey . . ." began Nell.

"That's beautiful?" said Tom.

And this time their laughter was low, intimate; nobody frowned at them.

"Okay, my turn," said Nell. "We both spend a whole lot of time looking inside people, trying to find out what makes them the way they are."

"Right!" he said. "Only you do it skinside outside."

"Skinside outside? You just lost me."

"Hiawatha? Ginny once—"

"That patronizing racist crap!" she snapped.

Acutely embarrassed and dismayed, he looked away, hoping he hadn't shattered the rapport between them. It was true, Nell and he did seem to have a lot in common, and he wanted Ginny to know this, for it would, in turn, surely draw her even closer to him. Then the same thing happened as had occurred when he'd glanced around the room and seen only Len Tullet. Tom's eyes, alighting on the etching beside them, picked out only what he immediately recognized: Ginny's shoulders, her throat, left nipple, hips, hands, swell and dip of belly. It bloody *was* her, at least in part, this nearer, lighter figure; while the more distant, darker, flatter-chested figure, which he had previously mistaken for a distorted reflection, suddenly suggested . . .

"Hey, I'm sorry," Nell Overton was saying. "You just caught me on the raw, I guess! I worked an ethnic arts program on a reservation once, and right nearby was the Minnehaha Motel where the goddamn tourists threw quarters to . . ." She stopped and asked, "Tom, what's up?"

"Nothing!" he said. "Nothing at all! You were saying?"

"There is something," she insisted.

"No, nothing!" he repeated.

"I changed the subject? You'd thought of another touch point?"

"Good God, no!" he said, with a violent shake of the head. "There's a limit to any bloody silly game."

Nell's eyebrows went up. "Wow," she said, "how come you're on the big back-off all of a sudden? I thought we'd—"

"Look," he said, pointing recklessly to the etching. "That's you, isn't it? You're in that!"

"Oh, I get you! Your images are never you, are they? Poor Tom . . ." And she ran a fingertip lightly down the glass over Ginny's long thigh. "God, I'd hate not to be able to express my feelings, this joy in something so beau—"

"Don't!" snapped Tom, unable to bear that word again. "What I meant was—"

"Don't?" said Nell, looking around at him. "Oh, hi, honey! What took you so long?"

It was Ginny, flushed at the throat and breathless.

"You didn't give me nearly enough money," she said to Nell. "So I ran round to the supermarket where it's a lot less expensive. Anyway, there's three more bottles of white, the extra red— they're on your table—and here's the change!" She dropped it into the waiting, open hand, which closed over her own for a moment, squeezing.

"Must go," said Tom, backing into someone.

Only then did Ginny turn to him, her radiant smile fading. "But you can't!" she said. "You haven't had time to—"

"Must!" replied Tom. "Should've told you—on call—accident coming in—sorry about this—must run—must . . . !"

He fled. Rushed down the library stairs, taking them faster and faster, trying to outrun even the most apparently mundane of the horrendous ideas now crowding in on him. There was no way, that he knew, Ginny could ever have afforded one hundred pounds for an etching.

16

One thing seemed clear to Tom Lockhart by the time he'd reached his car again, still in a total turmoil, but at least able to see where his duty lay.

Somebody would have to be told.

Ginny simply couldn't be allowed, in her innocence, to continue such a relationship, for who knew where it might lead. At best, she stood to be brutally shocked when its true nature was revealed, with every chance of her then becoming tormented by wholly inappropriate feelings of guilt. And yet, were he himself to attempt to do anything about it directly, the very fact he was male would surely trigger a response from the Overton woman for exceeding, in the misery it could cause, anything he'd been trying to prevent. No, the necessary intervention would have to come from somebody else, and obviously, all things considered, that somebody would have to be a woman.

Moira? God forbid! She'd never keep this to herself, not for a minute. Next thing, Hugh would be involved, unleashing all the righteous wrath of an outraged father—yet possibly forgetting in the heat of the moment what this would do to his horrified daughter, caught in the crossfire.

But if not Moira, who else was there? It would have to be a woman Tom could trust and talk freely to; a woman who'd listen with empathic understanding to all he had seen and heard; a woman unafraid to then take whatever action was needed to extricate Ginny.

Sylvia! he thought, chastened by finding the solution so obvious.

He was also immensely unenthused by it, and not unaware of certain ironies involved; but this lasted no longer than it took him to realize quite what an ideal ally she'd make, and this was paramount. Why, the pair of them could have another of their cozy "us girls" talks, during which Nell Overton could be casually mentioned, some notion gained of what the relationship actually amounted to at present, and then perhaps, if all went well, the first moves could be taken to end it. Alternatively, if Overton herself needed to be approached, nobody he knew was less likely to flinch at the prospect, nor more likely to effect a complete rout.

"Bloody brilliant," muttered Tom, getting out of his car again, and hurrying off without bothering to lock it. "We'll have you back here in no time, Sylv, me old love, just see if we don't. . . !"

When push came to shove, she really did have some virtues—and dammit, he felt proud of her.

When he reached his office it occurred to him he hadn't bothered to discover the number of the hospital to which his mother-in-law had probably been admitted by now; knowing her, very little could keep her out of an expensive private ward, given the slightest excuse. But his own hospital switchboard took that kind of problem in its stride. A minute or so later he'd been connected to Admissions, and then, even more quickly, his call was transferred to the old bitch's bedside.

"Hello? Dr. Lockhart's wife speaking."

Tom sighed. "Must you, Sylv?" he said.

"Tom?"

"Yes, I—"

"Where on earth have you been?" she demanded. "I've rung and rung the house, and thinking you might not hear me because you were tidying the garage, I've also rung the neighbors, who had some extraordinary story of your going tearing out as though—"

"I've just been to the—"

"Really, you can be most trying! Here's poor Mummy lying ill beside me, and as if that wasn't enough to worry about, you go gallivanting off—"

"How is she?" interrupted Tom, with as much apparent concern as he could muster.

There were the feeble, quavering sounds of a hideous cross being bravely borne in the background.

"Did you catch that, Tom? Mummy says she's as well as can be expected, thank you, under the circumstances."

"Excellent! Very relieved to hear it. And now, there was in fact another reason I wanted to ring you. It concerns—"

"I'm afraid it *was* a tiny stroke we had," said Sylvia, "but Dr. Fox is being terribly reassuring, and the staff here—I naturally let them know who you were, by the way—have been fairly good on the whole. Yes, apart from one little nurse, who really must get something done about a frightful walleye which revolts Mummy every time she sees her, I've very few complaints so far."

"Really? Only I must—"

"Poor Daddy, however, is *quite* a different matter, and Sister Pinkerton is being very unfeeling about the state he's in. She's actually had the cheek to suggest my time might be better spent up at Trade Winds, seeing to his waterworks and reading him his Agatha—"

"Be fair, they don't really have enough staff on at the weekend to—"

"Tom, I've had all I can stand of that sort of nonsense from Sister, so I don't propose starting the same argument with you—I simply refuse to. All I wanted to tell you is that I won't be coming back tonight, and may have to spend several more days here."

He said nothing, just shook his head.

"Mummy, Tom sends his fondest love," announced Sylvia in a loud aside, then added briskly, "Her tea's come, and it's bound to be half cold, so I must be quick. Did you say there was some other reason you'd wanted to talk to me?"

"Can't imagine why I might have thought that," replied Tom. " 'Bye."

Two fat pigeons landed on his window ledge. Vermin, the pair of them, going about, puffed up with ridiculous self-importance, forever on the bloody cadge. They each turned on him a beady, mindless eye, set in the side of a nervy head.

"Bastards," he said.

It shamed him to think of his wedding day, and of how flattered he'd been, the rough yeoman farmer's son, to be marrying into what had seemed the nobility. "This is Colonel Draycott, Grand-dad," he'd said, far louder than any onsetting deafness had necessitated, "Sylvia's father, late of the Coldstream Guards. He and Mrs. Draycott flew here from Africa only yesterday." "Bloody hell, must've cost a bit!" his grandfather had remarked sympathetically, only to be regarded in silence by the two Draycotts, as though deemed unutterably uncouth.

God knows what could have happened to their supposed wealth not long after that. They blamed "the wogs" of course, those barefooted upstarts who had taken it upon themselves to rule Kenya. But it had never been altogether clear to Tom—given that his in-laws had indeed owned the finest coffee plantation in the Highlands, and had been forced to accept peanuts for it—how their former, quite as white neighbors could continue to send them jolly postcards, air-mail letters, and the occasional food parcel.

Food parcel! Just what sort of picture of England in the late eighties were they, in turn, transmitting back to Africa in their own correspondence, the bloody old scroungers? A favorite theme, no doubt, would be communist-inspired strikes and drug-crazed black teenage muggers stealing army pension books. Not a word about three solid meals a day, a good sound roof over their heads, and the constant, most intimate ministrations of long-suffering Sister Pinkerton.

Late of Barbados.

Not a mention of the daughter who'd never been the same since their return "home," but had undergone a change, possibly in the extraordinary belief she now had "something rather special to live up to," which had left her all but unrecognizable by her own husband.

Tom, whose resentment of this had originally been colossal, before he'd simply given up the unequal struggle, suddenly felt it return even more sharply, more devastatingly than ever before. He'd just realized that should the future hold for him what he could only half dare hope, then he'd need enough money to run two households, what with Sylvia's alimony. And yet, as things stood, the Trade Winds bills would make this impossible.

"Bastards!" he exploded, startling the two pigeons from the ledge.

Then he had to laugh, for they defecated in fright as they took to the air, wings clapping. That, considering whom they could be taken to represent, was in character right enough.

The laugh came just in time. Tom, wavering on the brink of the blackest, most nihilistic mood he'd ever known, found he'd been cleansed by that harsh, gleeful sound in some sudden way—washed free of the last sticky traces of a sugary, cog-clogging sentimentality that for too long had bedeviled him.

His mind slipped smoothly into top gear, and almost before he'd posed much the same question again—What sensible, genuinely sympathetic woman could he ask to help Ginny?—the answer was already there, waiting on the tip of his tongue: Felicity Croxhall!

You know where you can always find me, Tom, she'd said.

Not on a Saturday, however.

The duty rota showed she wasn't on call but he tried her home number all the same, hoping the fine weather hadn't tempted her outdoors. No reply. He took a long shot and tried the operating room area, persuading himself she might be there after all, catching up on some paperwork. She wasn't.

That's when he would normally have given up, but too much was at stake here. He looked in the telephone directory, found her listed under simply *G.F.H. Croxhall*—the number corresponded to the one he'd already tried—and memorized the address beside it. Sad, he reflected momentarily, that single women had now to disguise their solitary status in this way, and hoped she wasn't going to have to fight his way past a pair of slavering Dobermanns.

As it happened, a very loud bark greeted Tom's clatter of the brass knocker on the front door of 4 Fisherman's Walk, a row of small, brightly painted terrace houses overlooking the river. Then there was silence, suggesting that, having performed its duty, the brute had retired to its basket, well content with itself. Or perhaps it had gone back to watching the cricket on *Saturday Afternoon Grandstand*, because faint sounds from a television set could now be heard. Nothing else, though.

"Got it," said Tom softly to himself. "She's popped out to see a neighbor, probably one with cats. Won't be long now . . ."

So he stationed himself directly across the road, pretending an interest in the duckling-rearing techniques of a bossy mallard, and waited. The drake, none to happy about this apparently, came ashore and waited too, pretending an interest in a tussock of grass near his ankles.

Phew, thought Tom. With the time to think at last, how thankful he was that his first, crassly impulsive idea of enlisting Sylvia's help had demonstrated its absurdity before he'd committed

himself to finding explanations for where he'd been that lunchtime and how he'd come to be Ginny's guest there in the first
place. Setting aside all other considerations, the Overton business
was far too pressing and important to be unnecessarily complicated in such a fashion. And with Felicity, of course, this aspect of
things need not even figure.

Yet would she, a stranger to Ginny, be willing to take some
form of action on her behalf, as Sylvia had been intended to do?
Tom hadn't paused to ponder this before, the turmoil within him
having been only partially overcome. But doubtless Felicity
would be able to suggest ways and means of achieving what must
be done, and there was certainly nobody whose counsel he
valued more, especially on the intuitive level.

"If you're really thinking of trying to walk on water," she said,
"I feel it'd only be sensible to grow a beard first . . ."

Tom looked up sharply as a green canoe scattered the ducklings, and then he needed a second or two to adjust before
returning her broad, lopsided smile.

"That was sneaky!" he said, grabbing the end of the paddle
Felicity now extended to him. "Didn't hear you coming."

"Downstream; the current's ferocious today, all that rain."

"Ah, very cunning. You've never said anything to me about
being a canoeist before!"

"And I can't remember you saying you'd be calling this
afternoon," she replied. "But I'm glad you have."

The very loud bark turned out to be a misshapen, floppy-eared,
coarse-haired, galumphing, cheerful black-and-white mongrel by
the name of Gluteus Maximus.

"Or Max, for short," Felicity explained, completing Tom's
formal introduction. "But don't ask me what kind of dog he is,
because nobody at the animal sanctuary had a clue."

"I think he's another of those Californian professors," said
Tom. "You know, Walt Disney makes documentaries about them.
They knock back weird bubbling mixtures in their labs, and—
flash, bang, wallop!—they end up looking like this and driving
Volkswagens."

Felicity laughed, dropping her life jacket on the stripped-pine
dinner table. "I'd noticed his weakness for calculus," she said.
"Like a lager? I'm parched."

"Um, yes, thanks," said Tom, impatient to have done with

these preliminaries, as cheering as he found them. "And then I wonder whether I could ask you—"

"Has it to do with what was on your mind the other day?"

"Well, in a way, yes . . . I—"

"Thought so. You fish the lagers out of the fridge, while I change quickly—my seat's all wet—and then we'll have ourselves a quiet chat. Won't be a tick!"

"Max, old son," murmured Tom, as he poured a little of the lager into his water dish for him, "you've got yourself one in a million there."

It was interesting, that kitchen. Virtually everything in it was old. The meat mincer was cast-iron and had a pattern of ivy leaves along the curved arm of its crank. The pepper grinder had a small drawer. The kitchen knives, hung in a row from brass hooks, all had irregular edges to their blades, having been sharpened so often. Interesting , too, was the vast range of foodstuffs, spices, and condiments, some very exotic; Tom had shared digs once with a Don Juan of a junior houseman who'd sworn that any female who delighted in eating well was almost certain to have other and considerable appetites. "Too many cooks," he'd say sagely over a bottle of cheap plonk at midnight, "are an impossibility."

Click. The television set in the living room had been switched off. A moment later, Felicity appeared at the kitchen doorway, just as Tom noted she kept only one place setting of cutlery to hand, while the rest remained in its presentation case up on a top shelf.

"Hungry?" she asked.

"No, the lager's all I need!" said Tom. "Here," and he handed her the other glass. "Lived here long? This kitchen's lovely and sunny."

"About a year, isn't it, Max?" she said, taking an oatmeal biscuit from a japanned tin. "Come, let's go out and sit in my little garden at the back."

Max went with them, and occupied the second deck chair as a matter of course, having to be shooed off.

"This is probably all going to sound a bit bizarre to you," Tom began, pausing for a sip of his lager before balancing the glass on his knee. "But what's happened is, I've discovered something very worrying about the daughter of a chap I was once best man to, and I'm at a loss to know what to do about it."

Felicity, dappled by sunlight beneath the small, twisted apple tree, nodded. Her long hair shone where it curved down over the fullness of her breasts, hidden by a smock in vivid mango colors, orange and deep green. One wisp of that hair wafted free, finer than the thinnest ophthalmic suture.

"Earlier, I'd only had my suspicions," Tom went on, "but today I went along to the private viewing of a new art exhibition at the public library. I wanted a closer look at someone who had made an etching I'd found disturbing."

"In what way, Tom?"

"Well, it was heavily stylized, and not what one would call a realistic attempt, but if one looked very carefully, one of the figures—female nudes, I'm talking about—had bits of detail in it that undoubtedly belonged to the girl I mentioned, my friend's daughter."

"What sort of bits?"

"Oh, ears, the hands, distinctive features, that kind of thing."

"Is she a model, this girl?"

"Wouldn't dream of it! But I'll go into that further in a minute. One of the first things I learned was that this girl—"

"Can't I know her name?"

"I'd rather . . ."

"Let's call her Jenny, then. Go on."

Tom spilled a little lager onto his knee. "Fine. Well, I was having a chat with an artist fellow, and he said to her—no, it was to me, once she'd gone to get something for someone—that she was in danger of becoming a groupie, a person people were prepared to take very unfair advantage of. By the way, why 'Jenny'?"

"Why not?" said Felicity, shrugging. "First thing that popped into my head. But I'm already a bit lost. Isn't there a beginning to this story, and how old is she?"

"Eighteen, I think. Yes, definitely eighteen."

"Ah, not a girl, but an adult, legally speaking anyway."

"That's the whole point," said Tom. "There is an adult involved, but—"

"Once upon a time—how many years ago?" teased Felicity Croxhall. "Really, Dr. Lockhart, if I'm going to be any use to you, you'll just have to be less circumspect with me, you know! I need the full case history, times and places, some idea of physical characteristics, what sort of personality she has. So far, she sounds, well, to put it kindly, a bit wimpish, prudish, and rather silly."

"Ginny's not!" Tom said.

* * *

Then he hurriedly began to sketch in *Jenny's* background, repeating the pseudonym in quick succession, five or six times. He told Felicity about the reunion at the Ashfords' the previous Sunday; about the anniversary present of the etching. He tried to explain how he'd changed his mind over it at least twice before seeing it for what it was; and finally, he gave, word for word, an account of his conversation with Nell Overton where it'd touched on *Jenny*; adding, for good measure, some notion of what it had felt like, seeing her hand squeezed.

"Hmmm," said Felicity, leaning forward to fondle Max's ears. "Wish I could see this etching for myself. Ignoring what you obviously see into it, how would other people react, do you think?"

Tom shrugged. "What does one make of a title like *Imago*? I suppose the one figure is chrysallislike, in that it's a bit shriveled by comparison, and the other figure, being in full bloom, as it were, could be the final stage of a woman after emerging." He snapped his fingers. "Yes!" he said, "that's it, isn't it? God, I should've been an art critic! Now I see why the figures are each cupping a breast and appear so much the same at a glance. To an outsider, it's the same woman, you see, looking back on how she was as—as . . ."

"An adolescent?" suggested Felicity. "They tend to be skinnier and flat-chested. I must say, this Nell Overton doesn't show much originality. I thought the art world had worked the caterpillar-to-butterfly theme to death years ago."

"Oh, but she was only using the imago idea as an excuse to put herself and Gin—I mean, Jenny, in the same picture, wasn't she?"

"Which can, you know, Tom, be entirely unconscious on an artist's part."

"Oh, no," he said firmly. "If she'd the eye to get that detail so exact, then she had the eye to recognize it."

"How have you been able to recognize these same bits of Jenny, do you think?"

"It's my job! You can't help developing a strong visual memory."

"No, what I meant was, you seemed to be hinting a few minutes ago that some of these details weren't what a well-brought-up girl would invite a Sunday-lunch guest to take a peek at."

"Did I?" Tom hid his face by taking a long swallow from his

lager glass, then coughed, as though choking, while the color rose in his cheeks. "Damn, sorry about that! Went down the wrong way! No, if I gave that impression, it wasn't what I meant exactly."

"Then you're not saying this Nell has somehow coerced Jenny into posing in the nude in return for a free print of—"

"No, but . . ."

Max leaped up, gave one loud bark, looked around at Felicity, and collapsed again under the apple tree, leaving one leg pointing at the sky.

"Someone at the door," she said. "I'll tell them to go away."

Saved by the bell, Tom thought—correction, the bloody brass knocker.

"Oh, boy . . ." he added aloud, once Felicity was safely in the house and out of earshot, ". . . *not* a good idea after all, was it?"

She had certainly listened to him attentively, making every effort to be sympathetic and understanding, but most of the evidence against Nell Overton had proved too subjective to convey clearly. Moreover, some of the most damning aspects of the matter were impossible to broach without revealing his actual relationship to the victim, and that, of course, had nothing at all to do with the issue under discussion. In short, Tom told himself, the whole thing was turning into a fraught, time-wasting, entirely pointless exercise, and so he'd just have to think of some other way of handling this.

He stood up, stretched, and said, "But it was a pleasure meeting you, Gluteus, old chap, and there are not many dogs I'd say that to. Any idea of a good excuse for my having to leave suddenly?"

"Oi," Felicity called out from the back door, a red first-aid kit in her hand. "Dr. Doolittle? My neighbors' toddler has chopped a bit off a finger in a door someone slammed. Would you mind holding down the hysterical mother while I do the necessary? Shouldn't take a minute."

It took an hour, and at the end of it, Felicity Croxhall told Tom Lockhart that he wasn't going to put a foot out of her house, on pain of never being permitted to enter it again, until she'd taken a quick look at her *Concise Oxford Dictionary*.

17

They were back in Felicity's living room, where, Tom noticed, several snapshots of a distinguished, affable-looking man with white hair were on display. One showed him holding up a large salmon he'd caught, an arm across his fishing guide's shoulders, and in another he was seated on a balcony overlooking a Mediterranean bay.

"Your father?" Tom said.

"No," said Felicity, hunting along the lower shelf of the books that covered the wall to the left of the chimney. "Good, here it is . . ."

She took the dictionary over to a wicker chair by the window, leaving Tom to continue his restless prowling about the room. He was busily stuffing his mind with quite useless information, leaving no corner in it for conjecture, for wondering what, in Christ's name, she was up to.

G.F.H. Croxhall, the room indicated, preferred *The Times* as her daily paper; bought every novel written by Fay Weldon, Kurt Vonnegut, and John le Carré; liked to collect glass paperweights; kept her driver's license and other such documents in an earthenware dish; and employed a cleaner. The pair of antique candle snuffs had been carefully replaced on the dusted mantel shelf, but were inverted.

"Imago . . ." murmured Felicity, running a blunt, practical finger down a page in the dictionary. "As I suspected!"

* * *

"What?" asked Tom.

"Sit down, while I read you this . . ."

He perched on an arm of the sofa.

"Imago," she quoted, "final and perfect stage of insect after all metamorphoses, e.g. butterfly."

"Virtually word for word what I—"

"Hold on! It does have another meaning. 'Idealized mental picture of oneself or another person.' That couldn't fit more exactly, could it?"

Tom frowned. "Fit what?"

"Everything you've told me about these two and the etching."

"Oh, come on!"

"No, you come on," she said a little crossly, putting the dictionary aside. "Can't you see why Nell laughed and thought you were being witty when you tried to drag insects into it? Her etching was about her feelings toward Jenny—and probably, vice versa. Didn't Nell tell you what a wonderfully good person she thought she was? As though she idealized her? Haven't they *both* said pretty much the same thing to you?"

"Er, yes, but later, when she touched the—"

"What was wrong in that, for goodness' sake? She'd touched the thing often enough, making it! And art almost revolves around the female figure, doesn't it? All those life studies at art school, with everyone learning to draw bottoms and bosoms before they even think of—"

"But she was talking about expressing joy in—"

"Tom, really! Can't one woman see the beauty in another woman, without you branding her a raving lesbian? I've often admired girls with lovely figures—especially as mine's anything but!—yet I've never wanted to go rushing over and hint madly we should start taking showers together! God, that's the sort of lorry-driver mentality I'd never expected to hear from—"

"But you're forgetting," Tom cut in. "The next thing she did was—"

"Squeeze Jenny's hand, in a nice, warm, appreciative gesture? Isn't that what one would automatically expect from Americans, who haven't the hang-ups we have about touching one another? I really don't see what the fuss is about. In fact, I might even have just given her a squeeze or a pat myself, not wanting to launch into a long-winded speech about how grateful I was, and interrupt the conversation. Weren't you two chatting happily away at that point, before Jenny came up to drop the change off?"

"Not happily, no. I'd just pointed out to Nell she was in the picture and—"

"Did she deny that?"

"No, but—"

"Goodness, you're being so pig-headed! Why?"

"Why?" said Tom, frowning. "Because it's all very well saying there was probably nothing to all this, but one of the first things I ever heard about Nell was how she reacted to words like 'poofter' and—"

"Nell's black, isn't she? Don't you think she just might be a fraction sensitive about blatant bigotry?"

"What I haven't told you is that—um, someone I know—noticed something cold about that etching long before I did. Said I was too puritanical to notice it myself, and so was Jenny, for that matter, and—"

"This someone," said Felicity impatiently, "was it she or he who first gave you the idea of lesbianism being involved?"

"There was also the sculptor who said she was becoming a groupie."

"And what does that mean? It's a word with heterosexual connotations for most people, I'd have thought, and surely to goodness, that print workshop or whatever has its males too! Although, personally, I think he was just on about her allowing herself to become a complete doormat. But back to the point I wanted to make: did the idea of homosexuality, gayness or whatever, originate for you with this certain someone who commented on the etching?"

After a moment's thought, Tom nodded. "Yes, I suppose so," he admitted. "That's what must have alerted me."

"Good at detecting that sort of thing, this someone?"

"Well, I . . ."

"Ever made similar allegations before?"

"Er—yes. Once, that I can remember."

"Was it proved right?"

He shook his head. "No, I'm damned sure it was wrong."

"Then we know who it is now," said Felicity Croxhall, "who has the problem! Because, if you'd only listen to me instead, you'd see that this whole Jenny-Nell business sounds—and probably is—perfectly innocent."

* * *

Tom slid from the arm of the sofa into one of its deep, soft cushions, and Max, stretched out there already, made room for him.

"Go on," said Tom, suddenly so weary.

"There isn't much more I can say I haven't said already. If Jenny is in fact anything like the bright, sensitive person you've described to me, then I'm sure we can safely say the etching has nothing prurient, immoral, or even vaguely nasty about it, and that's why she thought nothing of giving it to her parents. Let's suppose she does know that's her in it, then she could be secretly proud of the fact she's inspired a work of art. Alternatively, if she isn't aware of it, so what?"

"I don't follow you," said Tom. "There's the unconscious element to be—"

"Forget the etching! Listen, do you really think that, for one minute, an intelligent eighteen-year-old girl wouldn't notice someone taking an unusual interest in her? And, if it was the kind of interest which upset her, that she'd still want to buy any of their work? Not bloody likely, I'd have thought!"

"But—"

"Unless, of course—and frankly, Tom, this *is* the only alternative—the so-called Jenny is in fact that way inclined herself, and took the picture home as a means of breaking the news gently to mum and dad."

"Christ, no!"

"Then I must be right. You can't have it both ways."

He got up and went over to the doorway opening onto the back garden. He stood there, looking at the apple tree. Perhaps as much as a whole two minutes went by. Then he turned suddenly, smiling, wanting to take hold of Felicity Croxhall and dance around the room with her, sing and shout, shower upon her his grateful kisses.

"Here, Max!" he said, and knelt to hug him when he eagerly bounded over, tongue lolling. "Good lad, Max! Good lad! God, Felicity, you don't know what a weight that is off my mind, even if I do now feel one hell of an idiot . . ."

It was true. Although he'd not had time to order his thoughts again properly, the realization of how wrong he'd been in his assumptions needed no elaborate underlining; it was now as plain as that defect in Annabel's ventricula septum, and his blood could run red again.

Ginny, flushed at the throat and breathless, beneath him.

Max licked his cheek.

And Felicity said, getting to her feet still without smiling, "What I really don't know, Tom, come to think of it, is how someone, generally so sensible as yourself, could have needed my help in the first place. That's worrying."

"No, it isn't! Couldn't see the wood for the trees, that's all!"

She shook her head. "It was the opposite way around. You saw a wood and missed the trees."

"I don't follow you," said Tom, rising too, and pushing the dog away from him. "What wood?"

"What mirror?" she replied. "You keep doing it. Keep missing what's really there and imagining something else instead. Why? It's like someone obsessed by an idea, who must make everything else fit it."

"Oh, bosh!"

Her smile reappeared, lopsided. "There's a quaint old word for you!" she exclaimed. "And, one could say, there's our answer: you've been terribly old-fashioned in your thinking all through this, just like Geoff Harcourt might've! You know, seeing this Jenny—who sounds, as I've said, like someone perfectly capable of looking after herself—as some poor defenseless young creature being ruthlessly hunted down by a predatory adult! Geoff wasn't the one who started putting ideas into your head, was he?"

"Good God, no."

"But it surely must have come from somewhere, this hapless prey fantasy of yours—which is what it amounts to, you know."

"Look," said Tom, "I made a mistake, that's all! I overreacted, probably put myself in her father's shoes and—well, went a bit paranoid. You've got to admit that it's bound to be a bit of a shock, recognizing in a nude study someone you're practically related to!"

Felicity took the dictionary over to the bookshelf and replaced it. "Yes," she said, turning to him and nodding, "you could be right. I think I understand it now. Obviously you must've felt identified with someone else very strongly at the time for you to see things as you did, and her father would be, I suppose, the one you'd feel you had the most in common with."

* * *

He thought he swayed then, but Felicity Croxhall showed no sign of noticing this, as she started toward the kitchen and said, "Tea?"

Tom shook his head.

"Why ever not? You can't have to dash off as early as—" Then she glanced at the clock beside the candle snuffers, and said, "Goodness, it's after six!"

"Er, yes, and I—"

"What about some supper, then? I've a gorgeous asparagus soup I—"

"No, no, really, I must go! Must, I'm afraid!"

Oh, Christ, oh, Jesus . . . Not AGAIN.

"But I thought you told me," said Felicity, following him as he blundered toward the front door, "you were on your own this weekend, which was why you decided it was the perfect time to go to that private viewing and—"

"Yes, but—"

"But what? Has something I've said upset you?"

"Heavens, no! Couldn't have been a greater help! I'm very, very grateful! It's just—well, expecting a phone call at home from my wife. Yes, promised I'd be there—probably'll have to go shooting off with a suitcase of her things. Her mother's been admitted this morning, had a stroke."

"Oh, you hadn't explained that."

"So you see, I—"

"Yes, of course, although you could ring her from here if you liked."

"But the suitcase? She'd have to tell me where everything was, and I'd have to say whether I'd found it."

"Right," she said, catching hold of Max's collar as Tom opened the door onto the street. "See you get something to eat, though! Your belly's been rumbling."

"Has it? Must've been missing lunch. I'll grab a quick take-out—fish and chips, something like that."

"Get plaice," she said. "Nothing's tastier in batter. I love it."

He paused on the doorstep, trying to think of something to say that would ease his guilt about this rudely abrupt departure. Felicity Croxhall had done all he'd hoped of her—and more, God help him.

"Well, Tom," she said, "it's been lovely seeing you, so I hope you'll feel able to come back again whenever you want to . . . Take care!" Then she reached out and removed from his lapel a long, white dog hair.

The town center had a Saturday-night zing to it. Everywhere, young couples were hurrying, some into restaurants, some into cinemas, into discos, turning to smile at one another—or standing happily hand in hand, looking at rings in jewelers' shop windows. Older couples were moving more sedately, linked arm in arm, avoiding the packs of poorly dressed, loud youths kicking beer cans along, who whistled when a lone pretty girl went by, her eyes on the pavement ten yards ahead of her. Normal people doing normal things.

Tom Lockhart drove those streets for an hour, not altogether aimlessly. Obeying traffic lights and dodging jaywalkers helped to preoccupy the forefront of his mind, while way at the back of it a bowed, deeply shamed creature whimpered and licked its wounds in a cave.

Once he passed the public library, and wanted to brake, leap out, run up those stairs again, and say to Nell Overton that he craved her forgiveness on his knees. But she'd have left long ago, and besides, that sort of thinking made him feel he might be going mad.

Perhaps he was. He'd begun to hate those young couples out there, the older ones too, for having what he hadn't, and could never now aspire to. Not since seeing himself in that mirror. The one silvered by his last vestiges of simple decency but, until a good woman had given it a quick wipe, fogged over by hot, goaty breath, hiding what was reflected.

Yes, let's face up to it, he managed to say to himself at last. What you saw as Nell was really what, deep down, you felt about your own sly seduction of a lovely young creature; and that being so, here's an end to you and Ginny Ashford.

He wanted to weep then.

But wait! cried out the rabble, faint and shrill. That glance, six long years ago! A glance since then repeated. And, and, and . . . ! Why, she left you that invitation card; she schemed to go home with you; she covered a pie with pastry kisses; brought you a ladybug, when she'd become woman.

From a chrysallis that ladybug had come, Tom suddenly realized, remembering his biology. It'd been an imago.

Or had it been Ginny's way of saying of Sylvia, "Ladybug, ladybug, fly away home, your house's on fire, and your man is mine now"?

I am going mad, decided Tom Lockhart, bringing his car to a halt. Take a grip on yourself, get down to basics. No one my age has the right to risk taking advantage of anyone so immature and unworldly, no matter what her confused feelings might drive her to. God knows, he thought, looking down at the feather fob on his key ring, perhaps all she's seeking is a more convincing father figure.

And he shuddered, aware that he needed to be even more basic still if he was to survive the night without wanting to drive too fast, too long, until oblivion met him on the highway. So he tried switching off his mind and listening to what his kid brother of a body had to say. Captain to engine room?

For Christ's sake, Tom, it's bloody obvious! I'm tired and I'm hungry.

Then it began to murmur other things, as he released his clutch and went in search of some take-out food.

Where would he take the take-out? Surely not back to that chill house with its wide-apart walls. His body needed warmth. Somewhere snug to rest where his eyes wouldn't seek out a potpourri bowl, the end of a white sofa, the corner of a ceiling where his friend the spider had once spun its small web. Likewise, he needed a break from this video loop ceaselessly repeating the same shattering moment of self-diagnosis when his heart had darkened, stopped, beat wildly on again; it suggested a fresh set of vivid images to wipe it. All this, his body insisted, was what was wanted. Plus (if he knew what was best for him) to return, take up an open invitation, and find felicity in simplicity— allowing it to become his balm and his watchword.

"Right, guv, salt and vinegar?"

"Please," said Tom, nodding.

The pudgy hands shook the two dispensers simultaneously over the double portion of plaice and chips, then wrapped it swiftly in newsprint.

"Anythin' else yer fancy? Pickled eggs, onions? Saveloys is lovely tonight!"

"No, I don't think so, thanks. Is this what I owe you?"

"Spot on, ta! And now you, luv? Just the four Spam fritters, isn't it?"

"Excuse me . . ."

"Guv?"

"Would you know if there's somewhere nearby one can get a bottle of wine?"

People in the queue smiled and two tarty girls sniggered.

"Certainly, guv! Go out, turn left . . ."

"Turn left," repeated Tom. "And then?"

"That's it! The offy's bleedin' next door, see!"

Tom didn't join in the laughter. He just walked out of the shop, turned right, and continued on past the launderette three paces.

He'd had a gutful of the sort of thought and talk that went with wine, anyhow.

He pressed a doorbell.

18

It was almost a minute before the door opened and Carole looked out, frowning. Then her expression changed. "Tom, pet! Me knight in shinin' armor!"

"Am I?" he said.

"Course you are! Just didn't recognize yer for a sec, 'cos of that long face yer were pullin'. You all right?"

"I was just beginning to wonder if this wasn't perhaps an awkward moment for me to—"

"Got that Kevin with us."

"Oh, then in that case I'd better—"

"Don't you dare go nowhere, you hear?" she said, grabbing hold of his arm. "You'll see him off, won't yer? I knew he'd come sniffin' around, first whisper he got Harry were away, the randy sod. Only let 'im in 'cos he said he wanted his videos back, and I didn't know which ones they were, see? But now he won't shift, and—"

"But," said Tom, instantly regretting having never been brave enough to take up boxing at school, and picturing any friend of Harry Coombes to be at least the same size, "how am I meant to . . ."

"Here, give us that," said Carole, taking the parcel of fish and chips from him, and leaving it on a shelf beneath the telephone on the wall. "Now all you do is, act posh, pretend yer me doctor wot's come round 'cos I've rung yer about this pain in me stomach an'—"

"I can't very well," objected Tom, "totally unethical, and besides, I've not a GP's bag with me."

"Wot's that, then?"

"Only a briefcase containing confidential case notes that I didn't like to leave in the car."

"Too right, round 'ere it'd be gone in a flash! But I thought it were yer bag, y'know—ready then?"

"Wait a moment," said Tom hastily, fear tasting like a dirty penny in his mouth, "you don't seem to understand, Carole! I cannot masquerade as your GP, it could cost me my job. On top of which, what would I be achieving? This Kevin or whoever could be back again as soon as I—"

"So yer not goin' to help us then?" said Carole, her face falling. "Thought we was mates, Tom."

That did it. His adrenaline surged, flipped from flight to fight, and handed the good Sir Thomas his lance. Twice that day he had fled the field, but bugger it, there wasn't going to be a third time.

"Fair maiden," said Tom, "lead the way!—and fear not, I'm bound to think of something."

"Knew yer could!" she whispered, giving him a quick peck on the cheek, then turned and went back up the stairs.

My God, he thought, hastening after her, what an enchanting rump: as shapely as an apple and looking like two halves of a delicious idea rubbing together. A man could follow it anywhere.

The lout lounging in Carole's living room was a foot taller than Harry Coombes, had a head like Attila the Hun, and wore studded wristlets fashioned from black leather. His jeans, tucked into high boots and secured by a belt with a death's head for a buckle, were grease-stained and patched at the knees—wear and tear, Tom presumed, from all the spleens they'd ruptured. He had no shirt; simply a denim vest, possibly inscribed on the back: *Hell's Angels Are a Load of Wanking Fairies*.

"Kevin . . ." said Carole.

"Strewth," he growled, as Tom entered the room behind her, "what's this mother, momma? Yer fuckin' sugar daddy?"

"Good evening, sir," said Tom, seeing red, but touching a hand to the knot in his tie. "I hope I'm not intruding too greatly. Coeur de Lion's the name, Department of Health and Social Security."

"You gotta be jokin'! You bastids never work past five on a—"

"Special division of the department," Tom ad-libbed hurriedly, noticing Carole's expression and being afraid she might start laughing. "Have to catch people when we can, and because of the degree of discretion involved, this can't be when they're at their place of work, naturally. Weekends are often our busiest time in the CMD."

"The wot?" said Kevin, crumpling a lager can and leaning forward.

"CMD, sir: Monitoring Division. You've no idea how certain diseases can spread, one person to another, like wildfire, and unless each client is traced and warned of the position it's alarming how many can be infected. The new R-strain syphilis— not to mention AIDS, of course—has made our work even more—"

"Fuck me!" said Kevin, struggling out of the armchair he'd filled to overflowing.

"I'm sorry, sir, but if you're cohabiting with this young lady, I fear I'd consider such a course of action extremely inadvisable. Furthermore—"

"*Wot?*" exclaimed Carole.

"I'm off!" said Kevin. "Out of me way!"

"But, sir, I need to know your name, and find out who else you're—"

"Look, boss, I never touched 'er, right? Not the once! You've got me God's honor on that, so don't yer come round the 'ouse, upsettin' the missus an'—"

"Am I supposed to believe that?"

"Go on, ask 'er!" implored Kevin, edging toward the door to the landing. "Ask 'er, she knows! Never touched 'er! Christ, never will neither!" Suddenly, he lunged for the stairs.

"Hey, Kev," Carole called out, "yer forgot yer viddies!"

"Sod me viddies!"

"Now that," said Tom, turning to Carole as the front door banged open and then slammed shut below them, "is something I believe we could safely do . . ."

She burst out laughing and threw her arms around his neck. They staggered about the room together, whooping and giggling and snorting, and finally fell, all of a heap, on the double divan bed in the corner.

It was then Tom Lockhart discovered that a compound of extreme nervous tension, close physical contact, and unrestrained mirth produced a near-irresistible aphrodisiac. He returned Carole's kiss chastely, on her cheek.

"No, stop! Where you goin'?" she asked, as his weight left the divan.

"Down to the hall to fetch the fish and chips I bought us."

"They was for me, too?"

"Of course."

"You're lovely," she said, rolling over to face him.

How wonderful it was to stop thinking and concentrate instead on simply having fun. Because that's what it is, realized Tom, retrieving his newsprint package, this is *fun*, dammit—like love, something he'd not thought about in years. Only a bloody sight less complicated.

Carole had knives and forks, more vinegar, a bottle of tomato sauce, and two chilled cans of lager on the living room table by the time he had come, huffing and puffing a bit, back up those stairs. For a girl of her build, she could move faster than a wood nymph in satyr season.

"No, you sit yourself down, and I'll do the honors," said Tom, preparing to unwrap their take-out meal right there on the table, the hell with pretensions.

"Mmmm, just *smell* . . . !" she said.

"I'd have thought, living almost above the shop, you might have—"

"Never!" she said. "Can't get enough of it."

"Oh, really?" said Tom. "I might want to take you up on that!" Then he pointed at one of the two portions before adding, "Your plaice or mine, miss?"

And that was only the first of the witticisms he invented quite without thinking that came popping out of him to delight Carole, making her giggle and laugh, hurl a chip across the table, tell him he was loads better than any of them comedian fellas on the telly.

"You've gone dead quiet," she remarked about a minute later. "Worried one of 'em could've heard me say that, and it'll be jokes at dawn t'morrer?"

Tom shook his head. "I'm concentrating on eating," he said. "Before it gets cold."

This wasn't very truthful of him. He'd just had a thought gate-crash the party, spoiling his enjoyment for the moment.

* * *

It could well have hissed from Sylvia's lips: Really, Tom, what on *earth* are you doing here? Just look around you!

In a better area, the same basic type of accommodation would have been described by estate agents as a studio flat. Decoded, this would mean one L-shaped room, just large enough to swing a very small artist in, off which were to be found a kitchenette and cramped bathroom.

Again, in a better area, full use would have been made of these limited dimensions. There would have been an ingenious bed that looked like a sofa—or indeed, even an armchair—during the day. The rest of the furniture would have been equally compact, with wardrobe space artfully concealed behind bamboo curtains, and mirrors placed where they'd provide illusions of spaciousness. Care would have been taken with the colors in the main room too, of course; white walls and ceiling perhaps, with a tapestry that contained the same mustard yellow, turquoise and charcoal gray as the three, and only three, cushions had been covered in. Finally, to give the room its focus, there would be one good watercolor, an interesting piece of driftwood, or maybe a Japanese flower arrangement.

There were flowers in Carole's L-shaped room: a handful of daisies stuffed in the mouth of a milk bottle. Every other decorative element was pure kitsch, ranging from a plastic orchid to a chain-store picture, canvas-textured and in a bright gold frame, showing four white stallions cavorting in cumulus nimbus. As for the furniture, that had come directly from one of those late-night TV commercials for unbeatable warehouse offers. It was fake in almost every respect—for leather, feel plastic; for walnut, see veneer. Although comfortable enough, even its capacity to withstand the pull of gravity, particularly in regard to two of the chairs, seemed suspect. Besides, there was far too much of it, just as there were far too many colors in the room for the eye to rest anywhere for long, making it as undecided as a flea at a dog show.

Tom knew, having been surrounded by "good taste" these last fifteen married years of his life, that he really ought to have felt thoroughly repelled and ill at ease. But now, having been forced to reflect on the flat's effect on him, he declared it extremely agreeable and soothing, and wondered why this was so. A partial explanation occurred to him almost immediately. There were no mysteries. Nothing in that room belonged to anyone's past other than Carole's own; nothing had been placed in it to please anyone but herself; nothing in it contained subtle shades and hints of other meanings to be carefully read, injecting skepticism as one's contrast medium. Thus, it made no demands upon a guest to assess and then guess what sort of person really lived there—whether or not the leather-bound volumes of Dickens were ever actually read, the horse brasses polished lovingly, the antique clock valued for its own sake. On the contrary, this is Carole, it admitted honestly, Carole here and now, pet—love us or leave us, I can't be no different. Or in short, the room didn't need bloody X-raying to get at the truth, no more than she did.

"That's better," said Carole, returning from her refrigerator and handing him a fresh can of lager with a wink.

"What is?"

"You've undone yer tie, beginnin' to look a bit more relaxed, like. Maybe you didn't notice, but all the time we've been sat 'ere, your hands has never stopped makin' fists when yer didn't have yer knife and fork in 'em. I thought I was going to have to give yer a cuddle."

He looked up at her then, very directly, and said, "I'd have left my tie on if I'd known . . ."

Carole returned his gaze for only a second, then faced away as she yanked the pull-ring from her own lager can. "I don't like yer wife," she said. "But I'd never do nothin' just out of spite, see?"

"I, um . . ." said Tom, not knowing quite how to reply to that.

"Sticking with her why? You got no kids."

So Carole had troubled to find that out, had she? Must have been while he'd been holed up that night in the kitchen with Geoff Harcourt. "No, we've no kids, you're right."

Carole poured her lager into a glass. "Then why?"

"I'm not sure. Perhaps I used to think things would get better."

"Will they, you reckon?"

"Not unless one of us changes a very great deal."

Carole rounded on him, frowning angrily. "You mustn't never change!" she said. "Promise us!"

Tom placed his greasy plate on hers, and got up from the table. "Thanks, Carole," he said, his voice gruffer than he'd yet heard it. "But I've already changed quite a bit, just being here with you, you know. It isn't often I take on people like Kevin! And besides, you don't really know me. What I'm really like."

"I do," she said, taking the plates from him. "And you're not changin', Tom. You're just sort of . . ."

"What?" he asked, and followed her through to the sink. "Tell me."

She put down the plates and turned slowly to him, putting a hand on each of his shoulders. "I dunno the word for it, pet," she said. "P'raps you can tell it us later, after I've shown yer." Then she slid her hands around behind his neck and drew him down to her until their lips touched, parted, and her tongue slipped into him. His head jerked back violently.

"Oh, Christ!" Tom whispered, the breath taken from him. "I'm sorry, Carole, I'm sorry—it's just . . ."

"I know, luv," she said, taking his head in her hands again. "Been a long time, hasn't it?"

He nodded, his eyes screwed shut. "Yes, but it's not just that. It's . . ."

I'm flesh and blood and bone, he was telling himself. Not this vast, dark inner landscape, so vivid in my mind's eye, where starbursts are still going off in distant parts of me, lighting up the sky, inviting the next tingling thunderbolt to strike dead in the middle, deep into a powder magazine as big as a bloody hill.

"It's nice, that's wot it is," Carole murmured into his ear. "Loveliest feelin' in the whole, wide world . . ." And she licked behind his earlobe.

"No, don't!" begged Tom, unable to pull away without hurting her, she now held him so tightly. "Please, don't! It's for your sake! I won't be able to control myself. No, really, I think you're so lovely that I—"

"Smashin'," she said, reaching down to give him a grateful squeeze.

"That's torn it," said Tom, moments later, sounding weirdly matter-of-fact as he sank back onto his heels again, a warmth of stickiness on his stomach.

"Gawd, I hope not," murmured Carole, still into his ear. "Never was much of a one for that Frankenstein fella and all them black threads hangin' out of his stitches . . ."

"What?" said Tom, pushing her from him with an astounded laugh, his eyes wide open.

Carole grinned at him.

"You're incredible!" he said, laughing again. "Honestly, I've never known anyone like you!"

"That's good," she said. "Wot every girl wants to hear, isn't it?"

"No, what I was trying to say was . . ."

"Tom," she said.

"Yes?"

"Can yer just try and shut up for a minute? Go down, see the door's locked proper, and I'll do me little bit o' business in the bathroom."

"You mean you still want to—? I'm, I'm not sure if I can, er . . ."

"Shhhhh," she urged, placing a finger on his mouth. "You do like I said, then come back and we'll see about that. Can't yer understand I fancy yer rotten?"

He backed away clumsily. He knew his lust was showing bold in the bulge in his trousers, but, for once, he couldn't feel embarrassed. Because in that heavy, lowered gaze her own lust was showing, making of them one flesh even before they touched again.

And twice, hastening down to the street door, he had to snatch at the banister in the stairwell to keep his balance. It was literally dizzying, this realization that at last his animal self wasn't being acknowledged to be sighed over, but to be rejoiced in and used quite openly to meet needs matching his own, in all their wild, rutting urgency.

He made certain the door was locked fast, turned, wondered if he shouldn't allow Carole longer to get in and out of the bathroom. He stripped off his tie, rolled it up and put it away. He took his loose change and everything else from his trouser pockets, and transferred them to his jacket, from which they'd be less likely to spill at the wrong moment. He noticed the telephone on the wall. He removed the receiver and very coolly, without the slightest twinge of conscience about life-or-death messages, left it to dangle on its cord. Nothing, absolutely nothing, was going to intrude on the next few hours of his life, no matter what lengths he had to go to.

I'm changing all right, thought Tom Lockhart.

Then he went bounding back up that gray flight of concrete steps faster than Pan up Mount Olympus. The clatter of his leather soles, ringing as sharply as cloven hoofs, made him grin wickedly.

* * *

But it wasn't like that, not to begin with.

The first moments of their renewed touching was solemnly timid. They met at the foot of the divan, linked hands like children, and just stood there, looking at one another.

Carole, Tom noticed, had put on lipstick. It glistened and was the same vivid pink as one of the two long strings of beads she was wearing; a delicious, very edible, exciting cerise which he'd always associated with the candy cotton sold at seaside amusement parks. Her second string of beads, as round and shiny, were the softer, more subtle shade of mucous membrane. He also noticed how her golden hair, given a quick, dividing brush, now fell in a wave over one eye—creating a coy, peak-a-boo look that, presumably, was unintentional. For her other eye, bluer than a bluebell, almost lilac, showed desire so blatant it might have been chilling in its reptilian fixity were it not for how softly her thumbs had begun tickling his palms, describing small circles.

He bent forward and kissed the tip of her nose. She brushed flavored lips across his lips. He shivered, and tried to slip a hand from her interlaced fingers.

"No, not like this," she whispered. "Not with clothes in the way." And she turned him slightly, so he'd know to sit on the side of the bed, only then letting go.

They undressed back to back, the width of the candlewick counterpane separating them. Tom, fumbling at his shirt buttons and trouser fastening, his fly and his shoelaces, found himself observing his hurried clumsiness with detached interest. He wondered if this really could be him, for the man was showing not the least hesitation in readying himself to commit the mortal sin of adultery. Perhaps the man really did believe in other gods and was hoping, by means equally momentous for him, to delight the divine Aphrodite. Or maybe, Tom mused, the randy bugger just couldn't wait to get his leg over, and wasn't giving anything else much thought at all.

He certainly quite forgot about those ankles until Carole, approaching him with crossed arms at the foot of the bed, slowly and shyly exposed her breasts. They were patterned by two wide blue veins: one pair forking down directly into the broad areolas around the stubby nipples; the other pair, curving on around, faded away beneath the heavy globes.

"God, you're beautiful!" he said.

* * *

And then she was in his arms, her own flung around him, hugging him, kissing him, repeatedly, avidly, standing so high on tiptoe he almost entered her, but that would have been too soon. So he toppled her backward onto the bed and dived full-length to lie half over her, making them both bounce on the foam mattress, making Carole laugh and catch his hand and draw it tight against her throat, where a fat pulse beat. She kissed his forehead, cheeks, chin, nose, ear, brushed his mouth again quickly. He kissed her shoulders, her knuckles, kissed her lips, parted them with his tongue, then slipped his other hand to her breasts, fluttering, cupping, sliding away to skip smooth over her belly, returning, skimming a springy cushion of curls, returning, but never touching those stiffened centers until she reared them to him, dragging his mouth away from her mouth, insisting. He nibbled, suckled, lapped like a kitten, heard her cry out, moved over wholly onto her, sank as her legs opened wide, then raised himself, poised. She reached down, positioned him for his thrust, and looking up, very intently into his eyes, nodded. He made no thrust. Slowly, very gently, he eased into her, looking back into those eyes, penetrating deeper and deeper. This, he sensed, was the truly important moment, the one they'd remember longest.

Now they were joined, and as there could be no going back, they went forward, moving cautiously at first, then at a wild, carefree gallop.

And Tom, before he ceased being aware of anything at all, marveled. Even bent back, gasping, heaving beneath him, Carole remained gloriously beautiful from the chubby lobes of her ears to the silken clench of her thighs, and he told her so, told her so, told her so, panted out his joy and his gratitude. Until she grabbed his head, forced his mouth back down over hers, and paced the final plunging with rapid thrusts of her tongue, closing a circuit that suddenly blew, arcing a dazzling blue bolt of forked light right into the very center of him.

19

3:07 A.M.

Peering muzzily at his wristwatch, Tom realized he must have slept, utterly spent, six hours or more. A deep, ancient sleep, from which his gradual awakening had made him think of salmon spawn drifting up ever so slowly from a riverbed, reaching the surface with a slight ripple when the moon was out.

Many were the empty and desolate seas the old Tom Lockhart had swum—yes, he liked the ring of that, half dreamed—before knowing instinctively that the time had come to mate, die, and begin again. Many, too, were the white-water leaps he'd made blindly, over and over, on his long struggle up from the ocean, dodging the talons of gape-jawed bears and the nets of cold-eyed poachers, until at last, with a final twist and quiver of fin, slithering into a high, still pool.

Salmon and chips twice, if you please!
Certainly, guv . . . Salt and vinegar?

Tom chuckled softly, and Carole, one satiny leg flung across him, a warm nose nuzzled into his side, smiled in her sleep.

He knew quite how absurd and fanciful he was being, and that he wasn't properly awake. Nonetheless, he could still taste the salt and vinegar of their last kiss, when each had quivered before reversing position, twisting around to bring their slithery lips

176

together again in plenary affirmation of mutual affection and acceptance.

No, don't, Tom!
Unspoken: Why not, Sylv? Afraid I'll detect the ghastly cheap scent of the new spermicide I know you've taken to using?

But what had made him think of rivers? Tom wondered.
He glimpsed ducklings then, and opened his eyes to be rid of them. He saw Carole undulating, not in silvery grays, although indeed the moon was out, but in the sodium yellows of the lamppost outside her window. Basking fields at harvesttime.
He searched for the tares.
She had a tiny scar just beneath her nose, and a clipped hair growing from a mole near her mouth. He wondered about the scar, and imagined a young brother throwing his toy fire engine at her, enraged by a Christmas-morning bicker over who had the most presents. He sought farther. She also had an appendectomy scar, far too long, which extended into her tawny pudenda and left a narrow clearing. And then, darker now in this light, yellow and blue mixing to bramble green, there were those mammalian veins which he'd traced with the tip of his tongue, repeatedly.
How glad he was of these imperfections, for only goddesses were faultless, immortal, and that night he and Carole had already died several times together. Small deaths, but complete ones.

I am forever, Ginny had proclaimed, standing woman on her parents' doorstep, but your love could destroy you. No wonder he'd been afraid, even of the sight of her.

You're still not really awake yet, he told himself, tiptoeing through to use the bathroom.
Harry Coombes would have lifted this seat up. He must have done so, many times. Lifted it up, aimed, waited, like Tom was doing.
His mind didn't give a damn what it thought anymore. He felt safe now.
Picturing Harry led, naturally enough, to seeing again the pale, aesthetic features of Geoff Harcourt beside him. What a very curious relationship, suggesting a doglike devotion on the one hand, and on the other—what? Doctors as a general rule did not

associate with bricklayers, neither did they encourage former patients, even those they'd snatched back from the grave, to demonstrate their eternal gratitude. Yet Geoff had patently put a collar and leash on Harry—why and, indeed, wherefore? And who was right, Felicity or Sylvia: was the man a closet case or latent lecher? Had Harry and Geoff, gone on their holidays, booked a double or two singles?

He'd have to ask Carole her opinion on all this in the morning.

Tom took her in his arms again, closing them around her protectively. Reflecting on how frail, how vulnerable they both were, he fell asleep, dreaming. Lying potbelly down on his chest, smiling gummily at him, a baby poked fingers in his mouth, in an eye, gurgled and drooled, snagged a thumb in his nostril.

"Tom?" whispered Carole, cuddled less close in the rising heat. "You awake?"

"Mmmmm . . ."

"It's nine-thirty, luv. Sun's streamin' in."

They stirred from their languor and began to play, drowsily at first. He looped a string of her beads around a high, domed breast, tugging gently. "Awake!" he recited. "And Lo! The Hunter of the East has caught The Sultan's Turret in a Noose of Light . . ." She used her long polished fingernails to comb a comical central parting in his hair, which made her giggle, and then, with a smile, plucked a gray hair from his head, dangling it in front of him.

"Look wot I found."

"That's cruel," he objected, focusing.

"No, it ain't."

"It is!"

"Don't belong, see?"

"Look, just say it!" said Tom, drawing away from her, deeply hurt, his emotions all as naked as he was. "I'm old! Too bloody old to be—"

"Listen," Carole interrupted, drawing the hair across his nose, "if I told the girls at work, there'd be a queue right down them stairs. You're fantastic."

"Christ, don't start bloody teasing and then—"

"No, honest! You're like a real lover, y'know? The fella we all dreams about? You got love on yer hands—could feel it."

"How?"

"'S obvious. I mean, usually it's yer boobs get the one quick feel, right, then bang, up it goes, don't matter if yer still dry as a flippin' crisp packet, and he—"

Tom had hastily kissed her, unable to bear the rest. "But don't forget," he said, "you're more than fantastic. You're . . ."

"Wot?"

"God knows," he said. "Treasure Island?"

Carole laughed. "Oh, really? How d'you make that out?" And she balanced the gray hair across his nose.

"Not sure," admitted Tom, who had spoken without thinking, and then paused to puff the hair away. "Twin peaks, for a start, I suppose—one always finds them on a treasure island." He gave the string of beads another tug.

"Oh, yes?"

"Plus, of course," added Tom, touching her navel, "Ben Gunn's cave." Then he went on, his fingers walking slowly, "And down a long, downy slope to the jungly cove where the treasure lies . . ."

As good as effin' gold, Harry Coombes had said.

"Sauce!" said Carole. "Can't yer think o' nothin' a bit more romantic, like?"

"As a matter of fact," replied Tom, affecting a wounded look, "I was about to remark upon your superb adductors."

"Me wot?"

"Move these legs apart properly and I'll show you."

"Get orf!" said Carol, clamping her thighs hard over his hand. "I 'ate it when you lot start gettin' yer little torches out and—"

"There, you're holding me with your adductors," said Tom, his fingers trapped. "Those two taut, narrow groups of inner thigh muscle rising from the inferior pubic ramus. You've one set each side, stretching from the groin to the knee, and they can, I assure you, be admired from fully fifty paces without the slightest threat to a girl's modesty."

"Let's have a gawp, then," she said, sitting up. "Huh! Can't see wot's so special."

"No? Yours happen to be unusually well developed."

"And so?"

"Our anatomy professor used to say that adductors like these went with the three aitches: hoofers, horsewomen, and—"
"And . . . ?" prompted Carole, arching an eyebrow.

Gutsiest and Windfall—God, against the sun that day!

"Sorry?" said Tom. "Where were we?"
"Talkin' too much," said Carole, straddling him.
They kissed.
Tom's stomach rumbled loudly. "Sorry about that," he apologized. "Never has had any manners."
"Actually, I quite fancy a bit o' breakfis meself," she said. "Egg 'n' bacon do yer?"
"Be perfect."
Carole smiled down at him. "Seems a shame, though, fattenin' yer up again."
"Not sure what you mean . . ."
"This," she said, patting his midriff. "Gone almost flat since I first saw yer, Tuesday—never known anybody slim off that quick. You been on one of them crash diets or somethin'?"
He shook his head. "No, but I suppose I've missed quite a few meals this past week, one way and another—a lot on my mind. Been an odd time."
"Dead odd," she agreed, lifting his hands from her breasts to kiss his palms. "Not that I'm complainin'. Slice o' fried, too?"
"Er, perhaps not," said Tom.
And it was true: when he stood sideways before the full-length mirror propped against a wall in Carole's bathroom, his paunch really had diminished to almost nothing. He'd always known he was able to put on and take off weight fairly easily, but somehow this particular demonstration of the fact left him enormously excited in a way he neither quite understood nor trusted. So he covered himself again, using the spare dressing gown Carole had lent him, flushed the lavatory, and went through into the kitchenette, glancing at the divan as he passed it. The funneled, crumpled sheet, from which he'd slipped, still hinted at the shape his body had hollowed within it.

Chrysallis.

"Wot's makin' yer smile like that?" asked Carole, above the sizzle of bacon.

"Just a silly thought I had," said Tom. "Anything I can do to help?"

"Orange juice's in the fridge."

"Fine, I'll get it. Glasses?"

"By the bread bin."

Tom saw to more than that, and laid the table too, placing the daisies in their milk bottle in the center of it. He and Carole ceased speaking for a while. There was a brittle delight to be had in performing a routine domestic task together in silent unison, for this suggested they had shared it many times before, and would again in the future.

"Everythin's ready," announced Carole, putting her head out of the kitchen. "Oooo, isn't that nice! And the bed made too! I'm surprised they don't advertise yer on the telly."

"What, just plug him in and away he goes?"

"Mucky devil!" said Carole, laughing.

Tom flinched, and not simply because, in his elevated mood of the moment, he'd intended no double meaning.

Mucky devil! Carole had said the night of Geoff's party to Harry.

"I think I'll move the chairs around," said Tom, picking up his place mat.

"Why?" Carole asked, disappearing back into the kitchen. "We always sits that way when there's two."

"Er, because the sun makes me blink when it's glaring in like this."

"Suit yourself, luv! I'm easy."

Tom rearranged the settings then sat down with his back to the window, his stomach rumbling even louder now at the delicious smell of bacon. Yes, you are easy, he thought, sweet Carole: easy on the eye, easy on the mind, even easy on the conscience. True, she was at least fifteen years his junior, but somehow their age difference had never troubled him—most probably because her worldliness left no yawning gap between his and her experience of life as it really was, stripped of any adolescent idealism. She knew it was ugly, unfair, all too short, and its rare joys were to be snatched up and made the most of, the hell with convention. She knew that pretty things were far safer than the beautiful.

* * *

"So yer likes me horses," she asked, catching him looking at the four white stallions as she came in with a laden tray. "I've got names for all of 'em."

"Oh?"

"The one in front, he's Ned, then there's Chalky, Billy, and, at the back, Big Frank. Chalky's the nicest though: d'you see how he's sort of smilin'?"

"Just got news he's not been picked to ride in the Apocalypse!"

"Can't be run on the flat or I'd 'ave 'eard of it," she said, sitting down. "Me dad actually kicked the bucket down the bettin' shop, did I tell yer that?"

"No, you've not really mentioned your family yet."

"Oh, a lovely fella! Bald on top, big smile, and talk about *thin*. As me mum used to say, thin as a ferret inna string vest, he was! Well, it were all them fancy women of 'is, weren't it? And never sittin' nowhere more than five minutes till we got 'im in 'is coffin—even then, me Auntie Ede lost 'er sherry glass and still says it were me dad, sippin' a sly one."

"Heart, was it?" asked Tom.

Carole nodded. "Those eggs okay? Harry usually wants them all slooshy like his nan makes, but I think that's disgustin'."

Tom took up his knife and fork to try a mouthful. "Delicious," he pronounced. "But talking of Harry, there's something I've been meaning to ask you. I don't quite follow his friendship with Geoff, do you?"

"No, not really, 'part from the fact Geoff saved his life and all, but I mean, that's his flippin' job, isn't it? Wot he gets paid for, same as you."

"So what is it that keeps them . . . ?"

"Dunno," said Carole, shrugging as she sipped at her orange juice. "Harry's dead flattered. I mean, that sticks outa mile—tells all his mates about the parties and that, him hobnobbin' with a load of toffs."

"But on Geoff's side? The two of them don't seem to even talk very much."

"I—"

"Yes?" prompted Tom.

Again, Carole shrugged. "I got me suspicions, like. It's a feelin' yer get when yer go there, and I know another ex o' Harry's wo' felt just the same, gave her the right creeps it did, same as me. 'S not Harry, I don't think, Geoff's so interested in, it's us wot h(

takes along with him. Y'know, his birds? That Geoff's got eyes like a cold hand up yer skirt—honest. I'm sorry if he's a mate o' yours, but—"

"No, not a mate, not any longer, so you just say what you like. Go on."

"Well," said Carole, stiffening against a shudder, "after the first time, I got back here and I says to meself, is Harry tryin' to get us on the game or somethin'? Gawd, it were like bein' took round to tea by a flippin' ponce, it was. Only nothin' never happened, and I started feelin' a bit sorry for the poor sod. Sex-starved he is, 'cos he do it to every female I ever seen him with."

"Are you sure?" said Tom. "I know one who thinks he's queer."

"Never!"

"That's perfectly true. She even hinted that he and I might be— er, well, you know, having an affair, would you believe it!"

Carole laughed delightedly, spilling some orange juice down her front. "Oh, I believes it—known all along, luv!" she said. "No, it's her wot's got owt on 'er conscience, that's what it is. But you'd think they'd have at least sent us a flippin' postcard."

"Geoff and Harry? Where the hell could they have taken themselves to?"

"Not that I really gives a monkey's."

"Nor me," agreed Tom.

There was a sudden, sharp tap on the windowpane behind him, and he turned casually, true to his new self-confidence.

"It's only me sparrers, poor loves," said Carole, as one of the row of birds on the window ledge gave the glass another peck. "They does that, when they sees I'm piggin' meself, not given' 'em a bite to eat, and it gone eleven already."

Tom looked back at her, surprisingly moved by the bond she had created with this scruffy little band. "Well," he said, rising, "I'd better go and get them something, before the silly buggers concuss themselves."

"Oh, ta! Their seed's by the biscuit tin."

"I'd noticed. Won't be a sec . . ."

Tom scooped up a handful of crumbs from the bread bin, added some birdseed, and paused on his return to the living room, struck by the picture Carole made, standing silhouetted, as familiar and voluptuous as a Renoir, in her thin pink wrap against the light.

"Gone," she said, opening the window. "Went when yer got

up, but don't take it personal, luv, they don't know yer yet, and they'll be back, never worry. Just put it for them here by me potted plants, and you'll see, in they'll come." Then she turned to him. "Tom?" she said. "Wot's the matter?"

"Oh, nothing," he said, advancing to carry out her instructions. "It's just I like looking at you."

"I likes lookin' at you and all," said Carole. "Watched yer dreamin' last night. Must've been a nice dream, 'cos yer face were so happy, like God'd just given yer wot yer wanted most in the whole, wide world. New motor, was it?"

"Sorry?"

"With fellas it's usually cars," she said. "I've noticed."

"I honestly can't remember, but don't you think you might have been in it?"

"Really?" she said, her face lighting up as she reached out for him. "No wonder I'm so knackered this mornin', yer bugger—never knew I'd been on overtime!"

Tom laughed and kissed her brow. "And you?" he asked.

"Me? Usual flippin' nightmares 'bout the girls at work, I s'pose."

"Oh?"

"There's this new one, see, only eighteen, same as most of them, but she's really good, y'know, specially on the latest fancy stylin', and it's making all them others dead jealous the way the customers say, 'No, we wants Tracy, ta,' and me bein' the receptionist an' all, it's a right headache, I can tell yer, fiddlin' the appointments book and tryin' to stop the rest tearin' 'er eyes out."

In the queue right down them stairs.

"Carole," said Tom urgently, "please kiss me."

She kissed him, mussed his hair, drew his head against her bosom. "Oh, pet," she said, "you're a funny one."

"Why?"

"Just are. Wot made yer so scared then?"

But Tom had just smelled oranges on these breasts, white as angels' milk, and this made him laugh. Laugh so infectiously that Carole laughed too, bewildered.

"You're all sticky with the juice you spilled," he said, stepping back but keeping hold of her hands.

"I know, I needs a shower."

"Me too. And then? I thought it'd be an idea to go and find a friendly pub somewhere for lunch, perhaps by the river."

"Yes, let's!"

"Good. So I'll get the breakfast things cleared away, while you take first turn in the bathroom, and—"

"Clothes," interrupted Carole. "You needs a change, don't yer?"

"Damn, you're right." Tom stood undecided for a moment. "Tell you what, I'll zoom off in yesterday's things, grab what I need, and shower when I get back again. Won't be more than half an hour."

She pouted. "Boo-hoo, don't want t' let yer go," she said.

"Miss, there's times when a man's gotta do what a man's—"

"Then spread yer little wings and fly, me luv!" she said, smiling and giving him a push. "Go on, off yer go! Only see yer packs a big suitcase."

Tom stood very still. "You mean that?"

Carole nodded.

20

There wasn't much traffic, as was to be expected on a Sunday morning. Fifteen minutes out, fifteen minutes back; that still seemed a fairly realistic estimate. Tom Lockhart accelerated and glanced at his watch, intending to time himself.

Sunday?

Good God, he realized, it was precisely one week, almost to the very minute, since he had driven through Tuppmere, wondering whether he'd survive the tedium of lunch at the Ashfords.

How long ago all that now seemed. How long ago and irrelevant.

For he had just recaptured his last glimpse of Carole, soaping a shin beneath the shower. "If Gershwin could only have seen you now," he'd said, "it've been Rhapsody in Pink . . ."

So many pinks, from the beads she still wore to the coral soles of her feet, and no fewer than seven, if one counted them carefully, shades of yellow in her hair, from buttercup to golden syrup.

"Damn," said Tom, noticing his fuel gauge was registering near-empty.

He was tempted to take a chance on having enough petrol left to complete his errand without stopping, but drew in at the last service station on the way out of town, just short of the beltway traffic circle, and hurriedly half filled his tank. Then, taking a couple of five pound notes out of his hip pocket, he went into the service station shop to pay the cashier. She was brown-haired, nineteen or so, freckled, had a sulky, pretty mouth with lips smaller than they were painted. She could have been a pubkeeper's daughter, for she appeared a fraction world-weary for her years—as though having learned early on that the more people enjoyed themselves on a Saturday night, the bigger the mess she'd have to help clean up in the gents and ladies in the morning. Without expression, she took the ten-pound note politely handed her by a pleasant-faced young man in an open-necked shirt, registered the sale on her till, and put his change on the counter, all without once looking up. She placed Tom's change in his palm and smiled at him warmly.

He thought about nothing else for the next three miles.

Had she somehow sensed the tenderness he'd felt toward her, just for an instant? Had something in his manner declared that he had his own, gorgeous young woman, which meant she'd nothing to fear from him, not so much as a single degrading, lustful thought? Or was it something as simple as the old saying, All the world loves a lover? How very peculiar.

And rather exciting, he conceded, yet another mile farther on, when it became impossible to ignore small flickerings of arousal. Neanderthal must've stolen out for a quick peek at that smile, drawn his own very unsophisticated conclusions, and then dived back into his cave again, rubbing two sticks together to make a smoke signal.

She'd fancied him.

"Oh, rubbish!" Tom said out aloud, laughing, pushing his foot down on the accelerator even harder.

But no matter how fast he drove, the thought pursued him.

And it was joined by others, tumbling nubile, naked, hedonistic, all of a heap, like at the collapse of a couch at an orgy. Now that he knew he could bed a much younger woman and make her so happy, it was surely time he cast his inhibitions completely aside, spread the bliss around a bit, see how many other Caroles he could find in this world, how many other hairdressing salons. And as old Harv had remarked at the Red Lion, he was certainly in an ideal position to cast an eye over each new intake of student nurses and start having fun picking himself . . .

Tom throttled back, shocked. He felt especially ashamed of

thinking about Carole like that. It represented the first time he'd ever, except for a silly private joke he'd made about Page Three of the *Sun*, viewed her as some sort of sex object. Far from it: Carole was Carole, that was the first thing to be said about her—and the last, too, because what he valued most was her spirit, her uncompromising individuality, her courage, her enveloping warmth. Even the sex hadn't been just sex as such; she had rooted him in the earth again, and he'd licked up her sweat like raindrops.

Just look: sixteen sodding minutes gone, and he had only that moment turned off the highway.

"Oh, well," said Tom, resigning himself to having miscalculated, "no sense in killing myself."

Even so, he took the next bend a little too fast; something slid off the passenger seat beside him, clattering against his gearshift. He glanced down and saw the tape of Verdi.

Then he heard it, too, and saw Ginny Ashford beside him, eyes closed and lying back, listening, taking the breath from him without so much as a tiny touch.

Almost instantly, Hayden's Trumpet Concerto blasted out of the car's twin speakers, far too loud to hear properly but at the right volume to obliterate any other sound, real or imaginary. And Tom, keeping time by thumping a fist on his steering wheel, went: "Pah, pah, pah!! P-p-p-p-pah!"

At the top of his voice, which seemed to work. Within seconds, he could imagine Carole pah-pahing along with him, delighted by such rousing, cheerful stuff. That was another thing about her, of course: the way in which one could foresee, with a great deal of certainty, how she would react in almost any given situation. Even the surprising things she often said were part of a predictable pattern of quirky humor and candor.

Yet no sooner had he thought this, Tom regretted it, for she sounded so dull and boring. Christ, on the contrary, this was something else he cherished about Carole: the fact that in her company he could completely relax, feel secure, know exactly where he stood.

Eighteen minutes gone, and now his path had to be blocked by the inevitable country-lane hazard on the weekend: several young riders in hard hats, trotting self-importantly along, led by an instructor. He braked a good distance off, dropped right down to a crawl, and passed them with his nearside wheels on the grass verge. The instructor, an oval-faced, comely redhead in her early twenties, saluted him with her quirt and smiled her thanks. He smiled back, hearing thunderous applause as Dorian Williams, in the Earls Court commentary box, said: "And a clear round by Tom Lockhart on his new filly, Miss Complete Stranger, in only one minute fifteen seconds."

Hurrying on once again, he told himself: Now stop this. You're not God's gift to womankind. You're simply in heat, you evil old goat, and the sooner someone throws a bucket of cold water over you or you get back to Carole the better.

So he turned down the Haydn, gave himself to the music, and drove, glancing just once at the empty seat beside him.

Until he was home at last. Not that it looked like home, that first glimpse of thatched roof over a neighbor's mail-order conifers, but then it never had, not really. Tom had coveted an old mill house at Tuppmere, funnily enough, but Sylvia having done her sums (which included the cost of her drawn-out visit to Trade Winds each week), had won the day overwhelmingly. "After all, Tom," she'd said, "what'd we *do* with all those extra bedrooms? A teeny laborer's cottage is just right for us, and it *is* the quaintest, oldest building in the village." Which wasn't much of an achievement on its part, as there hadn't even been a village there before an enterprising builder had fiddled planning permission to construct one.

But if home was where a man packed his suitcase, Tom decided, he'd come to the right place. And he nosed his car into the drive, stopping just short of a small heap of pony droppings, round as pebbles.

"Sweet Zeus," said Tom Lockhart.

Then he thought quickly, taking a handful of music cassettes with him as he got out of the car. He dropped the lot right beside the droppings, and had to crouch down to retrieve them. In this position, his body shielding what he intended to do next, frustrating any watching neighbors, he reached out, and like an Apache scout, touched the nearest dropping to see whether it was still warm and moist. It was, distastefully so.

"Blast!" he said. "Can't have been more than a few minutes . . ."

He stood up, wondering what had come over him. He had Carole now, dammit—the sexiest, most adorable, cuddlesome lass in the whole wide world—and no man could possibly want anything more, let alone deserve it.

So he carried on up the driveway and with each pace he took, he listed one more item he should be sure of including in his case: dark socks for Monday; his old-school tie because he had that meeting with the health authority bigwigs at five; something casual in the way of shirts for Monday evening, when he and Carole would go and see a film, perhaps, with dinner at the Purple Cockatoo afterward; on Tuesday he'd need—

A violet envelope lay on his doorstep.

Tom let himself into the house, pushed the door half shut behind him, then tore the envelope open, not pausing to reach for the letter opener.

> *Sunday morning*
> *Tom my sweet,*
> *Ginny has told us that you were at the preview and said Sylvias away with her mother poorly and youll be all on your own this weekend with nobody to look after you poor lamb. Shes so sorry for you and we cant have that can we? Ive tried and tried to get you on the phone but as that hasnt worked heres a note to say youre more than welcome any time today and why dont you have all your evening meals with us here this week if S is away longer? Dont bother to ring just come.*
> *Lots of love!*
> *Moira*

He read it a second time, pausing at the part where it said how sorry Ginny had been for him, and then read it a third time, but between the lines. Nothing could then seem plainer than the fact that Ginny, perhaps bewildered by his sudden exodus from the preview, but still wanting to *SEE YOU!!!*—which she hadn't had a chance to do, what with the demands made on her by that hypocritical sod, Len Tullet, and by Nell Overton, of course—was behind this sudden very generous offer of hospitality from the Ashfords. If Moira or Hugh had really felt as partial to him as this, then surely he'd have been invited to join in their wedding anniversary celebrations last Friday.

And not only had Ginny coaxed her mother into writing the

note, but she'd obviously ridden posthaste over to his house to deliver it, possibly hoping he'd be in, with the telephone unplugged, disconsolately watching the cricket on television. Wondering why, at the private viewing, she'd seemed to be putting everyone else before him. Which wasn't really true, of course, because she'd actually planned that afterward he and she would . . .

"Carole," Tom said resolutely, and tossed the note onto the hall table. "Start packin', old son. Remember who yer mates are!"

But on the stairs, the accentuated cling of yesterday's underpants proved too much for him. So he decided, seeing how late he was already, it wouldn't matter much if he had a swift shower first.

That turned into something like a scene out of *Psycho*.

Tom was scrubbing an armpit, his eyes closed against the stinging jets of hot water that beat loudly against the plastic curtains, when he thought he heard someone turn the doorknob.

He switched off the shower and blinked, trying to clear his vision. The door opened, and a dim, female shape entered the room, silhouetted by the sunlight on the landing. Cupping himself, he asked shakily, "Who's that?"

The shape halted.

"G-Ginny?"

"What an extraordinary assumption!" said Sylvia with a delighted laugh, parting the shower curtains to smile in at him.

"Heavens, you're back," Tom heard himself say, with a lack of originality equaled only by his next stunned remark: "I wasn't expecting you so soon."

"Evidently! But why you should think it was—"

"She's just been here, delivering a note, and I thought she might've nipped back to use the loo, not realizing I was—"

"Yes, I've just read the note," said Sylvia. "I must say, it didn't take Moira long to dive in, did it? Need a towel?"

He nodded, hurriedly swathed himself in it, stepped out of the shower, and then grabbed up a second towel to hide his expression in, drying his hair vigorously. "Dive?" he echoed a little shrilly, his voice still not quite under control.

"Make a grab for you, while wifey was away."

"What on earth are you talking about?"

"Oh, come on," said Sylvia, as she crossed the passage into

their bedroom, "it's always been embarrassingly obvious she has designs on you. Why else do you suppose she talked Hugh into moving all the way down here? Probably timed it to catch you at your most defenseless, indulging in your midlife crisis, I shouldn't wonder. Easy meat for a minx like—"

"God, you do have an imagination, don't you?"

Sylvia made rummaging noises on top of the wardrobe. "Do I, Tom, dear?" she said. "Next, you'll be denying her passionate yearnings aren't reciprocated."

"What?" he said, moving to stand in the bedroom doorway. "Don't talk such—"

"I'm not," she replied nonchalantly, taking down a large suitcase. "Give me credit for having *some* feminine intuition, for goodness' sake. Not that it'd take anyone much of an effort to detect the very definite change in you after our arrival at Tuppmere last Sunday. I ceased to exist."

Tom toweled his hair again. Sylvia was saying all the right things for the wrong reasons, he thought. Allowing him the perfect opportunity to confess that yes, he did cherish another, and could they please end their marriage as painlessly as possible? But perhaps he ought to think this one out properly before dropping any blond bombshells.

"Silence is of course another way of admitting something," Sylvia remarked complacently, beginning to pack. "But, as I say, none of this comes as a surprise. What *does* intrigue me is how you managed to finish up at that private viewing of etchings yesterday! Did you seriously imagine Moira'd be there? In fact, how did you even get to hear about it?"

"Er, invitation on the piano."

"Oh, of course! Ginny's little cheerio, you mean. Now which shoes should I—"

"Cheerio?" queried Tom, tightening his towel against a dread hollowing of his stomach.

"You know, the note she left me after helping make that rabbit pie, which I showed her how to decorate. She was just saying how much she enjoyed the way we girls could just chat together, quite unlike with Moira, when I'm afraid Mummy rang up, one of her usual, rather anxious calls, poor darling, and—"

"Having reversed the bloody charges!" Tom interjected with sudden, flailing spite.

"You know Sister Pinkerton won't let her near the phone

otherwise. But as I was saying"—Sylvia paused to select a handbag—"Mummy did go on and on rather, until Ginny, the poor thing, simply couldn't wait any longer, what with her pony literally champing at the bit, and so she wrote 'bye now,' or something as charmingly juvenile, on the back of one of those cards she must've happened to have with her. Mummy had a frightful night last night, by the way, and they're keeping her in another week at least. That's why I've rushed home to pack."

Tom, his mind reeling, finally managed to say, "Oh."

Sylvia smiled as she carefully folded an evening dress. "I'll tell Mummy how dreadfully upset you were at the news," she said, "and that you send her all your love and best wishes for a quick recovery. Mark you, even after she's back at Trade Winds I'll probably have to remain on, giving her that extra bit of attention one can't expect from Sister."

"Oh," Tom said again.

"As a matter of fact," murmured Sylvia, partially preoccupied by making another choice from her huge wardrobe, "it mightn't be a bad idea . . ."

"What mightn't?"

"Your eating at the Ashfords while I'm away. I've a feeling Ginny is going to miss me, and who knows, maybe she'll find she's able to discuss at least some of her problems with you, the way she does with me. The child is obviously desperate for an adult she can really talk to, whose values aren't—well!"

A crooked smile twisting its way onto Tom's face made him turn and open his shirt drawer. "How is that obvious?" he asked. "I hadn't noticed it."

Sylvia laughed softly behind his back. "You're almost sweetly naive at times," she said. "Remember the night—was it last Wednesday—when you were so angry because I'd taken her home while you were with Geoff, and made you miss a chance of seeing Moira?"

"Now, look!"

"Sorry! But you surely didn't fall for Ginny's tale about hiding that etching here, did you? And being afraid to take it on the bus? She could have done so perfectly easily, and it would've been quite simple to hide it under her bed until Friday. No, that was all just a trumped-up excuse, and a fairly blatant one, to get in touch with us again, after that lovely chat we'd had on our own on the patio on Sunday—I think you and Hugh had gone to look at pumps or something, and Moira was seeing to the scones she baked us for tea. Oddly enough, I thought at the time, goodness, what a wonderful mother and daughter we'd make, and then, here she was, here with you in our living room, looking just as though she'd always belonged there, waiting for me. Since when, of course, she's felt welcome to pop over and see us whenever she wants to."

Tom froze, hooded by the clean shirt he'd been pulling on, and heard the firing squad raise its rifles, ready to tear his incestuous heart away.

"Oh, rubbish!" he snorted, quickly dragging the shirt down and reaching into his underwear drawer. "That can't be right! Ginny can't see you like that, let alone be so devious!"

"Consciously, perhaps not," agreed Sylvia. "And that's also why, knowing my dreams of having a daughter, I'm rather glad I'll be away for a while. Neither of us can afford to become too dependent on the other."

Tom stopped and turned, having heard something catch in Sylvia's voice, and he was right. Tears were brimming as she collected her makeup together. He experienced a sense of utter confusion: half of him wanting to hurry to her side and comfort her, the other half—the half she'd just hurt so badly—wanting to make her really weep.

His response was a compromise. He laid a hand gently on her shoulder and said, "Sylv, you know as well as I do there's never ever been anything to stop you having a daughter."

"Yes, there has!" she snapped, shaking his hand off. "Has, has, has!" And she spilled a compact of face powder.

"Then I want to know the new reason," said Tom. "*Now*. We've played this ridiculous game often enough. Neither of us is infertile, and we know it."

She looked at his reflection in the dressing table mirror. "I am infertile," she said. "I have to be. I've told you this before. You said you didn't want any of my babies. Once, when you were half asleep and had your guard down, you said—"

"And I have told you before," said Tom, keeping very calm, "exactly what I'd meant by that remark. You're taking something out of context."

"No."

"Then once again," said Tom, staring back at her reflection and feeling a wild rage rising, "you have to face up to the fact you're not acting rationally. You must have a desperate need to keep believing that, no matter what I say."

She turned and looked at him long and carefully. "Yes, perhaps you're right," she said.

"Fine, then why?"

"Because," began Sylvia, then shrugged. "I'm not sure," she said, "but you frighten me somehow."

"*Me* frighten *you*? That is a new one! How? I don't remember hearing anything about this on our honeymoon, or all those years we planned our—"

"Oh, no, it was different then. I think it began when you switched from ordinary medicine to radiology."

"Huh! Which was also when we could at last afford to start a family! So what was it, Sylv, cold feet? You were suddenly scared of seeing yourself swell up and having your spick-and-span little life disrupted by a dirty, greedy—"

"You changed," Sylvia interrupted, starting to pack again. "Or the way I saw you changed, because what frightened me must have been there all along. Before then, I suppose, I'd idealized you, which is easy to do with doctors, if you're like me and impressed by how their hands can take away suffering, by the long hours they'll battle heroically to—"

"Oh, please, spare me the sob stuff!"

"Exactly!" said Sylvia, and gave a small laugh. "Spare you the sob stuff, Tom! That's it in a nutshell. You couldn't take the suffering, could you? The days and weeks of watching that plumber die, and having to help not just him but his family, their demands on you. That's why you switched, wasn't it? Radiology got you safely away from all that! Oh, yes, now you could sit happily looking at pictures of ugly, ugly things, and come home and talk about them as though they were *beautiful*, those ghastly images of yours! How often—you just tell me—how often did you ever again tell me anything about a patient, the name of a *person* you'd treated? Except when one did something to spoil the picture, sneezed or had a fit, had the cheek to—"

"Christ, you have the most extraordinary—"

"Children get sick, suffer," Sylvia continued angrily, turning on him. "They do all the things a doctor's patients do, make the same demands on your emotions—only more so, because they're yours, part of you. But could you take that, Tom? Would you be a proper parent, a father? Or would you simply opt out again, when you couldn't cope with the pressure of your feelings, with too much reality, instead of a nice, shiny set of pretty pictures?"

"What," he said lightly, "and leave you holding the baby?"

Sylvia opened his wardrobe, handed him a pair of slacks, and said, "Get out."

"No, not until I've at least—"

"Get out," she repeated. "It's even frightening you could make a joke like that!"

He took the slacks, a pair of slip-on shoes, and a fresh pair of socks, gave her reflection one long look, and then went downstairs to finish changing.

"Who has she been talking to?" he murmured, because this latest outburst had sounded most unlike Sylvia in parts, being too glibly analytical by far. "Not that it sodding matters, when all she wanted was a bloody great row to end rows . . ."

Why? he wondered. But only fleetingly, before turning to what did matter—those devastating things she'd said earlier about Ginny. He could see how her version of events, as opposed to his own, was quite as possibly correct, and the implications appalled him—those he dared think about.

No, they did far more than that, he realized, as he made his way, still shaking, out of the house, with the sheet of violet notepaper in his hand. They had made it impossible for him to live another hour without finally learning the truth of where he stood with Ginny Ashford.

21

"**N**o," said Tom Lockhart, as he began reversing out of his drive, "bollocks to all this. You just get yourself back to town, and Carole'll kiss it better, pet!"

With a smile, he tried to picture that.

But all he saw was a candy-cotton blur. He would have telephoned the flat to say he'd be delayed by an urgent call he just had to make first, only he didn't know what her last name was.

Then, his car doing a dragonfly-streak toward Tuppmere along the last mile of straight Roman road, Tom sniffed twice and wound down his window. "Funny," he muttered, "stinks of Sylvia . . ." He couldn't think why. She had not been his passenger since the night of Geoff's party.

"Christ, her bloody powder!"

There, on his cavalry-twill slacks, which she'd handed him after spilling that compact. Tom slowed down to brush the powder away as best he could, but it still left a faint impression of her fingers on his thigh.

And that made him very angry.

"Bitch!" he said, accelerating hard again. "Get out of my bloody life, will you?"

Crazy, irrational bitch, he added silently, seething. She'd never even *liked* her parents before they'd returned to England—or at least that was what she'd always said, and nobody could deny she had all but neglected them entirely while they'd still been in Africa, writing to them only at Christmas. On top of which she'd made sure they had not gone into a home locally, but had selected Trade Winds, way off on the far side of the next county, to limit contact as much as possible. Yet after about only her third monthly flying trip to see them, everything had changed. Her visits had become weekly, she was away almost the whole day, and when she returned she was invariably in excellent spirits, often making her more aggressive than usual. How did one account for all this? Delayed guilt, followed by the immense self-satisfaction she now derived from being notorious as an utterly devoted daughter? But if she had become so devoted, then why hadn't she jumped at his idea of buying the old mill house, insisting her parents came and lived with them? Not that he'd have stood for this, not for one moment, but she could have compromised by finding them another nursing home much nearer. None of it made sense, and probably never would—the constant creation of confusion and impenetrable paradox was Sylvia's particular gift.

"Bitch," Tom said again, less vehemently, trying not to remember how he'd detected something of this when they very first met, and had then found it more and more irresistible the harder he'd tried to see what went on beneath that impeccable exterior.

He quickly wound up his car window again. The inrush of air was making one hell of a mess of his hair. He smoothed it down with a hand, and then quickly checked the effect in his rearview mirror. His hair looked presentable enough, but now he saw he'd quite forgotten to shave, idiot that he was.

Which reminded him: "Oh, it's beautiful, my sweet, and such a surprise—but should, um, the ladies in really artistic pictures be *unshaven?*"

Had Ginny really repeated this remark, word for word, to Sylvia? Had the pair of them really giggled about it for ages? And if so, then hadn't his so-called pursuit of hapless prey been more a case of one wicked-minded predator conspiring to join forces with another wicked-minded predator, the better to enjoy certain wickednesses?

"Steady!" said Tom to Tom Lockhart. "Steady. Slow you down, old son!" And pretended to be doing his own backseat driving.

It was true, he had just reached the start of the long, twisting section of road down the wooded slope outside Tuppmere, and proper caution was needed. Tom dropped speed, took his car carefully around bend after bend, and presently came to where, one gloriously beautiful morning, he had offered up thanks to a new goddess. A divine enigma, carved from marble the color of caramel, the workings of whose mind were enough to perplex any mortal man to distraction; these being, presumably, what she'd chosen to hide with her fig leaf.

Then he was actually in Tuppmere itself, and the clock on the church tower gave the hour as three minutes short of one o'clock. If he hurried, his arrival at the Ashfords' would coincide exactly with Sunday lunchtime.

"Look who's here!" said Moira, opening the front door to him. "Tom, my sweet, I am so pleased you've come! We weren't at all sure you would, not after turning your nose up at us last week like that, and disappointing Ginny on—"

"Last week?"

"You know, the invite to join us at the Cock Pheasant on Friday for our anniversary. But you had that meeting you wanted to go to."

"Had I?"

"Well, that's what Sylv said when Ginny went over—oh, and also to tell you about her friend and the aquatinting thingy on Saturday after the preview. Wherever did you go dashing off to?"

Tom, his fists clenched, just stared.

Moira touched a caressing hand to her hair, smiled, and said, "Oh, dear . . . You didn't know?" She had a hand very like her daughter's.

And Ginny touched my bloody arm twice at the private viewing, thought Tom. *Twice*—not by chance! Deliberately, so I'd notice. Aquatinting afterward. And then?

"No, I didn't know," he said, hoping to God that she wouldn't appear until he'd thought of some way of restoring her faith in him. "You and Hugh must think I'm a right . . ."

"Don't be silly, Tom! I think we've both always known where we stood with you—except the time you knocked me off that punt on the Cherwell! Come, give me a hand with something, will you?"

She pulled the front door closed behind her, and started toward the Volvo estate parked outside their double garage. Tom followed her, surprisingly warmed by that reminder of a summer's afternoon in Oxford, when rather drunk on white plonk, he had been teaching Moira the rudiments of poling a punt. He had stood behind her and they'd both had the pole in their hands, while Hugh had dozed with a copy of *The Wasteland* over his face. Time and again Moira's firm, rounded behind had bumped against the front of Tom's swimming trunks, as he'd helped her establish a rhythm, and then these small collisions had seemed to take on a rhythm all of their own. And so, with her engagement ring glittering on the hand that slid loosely up and down the punt pole, into the water Moira had to go—entirely by accident, of course. Hugh, ever gallant if terribly drunk, had jumped in to save her. Tom had jumped in too, hopeful that the cold shock would have vascular effects, and to wonder whether he'd been imagining things.

"Tell me," said Tom, noticing that the same bottom seemed to have changed very little down the years. "Those photos we took that day, whatever happened to them?"

Moira laughed, glancing around. "Don't you remember? Hugh still had his camera round his neck!"

"Oh, God, yes! And the poetry floating off downstream!"

"Even worse, do you remember there was a family picnicking by the Vicky Arms, just before that?"

Tom shook his head.

"I don't neither," said Moira, momentarily relapsing into her speech of the time, "but the man was on the same shift as my father, up at the works, and on Monday, when I got home from Marks, didn't I get a rollicking! Never found out exactly what the man said, but my dad swore he'd never been so ashamed in all his life. Nearly ended our engagement, that did, and Hugh had to get down on his bended knees to plead for forgiveness."

"Nobody's ever told me this before!"

"Well, we didn't see you again until the wedding, did we?" said Moira, with her smile broadening. "Your finals, your excuse was. And anyway, I've never had a chance to get you on your own since."

"On my own!" said Tom, realizing he must be being a bit slow about something.

"Well," said Moira, opening the back of the Volvo, "it's lucky Hugh was so tiddly that afternoon he couldn't remember what he'd been up to with me on the river, wasn't it?"

* * *

There was a large bale of hay in the rear of the Volvo, every detail of which Tom's eyes began examining, while, to his horror, Neanderthal puffed and blew into a smoldering handful of old leaves, grunting excitedly.

"Hugh hates looking after the ponies," said Moira, "so Ginny and me take turns getting their feed down to the paddock. Can you help me slide this lot onto that thingy?" And she indicated a hand truck against the garage wall.

Tom, eager to move energetically, said, "Oh, you can leave that to me, Moi!" He dragged over the truck, and then upended the bale on it.

"You're fitter than I thought you were! And you've lost weight."

"So I've been told. Where do we . . . ?"

"The paddock's this way," said Moira, starting off. "We've sort of worn a path now, so it's not too hard to push. Nobody's called me 'Moi' since—"

"Old habits," said Tom, cursing them silently. "Isn't your grazing good, that you need this stuff?"

"Don't ask me about ponies, that's Ginny's worry. Who looked after yours? Did you, or was it—oh, I'd forgotten, they were the next door farmer's, weren't they?"

Oh, no, you'd not forgotten, thought Tom, very relieved Moira had reverted to her catty, unappetizing self. "Yes, I'd gathered from Sylvia that Ginny knew a fair bit about them," he lied harmlessly. "You know she's taken to riding over to us?"

Moira, sucking a stalk of grass as she walked beside him, nodded. "So she's told us," she said. "Hugh's already a bit worried, because he thinks she could get too involved."

"Oh?"

"He has this thing about Ginny and her lame ducks," said Moira, shrugging. "She says she tried our present out on you two first. The etching?"

"Ah!" said Tom. "Yes, she did. What did you think of it?"

"I couldn't believe the price! Even if Nell did let her have it cheap in return for all the different jobs she's done for her, I still think twenty-five pounds was a bit much—took all her savings from her last waitress job. But there you are, typical Ginny!"

"Did you like it, though?"

"A bit sexy for downstairs, Hugh thought, where people with children sometimes come, but yes, it's lovely—very natural really, and the trees are just right, I think. Why're you smiling like that?"

* * *

"Oh, nothing," replied Tom, reminding himself that this was why he was at Cloud Hill, to get at the truth, dismiss the fantasies, and return to Carole a chastened, much better man. "I was just smiling," he said, "at the way the ponies have come cantering up, the moment they saw us."

"Huh!" said Moira. "Not that they'll canter when you actually want them to! I think Ginny overdid gentling them, if you ask me."

"Gentling?"

"Breaking in."

"Local word?"

"Oh, no, a proper one she learned from the man who taught her how to do it. But as I say, I had to practically *beat* that lazy fat animal all the way over to your house this morning, and all the way back again! An old lady frowned at me."

"Oh, so you were the one who—?"

"Yes, sorry about what's on your drive—but you can always put it on the roses!"

No, I'll put it on my head, thought Tom, as a penance. He knew his next question was going to cost him dearly, but having entered into a frame of mind that craved punishment, he put it to Moira all the same. "By the way," he said, "what are the ponies' names? Never thought to ask before."

"Guess," she said.

"How can I? Er, Adam and Eve?"

"You're warm. Ginny wanted that, but it wasn't very original, so I thought of Windfall—he's the one I've just been talking about—and Gutsiest. Ring a bell?"

Tom halted at the paddock fence, and tipped the bale of hay onto the ground. "Can't say they do," he said, and saw that Moira looked almost as disappointed.

The ponies' whinnyings broke the brief silence, giving him an excuse to laugh softly, and put his hand out to be nuzzled. God, that felt good, Tom thought, and found himself in a hurry now to get home to Carole.

But he knew he mustn't do that until he'd completed the process of utter disillusionment. "You mentioned 'lame ducks' a few minutes ago," he said to Moira. "I wasn't too sure what you meant by that."

"Here, give them some of these," she said, offering Tom a handful of sugar cubes from her jeans pocket. "Oh, they've been so many! That terribly neurotic boy, for instance, who first took her to the print workshop. Can't think of his name, but she found him at a club one night, sitting in a corner all by—"

"But how's that connected with, er . . . ?"

"Sorry, with Sylvia? Well, all of us were talking about how tense she'd seemed last Sunday, and thinking it was because she hasn't produced and the meno's on its way now. Hugh said she was probably very lonely, but now says he wishes he hadn't because Ginny—"

"I see," said Tom, numbed now. "So that's why she's been coming over."

Moira laughed. "Or so Hugh thinks! Personally, I think she's still got a bit of a crush on you, my sweet—and who could blame her? But I haven't asked yet."

Tom, by the time everything was in focus again, had fed every sugar cube in his hand to Windfall. He cleared his throat, and said, as casually as he could to Moira, who was behind him, fiddling with the hay, "Still got a bit of a crush? What an extraordinary statement!"

"Oh, come on," she said, joining him to offer more tidbits to the ponies, "I thought you had eyes in your head." Then she laughed again and nudged him, before adding, "But poor Ginny, either you're never in, or you're there two minutes, with her all dressed up, she turns her back, and you're gone again! You can be a bastard, Tom Lockhart."

"Gutsiest is due the larger share of those goodies," he said. "And Ginny's told you all this? You're quite a mother and daughter."

"Thanks," said Moira, and her smile was the prettiest he'd ever seen it; almost beautiful, and very like Ginny's. "At least she's always honest with me, when I feel I need to know something, but I let her have her privacy—you know, when it comes to, say, this secret thing of hers for you. I think I've known about it as long as she has, or even longer! Then again, I suppose it could be just—"

"Your imagination?" said Tom, feeling compelled to add, like a double agent, "Thank goodness for that!"

Moira glanced at him. "Hmmm," she said. "Mind you, it is a relief it's all so one-sided. I don't know how Hugh would react to you as a son-in-law, not after some of the tales he's told me about you."

"What tales?" snapped Tom, so indignant it was another split second before he felt the full, thrilling shock of what she'd just suggested.

"Tom, I'm just teasing!" laughed Moira. "You've always been the perfect gentleman, I know, I know—big sigh. One of the main reasons I've always fancied you was the thought of how lovely it'd be to *corrupt* you, my sweet, in the nicest possible way! Pity I didn't get that little flat in Oxford before I'd met Hugh and you felt I was spoken for. So, it's having you as *my* son-in-law I'd be more worried about!"

"I see," said Tom, needing to turn away. "I'll get this truck back to the garage."

They started back up the slope together.

"Then a swim," said Moira, "or are you famished?"

"I, er—yes, why the hell not? Sweaty weather."

"It's gorgeous, like that summer," said Moira, falling in step with him. "I'm glad, your ankle seems quite better."

"Ankle?"

"You twisted it in the changing room last—"

"Ah, yes! Slight sprain, that was all, fit as a fiddle next day."

Moira must have said other things, none of them consequential, on the way back to the garage. Tom was barely aware of them, merely murmuring the right sort of noises to keep her chattering. He was trying to grasp the import of so much he'd been told, and yet finding it like handling wet cakes of soap with boxing gloves. All that he was left with in the end, as the garage came in sight, seemed to be a delightful taste of bittersweet irony in his mouth and a sense of rising, compelling excitement.

Then, as he propped the hand truck against the garage wall, his mind cleared sufficiently for him to gratefully affirm that when Ginny appeared, he'd be a very different Tom Lockhart from the one a week ago—self-assured enough to join her very readily in the pool, and now armed with all that her mother had told him. How different Moira herself seemed today, he thought, probably because Sylvia wasn't around. He hoped that, somehow or other, he'd find his attitude to Hugh had changed too, making everything so much easier when it came to the gentling of Ginny Ashford.

That's right, he'd *gentle* her, in every sense of that wonderful word.

"I hope Hugh's looking after it," said Moira, motioning with her chin at the empty bay in the garage. "I'd only had it three days."

"Sorry?" said Tom.

"My new BMW sports car. He's gone up to Scotland for a week's fishing, and dropped so many hints I just had to let him try it out—after all, he bought it, the poppet! It's red, with the most super interior."

Tom, trying to keep a delighted smile off his face, said, "Oh? I hadn't noticed one was missing." Which was true, and he only wished he'd been more observant earlier.

"You're quite sure you don't want to eat first?" asked Moira, leading him into the house and then into the drawing room. "We were just going to have something very light anyway. Prawns on brown bread, lettuce, tomato, different cheeses . . . ?"

"Mmm, sounds delicious," said Tom, looking kindly on the videocassettes in their phony-leather cases. "Damn, I should have brought some wine."

"Hugh's a whole larderful, so don't let that worry you. White?"

Tom nodded. "I'll bring a couple of bottles during the week," he said.

"So you would like to eat with us?" said Moira, her face lighting up. "Oh, that will be nice, especially with Hugh away!"

It was none too clear exactly how she meant that to be taken, but Tom knew that he couldn't agree with her more. "Thanks, Moi," he said, smiling at her, "it's really kind of you to ask me." Then he wandered over to the patio doors and looked down the lawn at the pool, half expecting, with a tingling sensation in his stomach, that Ginny would be there, sunbathing.

"Well, what is it to be?" asked Moira. "Food first, or that swim?"

The pool and garden were deserted. Tom, deciding that Ginny must be up in her room, and wanting to see her again very badly, said, "I'm easy, so why don't we ask her to come down and we'll all take a vote on it?"

Moira looked blank for a moment. "Oh, you mean Ginny?" she said.

Tom nodded.

"But I thought I'd told you what a bastard you were," said

Moira with a laugh. "After all those phone calls to your house we'd given you up for lost this weekend, and she's gone out to lunch, poor thing! Didn't you take in how surprised I was when you popped up on our doorstep?"

"I, er . . ."

"So I've got you all to myself," said Moira, reaching out for his hand. "Come, we'll eat in the kitchen and try not to get tiddly."

22

I don't think I can survive much more of this day, decided Tom Lockhart as he took back his hand and leaned against a kitchen work-top, watching Moira open her refrigerator. Leaving Carole's flat that morning had been like quitting a deep, safe bunker, and ever since then it seemed he'd been crossing an apocalyptic version of the vast inner landscape he'd glimpsed the night before. For every dazzling burst of light he had seen, there'd been a shattering blast to follow it. With every step he'd taken, he'd moved farther into minefields. The parallel was too grimly obvious to be treated as mere fancy, and he knew, he just knew now, things could only get worse.

"Good God," he said, "is that the time? I'm much later than I thought I was! I really ought to get back."

"Back where?" asked Moira, taking out the prawns.

"I, er, am on call from one today," he said.

"Then ring and tell them where you are," she instructed. "Isn't that what doctors usually do?"

Which left Tom no choice but to return to the hall, where he faked a call to the hospital by ringing his own number and speaking to the dial tone. The hall table was booby-trapped: it almost tore him apart to see the hospital number jotted down on a pad in a firm, young hand, followed by his extension, and the human hearts someone had doodled beside it.

* * *

So he hit back cruelly.

"Please, Tom," begged Moira, toward the end of a meal dominated by one topic of conversation, "I can't *bear* to hear another word about Annabel! You know I haven't the stomach for gruesome subjects."

"But a man's whole professional career could be at stake, don't you see?"

"I don't bloody care!" said Moira, banging a small fist. "I can't eat when you're going on and on about catheters and the rest of it! Will you please stop it?"

"Ginny didn't seem to mind," he said, pouring his third glass of hock.

"God, you've *not* been telling her these kinds of stories!"

"What?" said Tom. "Didn't she debrief you?"

"Come again?" said Moira, slopping some wine on her hand.

"Oh, forget it," said Tom. "You'd never have made a doctor's wife, anyway."

Then Moira must have felt like hitting back, because she said, "Ginny might. She's having lunch with one."

It could get worse, and it had, thought Tom. Even though he'd prepared himself to withstand another shock, this shellburst caught him in the open. "Who?" he said, hemorrhaging.

"Can't think, but he knows you, apparently. Like to try some of this cheese with garlic in it?"

"No, thanks. Knows me from where?"

"The hospital, I suppose. Mind you, he's fairly junior, and probably only bragging. Cheddar?"

"Finished, thank you!" said Tom, tossing down his napkin. "How young?"

Moira shrugged, spreading a slice of bread very thickly with the garlic cheese; and taking a bite of it, she let some fall from her mouth. "I was in the loo when he came to pick her up," she said. "They've gone to the Cock Pheasant. Ginny'd noticed, last Friday, they have live country and western there on Sundays at lunchtime."

"Slim Panatella and his Smoky Mountain Boys?" said Tom scornfully.

"No, what she calls a 'brill' new lot, with even an LP. What's wrong with country and western, anyhow?"

"A bit far removed from Verdi!"

"That's Ginny," said Moira, dropping a piece of cheese down

her cleavage. "I wish you weren't being like this, or I might have asked you to fish for it."

"Oh?" Then Tom, seeing the real hurt in Moira's eyes, and knowing she was only half joking, felt shamed. "I'm sorry, luv. Bit upset, that's all."

"Your love life?"

Tom laughed, for the first time that meal. "Steady!" he said.

"No, I've guessed. You can't tell stories like that to Sylvia anymore, can you? From the way she behaves, you might as well not exist."

"Oh?" said Tom, very aware he was desperate to be distracted. "What gives you that idea?"

"Ginny. I think she's spent so long with Sylv hoping to find out bits and pieces about you. What she told me was, Sylvia seems obsessed with herself, her parents, and what sounds like a shrink, although she didn't actually—"

"A shrink?"

"You didn't know?"

He shook his head. "But *that* rings a bloody bell all right!" he said. "Wonder when she sees him? She's always around when one rings home, and—"

"Doing what? Ginny's hinted she's incredibly lazy. She had to show her how to make a rabbit pie look—"

"Oh, Christ!" said Tom with a barked laugh. "Time I got back to the Führen bunker!" And he stood up.

"The what?" said Moira, rising too.

"Look, Moi," Tom began, then shrugged. "A bad day, I shouldn't have come to see you. Not fit company for anyone, least of all someone I . . ."

Moira barred his escape through the back door. "Tom, what's really the matter? I know you haven't seen us for ages, but we're better friends of yours than you may think. I'll never forget the day you were so kind to Ginny when she was having such a horrible time of it at that boarding school we should never have sent her to. It was only afterward, when we were driving away, she finally broke down crying and told us how much she hated it, and why. She'd not wanted to let us down before that, you see, because Hugh wasn't well off then, and she knew how much the sacrifice of sending her there, which we'd hoped would be a good thing as she was an only, was costing us. But after you'd treated her like that, made her really welcome, even if you did seem shy, fussed over her when she hurt her knee—she kept that bandage you put on for ages—then, finally, she told us you were the first grown-up who hadn't put her down ever since we sent her to that dreadful place. Oh, yes, out it all came! And we were very grateful to you for that—we had her home that same week, and sent her to the local state school, which she loved. But that wasn't all you did for her."

"No?" said Tom, supposing his face must be burning.

"No," repeated Moira. "It's very worrying, having such an attractive girl for your daughter. We're sure that it was Ginny's looks and lovely nature that used to make those shriveled old bitches at her boarding school want to take it out on her. Worrying, because . . ." She had to stop and think, having lost her thread, and used the pause to brush his forelock back into place. "Oh, yes, what I was meaning to say was that she naturally has plenty of males buzzing around her wherever she goes, but she's always had you, you see, to sort of compare them with, and that gets rid of an awful lot we'd not want anywhere near her! Naturally, it's a bit glamorized, the way she remembers you from when she was twelve, and how she sees you now, but she worships the kind of work you do, your whole life spent helping people, and also the way you're always so friendly and—"

"Poor Ginny!" said Tom, grasping the back-door handle. "She'll never find anyone to measure up to *that* description—me, least of all!"

"You're wrong there," said Moira, putting her hand over his and opening the door for him. "You're a very nice man, Tom Lockhart, even if you are a bit of a bastard. I think you'd better go now."

Tom didn't ask why; her hand had lingered.

But once they were out of doors, with a good two yards separating them, it was possible to treat one another with the comfortable detachment of old friends. What made this most apparent was that they said nothing as they walked around the house to Tom's car.

"Well," he said, getting behind the wheel and buckling his safety belt. "I was delighted to meet Windfall and Gutsiest—give them my regards, won't you?"

Moira nodded. "If you want a good place to eat in town in the evening," she said, "then the Purple Cockatoo's very reasonable and the kitchens are clean. Ginny worked there once."

"I'll do that," said Tom, smiling. "I trust the BMW gets back in one piece."

Again Moira nodded, seeming equally aware of how much else they were saying to one another. "And I hope your friend didn't make a fatal mistake with that baby," she said. "You sounded, when you were talking about it, as if you loved him like a brother."

"Once upon a time, perhaps."

"You still do," said Moira.

Tom started his car, knowing he should tell her to take care, and then drive quickly off, with one backward wave of the hand. That would be the perfect ending to his visit to Cloud Hill.

But he blurted out, because he couldn't stop himself, "This doctor Ginny's with, you say you don't know his name?"

"Perhaps she told me, but it wasn't unusual enough to stick. She met him at the preview on Saturday, while she was going around the room, asking people if they knew where you were. She'd missed Nell, who'd followed you down the—"

"But I don't remember seeing anyone there that I knew."

"Then he must've slipped in just before you left. I don't think he was invited, but I've heard Ginny say previews often get people who just drift in, specially if there's free booze going. He seemed pretty knowledgeable, though, and got Ginny fascinated with—oh, I don't remember that either, but foreign films or something. Then he rang up this morning, just after we got back from delivering my note to you, and Ginny, who'd really gone down in the dumps, jumped at the chance of getting him to take her to hear Fox Mountain."

"Who wouldn't?" said Tom Lockhart, and tried to smile broadly. "Look after yourself, Moi . . ."

"You too," she said. "And take care, pet . . ."

Not "my sweet," he noted, as he drove slowly away from Tuppmere. If ever he'd received a clear indication from the Fates as to where he should go next, this was it. But Tom took the next narrow road forking left, and headed even farther from town, out onto a wide, exposed landscape.

He didn't think. He just went. One last thing remained that he simply had to know.

212 / James McClure

The Cock Pheasant did everything it could to keep a carriage trade visiting the once-busy village, now bypassed by a super-highway, in which it leaned picturesquely at a slight angle. It had pig roasts, Friday-night discos, jazz on Monday evenings, and a menu that undercut the prices in middle-range restaurants yet matched them for quality. Its barmaids, chosen with the greatest care, were as bright as they were a pleasure to look upon, able to exchange badinage with everyone from a motorcycle-gang leader (only there for the leer) to a polytechnic lecturer (pretending that leers were a serious social study of his). Naturally, it had a very large car park.

Which, right now, looked chock-a-block.

Tom nosed his car into it, spotted a young couple about to leave in a Land-Rover, quarreling about something, and took the space they vacated. He backed in, anticipating a need to perhaps leave again hurriedly, then switched off his engine. But it wasn't until he'd wound down his window that he heard the faint sound of "El Paso" being performed by, according to the prominently displayed poster, Fox Mountain Express. He sat back and wondered what to do next.

The music faded and he heard, loud and folksy, an amplified voice drawl: "Shucks, time we was a-goin', so me 'n' the boys gotta thank you, one and all—sure been the bestest audience we've had today! See you take care yo'selves till the next time, and if you've been hittin' on the Jim Beam, watch out on yo' way home, there might be some ol' bears out there—okay? And the gals among y'all, a special vote of thanks, it's helped a whole heap to have all these purty faces 'round 'bout us here to take a man's mind off knowin' this was *work*. So, from me 'n' the boys, good-bye now, yo' hear, God bless an'—" He must have added something else, but the laughter and applause through those mullioned windows was far too loud to pick it out. Then, briefly, the music sounded again.

Tom glanced at his watch. Buggeration: of course, this was Sunday, when the licensing laws brought drinking to a halt at two, and so there was no point in his going inside. He'd only draw attention to himself by his belated arrival—"Sorry, sir, last orders are over!" Actually, he was rather glad of this; he'd never really been cut out as a double agent.

But it wasn't until almost two-thirty that the Cock Pheasant's well-satisfied customers began to emerge into the car park. Many reminded him instantly of Hodgkins, and by the time the third gunfighter had swaggered out, dressed in black from his Stetson hat to the pointed toes of his high-heeled cowboy boots, Tom had started searching for his face among them. Preachers proved, surprisingly, an almost equally popular fantasy role. Their immense Bibles—strictly for burials up on Boot Hill, one assumed—were in fact possibly a deadlier weapon than the formers' cap pistols. Dance-hall girls there were aplenty, and remarkably authentic some of them undoubtedly were, being grossly overweight, sour-mouthed, and in need of much darning to their fishnet stockings. A Red Indian chief, who just *may* have been Hodgkins—it was impossible to tell because of his war paint—gave a wild whoop and threatened Tom's radiator with a tomahawk before touching a feather headdress to him, most apologetically, and scuttling off.

So unexpected and diverting was this sudden outpouring that Tom realized, perhaps too late, he might well have missed seeing Ginny and her companion among the larger number of people, dressed quite conventionally, who had been giving these enthusiasts a politely wide berth. Vehicles were now starting up all over the car park and, as he saw when he glanced around, a good many had already left.

"Damn!" he said, thumping his steering wheel again. "Now bloody what?"

He had no choice really, other than to hang on, hoping he'd not missed them. A rather perverse hope, he thought on reflection, but he was trying not to use his mind much and let it rest at that. There was a bright yellow sports car, an old TR7 with a hard top, parked right behind him and facing the other way, that he developed a certain, half-informed sixth sense about. It *looked* like the sort of flash . . .

By two-forty, Tom's own car was beginning to look conspicuous, being only one of seven left in the car park, and he knew he'd have to modify his plan. Firstly, he'd have to move to somewhere, across the road, say, where he wouldn't be quite so easy to pick out. Ginny had ridden in his car of course, and although black Metros weren't by any means rare she might associate one with him right away, if only half of what Moira had said was true.

Tom never got to consider his second point. At that precise

moment, he saw the unmistakable figure of Ginny Ashford, in jeans and her white cotton top, step lightly from the porch of the Cock Pheasant, carrying a turquoise scarf and with a hand-tooled leather bag hanging from one slight shoulder. Behind her came, dressed also in jeans but wearing a pink-and-orange-striped shirt, Ric Stephens—flush-faced, with an LP in his hands.

He handed it to her, and they turned toward him.

Tom ducked, his heart racing, and then realized he could possibly still have a shoulder showing above window level. He slid to the floor of his car, cramming himself into the space in front of his passenger's seat, his back hurting where it pressed hard against something knobbly. Then it occurred to him that this had been an utterly calamitous move. Should Stephens pass very close to his car and happen to glance in, he'd be bound (being the little shit he was) to offer a gleeful greeting, ruining perhaps more than merely a personal reputation, but a professional one too. No sooner however had Tom decided to wriggle around, and give the impression of mending a fault in the wiring under his dashboard, than it became obvious he was wedged in so tightly he could no longer move.

So he froze, thinking: I should have *not* had those second and third glasses of hock, because that's what has landed me in this shrieking nightmare of a mess! Yet simultaneously he conceded that when it came to anything connected with Ginny Ashford, he was quite capable of acting on totally self-destructive impulses cold sober—*and* with a smile on his face.

He tried one. Brilliant! He would claim he'd popped in for a quick Scotch, noticed their presence, and had decided to play this little joke on them . . .

Dear God, that didn't sound too convincing.

But Tom, his choices down to none, kept smiling.

Long enough for a shadow to flit briefly across the interior of his car from behind where he crouched, and then to see Ginny in profile, passing his open driver's window on the other side, a small, preoccupied frown on her face offset by a slight smile.

Oh, sweet Christ, I love you!

He just knew it. Didn't even have to think it. There it was, an absolute as ecstatic and terrible as that which had overtaken Saul on his way to Damascus, dashing him to the ground, blinded. Only Tom wasn't blinded: he saw, in the most acute, crystal-clear detail possible, that profile still before him, and it was good, it was *beautiful*.

Not simply in its lines or in its colors, of which there were more in a single curl of wild-honey hair, or in the gray of an eye, than could be counted. Not simply in its tender generosity of lower lip, or in the gentleness of every slight curve, the neatness of nostril, the wonder of tiny pores stippled in such subtle patterns. It was beautiful in a way which transcended all this, for the skull was visible too, where the flesh stretched thin, and so even death seemed imbued by the same luminosity.

"Yes, I love you," Tom whispered softly, opening his eyes again. "But what can that mean now, my Ginny?"

Then the TR7 behind him started up with a roar, backed into his Metro with a slight bump, and took off uncertainly, its faulty exhaust booming.

Tom, rubbing the side of his head which had struck the dashboard where its padding seemed hardest, grasped his steering wheel with his other hand and tried to extricate himself from his cramped and undignified position. It proved quite a struggle and might even have been amusing, had he not been trying to resist at the same time losing his temper. He knew he'd made the same mistake in car parks, getting in and forgetting he'd left the gears in reverse—but with Stephens, however much he tried, it was always difficult not to regard the man's every error as either a deliberate act of sabotage or a sly impertinence of some sort.

Back behind the wheel, knowing now what he'd come to the Cock Pheasant to confirm and having no further business there, Tom was about to start his engine when it occurred to him he'd better check to see if any damage had been done to his brake lights, although he very much doubted it. He had only just stepped out of his car, raising his eye level, when he saw the yellow TR7 being driven away toward Tuppmere in a manner that made his stomach turn over. The sports car wasn't traveling particularly fast, but it was using most of the road, including that reserved for oncoming traffic.

23

"**Y**ou bastard!" Tom exploded, jumping back into the driver's seat. "You drunken, irresponsible bastard!"

He started his car, revved hard, released the clutch, and went shooting backward crashing into a large, whitewashed boulder that marked the edge of the car park. "Oh, *shit* . . ." he said, craning around and seeing broken pieces of taillight on the tarmac.

But seconds later he took off again, hell-for-leather in pursuit. Never had he felt as angry at having to make do with an aging vehicle. To be fair though, he pointed out to himself as the speedometer swiftly swept to sixty and rising, his car wasn't called an MG Metro for nothing. He could remember feeling almost adolescent when he bought it.

A mile from the Cock Pheasant, traveling between high hedgerows, the yellow TR7 came in sight, following a much straighter course. Tom throttled back, trying to remember the road ahead. This particular stretch was too narrow and had too many blind corners for him to safely overtake the other vehicle and force it to pull up. If necessary, of course, he'd just have to chance that; but already it seemed as though the TR7 was slowing down a little of its own accord.

He fell in behind it, leaving a fifty-yard gap to preserve his anonymity, wanting the surprise element to have its full impact when the right moment came. Those fifty yards, however, likewise made it impossible for him to see what was happening through the TR7's small rear window, which meant he could only imagine Ginny shaking her fist at Stephens, warning him to drive more carefully.

Or perhaps, thought Tom, Ginny's telling him to stop and let her out as soon as it's safe to.

Not much farther on, he seemed to recall, the road widened and there was a proper grass verge instead of a ditch on the left, giving the TR7 somewhere to park briefly. And then of course, he would stop there himself and offer Ginny a lift home, saying what a lucky coincidence it was.

"Please, God," said Tom Lockhart, ready to trade anything for this once-only favor. "Please! You must love her like I do . . ."

It was another half mile, during which the TR7 had twice moved ahead with a sudden spurt of speed for no obvious reason, before Tom felt the awesome import of what he'd just said.

"Oh, rubbish!" he scoffed, closing the gap to forty yards and getting ready to sound his horn.

But the echo of those six words only grew louder and louder: You must love her like I do, love her like I do, love her like . . .

Like I must, thought Tom Lockhart.

How very, very simple.

The realization struck him with the force of revelation, confirming in an instant his only true or even possible relationship to Ginny Ashford.

"Bollocks," he said, but allowed the gap to widen.

Then he laughed. Why, the idea was patently absurd. God loved those *he* had created, not the children of other people! And yet neither had he fathered Ginny, which piaced them on something of an equal footing. They were perhaps equal too in another sense, Tom found himself admitting—entirely against his will, for he'd always denied this aspect of his love: he had also created Ginny, *his* Ginny, the most beautiful being in the world, from a clay that he knew everyone else seemed to see as merely "very attractive," "lovely," or, the devil take them, "very pretty." But that was of course because they concentrated their attention on the surface, utterly neglecting to look beyond that, deep into the very soul of her to where the beauty had its beginning. To be sure, in all fairness, the artist Nell Overton had come close. Yet she had not shown the pain that such a vision could bring, not once one had accepted that this glorious, gentle, all-too-mortal creature had been granted free will.

And that's something that I too must grant her, realized Tom Lockhart, allowing the gap to grow even greater. In an everyday sense, down here on this everyday earth, she is not my Ginny at all—not unless she wants to be.

The TR7 went into the next bend much too fast and its tail started to slide, suggesting that at any second the car was going to go into a spin, crash, kill or maim both its occupants. The hedgerow hid what happened and Tom, cursing the pompous, idle, bizarre fantasy he was indulging in, hammered his foot to the floor, flattening his accelerator.

Then he went through the same bend too fast, started skidding, and almost collided at speed with the TR7, which had slowed up again, only yards into the next straightaway.

Tom, badly shaken, dropped back, hoping he had learned a lesson. To test this, he continued to follow the yellow sports car, but without any intention of interfering in any way with its driver or its progress.

He no longer wanted to rationalize his feelings, nor to construct fevered apologia for them. He had decided to stick, calmly and honestly, to what he simply *knew* to be true in his heart, mind, and body.

He knew now, thanks to Moira, a sublime, ineffable link existed between him and her daughter; in revealing this, Moira had enabled him to place himself at his correct and proper distance from Ginny.

He also knew as he'd known all along, but had only a few minutes ago confirmed beyond doubt in the car park, that he loved her.

And finally, Tom knew that loving Ginny Ashford, loving her to the utmost of his being, meant he should never attempt to possess her or influence her. Instead, he had to watch from afar and allow her to go her own way, to find—if she sought it—her own salvation, even if the paths she chose were filled with peril.

In this much, he too was the Father.

What peace he felt, as he still tailed the TR7, now about to start down the wooded slope leading to Tuppmere. Delivered from all the turmoil and confusion of his emotions over the past seven days, if not much longer than that, he could at last think clearly, and even permit himself certain insights he'd avoided.

His first thoughts were of Geoff Harcourt.

What nonsense all that had been, first supposing he'd thought of him as the victim of professional prejudice, and then settling for the idea Geoff had presented an unacceptable threat to Ginny Ashford. The truth of the matter, which could now be faced squarely, had rested in exactly the opposite direction. Tom felt sure that during his conversation with Geoff in the kitchen the night of the flat-warming, he'd probably received, subliminally perhaps, an intimation of his friend's hitherto hidden alter ego. This, then, had been his real reason for wanting to keep away from Geoff thereafter: a terrible fear that he shared the same voluptuous yearnings that can edge a man closer and closer to madness.

"Jesus Christ!" gasped Tom Lockhart, skidding to a stop.

The TR7 had just broadsided around the first bend on the wooded slope, forcing him to slam his foot on the brakes, emphatically and without thought, just as the crowd leans forward when an athlete breasts the winning tape.

"Jump, Ginny!" he shouted, getting his car quickly into motion again. "Jump, you—!"

But cut himself short, knowing he mustn't intervene, and realizing for the first time what hell it must be to be God.

Again, when Tom had the TR7 in sight once more, he saw it moving at a much more sensible speed, even if it was still somewhat erratic in its approach to several of the sharper bends.

At this point he forced himself to begin glancing left and right, taking in vignettes of mossy logs, the tumbling stream, a bank of wildflowers; making himself act as though he were truly impotent in this horrifying situation, having deemed this only just, but not without a duty to survey the glories of nature abounding all about him.

"Good discipline," he murmured to himself, wincing when the TR7 vanished again too quickly, but keeping his foot off the brake.

"And this, my son, is merely the beginning . . ."

Ginny had spoken of travel, of the Third World, of countries where native buses plunged daily into ravines, overcrowded ferries capsized on river crossings, trains were derailed by buffalo and then splintered by expresses. Thomas Merton, the world-renowned Trappist monk, writer, and theologian, had been killed in his Third World hotel bedroom, Tom recalled, by a faulty bedside lamp.

At least if it happens to her here and now, he was very shocked to catch himself thinking, then I'll be right on the spot to provide immediate medical assistance. Even so, the thought remained a secret comfort, and he rounded the next bend almost half hoping to see the TR7 had been involved in a mild mishap that would prove salutary to Ginny. He just couldn't understand what had possessed her to—

"Oh, no . . . !"

The yellow sports car had already disappeared around the bend beyond, with a sudden burst of speed which could only indicate the effect of a last pint of bitter taking hold. The race was on, if Tom were to get ahead and prevent the nightmarish tragedy that seemed inevitable now. Those final, very tight corners, before the village itself began, were all potentially deadly.

"Oh, no," said Tom Lockhart, quite differently and firmly, hating himself for it, but knowing he had to learn that lesson, "this is as far as you go for the moment . . ."

He braked hard and stopped, not entirely by coincidence (although he tried to persuade himself otherwise), at the very spot where once, a very, very long time ago, he had offered up a prayer of thanksgiving to a goddess. Tom rather expected to be calmed by this, as he waited there long enough to feel he'd allowed Ginny her total freedom. But after an unbearably tense two minutes he shuddered violently, realizing this had been an ugly mistake, for his mind had suddenly insisted on associating a new pagan deity with virgins and consecrational rites demanding a blood sacrifice.

And so he immediately drove on again as hastily as he dared, earnestly and gladly offering up Dr. Ric Stephens—impaled by freakish chance on his car's radio antenna after a very minor collision causing no other injuries. That he should have even have had such an idea should have shamed him very deeply.

And so it did, when Tom reached the gates of Cloud Hill and saw there, glinting between the trees, a shiny patch of bright yellow. The Neanderthal in him, however, a simple sun-worshipper, cowed and silent this past hour or more, looked too, and gave a grunt of immense self-satisfaction. It was his crude belief that provided one had thought a horrible thought, it generally remained only a thought—the sun being a contrary bitch at the best of times.

"Hey, lad, what is this?" Tom Lockhart said to himself, smiling ruefully as he finally set off for what he now felt he could really start thinking of as home.

It proved a quick run to town. Only once did he encounter another group of riders half blocking the lanes he used as shortcuts, but nobody on the four lank, ill-groomed mounts acknowledged the courtesy he showed in slowing down; eyes fixed on the skyline ahead of them, they simply rode on. This drew Tom's attention to the gradual buildup of summer thunderclouds over the town, and by the time he'd reached the beltway traffic circle, the sky was darkening. So much for his plan to make up for the missed pub lunch by the river by suggesting to Carole that they take a picnic tea and spread their tablecloth under an oak in his favorite park. Perhaps he could switch plans, and they could go to the cinema at four o'clock, instead of tomorrow evening after the meeting.

Then he realized he'd not got that suitcase with him, his razor, or even a change of clothes.

"Bloody hell," protested Tom, with a sudden weariness so demoralizing that he took his foot off the accelerator and didn't much care where his car rolled to a stop, or how many drivers behind him were panicked into sounding their horns and flashing their lights. "I can't go back there now, not all that way back for Christ's sake. . . ! I've had *enough.*"

And as he sat on the side of the busy main road into town, still provoking loud and indignant blasts from other motorists, a more specific, and remotely alarming, reaction to his day set in: his throat contracted painfully and he wondered whether he, at his age, was about to cry. For a distraction he turned off his engine, took his ignition key, and removed the leather fob from its key ring. Without looking, he tossed the fob out of his window, under the wheels of the traffic.

His throat hurt worse. He turned on his engine again and noticed his fuel gauge was once more registering very low, which suggested there could be something the matter with it. In terms of actual miles covered, he'd not traveled any real distance at all that day. The thought made him laugh; a tight, constricted noise which he heard without interest.

He reached for the tape of Verdi. Again, without looking, he held it at his car window, waiting to toss it out into the wake of the next car. Then he hesitated, placed the tape in the cassette player, and switched it on. The music was as evocative as ever but now, when he turned, he could no longer picture Ginny Ashford sitting there beside him. He saw her instead some way off. Moira was with her, helping her feed the two ponies while they talked. Ginny pointed to the fresh bale of hay beside the paddock fence and raised an eyebrow, as though it had been her turn to take it down that day. Moira smiled and laughed, and so did Ginny.

Then Tom laughed too, laughed lovingly. Turning up the volume he drove on into town, thinking of Carole.

Sugar daddy. To be sure, the god-awful Kevin the Hun could have had a point when he'd made that crack, firing it at him like a poisoned bolt from a crossbow. And if it hadn't been deflected by a knight's shining armor, thought Tom, Christ knows what might have happened to the coeur of de Lion. Because, when all was said and done, only an idiot would deny that once again it looked as though the old predator was up to his even older tricks, ruthlessly exploiting his every unfair advantage in the pursuit of easy prey—as Carole had indeed virtually described herself.

Not that he would ever shower expensive jewelry and furs on her; such a charge could always be successfully refuted on the grounds of his not having enough money, abominating private practice, and being partial to seals. Yet as Tom had discovered, even on such short acquaintance, there was a wealth of equally dubious largesse he could bestow upon her. His respect for her as a person in her own right (which was only natural) Carole had already unwrapped, saying she couldn't want nothing nicer, not never. And this had caused him to feel most uncomfortable, just as it did when one of his witticisms went down too well, making her tell him what a flippin' genius he was. But he wasn't. Good God, the Oxford Union, say, was awash with men infinitely more amusing when it came to an adroitly turned phrase, although it was unlikely she'd grasp any of their allusions. And that was the crux of the matter.

For this time an inescapable class difference, rather than a difference in ages, seemed to threaten the future of an otherwise near-perfect partnership. Or did it? Tom, reflecting on all this as he approached the street where she lived (and trying to keep

Professor Higgins out of it), felt he'd grown sufficiently older and wiser that infinitely long day to cope with any problems they'd face in making a go of it. To begin with, he could cut out being so bloody patronizing—Moira would want to have his ears for some of the things he'd just thought—and then he'd discover what Carole actually wanted from him.

"Got it!" Tom murmured happily, as the flat above the launderette came in sight. "She'll really love that . . ."

He would take Carole out to meet Toby, an old reprobate of a retired eye surgeon, who now lived on a canal barge and spent his time fishing over the stern, cooking extraordinarily hot vegetable curries, and talking endless, perfectly wonderful nonsense. Once, Tom would always remember, Toby had solemnly explained to a particularly thick business type at a Rotary luncheon how the nation's future depended on building a reactor to split the infinitive. But Toby, he knew, would be very taken with Carole. For her benefit he'd go to great lengths to explain, in simple terms, why blue was the only color one couldn't turn upside down—or perhaps trot out that other favorite of his, the best means of curing gout in bishops, using only a turtle's egg, two sticky labels, and a trumpet. With the canal barge moored only a mile or so from the house, Tom would be able to nip off on his own, grab his things, and be back before Carole had time, or even inclination, to notice.

He parked on the fish-and-chip-shop wrappings and looked up at the flat's windows. The curtains were drawn, which made his heart sink a bit. With a frown he turned off the Verdi, and in the sudden silence saw Ginny again, stepping out of the Cock Pheasant with Ric Stephens in tow, which angered Tom and made him feel very disappointed in her. Maybe that sculptor bastard had been right and she was just anybody's, because no normal, sensible, self-respecting girl—

"Wasted enough time!" Tom snapped, unbuckling his safety belt, irritated that even it should try to evoke a memory of something extraordinary she'd once said to him. "And stop all this bloody talking to yourself—there's only one of you!"

24

The first fat patters of rain were falling as he crossed the pavement—unshaven, slacks creased from having sat so long at the wheel, hair untidy, even his brain feeling blustered and scruffy—to press the doorbell. He also tapped sharply on the door with his ignition key, just like—he realized as he did it—one of those hungry, disheveled little sparrows. Pure kitsch, and why the hell not, he decided, because kitsch knew a few truths of its own when it came to human beings.

His long ring on the doorbell went unanswered.

So Tom, trying not to leap to any sickening conclusions, and reassuring himself that Carole wasn't a spiteful person—not the sort who'd make him suffer before being given a chance to explain his prolonged absence—pressed the grubby, enameled button for a second time, holding it down even longer. Mariolatry no longer seemed quite as absurd to him, not when one considered that after all he went through, the Big Fella was bound to need a good cuddle.

Then, as he took his hand away, Tom noticed a faded label beneath the bell and saw printed on it: *C. Yardsley*. No "Miss," of course, for the usual sound reason. Those initials seemed to stand out somehow. CY? Why should that combination of these two capital letters tease his memory so? Where else could he have seen them?

But before an answer could present itself the door opened and

Carole, in a head scarf and raincoat, looked out, her blue eyes bloodshot with weeping.

Tom could have fallen to his knees then, so appalled was he, but she didn't give the opportunity. Carole flung her arms around him, hugged him so hard it felt as though it would be for the last time, and then, pushing him away from her, tried to speak.

"Tom . . . oh, pet . . ." she said, but got no further.

"What is it?" he said. "What in Christ's name has happened?" And he tried to take her in his arms, only she squeezed past him, and he had to follow her out onto the sidewalk. "Carole, you've got to tell me!"

She shook her head, with rain and tears beginning to streak her cheeks. "Gotta go round that Kevin's," she said. "Get a loan of some booze 'til offy opens."

"But we've at least five cans of lager left, and anyway, I'm not—"

"'S all gone. Look, Tom, best yer doesn't—"

"*Gone?*"

"Harry's back," she said.

He felt the blow, as though a studded wristlet had smashed him between the eyes, but no pain—only a numbness that enabled him to respond very quietly and calmly. "I see," he said. "I suppose I should have guessed, perhaps, but I'd have expected to see his Jeep outside here. I think he might have given us some warning of his—"

"Phone was off."

He felt that too, but it simply intensified his numbness. "Sorry, my fault. When did you discover I'd—"

"Harry did when he come in, 'bout dinnertime."

"Is that what set this all off?"

Again, Carole shook her head. "He never said nothin'," she said. "Just put it back. He were that upset, see, an'—"

"So you've told him? About you and me?"

"No, Tom," said Carole, reaching out to close her front door, "nobody's never goin' to know nothin' about that—it's for me to keep, see."

Tom jammed a foot in the door, and grasped Carole by the arm, not giving a damn if some kids were now approaching them on bikes, yelling obscene encouragement. "For pity's sake," he begged, "what *is* all this about? If we aren't the reason Harry's in a state, you don't have to make that sound so final and—"

"Please, Tom—let go, all right?"

He released her. "It's only I . . ."

Carole nodded. "Harry thinks yer 'ere 'cos I give yer a bell to come round," she said, turning her eyes on the grinning kids swooping around them. "I was to say he'll kill yer if you goes up there, but"—she turned back to face him, her eyes looking deep into his own—"but I think really it'd be for the best if yer did. Get it over."

"Get what over?" said Tom, turning pale. "Our ridiculous vendetta over Geoff?"

"C'mon, you was brave enough yesterday, remember?" said Carole with a weak smile, raising his hand to kiss it quickly.

Then she was gone, running through the rain, coat flapping, head scarf half off, pink soles showing with every flap of her slippers.

"Right," said Tom, enough of the numbness remaining to shield him against anything, "let's get this little lot sorted . . ." And then *he* was going to tell Harry Coombes about himself and Carole, his plans, and their future.

With all the curtains drawn the flat was very dim and difficult to see into from the landing, so he paused in the doorway, waiting for his eyes to adjust, hearing the rain now driving hard on the windows.

"Dr. Tom, I presumes?" said Harry Coombes from the divan, raising himself on an elbow. "How goes it, me old cock—a' right, is it?"

Tom advanced several paces into the room, stopping just short of the bed, and noting that Harry was presenting nystagmus and other signs of considerable inebriation. "Hello, Harry," he said. "Had a good holiday?"

"A cracker, Tom! Never sat still one minute, but down on them sands all day with me little spade and me bucket."

"I see, you two went to the seaside, did you?"

Harry nodded, and patted the candlewick bedspread. "Fancy a seat?" he said.

"I'll sit here, thanks," said Tom, turning around one of the dining chairs and straddling it, more for the slight protection it afforded than anything else. He had never felt in as much danger;

this man really did look intent on exacting the most terrible vengeance. "I take it Geoff had a good time too, did he?"

"Could've done," said Harry, lighting a cigarette. "The reason I took him, weren't it? Place is heavin' with bits o' spare. All yer gotta do is tell 'em yer a doctor, and they wants yer to prove it, get out yer little prober and that."

"Ah," said Tom, and had difficulty keeping his smile going.

"I mean," said Harry, "get yerself knocked up by a quack, and yer quids in, aren't yer? There was me to swear he weren't wed—Christ, they could *see* that—and even if he wouldn't come up with the ring, they could get him with a black, right?"

"With a black? That's a bit exotic!"

Harry sniggered. "Wot I mean," he said, "is they could say they'd been a patient, gorn to him with this 'oliday tummy, like, and then do the blackmail on the silly sod, describe his little willie to them medical council fellas."

"God, these women sound awful," said Tom, shocked.

"Be yer age," Harry reprimanded him witheringly. "They weren't all like that! Wouldn't let none of that rubbish near our Geoff, would I? Got him lined up with this nice little secretary or summat from a shoe factory—all he needed was to give her the wink, like, and Bob's yer uncle! That'd be last I'd see of Geoffers for two days, I reckoned. I mean, I've noticed—"

"But he didn't get his finger out?"

"Oh, Christ!" said Harry, giving a coarse laugh that made him cough on his cigarette smoke. "You near as bad as him, aren't yer? Effin' opposite, weren't it? That were the trouble! And I could see he were burstin' to. I mean, takin' our Geoff away like that, livin' in the one room, like, in this caravan wot we rented, you learn new things about a bloke, don't yer? I'd always known he were a bit randy on the quiet, fancied the bits I brung round 'is house, me viddies, but I never knew he'd not had it off yet, not with anyone. Never knew he wanted to do everythin' in sight, neither—oh aye, even yer missus, beggin' her pardon! Told us the first night, after we'd got a bit bevvied, and I thought, right, this fella's gotta get 'is leg over or there's gonna be trouble, be all over Sunday papers it will, and wotta waste, what a *waste*, when yer thinks wot he once done for the likes of us; crackin' good doc like that, and none of yer toffy-nosed bullshit to go with it neither. So I—"

"A waste?" said Tom. "Jesus, it'd be a tragedy! But I can't

imagine, if that was the state he was in, how he ever survived working at the—"

"Dead simple," cut in Harry Coombes with a nasty smile. "I mean, it were obvious, weren't it? Had this mate, see? Thought the world of him, he did, the stupid sod, 'cos he were such a 'thoroughly decent chap' and that, 'could trust him like a brother.' Fella with a right cow for a missus, but never did nothin' naughty, kept 'is hands off of the young nurses—real control, y'know? Sort of used him to keep hisself toein' the line, like. I remembers the once, watchin' this viddie, and him sayin' I was never to say nothin' about wot we was—"

Tom rose. "Christ, you're not going to hold someone else responsible for the insane beliefs he had about them? That's not bloody fair, Harry, and you know it!"

"But yer didn't have to go and tell fuckin' lies and breakin' yer promise all, though, did yer? Broke 'is flamin' 'eart, that did! I thought it were 'cos it seemed like he'd been through a whole lot for nothin', yer two-faced bastid, but he were really scared then, crappin' hisself, only I couldn't understand it. That was why he wanted to run away and all, and so I—you shit!"

Harry Coombes swung his legs drunkenly over the edge of the bed and made an attempt to get up, as if about to hurl himself at Tom, and the look in his eyes was terrifying.

"Hold on, Coombes!" said Tom, sidling to where he could make a grab at the bread knife on the table, so afraid was he. "What exactly are you talking about?"

"Like only pretendin' yer had took notice when he warned yer off this other tart for the sake of yer missus. I mean, he were dead shocked enough you'd even thought of givin' 'er one, but yer'd promised, and next thing—"

"I'd *not* thought of 'giving her one'!" Tom stormed back. "That was all Geoff's imagination! A misunderstanding, a ridiculous conclusion he just jumped to."

"Oh aye? But he says yer coughed to it, night of his party."

Tom just had to nod then, feeling sick to the pit of his stomach. "Put it this way, I didn't argue with him," he said. "But I did keep the promise I made. I never went near that person while he—"

"You bloody lyin' pile o' shit! Call yerself a doctor! Wouldn't trust yer with me nan's budgie, I wouldn't! You'd have its bum feathers off faster than—"

"Look!" said Tom, crashing his fist on the dining table. "I don't have to put up with this from you, Coombes! Let's get Geoff over here right this minute and we'll settle this once and for all! Do you hear me?"

Harry cut him short with a very odd laugh, and slumped back on the bed again. "Sorry, Tom, me old son," he said, "forgot me effin' manners, right? But first, lemme tell yer wot Geoff told us— 'bout ninety-two effin' times, I reckon!"

"All right," said Tom, warily straddling the chair again. "I'm listening."

"Tuesday night, you swears to him you'll never see this bird again. Come the Wednesday, there's this bit o' bother with a baby wot snuffs it after you two has a go at her. Geoff tells yer in the passage, just as you were leavin', that she were a goner, and then he thinks, bugger it, could do with a pint after them parents, and he wants to get yer across the Red Lion for half an hour, like. But you're already down the lift, see? So he gets hisself smartish to the window, so he can yell down to yer in the car park, only yer with this bird again, see? And she's all dressed up, different clothes on, ready for her big night out before yer gets her back to yer place and bonks 'er one. Can't believe his eyes, Geoff can't, not after yer promised—"

"Too bloody right!" Tom interrupted, with his own very odd laugh. "That wasn't the same person! It's a pity Geoff didn't try a closer look, instead of making absurd judgments over that kind of distance!"

Harry Coombes stubbed out his cigarette, scattering spark on the candlewick bedspread, and then lit another. "You're a bit of a goer, aren't yer?" he said. "Two birds in the 'and! Christ, how many did yer have in the bush, all queuein' up for it?"

"That," said Tom coldly, "was the teenage daughter of a friend I was best man to. I was giving her a lift home, that was all."

"Then yer mate better watch it, Doc, unless he wants 'er cherry done on the National Health, like, or somethin' 'cos—"

"Don't you say another filthy word about that girl!"

Coombes shrugged. "Bit sensitive, aren't yer?" he said. "Interestin'. Point is, Geoff's not to know this, right? Wot he sees is yer sittin' for bloody ages down there in yer motor, doin' the big chat-up, and this sets him thinkin' sort of, not that he wants to. He remembers that while yer was workin' on the kiddie wot snuffed it, this Aussie fella had said owt about yer with some surgeon down in the canteen at dinnertime. So he goes up, sees this fella, and bingo, he coughs—not knowin' it—that you and this same

woman doctor wot Geoff'd warned yer off, had had yer scoff
together, despite all yer promises. Shattered, he were, worse'n
seeing the Pope wavin' his—"

"Look, that lunch together wasn't my idea, and besides—"

"Don't want to know," said Coombes, blowing a smoke ring.
"You're a lyin' bastid, Doc, just admit that. Personally, yer can
'ave it away with any bit o' spare yer fancies, so far's I'm
concerned, and good luck to yer—only this time you really effin'
cocked it up, if you'll pardon me French, and there's wot yer done
to Geoff that I'm a bit annoyed about."

That weariness had suddenly come upon Tom again, demoralizing him, making him utterly indifferent to this whole
sordid business, irrespective of how much something was aching
inside of him, and how his throat hurt as though it had a hand
clasping it in a cadaveric spasm. So all he said was, in a mumble,
"Fine, I'm anything you like to call me. It's time, though, that
Geoff grew up a bit, don't you think? You can't always be acting as
his minder."

"Chucked it, Doc!" said Harry, blowing another smoke ring,
this time in Tom's direction. "Had to really, after what he done
Friday night."

Tom tightened his grasp on the back of the chair. "What was
that?" he asked.

"Depends . . ."

"On what?"

"If I can trust yer to keep a secret," said Harry, and made his
smile very unpleasant. "Don't know if that's wise, like, not with
the form you've got. Just for starters, our Carole better not get to
'ear it . . ."

"She won't," said Tom, knowing he'd turned traitor, but being
so desperate to know what Geoff had done, he couldn't help
himself. "I promise."

"If yer do let slip," said Harry, pointing his glowing cigarette tip
at him, "then I'm goin' come round and put this out on your
plonker—a'right?" Then he lay back on the bed and said, "I were
a bit fed up with our Geoff by Friday night, if I'm honest—dead
borin' all that talk, same things—and so when I pipes this little
cracker, down the pier, I thinks, why not? Dead easy to pull,
when she sees me motor, and so I says to Geoff, 'Look, mate, I'm
up the carrie for coupla hours, okay?' He says fine, he'll go for a
few jars down this pub we found, and I know why, 'cos there's

plenty o' nice tit he can look at, it havin' a good DJ and everythin'. Last I see of him, till 'round closin' time, and he comes knockin' on the carrie door. I mean, wot a bloody moment! This Bernice, or whetever 'er effin' name was, is goin' at it again, would yer believe, like a ferret and two pound o' liver. 'Sod off, Geoffrey!' I shouts to him, a bit arsy, like, as yer would in the circs, but he don't stop knockin'. So I opens the window on that side, Bernice hangin' on, and I tells him to give us another hour yet, and Bernice says, if he wants, he can join in, like. D'yer know, I quite fancied that? But, no, all Geoff want to know is if any coppers've been up the caravan, and say I bloody 'ope not, this Bernice bein' a bit on the young side and all. Only why ask us, I says—bit weird, isn't it? Geoff don't answer, just says can 'e have a loan of the motor, to go down this club the next sort of town, see, and I chucks the keys out. I mean, yer would, wouldn't yer? 'Cos Bernice wasn't wastin' no time, see, and I were nearly into me short strokes by then, and—"

"God, Geoff wasn't in trouble with the police, was he?" Tom broke in, getting to his feet again. "I mean to say, he has come back with you, hasn't he?"

Harry Coombes shook his head. "So I hears the Jeep go, and when I gets me puff back, I tells this Bernice she'd best bugger off, see? I'm worried about this business of the coppers, and I'm worryin' wot Geoff's maybe done, only I'm sayin' to meself, no, he'd never! Or could 'e, now 'is bottle's gone? Has he grabbed some tart down under the pier, like, an'—"

"Christ, Coombes! Just tell me what—"

"Wot Geoff done?" said Harry Coombes, shrugging. "Just listen, will yer? More knockin', see, and Geoff's right, three woodentops stood on me step, holdin' this receipt he got from rentin' the carrie, and it's got his name on. They seem a bit surprised, like, when I say, aye, that's me mate, wot yer bastids done to 'im? They say they done nothin', only he's down the 'ospital and can I get me clothes on and come, please. Then—"

"Harry, you're not saying . . . ?"

He looked up at Tom, his eyes glazed by drink and with an anguish that chilled to the marrow. "So I go down the 'ospital," he said, "It were terrible. Christ, as I'm always sayin' to 'im, 'ow you bastids do yer job, I'll never know."

"He'd crashed the Jeep?"

Harry nodded. "Took it up the cliffs where there's no road. Could've bin an accident, the bobbies said; they didn't know really, and he was a bit bevvied and that. Did a noser, missed this honeymoon couple out walkin' by about one hard-on, the young copper says—thought it were another of 'em effin' space shuttles."

"But if Geoff's in hospital, what are you doing back here and why in God's name didn't you get in touch? He can't not have let you! What did the doctors say?"

"Just the one doctor," said Harry, flopping back on the bed to stare at the ceiling. "Bobbies all knew him, havin' the same job and all."

"Don't follow you," said Tom, remembering—with astonishing irrelevance—how he had stared at the same ceiling that morning, contentedly counting all the small festoons of spiderweb. "Accidents, you mean?"

"Doc had this big room all to 'isself, cold, same as you'd expect, really. Said if it were goin' to upset us too much, y'know, to go inside, like, where they'd got the bits and pieces, they could bring the one out inna bowl, like, to show us in the office so's I could identify. But I must've still been a bit bevvied meself, 'cos I went straight in through the door. There was this sergeant, nice fella, took us to be sick, said he thought Geoff must've been stood up, see, and he caught his chin on the windscreen. Just the head, see, inna bowl. Then they said could I 'ang on, give 'em the next o' kin and that, and I said there weren't none, no brothers, nothin', and I give 'em 'is boss's name, then I waited, 'cos 'e said somebody were goin' to come down, only that were yesterday, and when they didn't, I thought best I get meself 'ome to Carole for a—"

"Must go, Harry," said Tom Lockhart.

He left the tape of Verdi, broken beneath his heel, in the litter where his car had been parked, and remembered little of his journey to the hospital, apart from very wet roads, some lightning, and a double-decker bus that had broken down.

Then, for a long while, he sat alone at his desk in his office, shivering slightly even though he knew that the fever had broken, and he was no longer gripped by its delirium.

Of those hours, he remembered nothing.

When night had come, he rang the hospital where his mother-in-law had been admitted as a private patient, and was told that she was asleep. Mrs. Lockhart had returned to care for her father at Trade Winds.

He rang Trade Winds and was told that his father-in-law was

watching television, and that Mrs. Lockhart had since returned to the Brunswick Hotel, into which she'd kindly moved so as not to monopolize the home's one guest room.

He rang the Brunswick Hotel and was told, by what sounded like a very young and inexperienced receptionist, that Mrs. Lockhart had left the hotel some two hours earlier, dressed in a lovely long evening frock, and it occurred to Tom that he had watched her packing it.

He rang the only other number in a dark world that still meant anything, and was told, yes, of course, he was always welcome. So he drove there.

25

It was almost a week before Tom Lockhart chanced to meet Ginny Ashford again, on the day of Geoff Harcourt's funeral.

After the funeral, he and Felicity Croxhall had made love for the first time. There had been no urgency until then, not in the slow, sure, intimate nature of their wooing, which had other means of conferring acceptance and affirmation. But both of them, having on occasion felt death come to human flesh beneath their fingertips—that jittery tremble—had found fierce need of a symbolic act of procreation to proclaim puny triumph over it, and Tom had bought sheaths from a machine in the pub where the brief wake was held.

They had, moreover, sensed that a part of them had died with Geoff. This was perhaps simply their own continuity, as had existed in the mind of another human being—but at least, distortions aside, Geoff had seen them as a couple long before anyone else had. And so when they'd watched his coffin bump and shake, as rigid as he had ever been, on its way through a parting of small doors to be cremated, their clasped hands had gripped tightly and their chief sorrow had been for themselves.

Or so Tom reflected, as he skimmed a palm lightly over the sumptuous spill of chestnut hair that flowed from Felicity's hard, round head on his shoulder, and out across his chest, hiding his nipples.

* * *

"Once upon a time . . ." he murmured. "Yes, I'm sure there was a fairy tale about you. A beautiful princess kept locked in a high tower, wasn't it? Until one day you spied a gullible-looking lad from your window, and lowered this lot down so he could climb up it and—"

"And talk endless nonsense," she interrupted with a chuckle, which was a particularly Felicity sound, warm and so immensely reassuring. "Tom, you're incorrigible. Remind me, when we've a moment, to tell you something fascinating I've found out about the title of that etching."

"Oh? What?"

"No, I think it can keep until you take me to see it."

"Last day today, only open a week."

"Is it really?"

"And the gallery closes at four on a Saturday, if my memory of the poster serves me right, which doesn't leave us much time. So why not just tell me?"

"I'm tempted. I'd like to go on lying here like this forever."

"Me, too," said Tom, who had not fallen asleep afterward for he'd wanted to savor and remember each separate and yet fused joy of their first union. Felicity had small, exquisite perfections to be discovered, one after the other, none obvious at a glance, but seemingly infinite in their number. He noted a stippling of tiny freckles near her collarbone like a small constellation. "You're beautiful," he added, impatient to make love to her a second time, and moved his hands to her breasts.

"Why is it so important for you to keep saying that?" she asked.

"Because of what Sylvia pointed out, that you spend all day looking at 'ugly, ugly things'?"

"I look *for* ugly things," he corrected her, "I don't necessarily want to see them, except to prove I'm doing my job!" Then Tom laughed. "God, the cheek of the bitch, turning up at Geoff's funeral with her fancy man in tow! Could hardly have been worse if it'd been at my own."

"Frankly, I was relieved she did, and that there were so many people from the hospital there. It gave all of us a chance to get things properly out in the open."

"And me a chance to drop a bloody great brick . . ."

Felicity's chuckle turned into more of a giggle. "Fancy," she said, "insisting on calling such a true-blue, Bulldog Drummond

type 'Sigmund'—you had him utterly baffled, and gave his stiff
upper lip an awful time of it."

" 'I'm Edward, old chap!' " mimicked Tom. "*Edward*—as in our
dear lady the Queen's youngest, what? How the hell was I to
know her so-called shrink had been come-cry-on-my-shoulder-
dear Sister bloody Pinkerton?"

"Poor Tom," said Felicity, giggling even more. "Don't forget
though, the Sister *was* psychogeriatric-trained, so what she
must've said about you—"

He interrupted her with a kiss, and then waited, his eyes
closed, for her to kiss him back.

But Felicity gently removed his hands from her breasts and
said, when he looked at her questioningly, "Perhaps we should
finish talking first."

"Can't imagine what about, not when—"

"I think we ought to, Tom. We've still a few ghosts to lay."

"My God," he said with a laugh, "are you hoping to turn this
into an orgy? For an outwardly very proper young woman, you
do surprise me!"

Felicity smiled only a little. "Many a true word," she said, then
added, "There's an old French saying, 'Every beginning is
lovely.' "

"So it was. Unbelievably."

"But we were both totally new to each other, which we can't
ever be again, and sheer novelty always concentrates things,
makes you focus completely on just the one thing, the one
person, the one—oh, damn, just put your hands back, that was
heavenly, and we'll pretend I didn't—"

"No, we won't," said Tom, keeping his hands where they were.
"Say what you feel you must say. Me and Max will just have to
wait for our walkies a bit longer, that's all."

"Oh, I do love you!" she said, impetuously kissing his brow,
before snuggling up again. "Have for ages . . ."

"Ghosts," Tom prompted her, hoping this wouldn't take too
long, but finding the delay already distilling his desire for her,
making it more intoxicating. "There is one obvious one I can think
of."

"Oh, I don't feel he'll ever be in bed with us."

"What?" said Tom, jolted, looking down at the top of her head.

"When I see that you have your eyes closed."

"Still no word of what might've made Geoff so frightened of the police," said Tom. "I asked Emmanuel while we were doing our pallbearer bit. They could be exercising discretion, I suppose, as it'd be a bit pointless now."

"Oh, I think it was probably mostly in his imagination; he had such a strong guilt that—Tom, you're changing the subject, you cheat!"

"Then if Geoff doesn't count, who does? What ghosts?"

"Carole," said Felicity.

Tom shook his head.

"Oh, come on, Tom. You're obviously still very fond of her."

"True, but as for the rest of it, that sort of sexiness has its limits. Two-dimensional, like a Page Three? You go so far, then you stop there. Hold it up to the light, and a headline shows through about a naughty vicar, a religious stripper, some titillating mass cliché— or an advert for corn plasters. There's always this grot factor to bring you down to earth with a bump. Oh, I don't know . . ."

"But you do know if you've ever slept with her," said Felicity. "That part of your story was never long on detail."

"Yes, once," said Tom, "only that was a dream."

And he couldn't believe saying any of this was wrong. He and Carole had been mates, and mates kept each other's secrets—just as they had to atone for any acts of betrayal. Yet he still waited very anxiously for Felicity Croxhall's response, knowing how astute she was, and that he might well have jeopardized everything he now lived for with the only words of deception she'd ever hear from him.

And while he waited, for what seemed an eternity, he thought of a joke he might make about Max, still scratching softly on the bedroom door. One midnight, unable to fall asleep on his makeshift bed in the living room, he had taken down Felicity's dictionary to read again the definition of *imago*. He then had paged on idly, stopping with a small grunt of surprise at *jinnee*. A spirit lower than angels, the definition had run, able to appear in human and animal forms, and having supernatural power over men. A better description of a certain hairy, irresistible beast could scarcely be imagined, and when Max, disturbed from his own slumbers, had come lolloping over to place a chin in his lap, he'd said to him, "Our jinnee . . ." But Felicity hadn't heard about this yet, and if he told her now, right now, taking his cue from the scratching sounds, it might prove sufficiently distracting for her to forget what she—

"Sleeping with Carole was a dream?" Felicity echoed, and then added with a lopsided smile, "I bet it was!"

Tom, trying not to hold his breath while he weighed the stunning ambiguity of those words, and feeling afraid to even blink lest this tipped the balance and Felicity left his side forever, just lay there.

Then abruptly, Felicity gave a chuckle. "Wicked of me," she said, "but I can't help *wondering* about Edward, as in youngest. Did you get the same impression?"

"Queer as a concrete parachute, you mean?"

"Really!" She laughed. "I wonder, sometimes, about the company you keep! Do you think there's any possibility those two might have, um, beaten us to it?"

"Hopped into bed with each other before today, you mean?"

"How long ago was it that Sylvia met him visiting his dear old mater at Trade Winds? I didn't catch that."

"Oh, two or three months back, so I'd say that they've spent at least the past six weeks going at it like two ferrets at a pound of liver."

"There!" said Felicity, laughing. "Now that's exactly what I meant about you! Wherever do you—"

"But to be serious," Tom cut across, wishing he'd resisted that, because some things still haunted him, "I don't think old Sylv's going to have to risk pregnancy too often, and why should she? He's a mummy's beautiful boy, if ever I've seen one, just *adores* helping her shop for clothes, and is, I'm sure, superbly toilet-trained. I think she's going to be very happy." He paused to kiss the top of Felicity's head, and then said lightly, "Ghosts all laid now?"

She nodded.

"By the way," said Tom, suddenly reminded, "Darby told me in the pub that Truman's called off asking for reports on Annabel, and that can't be discretion either, because it was a team job."

"What a relief for you!"

"Too right. That's something else I lumbered Ginny with, you know, but she reacted superbly. I hope when we have our daughter she'll have that kind of cool. It wasn't as if she's used to

Hugh coming home with horror stories from the world of marketing paint-stripper—God, I've just realized something!"

"What?"

"All ghosts laid indeed! You, Felicity Croxhall, are a devious, sly, cunning little cheat . . ."

"Me?" said Felicity, all innocence, licking a finger and thumb before taking his encased foreskin between them.

"*Your* ghost—just who and what is he? You know, the very distinguished one, who isn't your father, in the photographs in the living room? And will you kindly stop that while I'm talking to you?"

"Won't stop, because I'm not going to tell you."

"Look, in all fairness you've got to! I can't stand mysteries!"

"Tom, you know you love them, my love."

He wasn't sure why that observation should so arouse him, but within dizzying seconds, Felicity being as aroused and eager, Tom Lockhart was kneeling upright between her strong, sensible legs, perfect for standing and working hour after hour at an operating table, about to penetrate her. Neither had their eyes closed.

"Just you," she said, smiling as she gave him her hands.

"Just you," he said, smiling as he interlaced his fingers with hers.

Then he lowered himself, their hands now on the bed at her shoulders, and with a slight shake and a bump, moved into her very slowly, feeling their fingers tightening, the shock of sudden heat engulfing his rigid penis, and only wishing, at the very last moment before total extinction came, he'd not chanced to picture this happening through small doors, parting.

"Walkies, Max! Up to the library and back?"

"God, old Glute's not still in a sulk, is he?" said Tom, buttoning a clean shirt as he joined Felicity in the living room.

"He is, I'm afraid, but a good long walk should restore faith, which is important if you don't want to come home to chewed slippers!"

"Haven't any; Sylvia thought they were rather common. But do you think we'll still make the library in time? It's almost ten to four now."

"Oh, Max'll give us a quick tow behind his Volkswagen."

* * *

Tom was still smiling at that half a mile from her house. He walked with Felicity, arm in arm, his free hand gripping a taut leash, while passersby turned to grin at the straining, galumphing mongrel who'd once been a biochemist in Santa Monica. That was perhaps one of the most wonderful things about this wondrous woman: she remembered the things one said, understood all of them, and sometimes gave one or two back to you, gift-wrapped in her own glinty sense of humor.

Tom had never experienced such intimacy. He felt he had known her always and that in one sense she'd been wrong, they could never have been strangers. In just six days they had already proved just how much they shared hopes of the future, scars of the past, tastes, interests, the excitement of wanting to share even more, the tenderness needed before one could expose one's self spiritually and mentally to the other, making physical nakedness of little consequence. Tom, who had gone to Felicity at his most vulnerable, to discover she was curiously vulnerable, too, knew that only a great good could come of all this. He delighted in the picture they already presented to the world, with Gluteus Maximus panting in the vanguard.

"You mentioned a daughter," said Felicity, as they left the tow path and crossed the bridge, heading for the library. "I was wondering—"

"Oh, tonight."

She laughed. "I was going to say, what about our having a son?"

"Ah, better start at five, then."

"But we'll never get back from the library in time!"

"We will," said Tom Lockhart.

They reached the library at twenty past four, and went up to the gallery only because Max insisted and they'd walked too far not to. The glass doors of the gallery were closed, and the spotlights had been switched off.

"Hey, it's Tom," said Nell Overton, stepping out of the lift behind them, dragging an empty tea chest behind her. "Great to see you!"

"And you! Nell, this is Felicity."

"Hi, Felicity—I just love the pooch. He's yours?"

Both nodded, and Felicity said, "Max, say hello to Nell."

"You're just adorable," she said, crouching to pat him.

"Always wanted one just like him when I was a kid. You've come to look around?"

"I've just been telling Felicity about your work, only you look as if you're about to start packing things away."

Nell nodded. "There's another show moving in, and the janitor wants the keys back pretty soon, but you're real welcome to what's still up."

Then the other lift opened and Ginny Ashford came out, dragging a second empty tea chest.

"Oh, hello, Tom," she said. "I'm sorry about last Saturday, that private viewing turned into a complete muddle."

"Not your fault," he said. "I shouldn't really have slipped away when I knew I was on call and a patient was being brought in."

"Yes, isn't it a bind being on call?" said Felicity. "I loathe it and so does Max, who gets terribly bored—don't you?—having to wait for me in the car park."

"Hello, Max," said Ginny, and he licked her proffered hand.

"Felicity—Ginny," said Tom. "Felicity's one of the team at the hospital, but not a radiologist. Cardiac surgeon."

"Wow," said Ginny, "but you're young!"

Felicity laughed. "How much nicer that sounds than 'very junior'—I hope you're taking note, Dr. Lockhart, sir! Can we help with the packing up?"

"No, we'll manage just fine, thanks," said Nell. "Ginny's already taken half the stuff down—they should name a hurricane after her, the way she can strip out a place in five seconds flat, leave you with nothin'."

"You'd be in a hurry too, if you had my new boss!" said Ginny. "He's very strict about starting right on time, and we open at six tonight."

"What's this?" said Tom. "More waitressing?"

"The Cock Pheasant. I'm learning to be a barmaid."

"Really?" said Felicity. "I was one for two seasons at a holiday camp, in my third and fourth year. It's hard work!"

"Very," said Ginny, smiling at her. "I was surprised. And no tips, although some people offer to buy you a drink, and I usually take a half-pint."

"Of lager or Scotch?" asked Tom.

* * *

They all laughed and went into the gallery, where Ginny switched the bright lights back on again.

"If you two are in a bit of a rush," said Felicity to Nell, "I think I'll get Tom to show me just the etching he's told me is so wonderful, and perhaps I can see the others another day. I like to dwell on pictures."

"And I like to hear somebody say that," said Nell. "Tell you what, get him to bring you along to the workshop—these are all in the portfolio—and, if you want, I'll take you both through the whole process."

"We'd love that."

"*Imago*'s over here," said Tom, leading her across to it.

Felicity pondered the etching for a long while and Nell came to join them, leaving Ginny taking things off a desk in a corner. "Do you like it?" Nell asked.

"It's wonderful—and so sad," said Felicity. "The beauty in the imperfect image? You are using imago in that sense, aren't you? With the flawed reflection being only hinted at."

"That just kinda happened," said Nell. "What I started out with was more just Plato's basic theory that everything we see is unreal, because only the imago of something is ever real. You know, the original edos of The Woman, in capitals, The Dog, The Tree, that's the real imago because it's perfect, but all the trees, dogs, men and women in this world being a whole lot less, made in the image of, but still imperfect imagos—right?"

"To differing degrees of course," said Felicity, nodding. "Because I've always thought that Max—"

"Hey, he *is* The Dog, right?" said Nell, and laughed. "One glance and I just knew it! So I took that, I used dark-complected, light-complected to kind of set up negative and positive images, interfacing with the imago invisible somewhere between them, and—"

"Excuse me a sec," said Tom. "Max's about to criticize one of Len's sculptures in a manner all too figurative!"

And he hurried over and grabbed Max's collar, commanding him, "Now behave, old son . . ." Which reminded him of Geoff.

"Would you like me to take him outside for a bit?" offered Ginny, putting down a framed print wrapped in old newspaper.

"No, that's very kind of you, but we'll be off in a minute, thanks. Do you have to pack that stuff as well?" Tom pointed to

Len Tullet's sculpture. "It seems a bit of a cheek, expecting you to do that."

"Another reason for hurrying! Paws'll be here to do it himself soon."

"Yes, I gathered he—er, but talking of Third World Requiems, how are your plans in that direction going? Still off to feed the hungry?"

Ginny shrugged. "People anywhere can be Third Worlds," she said.

"Ah, so it's the thirsty now at the Cock Pheasant?"

She laughed and placed the wrapped print in a tea chest.

"It's just struck me," said Tom, keeping hold of Max by his collar. "You must've seen that barmaid's job advertised when you were out there on Sunday. Your mum mentioned where you'd gone, during lunch."

"Yes, and Fox Mountain was brill—I got their new LP, a signed one."

"Ric enjoyed it too?"

"He's not said?"

"Hasn't mentioned a word about it—or you, for that matter. I must admit I've been very curious to know the outcome."

Ginny smiled. "Poor Ric," she said.

"You don't sound as though you mean that!"

She smiled. "He's awful," she said. "He'd claimed on Saturday that he worked with you, but it didn't sound like it, not when I started asking him questions. Does he really, or was that another of his fibs?"

"Sorry?" said Tom. "Oh, we do angios together, yes, but—between you and me—I can't stand him and tend to keep him very much at arm's length! So you won't be seeing him again?"

"I don't think so. Besides, he's very cross with me."

"Why?"

"Between you and me?"

"Naturally."

"I played a trick on him, to stop him trying to touch me. I'm a really good driver—passed my test first go—but I made him let me drive back and I pretended to be *terrible*—it scared him half to death! The funniest part was, he wouldn't admit it, in case I told you how chicken he was."

Tom laughed. "But whatever would give Ric the idea you might spill the beans? It's not as if you and I often see each other, and you're so much—"

"He was right, though, wasn't he?" said Ginny with a smile he'd not seen before, then turned away to carry on packing prints into a tea chest. "If you don't wrap lots of paper round pictures, they get their frames chipped."

Tom looked at her, standing there in her jeans and white top under a strong spotlight, with her back to him, and saw she was shorter than he had remembered. He could see, too, that her feet, in their flip-flop sandals, needed a damned good scrub, and that her toes were an odd shape. He wondered about that smile, and whether she'd meant it to be enigmatic; he wondered what might happen to it if he told her about Geoff Harcourt. He acknowledged an unsuspected streak of devilment and arrogance in her, wholly at odds with a reputation for self-effacing goodness and kindness. He found himself conceding that, save for the odd remark, her conversation was largely banal; that she might well turn out to have hidden shallows.

Then Ginny Ashford, become woman, glanced serenely around at him.

"Well?" said Tom, as Felicity took his arm on the staircase leading down to the library foyer. "You and Nell seemed to hit it off! I hope you didn't mind being suddenly dragged away like that at five seconds' notice, but when a dog's gotta go . . ."

"*We* gotta go!" said Felicity, laughing. "Oh, Nell was fascinating, especially when it came to the Trinitarian aspect, and did you see that other print of hers, the one with the beetle in it?"

"No, I've never had time to—sorry, Max's spotted that lamppost, you'd better catch us up outside!"

But Felicity hung on to his arm, and together they reached the sidewalk in what seemed like the nick of time, only for Max to lose all interest in the lamppost after a single sniff, and then set his sights on a bus bench farther down the street.

"You were right," Felicity said to Tom with a chuckle. "We will be home by five if Glute carries on at this rate!"

But he stopped to glance back at the high gallery window, which was catching the sun, and tried to see through it.

Oh, Lordy, yours until the music stops, thought Tom Lockhart.
hart.